Not everyone who passes before the entrance of the *Excelsior,* luxury hotel on Venice's Lido, would venture across its threshold and mingle with those at the top of the social pile. This is the world of rich, beautiful, coolly elegant Gloria; it is not the world of Mario, a seedy young school-teacher living in a run-down tenement with his shapeless mother and catty sister. But Mario is good-looking, canny and propelled by his fantasies towards giddy ambitions. Turning his back on his stale, snivelling fiancée Luisa, whom he has got pregnant, and on the hornet's nest of mean little problems thereby engendered, he has set his sights on Gloria, splendid, serene Gloria. She is the way to the Better Life for which he imagines he is cut out.

Skilfully evoking the very feel of a hot Venetian summer, the sweltering alleys of the city and the sea-fresh promenades and beaches of the Lido, the author narrates the gradual development of Mario's relations with Gloria. His method of unfolding the story through the extremely subtle, complex mind of Mario, crowded with fantasies, riddled with self-doubt, by turns self-deceiving and painfully lucid, makes this novel a brilliantly successful psychological narrative, and provides the most sharply defined insight into the fine shadings of Latin sexuality.

Alberto Ongaro

EXCELSIOR

Translated from the
Italian by

Gilles Cremonesi

HENRY REGNERY COMPANY
CHICAGO

Il Complice
Milan (Rizzoli Editore), 1965

Excelsior
London, 1967

*The first four chapters are translated
by S. O'Donnell*

139070

I

MAYBE IT WAS only an excuse to justify his instinctive repugnance for his part in the daily pantomime featuring widowed mother, unmarried daughter, son (his part), son's fiancée, of whom anything might be said save that she brought anything new into a depressed and utterly hopeless domestic situation. But he had to admit that on that evening, at the very moment when he surprised his mother picking her nose with her little finger in the dark silence of the kitchen lit up from the outside by the lights of the neighbouring apartments, he had discovered the true essence of the relationship which bound him to his world. Never, as in that moment, had he felt so different from her, from Francesca who was typing in the dining-room, from Luisa whom he had just left. Yet the times he had been so ashamed of them as to dissociate himself from them had been so frequent, he could have counted them by the dozen. But he had never felt nauseated by them, even the day he received his teacher's diploma and his mother had waited for him outside the school, all in her Sunday best, with her little blue and white hat, her handbag, stockings, gloves, and her enormous body crammed into a black silk dress, faded from sweat. He himself was so slim, so—well—so different physically, so conscious of the absurd, lop-sided combination they made together; and when he caught sight of her he was on the point of turning back, of retreating into the school or hiding somehow behind the students who were coming out, to avoid meeting her in public and giving away, through the kisses and embraces she would have given him, his true origin, which he had hidden even from his friends. He had felt ashamed; he had blushed, and tried to drag his mother away in haste as if he had a

5

strong urge to return home, but that was all: the cup, it seemed, was not yet full; it could indeed be said that he did not then yet suspect the true nature of the uneasiness, the impatience and all the other aspects of the estrangement he experienced when he was with his family, and he was content to put it all down to age, to the restlessness which was said to be typical of his generation. But there was more to it still: he did not belong, he had never had anything in common with his mother, nor with his sister, nor with the others in that house and that quarter, still less with Luisa whom he had accepted just like that, listlessly, mainly because she had wanted him so much. He had wondered by what freak of nature a man like himself could have been born of that woman, and in that sweaty corner of Venice, when the fact of the matter was, he had only to glance in the mirror to convince himself that he was of a different breed and as such should have had a different history and above all a different destiny. Here was the point: because it was now too late to redeem the years that had passed; but what of the future? Must he spend the twenty, thirty or forty years of life which remained to him like that, in a state of obsessive deadening contamination? He had hurled the cushion against the glass door of his room and furiously struck the walls with his bare fists, so violently that he hurt himself. The tapping of the typewriter had immediately stopped and Francesca had asked what the hell had got into him; then she went on typing, unconscious of the fact that he was crying on the other side of the wall and promising himself that he would do anything, accept any compromise if only to get free. But from then on things had gone from bad to worse. Luisa had dimly divined that something strange and terrible had happened to him, something which concerned her too, her life, the chances of an existence with which she had always been quietly satisfied and which she could not see endangered now without protest. What did it matter to her if his mother picked her nose? And why in Heaven's

6

name shouldn't his mother pick her nose? Not that he had ever told Luisa about the kitchen episode, but all the same this had been the implicit meaning of the questions she had been asking him for over a year now without getting an answer, this was the beginning of the rupture between them and the remote, ambiguous reason why they had met like enemies, shortly before, on their usual bridge—where she displayed the threat and blackmail of her womb, and he was already so distant, present only with one part of himself, the other part in solitary flight to a world of different connexions where his mother, Luisa and Francesca did not exist. And that world was there within reach, rich with opportunities—the wonderful red cabin on the beach, the peace he had never known: he had known it again today, and the feeling of that contact still lasted mysteriously in spite of his long, painful conversation with Luisa. What had they done once he had left? And Gloria, what had she done? Perhaps she had remained alone and had tried, in the evening calm, to imagine the reasons for his departure, watching him as far as the landing-stage, following him on the *vaporetto* which was taking him to Venice and losing track of him in the crowded city where she did not know her way; and perhaps her brother had come to call her, it's late, let's go in. Is that what happened? Is it, though? Because if it was, he would have felt strong enough to face the scandal and Luisa would perhaps have stopped appearing to him as a horrible threat. But, quite apart from what had happened, he would not have given in to Luisa's prevarications. It was certainly easier to live with an unquiet conscience than with an implacable, unreasonable companion such as Luisa would have been. Disgust, intolerance, ill-will would break all bounds were his existence completely fused not simply with two women who were strangers to him as were his mother and Francesca, but with three, who would have ended up in alliance against him and identified as a single, inexorable, solid enemy presence.

7

He had felt them roused shortly before, rekindled by the idea that Luisa would arrive; she would come with downcast eyes, her face half hidden by her dark glasses, burdened down with fear and with the long minutes spent in the doctor's consulting-room, the dark, dusty room, foul with a thousand persistent smells, where she had gone two days previously to make arrangements. And now that he had left her they came flooding in like a wave, like a sob which cannot be suppressed—like an involuntary reflex. Certainly it had been painful for him to meet her. When she had appeared at the corner of the *fondamenta*, her head somewhat bowed as was her habit, he felt for a moment suffocated by everything that was about to happen, by her weeping, her appeals to duty, by her tender re-evocation of their relationship which was now wrecked; then he moved towards her with his heart pounding and a sudden sensation of cold all over; he looked at her coldly, as one looks at an enemy, and began straightaway to attack her with his eyes, thinking all the time that he did not feel at all certain how that meeting would end. She meanwhile stopped by a greengrocer's, among the baskets set out on the street. From a distance he had to admit that she made a striking figure. She seemed even calm—a girl who had just left the house for a few minutes, naturally elegant and in a way endowed with something that made her like him. She did not look as though, a short while before, she had been stretched out half naked on the doctor's white bed, smelling of antiseptics, beneath the harsh electric light, listening to the splashing of the boats and the cries coming from outside and trying not to think of what was taking place in her womb. She was choosing the fruit carefully, slipping it into her nylon bag, murmuring something to somebody in the darkness of the shop, just as he had seen her so many times: they were unmistakeably hers, those words and gestures. As he approached her, seeing her so much her usual self, so meticulously true to her habits, he had thought that perhaps it was all a mistake and that in a

8

minute, when he reached her, Luisa would say something
to him, he did not quite know what, which would make
him smile and deliver him from his anguish. But now the
memory of that brief moment of hope was good for a
laugh: it hadn't come out that way—not by a long chalk.
As he had walked towards her his heart had practically
missed a beat, such was his sudden feeling of relief: but
when he had caught her eyes behind the dark glasses—
in the useless artificial shadow which hid her—and recognised the soft, piteous curve of her mouth beneath her
lipstick, he had realised that Luisa was devoured by terror,
a blunt terror which was even more dangerous for him
than he had thought. He piloted her slowly among the
fruit-baskets towards the canal and well? he had asked,
how did it go? Luisa did not answer, but merely shook
her head and shrugged, an ambiguous gesture, between
desolation and anger. I don't know, she said; there's nothing more to be done, nothing. It's too late. They walked
side by side along the *fondamenta,* she perhaps seeking to
feel in the pressure of the hand which held her some sign
of their former complicity; he withdrawn into himself, on
the defensive, alert to forestall the impact of the news
she might have for him. Suddenly Luisa began to cry:
a noiseless, disagreeable weeping, cold as the hiss of a cat.
It had frightened him and he had at once looked round
saying look, please don't, and he had watched the street
hoping that no-one could see her. Then they had leant
on the parapet of the bridge, he with an arm thrown
absently round her shoulders, and he had watched the
canal where their reflections, repeatedly taking shape then
dissolving, seemed to him like an insulting reflex of the
waters separating and uniting them. Her back shook
beneath his arm. Don't, he had repeated, don't cry, people
can see you, then adding with constrained gentleness,
everything will be all right, you'll see. But meanwhile he
kept wondering what he could do. What, though? the
same question which was still tormenting him even though
it seemed to him that he had already decided; and at

that moment, whilst a boat emerged from the curve of the canal and a light came on low almost at the level of the bridge, illuminating the dark interior of a kitchen with a cast-iron stove-pipe, a rag hanging from a wire, a woman who at once disappeared leaving a vague shadow behind her flickering on the wall—at that moment Luisa had begun to talk, saying how she already felt ill, how her stomach was upset, her head ached and she had cold shivers all over; and she looked shivering at the dense, dark, perfumed waters of the canal, until the next thing had been that soft hiccup and that jet of whitish saliva. How he had stiffened then; what a confused sense he had experienced of disaster and of pity, and of fear lest at that very moment, were he not on his guard, the first cracks would appear in his life, the process of disintegration would begin, the slide towards the abyss. How he hated her, good God how he loathed himself the way he had softened towards her—his hesitation, his fear and bewilderment—which had not stopped him from pulling out his handkerchief and wiping her mouth, and saying, don't worry, everything will be all right, you'll see, while he would rather have got clear away from her and have wiped her off his conscience. Then that cry, you'll have to do it, and that heart-breaking conversation which had somehow or other been etched into his heart, word for word. This is what you ought to say to me, only this, I don't want to hear anything else. But he did not say it; he did not say the one word she wanted to hear, he never had said it. He had grown progressively more shut away ever since they had given up making love and he had realised that now he had to settle the account for all the times he had enjoyed her, under the prow of her brother's boat, in the store-room at home, in the cinema where he had had her for the first time. What he had to tell her was whether it had been all a game or whether everything that he had had from her committed him now, at this very moment, to assume the responsibility which fell to him. Now. Luisa had gone straight to the heart of the matter with that request of hers, dictated by her distress, and abruptly faced him with the necessity of making a decision, now, as she had said, at that very moment, precisely on that bridge where he had long awaited her, till a few minutes before, thinking—and how differently their minds worked!—that for many reasons, but above all out of respect for his own existence, he could never have tied himself to her. They had never faced the problem so directly since Luisa had come to him a week before to tell him that it was perhaps too late to do anything. From then on in their meetings, which were anyway less frequent now than at one time, the long silences, their mutual embarrassment was underlaid by the demand which she had made of him, or rather which she had flung so savagely in his face at that moment. He knew that after her visit to the doctor Luisa would have forced him, in one way or another, to put the cards on the table, to make a decision, and it did not therefore surprise him that she had chosen that moment to do so. What had surprised and shaken him, however, had been the violence, the fury, the aggressiveness of her words, the obscenity of her remarks, the hatred which he had sensed in her voice. Aha, he had thought, so that's how it is, is it? And suddenly everything had seemed easier to him; he had no longer felt himself waylaid by pity or by the daunting consideration of Luisa's suffering which seemed to him suddenly remote, almost abstract, no concern of his, anyway, for having shown itself in that fit of temper which was so out of harmony with her normal composure. Proud, therefore, in the security of his own detachment, he had succeeded in establishing a greater distance between himself and her. Ah, so that's it? He had been tempted not to reply at all, simply to break off the conversation; but instead, for some peculiar reason, he merely murmured: And you? Didn't you get a kick out of it? with a touch of bravado in his voice, but not enough of it to silence her. So Luisa had thrown the handkerchief in his face, turned her back on him, and left the bridge as though determined to go away, or, better, as though it were she who wanted to get rid of something that disgusted her. Good, he had thought as he watched her hurry off, go and kill yourself, do what you like, disappear—but without any hope that she would really do so. She went down off the bridge, her hair streaming over her shoulders, her nylon bag almost brushing the steps. But she would stop before she reached the *fondamenta,* she would turn, not to abuse him nor to take up the conversation again at the point where they had left off, but to go back to the starting point : to her vomiting, to the touch of his arm, to her hopes and his own cold anxiety, to the very substance of their thorny relationship. And this is just what had happened. She had stopped, one hand on the parapet, the other hand clutching her bag, and looked at him, saying, Mario, what will you do if the baby arrives? in a tone of such bewildered hopelessness that he had been surprised and touched in spite of himself. Look, he had told himself, now is the time, tell her before it's too late, tell her you've made up your mind, that there's nothing to be done, there's not the slightest question of doing anything. But instead, he had only managed to breathe a few ambiguous words—I don't know, honestly I don't know—and she had turned her back on him again saying, *I* do, in a voice which had become strangely calm and assured. He had stood still for a few moments until he had seen her disappear down an alley beyond the shop where she had been a little earlier. Then he had found himself far from the bridge, in the street which led·to his home, a lighted cigarette between his fingers, in his head a shifting tangle of fragmentary thoughts, a decision taken but all too difficult to realise, and a condemned feeling of not being able to return to the Lido because it was now too late, and of having to go instead back to the other two women in his life, his mother and Francesca, who were enemies like the one he had just left, and back to the house where his story had begun.

12

2

To be sure, arriving late gave him a confused feeling of guilt and hostility towards the official. Well, there it was. These things never change. He could not pay attention to him that evening, could not resume the lesson at the point where it had been left off : genders, the different tenses, the subjunctive and the conditional, the functions of the infinitive on which he had to dwell at length a day or two before, the infinitive used as a noun (*Cantare non è vivere, Volere è potere*), and the other rules of syntax which the official was now trying hard to apply in an exercise, tracing a string of words before his eyes, one after the other, with impressive deliberation : with huge o's that were curiously three-dimensional, like spheres, m's climbing up the paper, z's with a sort of horrible hook which he insisted on adding at the foot, like a g without the round upper part. . . . To be sure, he felt guilty towards him, but thank heavens he detested him : he detested his obtuse, utterly Southern placidity, and the tenacity with which he pursued his objectives, at once ambitious and sordid. Salvatore. The Customs barracks was not good enough for him; he had wanted to leave it ever since a gaga old music teacher had told him, you have great possibilities, my boy, but singing is education; first learn to write and speak the way God intended, then come to me for your voice training—singing is education. He almost had to laugh, with dismal mirth, imagining a dark room, a piano on its last legs and the voice—tenor? baritone?—of the official rising ambitiously up the scale, one, two, three and four, tra-la-la-la. What a world he lived in, a world full of snivelling girls who got themselves pregnant, of spiteful sisters, of little Customs men who came barging in right on that evening when he was feeling so disturbed and wretched, so terrified of the future, and drove him up the wall with their lunatic schemes. A singer who could take operatic roles and not, as he had told him without further explanations the time he first went to him, not just another pop vocalist. But now he heard his singer give a gentle cough beside him and mutter something which perhaps expressed some obscure doubt about syntax, some question whose meaning escaped him, but to which he replied, nonetheless, with a nod. What a lot he had to think about that evening: Luisa's womb, the number of days he would have to wait, and the ever-brightening image of Gloria smiling at him on the beach, shaking his hand and holding it a few moments longer than necessary. What else could have been meant by her holding his hand if not a sudden surge of emotion, which might be destined to last? But the open book was beckoning on the table and the official's breathing had the irritating regularity of a clock marking the time. How many minutes had passed since the beginning of the lesson? He felt tempted to go away, to withdraw into his room and wait till the man had finished the exercise, but something kept him by the table, in the light of the lamp: it was the hostile presence of Francesca which could be sensed as though it were a sound, a strident hiss coming from the other side of the house. Some teacher he is— comes in late, makes the fellow work on his own! He could almost hear Francesca's thoughts buzzing about angrily and see her grey eyes beneath her black brows, her hands as solid as a man's; how well he knew those hands—he could not look at them without recalling incidents of long ago, the rare occasions when they had gently caressed him and the more frequent times when they had tried to smack him hard in the face. He could even imagine the look that Francesca and her mother would have exchanged, Francesca standing at the kitchen sink, her ear strained to catch the furtive shuffle of his footsteps, her mother still seated at the table, her head nodding, her eyelids heavy with sleep and, beneath her eyelids, eyes lit

14

with a dull glow of disquiet, and the guilty ponderings that would have come into his own mind knowing that at bottom the unhappiness and weariness which united these two women in the kitchen against him were justified. Too many things had already happened, and if he wanted to avoid that day ending in a clash with Francesca he had to stay quietly with his pupil, whose presence was anyway not so all-pervading as to blot out the afternoon's events: Gloria turning to give him a second, gratuitous au revoir, Fenzo looking hard the other way, Alessandro's eloquent silence—memories that washed in and out like the sea. Anyway, it was certainly good to know that the next day he would be able to take things up again where they had been left off and perhaps rediscover the strange feeling of ecstasy that had come over him when he envisaged the possible consequences of his meeting with Gloria. There were, luckily, a few nice, convenient aspects to the situation. Fenzo would be glad to go on having him. There was no doubt on that score. He had told him endless times to come along, proud of his cabin on the most fashionable stretch of the beach, of his new friends and of all the things which, thanks to his father's overnight fortune, he had managed to win for himself in no time. He too had indirectly begun to enjoy this fortune. In the last two days he had breathed a different air from his usual one and felt a change coming over him; he had noticed himself slowly but surely adapting to a new environment. Of course there were obstacles, there was hostility to overcome, like those two whose names he wouldn't mind muddling up, Alessandro and Matteo or Matteo and Alessandro—they had been against him from the start, he'd realised at once. But *she* was friendly, the way she'd shaken his hand, keeping hold of it and smiling in that unambiguous way. How much had she taken to him? He had tried cautiously to find out, he had even tried sounding out Fenzo, but Fenzo evidently hadn't understood or had pretended not to. Something, it seemed to him, had certainly happened—he'd just need to find out more about it. Tomorrow, he thought, tomorrow. He was suddenly aware, to his chagrin, that tomorrow was still hours away and he felt as though stopped short by his very thoughts and driven back within the four walls of the dining-room.

It was hot. Outside, from the street, through the open window, there came shouts, laughter, the sound of footsteps, the clink of glasses at the cold-drinks stall, the ring of a telephone. Meanwhile the Customs man went on writing, but faster now, with the energy of a horse nearing the winning-post. He gazed absently at the gold fountain-pen moving across the paper, without troubling to check how his pupil was doing the exercise, but noting with a hazy sense of irritation but also of vague professional satisfaction, that he had finished it very quickly. A few minutes later he noted that the man had not made any mistakes; well, anyway, he thought, my lessons have been of some use to him after all, I've managed to teach him something. Good, he murmured almost unwittingly, grammar and syntax are all in order; but meanwhile he was asking himself what next, whether to give him another exercise or to start work. He looked at the man. Serious, sober as ever, he seemed to be waiting for the lesson to continue. Was there really no way of avoiding it? some way other than just another exercise to do on his own, something better thought out, more persuasive, too? Why, he asked suddenly, leafing through the pages of the grammar, did you become a Customs official? The man gave him a puzzled look, then wiped his hand across his brow. It's an honourable calling, he softly replied, somewhat disconcerted, as though he were having difficulty understanding the reason for the question. He closed the book and lit a cigarette. Tell me, he said, as though he was following some private method of tuition, in good Italian, as though you were writing; tell me about yourself, your life here in a strange city. You need to learn to express yourself properly. The man cleared his throat and seemed to be searching his memory for the distant motives behind his enlistment, the barracks in the South, the stages

16

of his journey across the country to this house. I made up my mind, he was saying, one day.... But now he was no longer listening to him, for there had been that long silence in the two cabins and her sitting, sort of relaxed, her arms hanging loose and her tanned belly all dry and her gaze falling on him every so often; and he sitting on the sand, leaning on one of the awning-poles, conscious of the rapport which was springing up between them. Alessandro and Matteo were away; no, only Matteo had gone, Alessandro had stayed behind; but he had this time barely noticed his prickly presence and had continued gazing down at her until she had raised her head and, meeting his eyes, had at first simply sustained them, but then she had cradled and caressed him for a long while, shamelessly. Had it been thus? Or had it gone differently? Then it was she who had said to him, when he had left, see you tomorrow, and to him it had seemed that she really was saying, see you tomorrow, my darling, now that I've found you, don't let me down. The Customs man's voice was like the irritating buzz of an insect in the background, but a wave of the hand could dispel it and bring him back to lie on the beach at the centre of this episode, which may have happened in fact or only in his imagination, it was difficult to say. And yet, and yet... Perhaps Gloria was not a figment of his imagination, or if she was, she might cease to be so. Something had indeed happened, something rather vague, perhaps, it was difficult to describe it, but in her company, in the unwonted surroundings of the *Excelsior,* he had felt himself sort of disembodied, he had felt a sense of alleviation, as though freed from a part of himself which was burdensome to carry. He could remember the very moment when it had happened. They were both watching the little girl who had suddenly appeared between the two cabins; she had shouted something in some unknown language and sat down cross-legged in front of Gloria's cabin. Then a woman had come, taken her in her arms and dashed off, kicking up flurries of sand. At once they had both smiled, and that

17

had been the precise moment. A knot had been loosened, and feeling suddenly alleviated, renovated, content for the first time in so many days, he had thought, am I really here? can this really be me? True, it had lasted only a moment, the interval of their simultaneous smile, but if he had immediately reverted to being as he was before, and here he was again at home, beneath the light in the dining-room in the evil presence of the Customs man, had there not, even so, been that moment? Something, he murmured, something has happened. But now he was aware of the man's look and of his silence. What was the time? Had he finished already? Go on, he said, go on. But the man had nothing more to tell; the thread of his memories had been broken off, and now he grimaced and gestured with his hand, as much as to say, that's all, or, I wouldn't know what to talk about. He took up the book of exercises. For next time, he said, and searched through the pages. It was still early, he realised, but he could hold out no longer. I don't feel well, he went on, d'you mind if we stop for this evening. The man got up, took his books, quietly said goodnight and left the room. He heard the door open and shut softly and could feel Francesca's silent surprise in the kitchen and her bitter, warped smile. What the hell, he muttered, I couldn't I'd had enough. He left the dining-room, went into his bedroom and dropped heavily onto the bed, all his memory afire.

But now that he was alone he found it more difficult to go back over the happy events of the afternoon and dwell on them without the whole time running up against that ghastly hour he had gone through before getting home, when he had sat on the parapet of the bridge waiting for Luisa and had reviewed his situation right from the start; and with Luisa's arrival he had felt himself hemmed in, threatened by a mysterious, implacable force. Now his thoughts kept returning to that hour, to Luisa going home, with her womb which would shortly start to swell, and to Luisa's room crowded with her thoughts, and to the

18

whispering in the neighbouring rooms, to the frightened questions, what's the matter with her, what's happened to her?, and to her weeping, and to the unsuspected presence of Francesca who, on the other side of the partition, in the kitchen, was surely passing judgment on him.

3

A LITTLE EARLIER, in the bathroom, with the first sounds of the household getting up, he had unexpectedly caught the reflection of his face, and as he looked at it a strange feeling had come over him, a sort of heady, insolent vitality. He had smiled at the fleeting thought that his was not the face of a man obliged to act against his will. True, he was in an ambiguous situation which would have to be cleared up quickly, though heaven knows how it had got that way. Perhaps it was a case of interference, some random manipulation of the cards which had resulted in his accidentally being dealt someone else's hand. That was probably it : and he had left the house to start setting things straight right away. He walked with quiet self-assurance along the streets leading from his quarter to the centre of town in the clear, pearly sunlight, with the few folk who were astir. He was going up the steps of a bridge when he was overtaken by a vague feeling of anxiety, almost a presentiment of imminent danger— possibly a phantasm escaped from the night hours or perhaps the result of his surprise at being, in spite of every-thing, calm. He looked round anxiously as though expect-ing to find someone watching him or to hear his name being called; but it was nothing, he soon realised, but his anticipation of a possible encounter at that moment with a boat laden with sacks, steered by a brawny lad who looked a little like Luisa. The boat appeared at a point of the canal, glided rapidly over the water sending up hostile sprays of green water and came alongside the quay with the aggressive confidence of an enemy craft. Quickly, he thought wearily, and he practically ran off the bridge to be out of the way before the boat appeared. But it was now as though he could no longer escape the encounter, as though the boat and the boy and the whole cargo were all to come surging into him and drag him in spite of himself into a brutal dialogue which once more invested Luisa's image, so distant, so strangely innocuous till a moment before, with all its menace. Yesterday she came home in floods of tears and shut herself in her room, what have you done to her? Perhaps Luisa had talked and her brothers were now looking for him to confront him publicly with the indelicate matter of her pregnancy and ask him questions he wouldn't know how to answer. He sighed. The miraculous equanimity of a moment before was quite gone, in its place there was a stinging wound, a burn like a ripped-up cloth. He was less sure of himself now as he walked, thinking that perhaps it was better to learn not to delude himself because it was to him, after all, that this was all happening. It was, he imagined hazily, like going into battle in the secure conviction of one's invulnerability. Instead of which, all of a sudden a bullet whistles up and hits you slap in the forehead in the same brutal and unexpected way that Luisa had struck his thoughts a little earlier. What would he do if they stopped him? Not that he was afraid of them, but if she really had gone home yesterday in a terrible state and had shut herself in her room and someone had heard her through the door weeping, she must have said something by way of explanation. Perhaps, he thought, it was better to speak up and have it all out once for all. But it was so difficult, so tiring to have it out. It was like discovering a damaged part of oneself, like standing a test without any warning. A prick of the lancet, a suture, and the pain would stop. Were he sure of it he wouldn't have hesitated an instant; but, he reflected, the analogy could scarcely be made to apply in his case. The operation might reveal a tumour, a gangrene, the rotten squalid roots of his decision. The thing was, he was afraid to give in. That was the long and the short of it. He was afraid that once he spoke out, his decision would strike everyone as so monstrous that

21

he too would see it that way. Which is why yesterday he'd hidden it even from Luisa. He shivered. Perhaps everything he'd thought of late, and especially yesterday, while he was waiting for Luisa on the bridge, was simply the sterile, yapping protests of weakness. Even his cruelty, which had seemed to him to be virtually the new measure of his life, was perhaps no more than the ephemeral product of an unbearable tension. Who knows how he'd act if it came to the point of deciding. Perhaps his ambiguous pity for Luisa, the scandalised shrieks, the violence with which he would be assaulted from all sides —would these not get the better of him? Christ! he thought. He felt a sudden need to grab hold of something more solid than the disgust and hatred which he realised, to his surprise, were no more than a disguise for his instinct for self-preservation; and all at once the Lido, the beach, the people moving about in it, Gloria, Alessandro and Matteo, assumed a concrete reality which they had hitherto lacked. They had been at first a vague presentiment, an allusion to unspecified possibilities, an extraneous current which occasionally impinged on his consciousness. He ran into them haphazardly when he had imagined, perhaps quite unjustifiably, that something new had come into his life. He had come upon them for a moment and at once had lost them, as they were swept away by more immediate, more painful elements. And yet perhaps he had not been mistaken, perhaps without his realising it the face he saw in the mirror, the grey eyes, the physique, acting as instruments independently of his consciousness and to happier effect, had established valuable contacts which he could now exploit. He almost broke into a run so as to arrive as soon as possible at the Lido, so as to establish as soon as possible whether what he imagined was true. He still did not know why, but he had a feeling that somehow or other he would find it easier to free himself of Luisa if he could win the friendship of Gloria, Alessandro and Matteo. He had a hazy conviction that somehow or other, if he were to learn their rules and

22

their language the ambivalence of his life would be resolved. He ran in the morning sunshine to get there the quicker, though the immediacy of his goal, the Lido, somewhat intimidated him. How would he be received this morning? Would he discover in Gloria the same experimental welcome, the same manifest addiction for him, or a new attitude more difficult to decipher? And the other two, Alessandro and Matteo, what was he to expect from them? We'll see, he said, we'll see, and he slowed his pace. He didn't feel quite prepared for the encounter, nor could he trust himself to rely on improvisation. He was up against three people, and two of them at any rate were hostile. Matteo had never addressed a word to him, nor had he said goodbye to him when he had had to leave them in the late afternoon. Alessandro had treated him with quiet indifference, unostentatiously so, just as if he did not exist. He had disliked them both and had scarcely been able to avoid provoking them openly. Perhaps Gloria had helped him by preventing his feeling too much of an outsider, but she had not been able wholly to eliminate the friction. What was he to do today if Alessandro's and Matteo's hostility became more explicit? He was certainly not going to beg for their friendship, but neither would he let them discourage him with their offensive taciturnity, their provocative indifference. That's it, he muttered, as though he had received some unlooked-for advice, some assistance. Whatever they did, he would act in a dignified manner, he would be cautious and on his guard and, in order to get better acquainted with them, he would observe them closely, though not obviously, without betraying the need he had of them. This above all he had to avoid. He was a little ashamed as it was of the importance he was according them, of the loneliness which impelled him to seek their company. Before he had met them, a painful awareness of his social inferiority had always kept him at a distance from their sort of people and every time that, in the random course of day-to-day encounters, he had happened to rub up against boys or

23

girls from a different material and educational *milieu,* his lower-class consciousness had made him smart bitterly. Pride, however, had always saved him from defeatism, a pride which was sometimes silent and tongue-tied, at other times unshackled and so violent that it was well-nigh indistinguishable from hatred. Admittedly, though, even on those occasions his state of mind was no different from his present one: a violent attraction, a quite shameless need for valued contacts, at all events, underlay his conduct. The difference was that formerly his need was frustrated from the start whereas now it was developing, it was growing like a fever little by little as he glimpsed the possibility of satisfying it. How shameful, though! How abject it was to feel oneself so greedy, soft, so dominated by squalid, murky ideas like these. Francesca would have laughed. Were she to know of them she would wither him with her scorn. But it was to himself that he had to account, not to the rigid morality of Francesca. And if he wanted Gloria to fall in love with him there was no reason on earth why he shouldn't satisfy himself. On this, he reached the landing-stage and boarded the *vaporetto* for the Lido. The air was now scorching, the paving stones of the quayside had a dazzling shimmer. What, he wondered, was Luisa up to? Perhaps she was still in bed, but this was not the moment to think about her. Perhaps she had just woken up only to rediscover, unaltered after a night's sleep, the anguish of the previous day. She would get up and slowly put on her slip, her eyes resting sightlessly on the objects in the room and focussed on the glistening walls of her fear. The day just beginning would hold no surprises for her. It was late, too late, even the doctor had said so in the dingy consulting-room where he had seen her; barefoot she would go into the bathroom, ignoring her mother's questions, how d'you feel today? couldn't you have stayed in bed? He could have wished that she too might have had someone to cling to, some patch of shade in which to rest. But she was like the desert—listlessness, unhappiness

24

without limits. Better not think of her, though, better stay out of reach of the echo of her fear. The *vaporetto* chugged ahead, someone on board was laughing, in the light of the distant beach she was on her way down, she was looking around her to catch sight of him, she sat down in front of her cabin, and refused, shaking her head, to leave the spot. No, she said, encouraging him to cruelty: and it was like a wrench for Alessandro who dallied a few moments beside her, then dropped onto the sand as though struck dead. Perhaps he would arrive to find no further trace of him, perhaps Gloria was helping him and her movements, her presence were the only reality of the moment, the texture of the day of which he held the thread. . . .

4

THERE WAS SOMETHING strange in the way Alessandro
was steering the launch. He drove it at full tilt on a
straight course, then swerved abruptly, first right, then left,
then again right and left, in a sort of restless, irritating
manoeuvre. Maybe he wanted to go back to the beach
as soon as possible and untangle his emotions, the knot of
vexation, pain and anxiety which was responsible for
the boat's capricious deviations. But he was still undecided.
Maybe Gloria, stretched out on the deck, indifferent as a
statue, was inhibiting him from any course other than
this disorganised careering back and forth across the bay.
But the sense of uneasiness was growing, it was increasing
every minute. From the moment early in the afternoon
that Gloria had come down to the beach with her usual
escorts, had caught sight of him and hastily invited him
to follow her—as if wanting to disguise some agitation—
there had been a subtle odour breathing in the air:
whether stifling or pleasurable it was hard to say. Certainly
this was his moment. That he was the cause of this
difficult situation was assuredly a motive for pride. After
the hours of waiting spent with Fenzo, after the thousand
questions: will she come? won't she? will she be changed
from yesterday? After the long agony when, lying restlessly in Fenzo's deck-chair or standing tensely in front of
the doors of the *Excelsior,* he had been torn endlessly
between fear and hope, it was, after all, a relief to be now
in her company. His anxiety had been somewhat mitigated
when they had boarded the launch and she had lain down
beside him on the deck. Then he had thought, this is it,
here and now, without knowing just what 'it' was, but
with a vague presentiment that at that moment two
realities, his and hers, had begun to fuse. Perhaps...

perhaps Alessandro and Matteo had realised that Gloria
was slipping away from them and they were fighting
against her deserting, the one with his petulant steering,
the other confining himself to a silent supervision. Because
Matteo was watching him. He had not taken his eyes off
him from the moment the launch had cast off from the
jetty. He had made no comment when he had accepted
Gloria's invitation to join them, but his annoyance was
none the less obvious. Matteo's gaze was even now fixed
on him, slipping and clawing its way down his body,
secretly telling him that in spite of his tanned skin, his
sleek brown hair, his opaque grey eyes, his cultivated
speech and movements, his origins had been recognised
and hence his place in their group was being challenged.
He felt a sudden cold anger towards this austere youth
who kept calm even in the heat of discussion, but at
the same time he was seized with fear at the idea that
Matteo may have not only seen through his origins but also
uncovered the soft, defenceless part of his nature—his
greedy little lower-middle-class nature—and the need he
had of him. Perhaps he had been wrong to accept Gloria's
invitation. It had left his dignity compromised and this put
him at a disadvantage *vis-à-vis* his hosts, for whom he
was merely an intrusive, a flashy, irritating and foreign
element, the one instrument out of tune in their
harmonious whole. Because, as he was now painfully
aware, Fenzo had been accepted without reserve: so it
seemed, at any rate, to watch him moving about the
launch, drinking cool beer from Gloria's thermos, laughing,
chatting without the slightest sign of caution on his part
or of annoyance on that of the others. Fenzo had been
accepted and he had not. And yet nobody could have
denied that there was a substantial difference between
him and Fenzo, not only in physical appearance, but
above all in the more secret regions of their character:
his with its components of pride and bashfulness, Fenzo's
vulgar, exuberant, coarse, for all the patience with which
he strove to soften it. Of course they had nothing to fear

27

from Fenzo, and this was perhaps why they preferred him; whatever Fenzo did, he would never manage to disturb the pattern of their relationship, he would never leave the slightest trace of himself in their dominant position. With him it was another matter. They somehow divined his furtive violence and were compelled to keep an eye on him for fear he might turn dangerous. Not that it could fairly be maintained that they seemed intimidated. Whatever reasons they may have discovered, searching their thoughts, for their hostility, Alessandro and Matteo behaved as though they were stronger than he was. Now too Alessandro surprised him with a sudden burst of laughter, the cause of which escaped him. Why was Alessandro laughing? Did it express joy, or did it disguise a fit of nerves? He watched him with the suspicion that he had not understood him at all; he watched Matteo through half-closed eyelids and found himself visualising them all elsewhere—for no reason he could recognise, but finding in the vision a certain ironical pertinence—in the act of coming down the stairs of their bijoux residences or of going up them and emerging onto a balcony overlooking the street, set there against a background of appropriate objects, in the quiet shade of a quiet afternoon, and identified with them. For an instant he saw life from their vantage-point, from just that balcony on the street, with the cars roaring past below and the launch careering madly across the bay, and he himself, the outsider sitting on the deck, engaged in a motionless struggle with them : and he suddenly had a vague feeling that those objects, those very objects right there on the boat served to feed their irritation, were reflected in the insulting curl at the corner of Matteo's mouth. Anger welled up in him, blinded him. He looked at Matteo and Alessandro almost without seeing them and poured out a silent stream of abuse at them. So his presence was not welcome? So they were challenging him, showing their open preference for Fenzo? Very well, then, he would accept their challenge and, forestalling their every move, would get his own blow in

28

first, at their weakest point. At once, though. He moved slightly on the launch and rested his eyes on Gloria. The girl seemed to be waiting for him. Half-reclining in the bows, her hair loose in the wind, her soft body tanned by the sun, Gloria met his gaze and suddenly seemed resolved to hold it for a while, just so, calmly, neither provocative nor impulsive. So, he thought, as his heart began to pound, so you're really on my side, you justify my presence even against those who don't want it; so long as you look at me like this nothing can happen to me. But if he wanted to strike a tangible blow now against his hosts he had to do it in the best possible way. He had above all to disconcert them, avoiding actions which were all too easy to foresee, and to mystify them, showing himself different from the preconception they had of him. Gloria's body now seemed to be impatiently waiting for a gesture from him, some gesture of complicity from his fingers, some movement of possession from his hand. It would have been infinitely easy to take up the tacit offer which Gloria was making to him: if he had moved his hand towards her he could have caressed her arm, lying carelessly on the bow, without being seen. Ancient, slumbering tremors, lost traces of other contacts stirred now, tingled on his body, forcing it towards Gloria's. He had only to move his hand a little and it would have been like crossing an enemy frontier and being safe, finding shelter with an accomplice. But his hand still remained riveted to the deck, constrained to deliberate immobility, for better or for worse he did not know, but it seemed to him that if he had given it up he would in some sort have betrayed himself. And yet, if he did not want to stifle with rage, he had to act now. He could no longer endure the way he was being treated and felt the need for immediate retaliation. But it was, he realised, a need which arose all of a sudden and was at once frustrated: to act at that moment, to show his hand in some motion of challenge or of possession was not so easy as Gloria's invitation might suggest. Gloria was making advances, true enough, but how far would she go? what would have been her reaction if he had openly leant over to caress her or simply reached out behind him until he touched her? Now that she had placed herself almost behind his back, at an angle to her earlier position, Gloria was no longer an absolute certainty, she assumed a sort of unnatural ambiguity. Perhaps he would do better to hold his hand in spite of everything, and wait for a more opportune moment, confining himself for the time being to titillating Gloria's desire by turning round to her from time to time to seek her eyes and smile at her. Maybe, he thought, it was better this way; but suddenly a hand insinuated itself into his thoughts and he felt it drop onto his back and stroke it gently and shyly, then slide down as far as his haunches, and heard it fall softly back onto the polished planking of the bows. Gloria's hand took him so much by surprise that he needed a moment to realise exactly what had happened; but when Gloria, perhaps surprised at his lack of response, perhaps determined to find out how much he wanted her, perhaps simply incapable of controlling her own agitation, when she repeated her caress, he turned to her, quietly and firmly took her hand, drew it to his face and brushed her open palm over his lips. All this he did openly, gravely, before the astonished eyes of Alessandro, Matteo and Fenzo, careless now of their judgment, forgetful of the caution which up to a few moments earlier had seemed necessary to him and of the subtle, neurotic calculations he had made, but quickly calculating still that, for the ends he had resolved on, it was essential to show that no arbitrary presumption had driven him to behave in this way, but an unequivocal, insistent and deliberate invitation by Gloria. And so, after briefly holding the girl's hand against his lips, he let go of it to resume his original position. But Gloria's arm slipped down to his thigh and remained there preventing him, with a slight pressure, from moving. Then, as it was clear that he could not do otherwise, under the touch of that full, rounded, consenting arm on

30

his skin, he placed his fingers on it and stroked it gently and possessively. Alessandro blushed violently, then altered course with a brusque movement and steered the launch towards the shore.

5

HE'D SPENT the past few hours with Fenzo under the beach awning, then at a restaurant, and finally in the crowded little bar on the piazza not far from the *Excelsior*. It had been a confusing evening, full of unpredictable events that just wouldn't tally. First she had suddenly turned cold and aloof, then she'd snapped goodbye to walk off with Alessandro and Matteo, and finally she hadn't returned to the beach. This incredible change of attitude had thrown him off balance, toppling his certainty that the boat incident had committed them both to a serious relationship. He had risen to the occasion with dignity, concealing his annoyance behind a polite, mute nod as she left with her escorts. He was overtaken by a sense of total failure which was not to leave him until much later when the situation, so it seemed to him, took another turn. In the meantime he submitted himself to a cross-examination. Had he been wrong to react to her tacit encouragement? Perhaps she stroked his naked back by way of an opening move. True it was a telling gesture but one calculated to give a vague, equivocal impression. Perhaps she hadn't counted on any reaction at all and his casually possessive gesture may have come as a complete surprise, and an unpleasant one at that, for he had to admit that his temerity had put her in an awkward position. It had exposed her, compromised her in Alessandro's and Matteo's eyes and even in Fenzo's, who had obviously endorsed his hosts' standards and judgments. As Gloria jumped up to hop off the boat before it had even bumped against the jetty, his sense of accomplishment vanished. Victory crumbled to defeat. Her arm, so affectionate a moment before, instantly became rigid, undemonstrative, and then positively hostile. She had reversed their roles, allotting to him that of the furtive aggressor who had been so bold as to caress her, and to herself that of the offended party responding with a slap in the face or an insult. The episode had scarcely concluded when it began to disintegrate and lose shape. He reconstructed the scene for hours on end, churning it over and over as he lay in the sand waiting uselessly for her to reappear, reliving it all as he wandered aimlessly through the streets of the Lido with a cool Fenzo at his side. Then when he'd mustered up enough courage to penetrate the serene, elegant precincts of the bar opposite the Casino, he sat down, and there he was, back on the boat: Gloria caressed his back and he submitted to the gesture, simulating indifference, or at any rate placidly, with none of the eager responsiveness of before. This time round Gloria didn't walk off; she stayed at his side on the beach and it became obvious to everyone how much she cared for him. And so on, for hours. As he tried to calculate just how final her gesture had been, and whether he could expect Gloria to be anything but cool and Alessandro and Matteo anything but vindictive after what had happened, a clock struck near by reminding him of another unalterable fact: he was still away from home and it was time to return. He'd noticed lately that wherever he was, and particularly at the Lido, the awareness of his predicament invariably sharpened at his homing hour. He knew that once he'd set foot in Venice, Luisa's presence, and all the other fears that Gloria's company had dispelled, would fall ominously about him. At this very moment they'd be expecting him on the other side of the lagoon. His mother's house started to take on the sinister appearance of a trap. As the clock finished striking he felt winded, as if he'd heard the trap snap to. He couldn't go home; he would have to stay out all night, at a safe distance. But annoyed and bitter at the irony of it all, he renounced the adventure, reasoning that if he didn't return home tonight, how would he be able to face it tomorrow or later when things really

33

came to a head. Then Gloria came without her usual escort of brother and fiancé. Instead she was accompanied by an elegant middle-aged woman whom he didn't recognise and who was obviously a close friend of hers. She saw him and nodded. She sat with her friend near by at one of the few vacant tables and ordered a gin and tonic. He listened in silence for about an hour, occasionally answering Fenzo who was now his talkative self again. He was deaf to all voices but Gloria's. Her conversation reached him intermittently like a moth flickering in and out of the light: a blue-green bikini, the usual cut, not too indecent . . . blue-green, such a pretty colour . . . sets off one's tan. The voice-moth faded out, then back into the lights and the sounds of the bar. He strained to catch it and gathered that she would be going to Venice tomorrow at ten. She was going to Pettinelli's where she had ordered the bikini a few days ago . . . Oh, the usual life, you know: beach, hotel, bar, bar, hotel, beach, with an occasional evening at the Casino night-club . . . yes, quite . . . . It was the other voice: she agreed, except that, unfortunately, she was no longer so young, you know, and perhaps at her age it was better to spend the evenings quietly at the hotel with the usual people, among whom, furthermore. . . . Suddenly he had had the suspicion that Gloria had intended him to overhear, that she was covertly inviting him to meet her in Venice the next day. She darted him a look, which he caught—a look of tender complicity that belied her earlier severity. She had indicated the hour of her arrival at Pettinelli's, around ten o'clock which seemed reasonable; and she'd added that she planned to spend the whole morning in Venice. He felt better and more self-assured. As he re-examined the situation in the light of Gloria's latest comportment, he concluded that perhaps he hadn't committed any blunder after all during the afternoon's outing. The sensation of failure vanished and with it the fear of going home. He got up, said good-night to Fenzo, and smiled openly at Gloria and her friend. He left the bar and made for the wharf to catch the last boat back to Venice. What else had happened? She had reacted to his smile and his look as if distressed to see him leave. There was a curious gleam in her eyes, perhaps a flicker of intelligent approbation which confirmed his conjectures and suggested even more optimistic ones. For the first time in many days he returned home whistling softly, and for once he wasn't repelled by the hall, nor by the acrid smell of the rooms, nor by all the shiny modern furniture which had always epitomised his family's condition for him. It just didn't affect him. He was mentally and visually absorbed by less immediate images, by Gloria's cabin, by the beach, by the thought of meeting her alone tomorrow without the hostile surveillance of Alessandro and Matteo. He was certain that Gloria could be the decisive factor in his future, a positive asset, and this certainty had nothing whatever to do with what feelings he might have for her, which were in any case so vague and indefinite, and so flimsy as to evade assessment. She would be the miracle of his unmiraculous life. Once in his room he sang her name as he undressed. He recalled her fresh, expressive face, her light silk dresses, her gentle eyes, her warm cultivated voice, her every gesture that accorded so harmoniously with that serene, temperate, comfortable background which differed so vastly from his own. Then something happened. The hall light switched on and a shadow fell abruptly across the glass door, interrupting his train of thought, cancelling its images. He was afraid. An animal need to defend himself was succeeded by the realisation that defence would be useless. The thought flashed through his mind that something serious must have happened in his absence. Francesca had been waiting for him. Now she came into his room and came right up to him. It was late and she wasn't undressed yet, probably because she'd been out all evening and had only just returned. He didn't ask what she wanted. Her troubled face cut by the half-shadow of the doorway was set in an aggressive, pained expression. Somehow or other she had found him out. She knew

35

about his relations with Luisa, knew about the girl's condition and knew, what's more, that he had decided to break it all off. Well, here we go, he thought, it's no use, we'll have to have it out. But something inside him recoiled, refused to allow him to slip into his old attitude. It made him wonder what had happened to that cheerful fellow who had just come home whistling, what had happened to his unshakable faith in the morrow? Francesca began to speak. She said she'd been to see her—how else could she have found out?—to see Luisa's mother, who was shattered, absolutely desperate about her daughter who had been locked in her room for twenty-four hours. Hadn't it been longer? Hadn't it been a week, a month, a year since he'd seen her at the foot of the bridge, her nylon bag bulging with fruit, her eyes bulging with resentment? Her mother had turned to Francesca for an explanation of Luisa's sullen bitterness. And she, in turn, had come to him, as always, because he was bound to know what had happened. He imagined her waking up in the morning, while he was on the boat speeding towards the Lido: she put on her slip and gaped at herself like a doll with its eyes rolled up. What had happened? The questions didn't take him by surprise; it was something worse, more abrasive, that graceless stab in the back that put him in his place and made a mockery of his reflections on the miraculous nature of his encounter with Gloria, and on the possibilities of her helping him to find a solution for it all. Damn it, he thought, I can't escape for a moment before somebody barges in to rub my nose in it all. But he had to admit that he wasn't really very ruffled. Francesca had made the mistake of donning the same damned worn out old image of herself, that of his eternal censor, which made it easy for him to fend her off. Well then, out with it, what had happened? He was amazed at himself: after the initial panic, he felt cool and courageous as never before. He said Luisa was pregnant, and that he had no intention of marrying her. Luisa had removed any hope of interrupting the pregnancy,

36

perhaps deliberately, by telling him too late, and a natural miscarriage was unlikely. He felt a bit of a heel, but guilt and remorse, however painful, could never persuade him to sacrifice his life for a woman he didn't love. Her schemes for holding on to him hadn't been exactly honest. All this and a lot besides had contributed to his decision that she wasn't the right match for him. Anyway, it didn't all boil down to his self-centredness. There was something bigger, older, deep within his very being. It was ... Did she really want to know? It was his survival instinct that drove him to sacrifice someone who would otherwise destroy him. He spoke without raising his voice, without any sign of emotion, surprised at how reasonable and sincere he managed to sound. Regardless of what she might think, he didn't feel he was being shabby. His self-restraint had made him courageous and noble. There was a long pause. He waited for Francesca's reply, bracing himself for what he knew would be a violent outburst. He wasn't afraid of her as he had been since he was a boy whenever she'd hauled him over the coals. He felt the silence quicken as he eyed her impatiently, mutely querying her hesitation, wondering why she hadn't started passing judgment on what he'd just said. She stood before him, tall, pale, quiet, and remotely unfamiliar in her afternoon dress. She seemed at a loss for words. As he watched her, he realised, perhaps for the first time, that she was no match for him. He wondered if his bluntness might have embarrassed her. He sneered inwardly, knowing ironically that it was a realisation he would have relished under any other circumstances, but which afforded him slim pleasure now. The atmosphere was too icy, and, to his surprise, her face had lost all traces of aggression; it looked more delicate and tired, almost as if it belonged to some-one else. How odd to see her like this. He felt almost sorry for her. He wondered whether she would retreat before his determination; instead, she began to speak: what about the child, then? As her face began to take on the menacing look it usually acquired at such times, he realised that so far he'd only conceived of the baby in a vague, abstract way: the irritant responsible for the sorry pickle he'd got into. That the baby should have a future at all hadn't crossed his mind. It now started to grow, to take on a form, and come to life within him. The glorious image that grew out of Francesca's voice threatened to overpower him. Baby. A cruel, absurd word. If they kept calling it 'the baby' it would be crushed, reduced by this label to the status of an object. Who was it? what was it? and what did it want of him? He said, I don't know, I can't think about *that*. There was still a chance it wouldn't be born. But he didn't believe what he was saying, nor did he suppose Francesca would have any such hopes. She confirmed this by stirring out of her strange torpor. If he hadn't given the baby a thought, what had he been thinking of? she inquired, still keeping her voice down but starting to become more and more agitated. What on earth had he been thinking about? What could he say? The previous days' thousand images suddenly thronged together, then contracted to a single point in his memory: the bridge where Luisa had gone down the steps and the dirty handkerchief she'd thrown at him which had wet his hands. There's only one thing left for me to do, she had shouted. That was the first step in her plan: she would stubbornly lock herself in her room, then he would supply the geometrical parallel by locking himself in his. He was only thinking of himself. That's all he was thinking of— of how to get out of this terrible mess. Couldn't she understand that? he said. Francesca shook her head, and he realised a storm was gathering. Any minute now all that aggression of hers which she'd suppressed momentarily would surface in an explosion. But he wasn't terribly worried. If the collision was inevitable, he'd just as soon have it over with. At least he'd be able to define his own position, listen to her arguments, throw them back, dispute them, even shout at her, attacking and counter-attacking. He could then consign the whole episode to some dark corner of his mind. He would have liked to

38

persuade her that his motives were fundamentally honourable. He would have liked to win her over to his side. It was no small achievement that he'd managed to shock her, sicken her with his bluntness, amaze her with his lucid resolutions; it was more than he could have counted on. He'd made an impression on her, struck her with his sensitivity, his maturity. In spite of everything, at least he'd convinced her that something more serious than pigheaded defeatism lay beneath the superfice of his ruthlessness. Their conversation wasn't over yet. Francesca was arming herself for a bitter offensive. He felt himself becoming what he'd always been with her—the deceitful bungler, the outsider, the purely destructive force. Francesca emerged from her stupor with doubled force, shooting a round of precise, meticulously aimed, abusive accusations. She scornfully accused him of being an unscrupulous seducer, a parasite, a blind egoist, incapable of seeing the pain he was causing Luisa and her parents, and his behaviour was unutterably shameless. What absurd illusions he had about himself. It all boiled down to nothing more than his usual duplicity, his wild, insane opinion of himself and of his own worth, his incapacity to accept himself as he really was and finally his damned swollen-headed pride that conspired daily to shove him further into isolation and further into that preposterously delirious dreamworld of his. Yes, of course, he thought, it was true, quite true, that and much more. But wasn't this explanation enough for her? He felt calm and unusually sure of himself. The insults and accusations bounced off the padded surface of his sensibility which diminished the impact and left him unscathed. What was she getting at? Who was she trying to get at? Where would she go from here? The little he'd done to date he'd done begrudgingly and sloppily, and the results of what he'd done were so clumsy as to be ludicrous, because he'd thought he was meant for better things. That's how he'd always been at school and that's how he was when he started teaching. That's how he was being now with

Luisa and how he'd go on being for the rest of his life no matter what he undertook. That wasn't true. He wasn't like that about everything. True there were some things which on their own merits he turned down, but he was quite prepared to throw himself wholeheartedly into something worthwhile. His almost perverse pride had often been the source of enormous shame. At this very moment, for example, it was the cause of his discomfort and weighed on him like some gross physical deformity. He couldn't rid himself of it, he'd tried time and again and to no avail. She went on. How could she take him seriously when he claimed it wasn't his self-centredness that was to blame but rather something deeper had motivated it all? What had he ever done to better his condition other than refusing to accept it? He'd just wallowed in discontented self-indulgence, feeding off resentment and recriminations, treating everyone around him perfunctorily, as if contact were some kind of unfortunate accident. Did he really believe Luisa would have destroyed him? On the contrary, she'd save him, cut him down to size—the size of a man who couldn't even make love to a girl without getting her into trouble. He smiled feebly. How could he have been stupid enough to believe that Francesca could be silenced even for a split second? He was trembling. It had been a storm, a barrage of stones aimed at his weak points. His flexible padding had withstood it, sounding mutely, even pleasantly when struck. In any case he knew it already. He knew what Luisa was going through and knew what Francesca was getting at. What difference did it make, when he knew damn well that he would be drawn and quartered if he were to give in? He coughed. It was time to speak up but his vocabulary coagulated in his throat. He didn't refute her accusations, but he objected to the account she'd given of his motives. She was just being nasty and negative, he said, prejudiced by her old hostilities. He was on the point of launching into an analysis of himself and of his relations with his family when he stopped short. He felt lost. During a momentary

40

wave of nausea, he imagined the entire conversation which might have ensued. He could hear himself talking about himself, about the years he'd spent with his family, those clandestine years he'd lived locked away in himself alternately consumed and paralysed by the awareness of that very duplicity that rent his life. He could hear himself explaining the times he'd looked at himself in the mirror to try and find a single shred of evidence which might tip the scales one way or the other. He could hear her replying in the name of some non-existent clan, that he couldn't distinguish himself from his station, from their code, that he was bound by the self-same station and code which bound her and her mother and Luisa. He had no choice, no choice whatever. And he could see himself struggling to make his secret life intelligible to her. The wave of nausea that had threatened to overtake him and the ensuing feeling of impotence and confusion engulfed him. He stopped dead. Francesca, quick to notice the collapse, slapped him across the mouth. A wound opened on his lip and he tasted blood. He slumped onto his bed, his eyes clouded with tears. His head was on fire. Caustic, disconnected syllables and words crowded the room: you'll do it, I tell you, and fast... fast.... Through his confusion he realised that Francesca had hit him again. Without a word he sprang from his bed, threw himself at her, lifted her and hurled her through his open door; her arms waved wildly clutching for support as she hurtled rustling through the half-lit hall to wind up with a great thud against the kitchen door. The noise reverberated throughout the house. There was a distant cry followed by a heavy clacking that drew nearer. Someone turned on the light, tripped, knocked against a chair. He looked at Francesca stunned on the floor, her back propped against the door, her skirt up, her hair a mess. I warned you never to touch me again. His mother erupted into the hall, half-asleep, half-naked in her astoundingly short nightgown ... her painfully embarrassing presence. She looked confused, like a great dumb animal startled in its sleep.

41

He looked at her, inwardly surprised to find himself coldly considering how unnatural, how deformed her body looked in that absurd nightgown. Before she had the chance to open her mouth, before she could come out of her perennial hibernation and take in what had happened, ask why, take sides, he went into his room and slammed the door behind him.

He lay stretched out on his bed in the dark before the rectangle cut by the open window. He heard Francesca get up. His mother's voice asked what had happened and his sister's voice answered that he had proved once more just how low, selfish and worthless he really was and how he couldn't be relied upon to show even the most elementary consideration for his fellow human beings—no, not even the most elementary consideration.

Later. Clouds passed low in the sky. The whole neighbourhood slept in a hot, heavy sleep. Those muted voices had stopped. His room was hot. He lay thinking that he'd accomplished a lot but he still had to expect an assault from Luisa's family. It was a struggle to freedom. He heard someone approach his door calling him softly. His mother was begging him to open, she wanted to talk things over, she wouldn't scold, only talk. An unusual tone of real live concern had crept into her voice and made it unfamiliar. She must have been really shocked if she'd managed to shake herself out of her usual apathy to intervene in a domestic drama. He lay motionless on his bed, fighting against a sudden urge to give in, to get up and open the door. This clumsy attempt to assume a motherly role by such an insignificant, bungling person was maddening but at the same time he was taken aback and pained by her pathetic attempt and felt perhaps that he really loved his mother more than he had ever loved her, or even for the first time. He recognised the danger of surrendering at that juncture to anything as unfamiliar as filial love. He shouted at her to go away, to leave him alone because he had nothing to add to what had already been said.

6

HE WAS APPREHENSIVE about seeing Gloria since the chances of meeting her were doubtful and since the previous night's argument and fight with Francesca had upset him. He left the house early, at exactly seven o'clock before his sister was up, thus avoiding any possibility of an encounter. It had taken him ages to doze off because the row had kept ringing through his mind. He'd woken up sweating heavily and feeling utterly exhausted. It had been a rude awakening all right: all the horror of the previous evening stung him anew as if he'd just been slapped again. The horror was shortlived; it was the horror of one who suddenly trips on the edge of a precipice. He forced himself to relax. He shifted wearily in his bed and tried to turn away from the abyss and take refuge in the still undisclosed possibilities of the day ahead. There were other things in store besides the precipice. The house was quiet, split open by a cold silence. He heard a faint, persistent sound like the cooling sigh of a conch. He had to get up. He got ready quickly, determined to leave before anyone in the house had woken. He had breakfast, and hunted round the kitchen for something edible to put in his old canvas beachbag. There was nothing in the larder but a bit of meat, a plate of potatoes and the leftovers of some unappetising soup. The day had dawned with the same equivocal balance between hope and despair. Yesterday and today swiftly melted into a single, shapeless day of straddling hours that dovetailed in a haze. He left the house wondering whether he would be more influenced by what had happened last night than by what might happen today. The stormy quarrel with Francesca had apparently drained him, robbed him of the vocabulary and gesture he'd rehearsed for Gloria. Perhaps a glimpse of her would refurbish his strength. Even if he were to ignore yesterday's events, today's seemed riddled with pitfalls. What if he did actually meet Gloria as he hoped? He would probably have to take her out to lunch and foot the bill and he only had 3,755 lire to his name, which he counted as he walked downstairs. What a pathetic sum! He might have been able to make them stretch; or he might blurt it out and say, Gloria, this is all the cash I have on me. But then he would run the risk of unmasking too hastily the man he paraded before her. Were he to reveal the minutest crack in his façade, Gloria might see through much further—through to his home, his mother, Francesca, Luisa, all the characters that peopled his life and even his involvement in the squalid little incident of the night before. How would she react? It was essential that he not give her the impression that he flashed money around. He would have to make his impecunious position clear from the start so as to avoid the danger of being put in an untenable position, because the resulting shame and embarrassment would render any sincerity impossible. His anxiety of being subjected to her scrutiny already threatened him and he blushed. He wouldn't allow this to happen. He had to find a way of mediating between the two, between appearance and reality, truth and fantasy, between his own conflicts. He refused to reduce himself to the level of the paltry sum he carried in his pockets, to the level of the man almost effaced by the contempt of the previous night. He had other reserves, other trumps to keep him in the game. We shall see what we shall see. Anyway, all these considerations were quite pointless at this stage. The immediate problem was how would he bide the time before the appointed hour. It wasn't even eight yet. The hours dragged by. They'd pass eventually, he thought as he abandoned his calculations. He would soon find himself at Pettinelli's amid the crowds surging into the Mercerie, mingling with the street cries from the neighbouring market. He looked for her from a distance, from his vantage point, and slowly approached

44

until she noticed him from inside, until she became aware of his presence. She recognised him. She wasn't surprised. She laughed as if to say, ah, I knew you'd turn up. She was holding the blue-green bikini. Her complicity grew as he said, not too indecent . . . blue-green, such a pretty colour . . . sets off one's tan . . . and she laughed. Goodness, how she dawdled while the salesgirls displayed green, red, yellow bathing suits, then blouses and trousers and rustling skirts. He looked out onto the street, his heart thumping impatiently. They were together. Soon they would be out there together. Was he happy? He found it difficult to tell. He was more moved than anything. He was not entirely absorbed or conquered by her presence. His anguish prevailed. What would happen? He knew that sooner or later there would be a visit and a discussion to sort things out. It wouldn't come immediately. Last night's exchange had gone a long way. Situations of such delicacy had to be approached calmly and bit by bit. He realised the importance of avoiding bringing matters to a head prematurely and to no purpose. So far nothing had really happened. Disaster pended but its presence wasn't overbearing as yet. In fact, there was no visible evidence, not even Luisa's stomach. He wondered whether Francesca had tried—and with what results, if any—to reach her through the locked door. Everything was so uncertain and last night's brutally terminated conversation hadn't clarified a thing. He didn't even find out how much Luisa's incredibly obtuse parents knew. They seemed to have grasped nothing. How much longer did he have to wait? Would they spend the whole morning in the shop or would they leave early? Would he hold her hand, or her arm? What would he say? It wouldn't be easy. She was being aloof and evasive. She might be embarrassed by her unresolved reasons for showing up. He held on to her arm working round her evasions, resolving patiently to wait for the right moment. He sat on the parapet of a bridge and waited. A *vaporetto* full of passengers blinked between the distant houses. Time ebbed past slowly. Nothing but difficulties. The hours splintered into minutes and the minutes into seconds before they had time to start; he could hear them accumulating within him, tick upon tick. Disjointed empty thoughts moved through his mind: a chalked diagram on a blackboard, the lips of an amphora, the flattened curve of a comma. He wasn't alive, he wasn't living. He tried desperately to isolate this waiting time and will its abolition. His efforts sent him skidding back to the same old time track, returning him squarely to the start mark or to some even greater handicap. Back, he was back in his room again. He could hear Francesca talking with her mother again; her accusations were even more virulent than they'd been last night. She was explaining why he had left early to rob them of their chance to sort things out. She was shouting, and his empty room and unmade bed cruelly accentuated every word, but he was too tired and listless to retaliate. Her cruelty paralysed him. Softly please, couldn't they please speak more softly. If only his hourly vagrancies could proceed silently, unobserved. As it was, words grew and swelled in the house, then burst into an uproar. He jumped off the parapet and ran from their voices. Blast you, he muttered to one and no one. Why can't you disappear, cease to exist? He walked on and on forcing his mind to blank, crossing alleyways, streets, bridges, canals, unaware of the circles he was turning and returning upon, until finally, as if emerging from a labyrinth, he found himself before Pettinelli's just before ten o'clock. The shop was empty and Gloria hadn't yet arrived. It's early, he thought calmly. He was feeling a little better. Now the wait was over he was over the risk of being bogged down by memories, or of having to straddle the present moment and take refuge in promises to come. At this point the present could contain him. He paused to look at the clothing displayed in the window, all the silk shirts and summer jackets. He wasn't killing time now; he was enjoying himself; he liked smart clothes and enjoyed window shopping from one display to another, dawdling lazily, comparing prices and making mental notes from his evaluations. The shopkeeper caught his eye through the window and waved to him. He waved back and started towards the entrance. Then he stopped at the door restrained by a sudden elegant consideration: mightn't Gloria prefer to bump into him accidentally, as it were, outside the shop among the strolling crowds, rather than meet him inside? He backed into the street and began to walk slowly away from the shop towards Piazza San Marco. At this slow, slack time of day the street was almost empty; the shop-assistants leaned on the counters or lounged in the doorways chatting to each other. The small clusters of people strolling about were mainly foreign tourists or locals on holiday and they were going towards the Lido. Even if he were trying to avoid her, he couldn't possibly miss Gloria among these clearly distinguished types. He would probably see her if he walked down the street as far as the Piazza. She might have taken the ten o'clock boat into Venice, in which case she'd be getting off this very moment, walking with her characteristic light, swaying gait that had first excited his attention: how revealing she'd been that first moment, her fair hair still damp, her grey eyes shining for him and her open surprise. That moment had revealed a good deal of himself to him. He had seen all the repressed potentials of his life unfurl before him, and she cut them loose, freeing them with her presence. Now she, in turn, was coming to free herself from her remaining inhibitions. She would confess her complicity in the allusive, equivocal and clandestine games of encouragement that they had been playing with each other. 'Oh, lucky little fan that fans your cheeks and fans your breast...' the words of the funny little song that Gloria had sung to the child she held on her lap, which reminded him of the surprise he'd felt as he'd listened to her. The strange little ditty and the sweetness of her singing seemed somehow to affirm the existence of a world he'd never known before he'd met her, a world he'd only envisioned indistinctly during his long years of searching and waiting. Oh lucky little fan, he whistled the tune wondering who could have composed it and why hadn't he heard it till then. Perhaps it was one of those family jingles that had been handed down from generation to generation like a family secret and then Gloria had suddenly decided to broadcast it to the world by singing it before him. Was she betraying her class, or was he encroaching upon it? It would be fun to bring it up with her. He noticed that he was in San Marco and realised that he still hadn't come across her. It was just after ten. The streets and the Piazza were getting more crowded but there was still no sign of Gloria. It suddenly struck him that she might have taken some other street; there were other streets that led from the San Marco landing to Pettinelli's; there was that dark narrow little alley that ran past the Ducal Palace dungeons and could serve as a short-cut if you were in a hurry to get to the shops. She may have gone that way to stay in the shade and now she'd be nearing the shop, unaware of his efforts to meet her in a different direction. Unless, of course, he thought—the possibility dawning on him for the first time—unless last night at the bar she hadn't meant to be quite so definite as to the exact time of her arrival in Venice. That must be it, she hasn't even left yet, she's still at the Lido, she's still asleep or she's just getting ready to leave. These alternatives, which somewhat delayed their meeting, didn't stop him from hurrying back to the shop just in case she had arrived. But she hadn't. For the second time she wasn't there. There was no one in the shadows of the shop behind the clothes he now only pretended to examine—no one except the shop-assistants in the same slack atmosphere of a few minutes ago. He stepped away from the window to conceal himself from sight, but he didn't move away this time. He didn't want to risk missing Gloria's arrival; she might go away before he got back. He would remain in the area, not immediately in front of the shop, but at a good scanning point, on the corner there where he could keep a check on those arriving from the Piazza. He began to feel worried. Her delay dented his resolution, created a cradle for his anxieties. As long as she comes, he thought. He looked at his watch: twenty past ten. In the normal course of events, he would almost expect to be kept waiting a good twenty-five to thirty minutes by a woman; and the delay in this case was more than justifiable since Gloria and he hadn't even made a real appointment. There had only been that tacit understanding between them, and possibly not even that; he may have been under an illusion; he may have read the invitation into her conversation when it just wasn't there. There was only that look really that she'd given him as he left and nothing more. But it was such a tender look. He lit a cigarette and glanced over to the shops. More and more people were walking about. Two women entered the shop, others clustered round the windows, a group of tourists emerged from a side alley, hesitated between one direction and another, then abandoned themselves to the mainstream and moved along to the Piazza. The minutes accumulated and he began to play his game of superstitious predictions: Gloria will arrive before the two women leave the shop; she'll appear at the top of the street before that man in white reaches me, or she'll come from behind me because she'll be coming from the opposite direction. What if she didn't come? Yes, she would. She's coming now, but you mustn't turn round, you must let her come up to you, slowly, let her pass even without seeing you. Before the boat whistle blows again, or just as the boat is pulling away ... If that woman in black goes into the church ... As soon as that newsvendor has sold three more copies ... Before ... After ... If ... He realised she wasn't going to turn up when a clock struck quarter past eleven. He decided to wait another quarter of an hour before leaving. He didn't know what to think; had he really misunderstood? had she really not extended a secret invitation? Even if she hadn't meant anything, why hadn't she come to pick up her bikini? Was she having him on? After the tensions he had undergone waiting for her he didn't feel capable of interpreting her strange behaviour. He couldn't decide what to do. Should he hang on or should he go to the Lido and look for her there? Should he give up the idea of seeing her, today at any rate? He was terribly hurt. He had squandered four whole hours since leaving home, four useless hours of wandering, of anxious calculations, of empty conjectures. He felt a fool in the context of his elaborate preparations for the meeting and of all the neurotic assessments of the possibilities and risks implicit in the meeting. She hadn't come and her failure to do so made him almost grotesque in his own eyes. Beside the pain of betrayal he was experiencing, he felt a contentious energy rising whose resulting anger was levelled at Gloria. Her sort always have the upper hand all right. They always come out on top, he said, yielding to the love-hate he felt for Gloria's class, confusedly identifying her with her brother, fiancé, the *Excelsior* crowd and the very cabins on the beach. They remain omnipotent, heedless of their circumstances, of their relationship with those who happen into their circles or those who actively try to penetrate their sphere. It is they who are both the bene-factors and the bestowers of largesse, who manage to remain healthy and strong; it is they who hold eminent domain over those who stray across their paths, who are totally indifferent to the injuries they inflict. He felt the same rage he'd had difficulty in controlling the previous day on the boat, the same violent desire to avenge himself on his offenders. As the minutes wore on, his anger replaced his discontent. His irresolution began to fade and he saw what he would do. A detailed programme for the day took shape in his mind. He left his waiting post and made for the Piazza once more, hurrying now to catch up on lost time. He'd go to the Lido, but not to ask her to explain why she hadn't turned up or have her justify his wasted morning, but rather to start treating her as he should have done from the very beginning, regardless of the whys and the wherefores of her absence. He wasn't sure that he knew exactly how, but he did know he should have been more calculating, more restrained, malicious, even spitefully indifferent. This positive line of action led him out of that maze of conjectures, returning him to his conviction that Gloria had, in fact, even if only for a moment in their whole association, recklessly thrown herself at him. This was the one, single, absolute fact. He had to go back to it, as if time had stood still, as if the night and the whole morning hadn't gone by, as if he were still lying in the boat and her hands were still caressing his back. He had to start all over again, he thought angrily, and bury all he'd thought and done these past hours, to uproot every self-pandering forecast he'd made. He'd have to hold onto one idea, even if it meant petrifying with determined self-control, that if he ever wanted anything from her, he would have to distrust her all the way.

A boat from the Lido was arriving at the San Marco landing on the other side of the Piazza, tracing its wide curve and nosing up to the wharf. He saw it moving in the background and hurried towards the gang-plank to catch it before it left again. He strolled aboard amid the usual crowd of tourists fresh from their hotels, young people and boisterous children; as he went on board he looked to see if Gloria were among the passengers going ashore, half hoping not to see her among them. After the violence he'd done to himself while he'd been waiting, and after having decided upon a determined programme for the day, a belated encounter would probably throw him off balance again. He didn't want to see or talk to her at this point. On the other hand, that possibly wasn't the reason. Perhaps it was that the signs of his recent humiliation were still too obvious for him to be exposed to the one who had caused them. Anyway, there was no Gloria. He sat down on one of the side benches and was soon joined by another passenger. He glanced at the fellow and didn't see him through the weave of his thoughts. The boat cast off and headed out across the basin, making for the Lido. The fresh air and the sound of the boat under way threatened to disrupt his isolation, but other

51

sounds and figures snaked through his consciousness and he only noticed a distant whistle and a gentle remote vibration. He was in another time, submerging in an orgy of emotions: Gloria hadn't shown up; Luisa thrust forward again; Francesca got up this morning and went to look for him; his mother gauchely tried to regain his confidence and intimacy; the Lido was not the long green streak that approached the boat, but an evasive, distant goal. He felt sick again. He was forced to recognise that his recent fury hadn't lasted long enough, that he had pried too far back and that subsequently he was having to struggle to hold his memories at bay. They weren't memories really, they were live presences, words just now spoken in his ear. God, he was going to have to convince himself if he was to convince anyone else. They were the usual random accusations dictated by her blind preconceived hostilities. He wasn't wrong. He really was like that and there was no room for doubt or shame. He had copious evidence to support him. Ever since he was a child, he'd felt detached from the family, out of place, an anomaly in his surroundings, different, even if the word did sound false and indulgent; had he been able to find some other word, a more persuasive word, he might have felt more sure of himself, but there he was having to support the weight of his resolution on this fragile word which lent itself so readily to ridicule; he'd have the last laugh, though, he wouldn't marry her. If the baby were born, he could take it, he could even give it his name because for the time being he felt it was easier to be a father than a husband. Let them scorn him if that was all they could do; he didn't care a fig for their judgments. Anyway he knew that they would never respect his. He had figured it all out for himself and knew how and to what extent his judgments could be condemned. All right, what then? It all boils down to this, my dear Francesca—it is far better to be condemned out of hand than to sit back and be destroyed. God, if only Gloria had been more forthright, if only she'd not forced him to struggle like this, he might have been able to break away entirely, to forget all the accusations and condemnations from all those who felt it their duty to pass judgment on him and his actions; and he could throw them all out, all the names, all the memories, all the ties. Her undecided, ambiguous attraction to him had the effect of either confirming his decisions or rejecting them, almost as if she wanted to deny him the right to do what he had done. He just couldn't go on like this, he would have to learn how to live in a state of constant, ruthless indifference. A few days, or even weeks, might see him come through victorious, so hardened as never to feel pain again. Perhaps then . . . he thought, but for now . . . He got ready to land; the boat had arrived. A few minutes later he was walking along the street that went diagonally across the residential area of the Lido, a short cut leading to the *Excelsior*. The sun was high, scorching. A few cars and silent bicycles moved along the street. The air, the breath of the sea filtered through the tall trees.

7

THE CASINO PIAZZA looked opaque in the mid-day heat, fogged as dusty glass. Two fellows watching him approach—he'd recognised them from a distance and was making furtively for the beach entrance—moved up to greet him with a jolly: hello, where are you off to? He hesitated before answering, suspicious and all too familiar with this kind of assumed affability. He decided to refuse whatever they were about to ask. Going to the *Excelsior*? they smiled, lustily swelling in their tight cotton T-shirts: the usual smarmy types from his neighbourhood, holding flashy little bathing trunks in their hands like posies. Yes, he was on his way to the *Excelsior*, but he had no intention of taking them if that's what they were after. In any case the cabin wasn't his and he couldn't possibly take anyone else. Dark, silent figures, looking strangely dominical for a work-day, were standing on the Casino terrace that rose beside them, gazing out at the sea, at the crowded jetties and the cabins. Just for a second. You know. Just to change. No, he said, I can't; suddenly he felt drained. Wherever he went, there was always someone to drag him down, a neighbour, someone he'd known at school, some tatty customer from his mother's shop. His past reclaimed him, persistent in upturning a thousand characters in his path all slyly winking in recognition. And now he had to struggle against the calculated sweetness of their voices—we'll only be a minute, we're pals, aren't we? we'll just go in and change, leave and come back later—struggle with the cruel validity of their nagging that would render him speechless. Hadn't anyone noticed how he'd changed years ago, how different he was? Had everything he'd done to date been futile: his proud isolation; the calculated violence which he'd used to break with his surroundings; the rift he'd deliberately opened between himself and his family? Here were these two insignificant little types, whom he'd purposely ignored, blithely barging in on him to propose some kind of smutty truant's pact. It offended his dignity precisely because it presumed that nothing had changed, that he was still one of them, and duty-bound to help them in the name of their common origin. They should have felt intimidated when they saw him, avoided him totally, greeted him with respect, or even gone out of their way to ignore him. Blast, he exploded, making for the beach almost at a run, muttering Fenzo's cabin number as he passed by the guard at the entrance. A volley of insults, imprecations, slashing abuse blasted behind him like rifle-fire on a fugitive. There was almost a tragic tone of indignation in that rattle of insults, as if his retreat were tantamount to treason, a despicable, shameless betrayal. God, what a world, ever trampling his individuality, ever presuming his indebtedness to it without giving him the slightest consideration. Voracious world, jealous of its departing son even unto barring his way, obsessive, deceitful world. Had he been anywhere else, he would have turned back, but here in the shadow of the hotel, perhaps under Gloria's very window, near Gloria anyway, and obsessed by the mad suspicion that the scene had not merely been a coincidence, but had in some obscure way been predestined, preordained, it was surely wiser to ignore the insults and keep on the cabin path to where Fenzo was sitting peacefully in the sun reading his newspaper. He walked towards him trying not to glance at Gloria's cabin, unable, however, to exclude the red awning from his field of vision, or the lilo swollen on the sand, or the deck chair open to the sun. Then, as the previous scene vanished without a trace and his heart beat wildly, because he perceived at a glance that Gloria wasn't there, that Matteo wasn't there, that Alessandro wasn't there, that the cabin was, in fact, deserted, he was overcome with disappointment and emptiness and a feeling of rejection.

55

He became witness to a strange, painful internal experience, not a loss of control, nor another outburst of rage,
but a sudden mortal fatigue in which the sea began to
dissolve and the sweetly languorous figures stretched out
on the sand, the gaily flapping awnings; these things, these
people in this beachscape, the only imaginable foreground
for him at this moment, faded and slowly mixed into a
spectral vision of his home, his neighbourhood. She's not
there, he thought bitterly, she's not come. Then as he
surveyed the empty cabin and Fenzo still hiding behind
the screen of his paper, he realised by means of an effort-
less clairvoyance that there would be no meeting with
Gloria that day. He felt frightened again anticipating the
long useless hours of waiting alone, and another long useless
inevitable trip home. He thought of Gloria's absence,
mentally summoning her before him and charging her
with it—why, he said, didn't you turn up here either?
It was a weary reproof, lacking in the anger that had
charged him a few minutes before, that had made him
positive about her, bereft of the energy to decide what to
do: to stay and wait or make up his mind to leave. His
assurance had fallen before his presentiment of ensuing
disaster. He saw Fenzo fold the paper, drop it onto the
sand, flex his arms, grope round on the canvas stretcher
for a packet of cigarettes and finally turn his gaze on
him. He went over to him feeling unpleasantly hollow,
oppressed with the fear that Fenzo had surprised his
moment of anguish and would want to pry. But Fenzo
obviously hadn't; he got up from his deck chair and greeted
him, asking why he'd come so late that morning. He
replied in vague, distracted terms, mechanically going
through the accompanying set of gestures, then went into
the cabin and began to change. Fenzo was talking near
by: he heard the words indistinctly as he concentrated on
picking up the sounds which would indicate her arrival,
trying to fathom why Gloria hadn't come, puzzling
whether she had gone to Venice after all and he'd missed
her in spite of his vigil and his search—until he became

56

aware that Fenzo, without knowing it, was answering these questions: he was saying that Gloria had stayed in bed that morning because she wasn't feeling well, he'd got this from Alessandro who had come to get something from his cabin. Alessandro was leaving. He had been sullen, surly, something must have happened between him and Gloria, maybe something irreparable. He'd hardly said hello, had utterly refused to explain it all. He'd replied short and sharp to Fenzo's questions: no, he didn't know where Matteo was; Gloria was indisposed; yes, he was leaving right away; no, he wasn't coming back. The shape of things changed again. Fenzo's news completely dispelled the doubts that had rent him for so many hours, the reasons for Gloria's mysterious behaviour became clear now and were so flattering to him that if Fenzo hadn't been there he would have given vent to a boisterous expression of joy. Triumphant thoughts assembled in his mind. So that was it. Had he known earlier he could have spared himself a lot of pain. Those long, tiresome past twelve hours must have bristled with events for Gloria. It wasn't just a coincidence that Alessandro was leaving, nor was it just a coincidence that he had answered Fenzo's questions coldly. Something serious must have happened between him and Gloria. Her restlessness during the motor-boat trip, her display of tenderness to her guest must have demanded an explanation afterwards and given rise to a trying debate which Gloria must have had with herself first and then with Alessandro and Matteo. Me, he thought with pride, it was because of me. His recent anger, the anxiety and the bitter sense of failure had faded into a distant memory. Now he was certain he'd been the cause of everything that Gloria had thought and done in the past hours. He'd caused her absence, her isolation, caused the family row which might even have erupted at the same time as the one in which he'd been the protagonist. He'd caused Alessandro's unconditional surrender and his eventual decision to leave. And he even had proof: Fenzo, smiling like an accomplice, not without a touch of envious malice, expressed his belief that Alessandro's departure was connected in some way with yesterday's incident when he . . . but how in heaven's name had he found the courage?—he'd actually taken and kissed Gloria's hand in front of everyone, and to her obvious pleasure and the others' obvious irritation. Now he was all ears, feigning indifference, hoping Fenzo could prove what he was saying by recalling some word of Alessandro's or some gesture of Gloria's whose significance had escaped him. But the only thing Fenzo was sure of was that Alessandro had decided to leave, looking as if he were about to declare himself bankrupt. Was this enough to reassure him? He thought it might be. If nothing else, he thought, Alessandro's departure would allow him to advance more easily, to press on to less hostile territory. The first enemy was in flight. It had been easy, all right. But so what? Who on earth would have wanted it difficult? Of course he didn't, as he rubbed his hands with satisfaction and thanked heaven that Gloria and Alessandro had been on even more precarious terms than he had dared hope.

By the time he stepped out of the cabin, his mood had changed radically from the one he'd been in as he entered. He lay out on the stretcher in the sun a different man from the one who had halted, as if stupefied, on the beach, but still not so self-assured as to feel safe from the irregular circumstances which assailed his life these days, the abrupt shuttle of reverses, the oscillation of feelings that jolted him backwards and forwards from hope to anguish in a matter of minutes, from anguish to hope, and still again from hope to despair. Now that Gloria was again a possibility, he naturally felt more peaceful, as if relieved from a great strain. But how could he forget that a mere nothing, the slightest provocation, a sudden misgiving or a memory grown doubtful were enough to upset his tenuous balance again and send him plummeting into confusion? But maybe this time, he thought, things were different; if what Fenzo had said were true, the situation had changed and he had finished with the oppressive pendular swing. Meanwhile vague images, snatches of words, the distant rhythm of a conversation drifted out from the hotel rooms where the night before, or this very morning, Gloria and Alessandro had fought about him. The phrases were disjointed, barely perceptible, because he didn't know how Gloria and Alessandro spoke to each other, he knew nothing of their secret language. Are you in love with him? tell me, do you love him? Yes, and I want him—seemed too explicit, no they couldn't be the words they'd use. Maybe the discussion went on in silence, with rapid facial expressions, fulminating glances that struck down questions and retorts. Not likely. He couldn't see them behaving like that. Why should they speak any differently from any other couple having a row. In any case, these undecipherable sounds emanating from the hotel, this confused mumble prevented his discovering from her replies how far Gloria's feelings had progressed. He himself, moreover, hadn't really decided what he wanted of Gloria. Up to now, having her had been a positive, definite goal, but the multiple impulses which thrust him towards her had never been clear to him, or rather, he hadn't had time to specify his ulterior purpose. In the first place, he needed an escape from a stifling reality. Secondly, he'd felt attracted by Gloria, attracted beyond all calculated motives, completely spontaneously. And he'd become involved in her fascination, in the gradual revelation of her delicate, quiet beauty. She had appeared to be the emblem of everything he wanted but couldn't have. Finally, there had been his contentious will to assault whoever was stronger than he. These had been his impulses; only he'd been forced constantly to devote himself to the conservation of balance, and he hadn't really had time to see them in their true perspective; which in fact exceeded a mere momentary possession of Gloria. He lay in the sun waiting for Gloria to appear, receiving the voices from the near-by cabins without listening to them, hearing Fenzo, whom he

59

answered with a distracted grunt, rousing him because it was time for lunch. Now he realised that he wanted everything from Gloria, a total and immediate surrender, a guarantee that he would be safe during the subsequent days, but, above all, afterwards—this was exactly what he wanted—afterwards when, thanks to her, he'd released himself once and for all from his destructive fury and had freed himself completely. Boundless. The possibilities Gloria offered were boundless, he could even marry her, his whole existence would change. He had noticed already the first signs of a metamorphosis, his consciousness of time was less oppressive, space dilated, even now he was both here and far away. He listened, as if split in two, to his life breathing elsewhere; it was not an anticipated sound but a certainty of also being there, elsewhere, and of being strong, self-assured, a certainty of finally arriving back on his native soil after an interminable exile. A wave of gratitude swept over him. In the past few hours since he'd last seen her, Gloria had been silently at work seeing to it that all this would come about. He even felt guilty, felt he had to atone for having reproved her. Well, he thought, without asking himself how tenable his fantasies were, while I was feeling betrayed, Gloria was fighting, breaking off with Alessandro, presenting her brother with an accomplished fact, learning to respect me, to make others respect me. As luck would have it, Fenzo called him just at the point when, overcome with gratitude, he was clasping Gloria in his arms caressing her head on his shoulder. Slowly, reluctantly, he got up and set out for the restaurant with his friend, not the *Excelsior* restaurant, which was too dear even for Fenzo, but a little bar on the beach, where one could eat quickly and cheaply. There were few people at the bar. Fenzo chattered noisily, hummed, clapped and stamped about to the sound of the jukebox, breaking out occasionally into fast, jumbled drum solos. He said nothing, answering Fenzo's chatter in monosyllables, absorbed by the thought of Gloria that pulled him away like the tide; he would go straight towards her when he saw her, no longer hiding behind the mask of indifference—a pretty crude contrivance, he had to admit—which he had worn while he still felt Gloria was eluding him. Now he wouldn't have to subdue himself; on the contrary, he felt and endorsed his need to be open with her, to rest a while after so many hours of struggle. Naturally, he would be careful enough not to betray his anxiety over Luisa, any more than he would try to mask it in a prevailing pensiveness which—an unconscious smile moved across his mouth—she would probably like anyway. But if Gloria tried to pry into his feelings, what would he say? What questions? He could certainly tell her, without feeling he was lying, that he loved her, that he couldn't live without her. But did he really love her? He stood for a moment in bemused curiosity, absorbed in this consideration for the first time. But the question, which he had, in any case, raised almost timidly, met with ambiguous, counterfeit answers: of course; who knows? Determining the true nature of his feelings was hardly what mattered. What did matter in these circumstances was that Gloria loved him, and not whether he loved her. He wondered if she agreed with this? Certainly if he did love her everything would be different, he would be able to regard his every gesture from a less rigorous angle; even his desertion of Luisa would be judged more favourably by his censors. It would really be marvellous to love her, to be able to live only for her, to need her so much that he could forget everything else but her, and feel himself dying without her. It would be marvellous, he repeated, but immediately he realised that despite his need for Gloria he'd never succeeded in obliterating the pain of Luisa from his conscience, the premonitions of scandal, the certainty of destroying a life to save his own skin. He felt dispirited, sensing that even his relations with Gloria were blurred, ambiguous, as they had always been with Luisa and Francesca and his mother. He wondered whether this were not in fact his natural condition, his immutable, essential mode of being:

61

an outsider, always an outsider, alone, unable to define either himself or anyone else, confined like an outcast. Fortunately he felt himself capable of answering these questions. No, he wasn't like that. There was evidence to the contrary. He was only estranged from the few detestable creatures among whom he'd grown up. Otherwise he wouldn't have responded so readily to that something in Gloria that betokened everything he felt he lacked. He had to struggle to find his level only because he lacked freedom. But had he had freedom his whole life would have developed harmoniously and he would have loved Gloria from the moment he saw her. That was the point. But there were Luisa, Francesca and his mother; there were his fears of the irreparable and the persistence of his remorse both conspiring against him to cut him down every time he tried to escape. He sighed wearily. The sore spot was always the same. One way or another, his thoughts returned to it as if drawn or constrained by an occult mysterious force. He began to be uneasy again. Then something would come to soothe him and then uneasiness would return again. And so on, and who knows for how long. While Fenzo was getting up, preparing to leave, he was tempted for a second to stop him, to tell him everything, to talk about Luisa, about the baby, about Francesca, and his hopes for Gloria. Instead he also got up, without a word, and went out into the glaring sun of the beach.

It was two in the afternoon, the time when the Lido was sleeping. From the cabins came muted voices, short bursts of laughter, rustling sounds. The life of the beach was spent in the afternoon of inertia. In the *Excelsior* restaurant, half hidden by the rows of trees and the ivy that hung down from the terrace, muffled sounds of crockery and the scarce voices indicated that lunch was drawing to an end. Glancing over the balustrade he looked for Gloria among the few remaining people and among those who were slowly climbing the marble stairs up to the hotel. Unable to find her, he hoped he might see her in the cabin shortly, alone, without the usual train of escorts, willing to resume the mute dialogue that they'd opened the day they'd met and suspended the previous day at the end of the motorboat trip. But Gloria wasn't there. The cabin was still deserted; only something was different, the arrangement of the things had changed slightly: the stretcher had been moved, Gloria's tiny bathing suit lay inside out on the canvas, wrinkled in the sun that dried it. He started and cursed to himself. Had Gloria come in his absence and then gone away? There were other indications than the bathing suit to confirm it: the door of the cabin, closed before, now stood open, a packet of cigarettes lay on her deck chair, a newspaper lay half-buried in the sand. Gloria had come and the damp spot left by her bathing suit on the stretcher indicated that she had been gone only a moment. He was furious. Why had he followed Fenzo? Why had he left the cabin? If he hadn't gone, if he had only waited a moment longer he could have seen her, he could have spoken to her, heard it all from her, been able to compare the disparate conjectures he'd made up to now with her own version. What a chance he'd lost. Perhaps Gloria had come to look for him and he'd missed her. Now he had no recourse but to wait, to return to his vacillating thoughts, to his distorted perspective, his kaleidoscope of asymmetrical images. He would have to spend hours like this. He collapsed irritably onto Fenzo's deck chair where he lay motionless for a long while, staring gloomily at the empty bathing suit, then at the open door of the cabin and at the other traces of Gloria's hasty visit. To go and look for her, ask for her seemed too risky, too precipitous, hardly appropriate. She would probably come back. If she had come once there seemed no reason in the world for her to spend the whole afternoon shut up in the hotel. Now that she knew he was there, she might come back to find him any time now. She would suddenly appear and silently take up her place at his side. He had to wait, though. Wait again, always waiting. If he fell asleep, it would help to relieve the tedium. Fortunately he had hardly slept a wink last night and so felt enormously drowsy, irresistibly sleepy. When she arrived she would observe him sleeping and he would feel her presence and wake. Perhaps she would be touched at finding him asleep. She would smile tenderly and stand watching him for a long while. He lay back in the deck chair. Way up above his head white clouds passed before the sun. A seagull plummetted towards the sea. He closed his eyes. The anger was receding, a sweet anticipation of repose filtered through. Then a shadow skimmed across his eyelids and at once he plunged into sleep.

8

THE STREET WAS almost empty but for a small group
of people silently clustered round his doorstep. They were
waiting for something. As he drew near he recognised
them and stopped short in the shadow of a bridge. He
stood still and watched them for a while. He felt surprisingly calm, which was not what he'd expected to feel when
the time came. Their presence was no shock because he'd
known all along that catastrophe was bound to ensue and
now that it faced him, a stone's throw away, he stood
waiting for it undisturbed and unafraid. It left him cold
and his coldness didn't weaken his capacity to calculate
whether it was wiser to fall into the ambush or side-step
it entirely. They couldn't have seen him yet as the bridge
concealed him from view, but they would notice him if
he lingered on much longer. What was the best move?
Was it worth facing the music if he had no earthly intention of capitulating? Was it worth the wrangling and the
clashing and the slamming if his relationships and their
attitudes would remain unchanged? His eyes scanned up
the façade of his house to the lit dining-room window.
Francesca and his mother were up there waiting for him,
or Francesca may have come down to stand there in the
street among that silent group gathered round his doorstep. He studied the shadowy wavering figures and tried to
single her out but she wasn't to be seen. The others,
Luisa's brothers and a shape he didn't recognise, looked as
though they'd either just come down into the street or
just arrived. The doors were open behind them. One
lounged before them and another was propped against
the wall as if suspended in the darkness. Marco crossed
over and sat on the embankment wall with his back to the
canal. As he stood there watching them he wondered why

they were waiting for him in the street and not upstairs in the house. He saw dark, restless shapes moving across the dining-room window like hostile shadows in the house's vacant, luminous eye. Luisa's mother and father and even Luisa might be waiting up there. They'd be tearing him to bits up there, tearfully denigrating him, not out of any particular conviction but just for the drama of it all. He didn't have to ask what had been going on because he'd known the moment he'd espied that cluster on the pavement that she hadn't been able to contain herself, that she and her whole clan had come for his blood. It was strange how impassive he was before the siege of his house, how unperturbed before a reality that relentlessly, swiftly felled him at every attempt to break loose. He felt a new sensation welling up within him, one that seemed to spring out of the previous days' confusion. His tension was gradually replaced by a coolly relaxed confidence. Marco got off the canal wall and peered at the bridge as if he'd seen him. He muttered something and someone else whined tearfully back. Then Marco cursed out loud and a shadow slithered up to him and tried to drag him off: let's get out of here for God's sake. Marco pushed him off. A couple sauntered past, turned and stared, then walked on a bit, then turned again and stared. He gathered that Marco was itching to lay into him and that the others wanted to drag him away to avoid a scene. All right, then, he thought, here I am. His first instinct was to step forward and be seen, but he didn't move. His thoughts reeled on without absorbing his attention, whirling round a single, hollow vortex, which he couldn't locate. What was he after? He couldn't understand what arrested him there in the shadow of the bridge, what stopped him from either confronting Marco or walking off. What he did know, however, was that he wouldn't be able to move until he'd sorted things out—not that he was confused. He just felt completely indifferent. These actual happenings seemed to be taking place not in the immediate, live reality, but in his memory. They paraded past like memories of by-gone moments. The figures on the other side of the canal were so many images from another time, from situations he'd managed to survive a long time ago. Had he already faced Marco? or had he simply slipped away, just as if he hadn't seen him? Marco, however, was still there and he existed independent and heedless of these feelings. He was physically present and somehow or other he had to be faced. Yes, he would have to face him. He peered over the wall, across the canal, trying to pull him into focus from afar. Under his defiant gaze Marco's self-composure seemed to melt and fade into precisely the posture he would assume once he himself had stolen off unseen or boldly thrust forward. He said he wouldn't marry her and Marco, the sole member of her family who didn't have any illusions as to honour codes, leapt on him. He leapt on him not to force his hand but to castigate his evasion and his weakness. He named him coward and bastard. Maybe he didn't fight back at Marco because he wanted to redress the balance of their relationship (it was the very least he could do for him), or maybe because Marco had been stunned by what he said: what do you want? what can you do about it? put yourself in my shoes. Marco was disarmed, Marco was completely in the dark, he couldn't do a thing to him. You see, this is all you can do and now that you've realised how useless it all is, that's it, mate. But he frowned, he'd be a fool to count on any such outcome while planning his moves. There was a touch of the heroic in facing it head on which even Francesca would appreciate, and which would enable him to emerge feeling satisfied with himself, even relieved. On the other hand, things might turn out very differently. Marco might retaliate in kind, instead of being stunned, might confuse him with a thousand arguments he'd never considered. And there were the others, too. Once he'd stepped out into the open, Francesca would swoop down and force him to remain and hear the obscenities she'd screech. He wasn't frightened, but it might be wiser after all to turn away, withdraw before it was too late. What did he have to lose? the opportunity which he might later regret? Tomorrow, or even earlier, he would catch himself wondering, what if he'd spoken out: it would all be over and done with, you'd be a free man if you'd gone through with it all. But if he did go through with the blasted thing there mightn't be a tomorrow anyway. Come on, let's get out of here, he decided, but he was glued to the spot, halted by the suspicion that he was afraid of Marco. The idea irritated him enough to prevent him from shrugging it off. He couldn't afford to be afraid. So far he'd behaved honestly —as honestly as the circumstances allowed. If he were to withdraw it mustn't be a retreat. It had to be an unemotional, coolly calculated act. He had enough things to worry about without adding shame to the list. He wasn't afraid, though. He was absolutely positive about that. He was withdrawing only because the idea of facing the outcries of Luisa's family was repellent, as was the prospect of Francesca's vociferous tirade and his mother's probable reproofs. That's why he'd leave. He had no intention of jeopardising his future with a senseless act of heroism. No, it wasn't fear, really, but common sense or even tact. And if tomorrow he suspected that fear had motivated his withdrawal he would face Marco, phone him and arrange to meet in some quiet secluded spot where they could talk it out. He would tell him everything tomorrow. Tomorrow would be better. He was drawing back from the bridge. He had decided to leave and burn the last of his uncertainties behind him. Perhaps his character would be scarred for life, he didn't care. On the contrary he was quite amenable to the prospect of a sinister outcome if there were any guarantee that it would free him once and for all of the worries and tortures he'd suffered to date. He was amazed at how calmly he turned his back on Marco, Francesca, and Luisa. He retraced his steps. He was acutely aware of the melodrama of his gestures. But something didn't quite

68

fit. As he walked away, he heard a shutter creaking open, a load of rubbish fell with a splash into the canal, a cat hissing viciously—they were the last gloomy farewells to his neighbourhood. Well, that's that, he sneered.

He didn't know where to go nor where he'd spend the night, and it didn't worry him. The only thing that really mattered was the sudden silence, the absence of emotion, the cool peace into which the long years of strident confusion had jelled. Had all the anguish really disappeared forever? Had remorse, troubled conscience, neurotic shuttling between hope and despair really finished? He was turning his back on his besieged house, turning away through the dark streets. He vaguely distinguished the nocturnal sounds: clusters of confused voices against the silence, snatches of songs, the water slurping as the boats passed, the hurried footsteps. As he walked along slowly, his knee bumping rhythmically against his blue beachbag with its empty lunchpot, knife, fork and bathing suit, he was dogged by the picture of that group round his doorstep but he himself was totally unaware of its presence. How much longer would they wait there? All night? They weren't likely to persevere for long, but still he wouldn't go home to Francesca and his mother, who would undoubtedly be waiting up for him, because he didn't feel like seeing them or listening to their arguments. He knew what they'd say and the obvious, banal, harsh language they'd use to break through the shell of cold inscrutability that protected him. You and your selfish pride, you're so selfish. God, if only you could see yourself as we do. But no, he was the man apart, immunised and hermetically sealed against such onslaughts. He shuddered at the thought of cracking. What on earth should he do now? he sighed. Was he going to walk about all night long accompanied by the maddening metallic clinks from his beachbag, or would he find some place to stay? If only he'd left his bag at the cabin at least he wouldn't have that stupid tinkle heralding his way through the town like some leper's bell. The alternative was to stop

69

somewhere or other and wait the night out. He paused to look up at the sky, but the prospects weren't encouraging. Morning was hours and hours away and the sky was totally dark. He'd definitely have to do something. He wouldn't really mind spending the night outdoors but he probably would be better off going to a hotel. He might end up in one of those boarding houses he'd taken Luisa to a few times, the ones with the unlit corridors, the filthy rooms looking out onto sordid alleys, if they had any windows at all. At least they were cheap and easy to come by and the beds were fairly comfortable. If he was going to spend the night at a hotel, he'd have to borrow some money off someone, some five or ten thousand lire to add to his paltry two. He'd need it for tomorrow too. Fenzo came to mind, but he didn't think he could take Fenzo's sniggering, self-satisfied grin. He set out gingerly walking along the *fondamenta* that would take him beyond the bounds of his neighbourhood, of his house, of Fenzo's house and into the centre of the town. Perhaps, though, his predicament made the humiliation worth facing and it probably wouldn't be that painful anyway. He turned back stoutly. He didn't follow the *fondamenta* all the way back but turned off right into an arcade at the end of which a tree began to take shape through the funnel of darkness. Through the prevailing silence he heard the gentle trickle of a fountain. That's it, I'll go to Fenzo's. He'd go to Fenzo's but he would have to start steeling himself in case of Fenzo's irritated reaction.

He looked at his watch. It was almost eleven o'clock— not the most convenient hour to go knocking at someone's door, but still within the limits of acceptability. With a bit of luck he might actually succeed in borrowing the money he needed so badly, he might soon have it in his pocket, he thought, unless his determination to be unaffected by Fenzo's reactions dissolved just as he reached Fenzo's house, unless he began to falter, to test his pride with the usual questions: shall I go? shall I stay? shall I call him? shall I not? He pressed forward taking the first turning on the left down a tiny alley no wider than a railway track.

When he finally reached Fenzo's house, he couldn't move. He couldn't decide whether to ring the bell or not. The dining-room window was alight and wide-open; the other rooms were dark. Was the idiot asleep or was he out? What's up? he thought absurdly, as if he had expected to be met at the door; it was amazing, every time he wanted Fenzo he was impossible to find. The lights in the dark house were somehow repellent, infinitely distant and dead, even if the red house embedded in the depressed setting of the neighbourhood was so familiar to him. His first impulse was to retreat, but the courageous ordeal by humiliation which he'd just envisaged thrust his hand towards the door in defiance of his timidity. He still couldn't bring himself to ring the bell. Blast, he swore, uncertain whether it was Fenzo he was blasting, or the effort he'd have to make, or the present situation, blast it all. He couldn't decide. He was cross and sorry he'd lost a friend. Things would have been so different, he thought, if they had had a straightforward honest-to-goodness friendship. It would have been so easy to turn to Fenzo at any time of the day or night. As it was, his relations with Fenzo, as with everyone else, were troubled and strained. Things could be different, he thought. He felt a helpful surge of bitterness about his friend which made him insensitive to what Fenzo might think of his midnight visit and his request. So he abandoned the speculations, and found himself ringing the bell with peremptory insistence. Damn it, he mused as he heard the ringing penetrate the house, damn them all. A dishevelled shadowy image appeared at the window. He moved back almost defiantly to the middle of the street, stood beneath the streetlamp and asked if Fenzo were there. He's out, he's gone to the cinema, the Rio Marin Arena. Do you know where it is? Fenzo's mother looked surprised. She'd probably been startled by his vicious ring, by having to go to the window to ask who it was at this hour: and what

71

a time to go round ringing bells. He gave her a quick, sharp smile; I'm sorry, he said, it doesn't really matter. I'll wait for him outside the cinema. As the shadow started to withdraw, he waved good-bye and moved away. His bitterness returned because he felt that Fenzo's absence was somehow proof of his doubtful character. He felt relieved, however, as his plan could be postponed for a bit and it would be easier to put into effect away from his house. He walked slowly towards the Rio Marin Arena which was an outdoor cinema in a courtyard squeezed between tall working-class houses. Of course he knew where it was, what a silly question, as if there were any other summer cinemas in his neighbourhood. He'd often gone there with Luisa during their first, almost happy year and after that as well. It had been ages since he'd been there with her. When was it? It must have been at the beginning of the last summer when affairs had become strained. One evening Fenzo had gone with them. Luisa had told him afterwards that Fenzo had tried to stroke her knee once or twice and that he'd persisted clumsily, but that she had stiffened. He had been almost tempted to have it out with Fenzo, to teach him a lesson, but he had done nothing about it because he realised that he could quite easily have given her up to Fenzo. He had begun to hate her. Luisa. He shuddered at finding himself thinking about her again, as if she'd been crouched, waiting for a chance to slip into his thoughts. He'd left her on the other side of the bridge outside his house, but she'd skulked in his footsteps because she wanted to continue their dialogue. But my poor, desperate little Luisa, he thought, even if he'd only just realised that he was vulnerable, very much more vulnerable than he'd believed until just recently, he really didn't have time to chat things over with anyone. All he had time to consider now were his own immediate problems which needed immediate solutions. Fenzo, he muttered, Fenzo's the man. He could wait for him at the exit; or better still, if they'd let him in without a ticket, he could look around for him in the courtyard. It was just after eleven and he could count on the doormen being tired, confused with sounds and blurred images, and neglecting their duties at the entrance. He might even be lucky enough to see the last part of the film. If so, the last empty hour before midnight wouldn't be so hard to fill. He hurried along almost gaily. He'd soon covered the distance through the maze of *fondamenta* and alleyways which brought him out in front of the cinema. The clear, bright, unnatural sounds of the dialogue floated out through the entrance, through the trees that overhung the walls where the crowded windows of the surrounding houses started. Before entering he studied the titles and the few grey photographs billed on the wall outside, from which he gathered that it was a whodunnit he had never heard of but which looked fairly promising. All right, he thought, I'll go in now, maybe I'll even pay for my ticket, but, as he hoped, he didn't have to because the old woman in the box office who was arranging piles of banknotes and coins behind the counter nodded absentmindedly to his timid request to go in to look for a friend. He was inside the cinema, standing before the screen which teemed with light and shadow and sound. The crowd was silent, intent. He'd look for Fenzo later when the film was over. He didn't want to barge in now at an exciting moment. He wanted to catch his breath, to enjoy the odd sensation of relief at being able to let himself go for an hour. He soon realised, however, that it was no small task to forget himself, not just because the film was too near the end for him to understand what was going on, but because a kind of neuralgic spasm kept interrupting his consciousness to thrust forward thoughts of Luisa and the group standing round his doorstep. The images filed before him spliced with the images on the screen. The film would capture his thoughts momentarily, he would relax, then another spasm would assault his consciousness. Somehow he still managed to cut himself off, to freeze his mind as he had done before, to keep his balance. The scene with that

73

dining-room light, with the shadowy figures waiting for him below and with his own immobile figure looking on from behind the bridge hung menacingly in his mind.

The end of the film suddenly overtook him. The lights went on while the deafening sounds still thundered and the last images lingered on the screen suspended from the trees. He rose, stepped into the aisle and looked for Fenzo's face among the crowd. Men, women, entire families, little swarms of noisy children passed by, their comments assailing him: remember when he ... but after that, after ... what do you mean? he'd already understood ... They knocked into him shoving him helplessly towards the street. He caught sight of Fenzo threading his way down the far aisle with a group of young people that were pushing, yelling, jumping up to snatch at the branches of the trees as they passed. He forced a passage through the crowd, hurdled over a few rows of seats, brushed through a group of boys who were in his way and got into the jostling mass of people slowly emptying into the street. He was out before Fenzo. He lit a cigarette and settled down to wait. Fenzo emerged a few minutes later, crooking his arm round a girl's shoulders. She looked cheap. Her head was tossed back and she wriggled with laughter as they went down the steps. Fenzo passed by without seeing him and he just couldn't stop him; he lost his nerve at the very last moment. Perhaps he had realised that he couldn't ask Fenzo until he could get him alone. I can't, he thought, I simply can't. He knew that crowd strolling away too well. He couldn't bare himself before them all. They had been his friends at one time. Now they regarded him as a traitor; his disdain was an insult to their obtuse dignity. He could see the ironic glimmer in their eyes, hear their insults as he went off. He could feel the overbearing weight of Fenzo's self-sufficiency: did you see him? that sniveling pauper, you shouldn't have lent him a thing, you're crazy, you should have told him ... They wouldn't have stopped talking about him until they finally went to bed. He stood beside the cinema

entrance until Fenzo and his companions were a good
way off. He moved slowly, tagging on to the last batch of
spectators to come out of the Arena. Behind him they
were taking down the posters from the wall. The lights
were going out in the windows of the surrounding houses.
He caught a glimpse of Fenzo and his friends again a
hundred yards on, gathered round a closed news-stand
at the foot of a bridge. They were all talking at once in
that choral mode he remembered so well, happy, amused,
still exhilarated by the film, excited by the girls. They
commented, reconstructed episodes in the film, rehearsed
the actors' gestures, garbled their foreign names, calling
each other by them. Watching them he felt annoyed and
slightly envious, nostalgic for their carefree air, regretful of
a past epoch when he, too, could have joined in their
games but hadn't. Perhaps he might have liked to jump
up and down, run round the news-stand, pinch the girls'
bottoms, and giggle with them all. What a stupid, banal
idea, he thought. Would he really have liked to be one
of them, laughing with them, running round the news-
stand, sitting on the steps of the bridge until it was time
to go home to sleep, and then repeating the same charade
the next day till bedtime and the next, because they
accepted the logic of their way of life without ever questioning it? To hell with their sort of frivolity, he thought,
he could do very well without their bloody giggles. As
far as he was concerned he was convinced that the
estrangement he suffered was to his credit rather than
otherwise. He would go on feeling awkward only so long
as he hadn't found his level. After that, there wouldn't
be any more doubts, he'd know what he was about and
everything would be different. All his relationships would
be natural, spontaneous, like those of the four animals
roistering round the news-stand a few yards away. They
had no conflicts, they were fully realised beings. He was
proud of his solitude, of his capacity to face it alone
without anyone's help and without too much distress.
He decided he would not humiliate himself by waiting a

minute more. He wouldn't ask Fenzo for a penny tonight and maybe not even tomorrow. It was hot, the sky was clear. The city by night was an enchantment—he'd heard it said so many times—empty, silent, echoing. He would walk around slowly, stop occasionally on a bridge, on the edge of a canal, until day broke and then he could return to the Lido. Calmly and without regret he turned his back on Fenzo, on the plan he'd so long nurtured. He went into the Camp della Lana and headed for the Riva dei Tolentini, past a low, grey building and a long line of doleful windows. He followed the *fondamenta* along the quiet canal. At the bend it was brightly lit by a hotel, but beyond, by the solid Ponte del Gaffaro, the lights were all out. He had forgotten Fenzo and his companions. He'd forgotten so many things. Gloria sprang up into his solitude, Gloria who hadn't returned to the beach that afternoon. He had caught a new look on her face when he saw her briefly from a distance before leaving the beach. He thought of his own predicament of having to spend the night out of doors. He wasn't very worried, though, because Gloria had been sitting on the hotel terrace beside the empty seats of the orchestra; he'd looked at her for a long time. She wasn't alone. Alessandro must have actually left the Lido, then, but Matteo was with her and so was that elegant woman whom Gloria called Elena. How beautiful she'd looked just then, and seeing her there like a sweet dapple of red and gold between the marble and the ivy, he felt an odd mixture of yearning and embarrassment. He didn't know whether Gloria had noticed his excitement as she saw him pass close by or whether her own excitement had dazzled her perception, but he was sure that the quick accidental encounter had been important to her. She couldn't have foreseen it, even if she'd realised he had summoned the nerve to take the exit through the hotel lobby to the street instead of simply leaving by way of the gate on the beach. How else could he explain that quick jerk of her head and that long look which followed him until he'd entered the hotel? As he crossed over to the exit, he wondered why he hadn't called to her, why he hadn't sat down next to her in spite of her brother's presence, or at least at a near-by table, leaving the initiative to her. He was furious with himself, he felt miserable but he carried on towards the entrance. In spite of his pressing need to see her again he felt propelled, overwhelmed by the enormous inferiority complex that the hotel always managed to arouse in him whenever he was anywhere near it. He wanted to go back but pressed on reluctantly to meet Fenzo in the street. Fenzo had just come out and was waiting for him. He couldn't imagine what welcome Gloria would have given him if he had stopped. He might have behaved off-handedly as if he'd known her for ages, or he might have pretended that even though he'd only just met her, their vague hasty relationship justified his sitting down. Others would have sat down, that is, other members of Gloria's world; and he might have done so himself if she'd been alone, in fact he wouldn't have hesitated, but it would have been excruciatingly awkward to do with Matteo and Elena there. Who was this Elena, anyway? A relative, or perhaps one of her more mature friends. She, too, had looked at him with interest as if she already knew about him. Gloria may have pointed him out to her the night before when he'd passed by their table on his way home. What a day it had been, and what a night. His argument with Francesca had been a nightmare, but he had performed fairly well. He'd defended himself with dignity and courage and without lying. That was a fact, wasn't it? He would behave similarly with Marco tomorrow or whenever he decided to see him. He would say everything in a few calm, decisive sentences and no offences as they were completely uncalled for: look, put yourself in my place, tell me honestly what you'd do if you didn't love her and you knew that she didn't love you, that she wanted to have you at any price because she was afraid, what would you do? What would he do? What would he ask? If he

77

could meet him half way he wouldn't hesitate, but there wasn't a chance, there simply wasn't any room for compromises. Even the idea of giving his name to the baby was senseless now, as was his earlier decision, which he'd made absent-mindedly while waiting for Luisa on the bridge, to care for the baby himself : too much had changed. Previously his main objective had been to avoid a permanent commitment, but now there was Gloria. Gloria didn't deserve to be disgusted or offended. Was there any chance of her taking him as he was with his long sad story of squalid involvements, mother's tears, sister's screams, people waiting round his doorstep? He didn't know. Perhaps later on. Right now it was useless to think about it. He tried to visualise Gloria visiting his house, holding his hand to prove that she was his, but it was too ludicrous for words. He could have no illusions about that; his relations with Gloria were still dangerously fragile. If his true circumstances came to light, Gloria would immediately stop fighting herself, stop hesitating, stop questioning. She would revert back to her old self. She might even feel the same disgust for him that he felt for his family. He felt his heart contract. A chance like the one Gloria offered might slip through his fingers any moment. He must persist with dogged, even vicious determination. A word, a gesture, a mere nothing might do it; his condition would be exposed and Gloria would become a contraction of the heart such as he felt now. He would be crushed, humiliated, repulsed to solitude and ignominy. No there was no hope of falling back on compromise. He had to be free of all the old ties, unburdened by problems, with a clean slate and fancy free as he thought he'd appeared to her the first time they'd met. Gloria was neither strong enough nor sure enough of herself to accept him on any other terms. It was marvellous, he reflected, to be perfectly certain of what he had to do. His new plan was requiring much more conviction than he'd originally imagined when he'd first decided to give Luisa up and had idly imagined he could do so on the sly. He knew now how impossible it was; he understood why he had waited until now to admit that it was all over with Luisa : because he'd been afraid of her desperation, afraid that it would tarnish his own petty self-respect. He had had intuitions of this frequently, and in his moments of greatest anguish he'd even felt Luisa dying. But until she'd returned with her news from the doctor, he'd always deluded himself into thinking that nothing had really happened, or at worst that he would take care of the baby if it was born. Now he realised that his hesitation, his reservations, his fears, his anxieties, which had grown parallel to his break with Luisa and had compounded the difficulties, were a mere extension of his incapacity to accept the transformation and its compensatory twinges of conscience. What they actually reflected was his refusal to be what his choice implied : in a word, his refusal to be a cad. He also realised that if he'd accepted himself as others saw him, the anxiety which tormented him would probably subside. The tendency towards a new form of existence, towards a less hypocritical definition of himself must have taken effect from the moment he had spied on Luisa's clan gathered outside his house, and had turned his back on them with supreme indifference. Only his unconscious acceptance of the fact that he was a swine and that he could behave like one without damning himself in his own eyes could have produced that feeling of indifference. These were not discoveries about himself which he could accept without a struggle. On the contrary, they were accompanied by a feeling of overwhelming weariness. The objective reality was that his side of the story didn't count a damn, and his own instincts and revulsions didn't matter to anyone, nor did his certainty that he was only one of the guilty parties. As far as the outside world was concerned nothing really mattered but the fact that an illegitimate child made the mother an innocent victim and the father a cad. There was no escaping it unless he sacrificed himself to save Luisa and win the others' approval. It seemed that he had achieved a complete grasp of his situation now without any of the previous uncertainties. Once again he considered the cost of his freedom and it seemed a reasonable and desirable sum to pay, even if some tiny vestige of doubt insisted on making him feel perfidious. If circumstances made freedom possible only if he was a cad, then, god damn it, he would be a cad. He would leave Luisa and the baby to their fate, refusing to have anything more to do with them and denying, when necessary, having had anything to do with them in the past. What counted was to have a clear field ahead and no ties to drag him back. If accepting the fact that he was a cad could put an end to all his anxieties, then that's what he'd be. He would welcome peace with open arms as the blessing he'd gone without far too long for there to be any question about accepting it.

He'd walked on without noticing that he'd followed the same route he always took to go to the Lido. He came out into Piazza San Marco, which was almost deserted. The café lights were out. A group of fellows lingered among the tables of the Café Quadri. A couple strolling under the arcades of the Procuratie stopped as if to be sure they were going the right way, then walked on. He considered sitting at one of the cafés in the dark and waiting for time to pass; but it was too early to stop, and he didn't feel tired yet. In any case he had better things to do than sit down like a vagabond in the Piazza, trying to look inconspicuous. As it was, he could see a tramp approaching with a paper bundle under his arm— or maybe it was a blue beachbag like his own. He rolled about, stumbling under the street lamps, wandering between the tables, waiting until the square was completely deserted. This was not for him, so long as other possibilities remained. Objectively it seemed a much better idea to continue his nocturnal saunter. He might head for the Riva degli Schiavoni, follow it through to the end, then look for a deserted landing-stage where he could stretch out without being seen. He left the Piazza and made for the Riva. He walked slowly, settling on a gait, however, which was not too suggestive of vagrancy. He even pretended to himself he had a definite destination. He lingered a moment at the Ponte della Paglia, examining the quiet structure of the Ducal Palace, which gave him pleasure for some reason. It stood pale in the light of the street-lamps, its empty arches supporting the walls, flanked by the dark and bottomless canal. The lights of a *vaporetto* caught his eye, shimmering out in the dark of the basin. Suddenly he knew what he'd do, where he'd go and how he'd spend the rest of the night. He dashed off the bridge and crossed the *fondamenta* to the landing. The landing-stage was deserted; it moved gently under the impact of a wave which had just reached it from some remote part of the lagoon. Through the glass partitions of the shelter he could see the *vaporetto* approaching; dark figures sat in the bows; a sailor unwound a coil of rope. It wouldn't be long now; he was in a frantic hurry to be on the boat, to leave the city behind him and have the Lido ahead, but the boat seemed to be moving at a snail's pace. Still, its unexpected, brilliant arrival was a thrilling sight. He felt relieved and almost happy, not to have all those dreadful hours yawning ahead. The boat drew alongside, a few people got off and he clambered quickly aboard. He lit a cigarette and looked round. There were only two other passengers left on deck, a couple who were kissing in the dark, and no one else had got on with him. Thank goodness for that, he mused as he looked at the couple. Then as the sailor unwound the hawser from the wharf, the hull and the thin metal sheeting began to throb, the run towards the Lido was resumed. What luck! Why did the realisation of being on board, the sensation of damp wooden seats and sea air, that showered him now and then with that invisible spray out of the dark water, why did they make him feel exhilarated, drunk with the delightful feeling of setting out on a journey? His destination, that luminous streak, that shimmering reflection of the city, was only a few minutes away; yet he felt as though he were really leaving for good. He experienced all the emotions of departure: relief, hope, and farewell. As he bore down towards the watery reflection, all his hopes, his needs, all his recently formulated ambitions were stimulated violently by the voyage, which was carrying him to his natural dwelling-place amid the lights displayed before him. It was there more than anywhere else in the world that his existence seemed to have some meaning. So what did it matter that he had to wait till morning?

When he landed he found the bars on the square still open, but they were empty and silent and would soon close. Beyond the square the Lido was sleeping and the great tree-lined avenue was sleeping, almost dead without the usual hubbub of cars and trolley-buses, without the life of the day-time crowds. He walked slowly, passing the silent hotels, the dark shops, the tightly shut souvenir-stands that looked like strongboxes, the cars parked along the pavement. As he reached the circus at the end of the avenue from which radiated all paths to the beach, he encountered the whole body of the sea. To the right the streets led to the big hotels, the *Des Bains,* the Casino, the *Excelsior*; to the left, to the working-class area. He faced the central terrace of the circus, which overlooked the seashore. The sea slept, calm and dark. He stood staring into the distance. As the cigarette he held between his fingers burnt down, he felt magnetically drawn towards the *Excelsior.* He threw down the cigarette, crossed the circus and took the street that led to the big hotels. He strode along without the slightest idea of what he would do when he reached the other end. He began to realise somewhat hazily that his flight from Venice had unconsciously been directed towards the *Excelsior,* that when he reached the *Excelsior* his escape would be complete. As he approached the Casino a few minutes later he was dazzled by the glare of the lights and by the sharp contrast of the dark terrace, where a few couples were dancing closely in each other's arms. He stopped short under a tree, looked towards the terrace and strained to see the dancers' faces. Conflicting sensations superimposed themselves onto his visual perceptions, but not to their detriment, as he was so accustomed to conflicts that they couldn't reduce his capacity to snap the dusky figures into focus. He both hoped and feared that Gloria would be on the terrace. Now, when he least expected it, he felt like resuming their dialogue; but he was afraid that the irregular circumstances that brought him there would make it difficult to face her. He both hoped and feared that Gloria would not be there; he feared and knew that if she were, he could not be alone with her. He peered at the entwined dancers through the ivy-covered trellis, but he couldn't distinguish their faces because the dim lights, the dancers' movements and their embraces conspired against his vision. It was useless to observe them from out here. If he wanted to find out if Gloria were there, he would have to enter the Casino, cross the foyer, and perhaps a corridor and a lounge, and sally out onto the terrace. But the temptation to move was checked by the embarrassing, unpleasant certainty that he hadn't enough money to meet the admission charge and not enough courage to venture alone into a place which, like the *Excelsior,* always managed to paralyse him with timidity. Even if he had to renounce the idea, he wouldn't budge from his vantage point. He sat down on the roots of the tree and wondered whether he should thank his poverty or curse it for having immobilised him. He no longer studied the undulating shadows on the terrace, but he could still see them. He became acutely aware of something that had never caught his attention before : Gloria's faithless, permissive form dancing in a mythic nocturnal world peopled by objects and figures he'd never imagined existed. He painfully realised he'd never seen her in such a context before, and his awareness of this night-life grew to a menacing nightmare. For the first time, he felt jealous. Every evening as he left the Lido and wearily truncated his day, Gloria's life went on without him to pursue untold possibilities that might blossom into new relationships with other people —other men. What if someone stole her in the dead of night while he was miles away? What if she were drawn to someone else and robbed him of that tiny part of her she'd given him? What recourse would he have? Another nervous spasm shivered through the tenuous web of their relationship edging him into further conflict. How could he have been so naïve, so presumptuous? Was he the only man on earth? He saw Gloria smiling; she was holding hands with one of the shadows, leaning against it as it engulfed her. How could he have been so sure of himself as to ignore the possibility that Gloria might be attracted to someone else? There she was again standing next to a quiet, positive silhouette, and although he hadn't detected a single compromising move, he knew she was lost. He choked and struggled wildly to see how things really stood. Yes, I need her, I want her, I've put all my hopes on her and here I am expecting her to take the initiative while I lounge around despairing and procrastinating indefinitely. I spend days on useless conjectures, on interminably evaluating my overblown speculations. He was disgusted with himself, with his passivity, with his vapid conjectures about her. He began to feel it was absolutely imperative that he act immediately, that he find Gloria now, now, this very moment, talk to her, that he wrest her from the hands of whoever was holding her. He sprang to his feet and made for the Casino entrance. His heart thumped madly. He hoped he would find her now, without even considering what she would think when she saw him. He wanted his arrival to shock her. He didn't even bother to worry about the entrance charge. He ran up the steps and entered the foyer. He looked so sure of himself that he might have been one of the regular visitors; he headed for a corridor which he thought would lead to the terrace. He did not know whether to feel relieved, hopeful or annoyed as he realized how easy it was. No one stopped him, no one asked for an admission ticket, no one contested his right to cross the lobby, to step on the red carpets or to walk down the corridor. A waiter about to carry a tray of glasses out onto the terrace stepped aside to let him pass. The head-waiter approached and respectfully motioned him to a table, but stopped almost intimidated as he swept past without looking at him and made for the dance floor. It had all been very easy, but equally useless: Gloria wasn't there, there was no one to spy upon, and what's more there was nothing either dangerous or mythical about the nocturnal hour. The spectral couples embracing on the dance floor, the tiny islands of men without partners, and an odd girl or two sitting it out alone at the tables betrayed the boringly middle-class character of it all. The little lights and the orchestra and the Coca-Cola bottles lent the terrace an air of thinly-veiled squalor. He had the feeling he was surrounded by ambitious little social-climbing blood brothers, who, like himself, had come to roost in this place as the goal of an angry rebellion. They were identical to him; they were nauseatingly exact copies. He left the terrace as decisively as he'd entered. He had come counting on exposing Gloria's secret nightlife, and now he left for fear of becoming involved in the home-from-home frustrations that paraded the terrace. God only knows what I hoped to find, he mused, and instead I wind up bumping into a couple of lousy spivs with ulterior motives like mine. Where, then, do Gloria and Elena and Matteo and people like them go at night? He blushed inwardly as it occurred to him that they'd probably given the place up so as not to have to mingle with intruders of his sort. He was in the piazza again, facing the hours to dawn. He started walking instinctively towards the *Excelsior*. It was only a few yards away, massive and silent, the end of his journey. He looked up at the tall dark walls and then over to the lights suspended on the deserted terrace. The whole building was submerged in a thick, respectful silence. What now, he wondered calmly. The hotel and the beach behind began to warm his lonely

85

solitude; he felt at peace. The long journey hadn't been in vain; it did him good to be near Gloria, even if circumstances weren't the most propitious. Her proximity stimulated him, kept his interests alive and active, banished the haunting spectres. In fact, he thought, his nocturnal journey had made him discover an entirely new dimension in his interest for Gloria. He wasn't carried away into believing that he loved her, just because he'd felt jealous for the first time. It didn't necessarily follow. But all the panic and fear he'd felt and his need to grasp the hidden, unvoiced nuances of his relations with her indicated that his feelings were stronger than he'd thought. It wasn't all cold calculated strategy, he thought; there was more to it than that and this something gave his actions a tinge of romanticism, a saving grace. Perhaps he wasn't such a cad, after all. Perhaps he could afford to be a little more indulgent with himself. His midnight trip to the Lido had been a real inspiration. He felt calmer, richer, and much more at peace with himself, but still aware of how he fluctuated, how his emotions swung pendularly to and fro. He wouldn't be at all surprised if tomorrow everything was exactly as it had been before, if he were again to see himself through Francesca's and Luisa's eyes, if he fell to tormenting himself again, to arguing and casting about wildly for justifications. But just for now, for tonight at least, it didn't matter, for he'd secured a short respite for himself. He walked almost jauntily away from the piazza towards the dimly lit entrance to the *Excelsior*. The glass door was open and the foyer deserted. He stopped in the middle of the street and looked at the huge empty armchairs stranded in the middle of the lounge, the thick carpets and the window that overlooked the sea. He saw the lights of the jetty like a ship anchored offshore twinkling across the intervening darkness where the beach and the cabins and the bright sun and the looks he and Gloria had exchanged and the gestures, the hopes, his life—all hung suspended, invisible, asleep. The quiet darkness of the beach close by tempted him. All he had

to do was enter, cut right across the hotel and he would
be where he'd been a few hours ago, where he'd left
part of himself behind. But he couldn't risk it, it was a
crazy notion. What if someone saw him and asked him
where he was going and booted him out without more
ado. He moved away; about a hundred yards further on
he reached a spot where the wire fence separated the
street from the beach; he retreated leaving part of himself behind. His thoughts winged back to the lights of the
entrance like a host of moon moths back to the vision
of darkness and quiet he'd seen beyond the foyer. Don't,
they whispered, don't go, don't go away again, this is
where you wanted to come .... you're here. That vaguely
formulated temptation suddenly developed into a conclusive moral imperative with undertones of needs and
ironical urges that had to be gratified immediately: it was
imperative he go onto the beach, he really had to. He
would go to Fenzo's cabin and take refuge for tonight and
for the nights to come. He would never go home again.
Now he knew for certain why he'd walked all this way
to the beach. He wanted to transfer himself completely
and permanently, or at least until his present circumstances changed. He had been slow to identify his final
destination, unconsciously confusing it with the Lido in
general, then with the Casino terrace, finally with Gloria's
hotel; but now he knew that it was Fenzo's cabin, that
lovely red cabin that was his day-time haven and now his
nocturnal refuge, a place to rest, to sleep, to live safely
from all that oppressed him. Here he would find the
true axis of his existence. Thank God, he murmured,
almost attributing divine origin to his fresh illumination,
thank God. His utterance of gratitude was feverishly excited, because his latest plan was a dangerous and
provocative act which unnerved him. The street had
narrowed into a path. The *Excelsior's* wire fence had
joined that of the adjoining beach, the *Ondine,* and it
lay low and unhinged from its stakes, permissive among
the dunes and bushes. He stopped to examine the street

87

furtively but thoroughly, like someone reconnoitring enemy territory. Not a soul. A street-lamp above him ten yards away loomed glumly against the shadows. It would be awfully easy to climb over the fence if he did so at once. No one could see him and no one would stop him, but he would have to do so now before anyone came. His heart beat wildly as he leaned against the fence and shook it to see if it would bear his weight, not buckle beneath him, and spring back into place after he'd jumped over : it was just the job. Now, he said, now. He looked round quickly, climbed up and leapt over like a huge stealthy cat, whereupon the fence sprang back with a metallic clash as he landed silently among the sandy scrub. He stood up, clutched his blue beach-bag under his arm and ran down the dark slope, jumping doubled up between the reed clusters and the hewn stubble towards the small skeletal cabins of the *Ondine,* which spread out in a row along the water's edge. He stopped once he'd passed the cabins' fringe, reached the wet sand and caught sight of the sea before him. He took off his rope-soled shoes and rolled up his trousers to the knee. Then looking round absentmindedly, he made his way to the massive hulk of the jetty which separated the *Ondine* from the *Excelsior.* He knew his way. On his right the sea lapped persistently, slipping its cold tentacles between his shivering ankles. He still felt sure of himself, excited and somewhat amused by the prospect of leaping over the next hurdle of iron and concrete. It was a frontier between two worlds, he thought; it could be surmounted, but its presence haughtily forbade all but those who felt personally authorised to do so. I am here, he laughed to himself, and I am prepared to cross the frontier.

His feet squelched among the occasional clots of rubbish, algae, slime, tins, rotting waterlogged driftwood deposited during the night. Even at night the beach was pock-marked with the million prints of ragged bathers who passed daily up to the limits of the *Excelsior.* The crowd was awed to silence now, holding its breath as he set out with jovial impudence, as he marched along the bordering path with the brazen effrontery of a stowaway, with the feline furtiveness of a smuggler jealously guarding his precious cargo to the other side. Was it really he who moved with such certainty? The adventure was exciting, it was fun, it was doing him a world of good. He not only needed to find a refuge, he needed to challenge the *Excelsior's* inviolability, he desperately needed to prove to himself that all the fears in the world couldn't prevent him from gratifying his urges, he needed to prove that he could rely on his own powers, that he didn't have to rely on anyone's help. The cement wall came into sight. It divided the beach in half, separating the sea like a promontory. A long iron railing ran on top and beyond the sharp palings, the beach. It was narrowed considerably here, but on the other side it widened miraculously into a vast, dry, meticulously-cared-for expanse. Specks of light shone in the shadow of the *Excelsior* and beneath them, between the trees, were the shiny red cabins where he was soon to be. But he wasn't there yet, he quickly reminded himself. He still had a long way to go. He wouldn't be able to jump over the railings without risk of getting hurt. He couldn't straddle it, nor could he climb round it at the end because there the spearhead railings swung round in a semicircle like so many lances poised at the enemy. He finally concluded that the only way to reach the other side was to wade out along the jetty as far as he could, then swim round when he got beyond his depth. He opened his bag and dug out his bathing suit. He undressed quickly and put it on, then kneeled on the wet sand with his naked back to the night air and stuffed his pair of shoes, shirt, and trousers into the bag, which bulged out like a wineskin. He just managed to zip it up. He got up and tiptoed out to the sea. The cold water bit into him, cutting his breath. He stood still for a moment ankle-deep, the bag under his arm, his whole body refusing to budge. Then he started forward again, an outline in the shadows of the night, a weak vibration against the solid blackness. He pressed on, sinking slowly to his knees, his thighs, to his stomach, God . . . His body contracted, stung, his chest exploding in contact with the water which grew colder as he waded farther from the shore. He lifted the bag stuffed with clothes high above his head and swam with one arm as the bottom dropped out abruptly from under his feet. He fixed his eyes on the far end of the jetty. Rounding the point was tiring and laborious. His foot scraped against the rocks beneath the wall, which nearly lacerated him; then a wave rebounded off the wall soaking his bag and lashing across his eyes. Christ, he spluttered, enough's enough. Why is the shore so bloody far? He must have been mad to throw himself into the sea like this. It was like being naked in winter, buried in ice, abandoned, unarmed, in danger. The bag weighed a ton, he should have thrown it across the railing. This was no simple midnight swim, no innocent mid-summer madness. It was another ordeal, another of the many ordeals he'd been forced to undergo just recently. His foot touched sand. He'd arrived. The water swelled against his back, then sank beneath his chest. The night air on his wet body made him shiver horribly. He struggled against a couple more waves, then dragged himself exhausted onto the shore. He was so cold that he didn't stop to rest a while but painfully got up, squeezed the dripping beach-bag under his arm, and ran along the shore until he came to a point that would more or less be parallel to Fenzo's cabin. He was thinking clearly again. No one could possibly have seen him; the beach was so dark that he could scarcely see a few yards ahead. Even so he hesitated for a second; he stood still and he held his breath. He scanned the darkness straining to catch a glimpse of anyone who might be there. He stepped away from the water's edge, reassured by the all-prevailing silence and the distant neutral light of the *Excelsior,* and started to run soundlessly up the tidy beach, kicking up a spray of dark sand in his wake. His lungs were bursting by the time he reached Fenzo's cabin. He leaned shivering against the door and looked about him once more. The darkness he'd just crossed closed in again, erasing all traces of his presence. The natural sounds of sea and wind hung in the air. There was no sign of alarm along the lighted paths. He'd succeeded. All he had to do now was remove the chair which leant against the door, slip his finger into the ring which served as a handle and open the door slowly to avoid the squeaks. The door opened easily. An odour of warm wood and damp objects slipped out, sand scraped familiarly on the floor; the towels that hung from the central beam invitingly suggested themselves as bed clothes; he touched them, then ran his hand eagerly along the length of the stretcher in the corner, over the rubber cushions and the heavy bathing wrap. He inhaled the familiar warm odour exuded by the walls and he felt at home at last. He wrapped himself in a towel, rubbed hard until he'd banished all traces of numbness and began to feel warm again. Then he stepped out of his bathing suit, put on the thick bathing wrap. He felt better than he'd felt for ages. He was torn between feeling sorry for himself and feeling proud of himself: a truly marvellous deed worthy of leaving one speechless with respect. He was so proud of himself that if someone had walked into the cabin now he would have welcomed him without the slightest hint of timidity, secure of his proven certainty that he didn't need to explain himself to anyone: so you want to know what I'm doing here, do you? It's none of your business, I go where I want when I want and do as I like. But no one will come, he thought. Even if he left the door open, it would stay open all night, and curiously enough, he rather wanted it to stay open as it would be another challenge and one he was quite willing to take up, so much was it in harmony with his present provocative, self-gratified state of mind. Although it was an amusing idea, it was foolishly risky, useless, and silly, and he'd soon live to regret it. I must be mad, I'd better go close it, he thought, even though the chair could not be put back exactly as it had been. He'd have to open the other half of the door a little, leave the first leaf half-open until he'd arranged the chair and finally pull them both to. It would look closed from a distance. The chair, of course, would be in a slightly different position, not exactly in the centre of the door, but not out enough to draw attention. The attendants might notice it in the morning when they came to straighten the cabin, but he'd be gone by then. Before he left he would close the door properly and put the chair back in place. The manoeuvre took a few seconds and then the door was shut. He was safe until eight or eight-thirty tomorrow morning. It was a great relief to know that he could count on his refuge for tomorrow and the next day. He wouldn't let anyone take it from him, not Fenzo, not even the attendants if they ever discovered him. He smiled. He'd have to be careful not to give himself away, and he'd have to leave early and hide somewhere till the beach reopened. In the meantime, he could stretch out, rest, sleep in peace for a few hours. He could even get himself some coffee, eat a little something : coffee, chocolate, biscuits—Fenzo's cabin always contained all of God's bounty. He wouldn't even hazard going hungry in that marvellous little cabin. He smiled at his luck, tucking the wrap round himself tightly. He moved quietly in the dark until he came upon a cabinet next to the wall. He groped blindly further to find the little methylated-spirit stove, the pitcher of water and a tin of condensed milk. He took them out of the cabinet and set them down on the floor. Then he twisted round, stretched out his arm for his canvas beachbag, which he'd tossed onto the stretcher, opened the zip and pulled out his trousers, shoes and shirt. They were soaking, but maybe they'd be dry by morning. He left his shoes on the floor and hung the shirt and his trousers on a hanger. He fished out his cigarettes and matches from his trouser pocket and lit the spirit-stove. He poured water into one of the pans and sat down on the stretcher. The cooker's dim light among objects that were scattered round the cabin looked like a distant camp fire. It trembled silently in the draughts that came in through the cracks. The sea panted faintly outside. Everything seemed miles away. Even this past day and all its happenings were buried in opaque, silent memories. Luisa, Marco, Francesca, Francesca, Luisa, Marco, the baby, his mother, Venice—they were there but only as pale reflections, like wan images of some city sunk beneath a lake. How much longer would they be like this? Would this single night of vigil suffice to open an unspannable rift between them? or would they reappear before him in the morning immediate and aggressive as ever? He shook his head as he felt a new wave of panic overtake him. Grey disconnected thoughts slowly corrugated the surface of his consciousness. The fact was that they were much closer than he'd imagined a moment before. He only had to remember where he'd left them and a window flew open in his memory. They came filing into the cabin with Luisa at the fore, like a swarm of angry bees, to claim back their recalcitrant slave. He had to erase and banish the twisting, curving rings of anxiety before it was too late. He swore and cursed himself aloud. He lay on the stretcher and curled up in defence. The water on the stove was boiling. He turned over, got up, opened the cupboard and took out a cup, the tin of coffee, and the sugar bowl. He dumped a spoonful of coffee into the cup, added water, a bit of condensed milk and some sugar. He drank it slowly, savouring each little sip, forcing himself to think of other things, of ordinary, inoffensive things. He considered the pros and cons of drinking in the dark and came to the conclusion that things tasted better in the light and this was why he'd left the cooker lit. He wondered what the time was. He would get his watch from his trousers. It was marvellous to be there drinking coffee with condensed milk. He didn't feel self-pitying or calm as he had when he first entered the cabin, but then he didn't feel the anxiety any more either. For better or worse, he could manage a moment's peace for himself if he wanted to. When he'd drunk the coffee, he found his watch in his trouser pocket and strapped it to his wrist. He lit a cigarette and turned the cooker off. Tying the wrap round closely, he lay down on the stretcher and rested his head on a rubber cushion. I'll go to sleep now, he thought. It was quarter past three and still pitch black outside. I'll go to sleep now. He was not afraid of oversleeping. He never over-slept once he'd decided what time he had to get up. That wasn't a problem, but he was afraid he wouldn't be able to fall asleep in his present condition: the canvas stretcher was abrasive to his skin, his neck was wet and irritated where it touched the cushion, but it didn't really matter. It wasn't even worth getting up to fetch a towel to put beneath him. To hell with it all, what more did he want? He was so lucky; he should be thankful for his lot. He liked lying there smoking in the dark, and he liked lying awake listening to the sea. He was at the *Excelsior,* what's more, in the shadow of the hotel's walls, there where Gloria slept. She was behind one of the dark windows that overlooked the sea. She was asleep, her long body stretched out on the bed, her hair loose, soft, tender like the night. What would she think if she knew he was so near? What would she have thought if she'd seen him jump over the fence, swim round the jetty, and steal into Fenzo's cabin. He smiled again. He was sure that the intrusion itself, his furtive and courageous invasion of the beach would not jeopardise her opinion of him. In fact, it would strengthen it, if she could see it as being somehow connected to their tale; to hear that he'd spent the night at the *Excelsior* might be of some value, strategically speaking. He might tell her tomorrow. He would obviously keep the real reasons to himself, but he could proffer other explanations: his inability to keep away from her, his desperate need to be near her morning, noon and night. It wasn't a bad idea, not a bad idea at all, but he couldn't count on it. How would she react? He might launch their official relationship with this story which was, after all, spectacular, irrefutable proof of his feelings. He smiled at the prospect of seeing the flattered look of surprise on her face. He couldn't decide: perhaps it would be better to wait and come out with it on the spur of the moment, rather than fix a programme he'd have to follow from now on. But one thing he did know—he could no longer wait for the convenient opportunity; he'd have to confront her when she arrived at her cabin or go and look for her at the hotel if she didn't show up. The time has come, he said to himself, and I mustn't let it slip away, so perhaps.... Meanwhile his long day was closing round this decision. He was happy and comforted at the thought that he would find it unaltered when he woke in the morning. He let the cigarette drop and settled down on the stretcher, folding his arms over his chest. He could see nothing in the cabin but the cigarette-end which was slowly going out.

9

HE SUDDENLY came to and realised he'd been sunk into Fenzo's deck chair. He opened his eyes. The sun was high. The beach was crowding. That's enough, he murmured, up you get. He didn't move. He was still paralysed by drowsiness. As he tried to get his bearings, he thought for a moment that he was waking again from the frosted sleep of the previous night and that he would have to get up again to dress quickly, to sneak out of the cabin and hide in the lavatory—the way he'd done till the beach had opened. Now he was there, in his bathing suit, his feet buried in the hot sand, and with the cabin door legitimately ajar. The stove, the coffee tin, the cup were back where they belonged and the wrap was hanging in its place. He heaved a sigh of relief. It's a damned good thing, he thought, that he didn't have to spy out the land from his hiding place in the lavatory, nor did he have to pull his damp clothing into shape again because he'd already done all that three hours ago, while he was waiting for the beach to open. It was a quarter past ten now. It was hot, but the sea was dark and there were thick clouds up in the sky. That's enough, he repeated. Determined not to doze off again, he resumed his vigil over Gloria's cabin, which was still closed, and over the paved paths along which he hoped she would appear at any moment. Something, though, was wrong. The suspicion that he'd harboured yesterday that his determination would tail off today was becoming more and more of a reality. He felt on edge, and this in spite of a slight numbing of his nerves from sleep. He jumped at the sound of every passing woman; every approaching voice made him weak. It wasn't that his courage had waned, nor his conviction that facing her would relieve his anxieties. But waiting for Gloria's imminent arrival made him dizzy, as if he were at the brink of tumbling into a void. Now that he'd shaken off his sleepy grogginess and was wide awake, the new day, which had scarcely started, yawned like a great bottomless chasm. For God's sake, he said clutching for control, what on earth is there to be frightened of? you've accomplished a great deal, you're here, aren't you? if you reach out you can touch her cabin, just think and have a little confidence, no one's trying to get at you now. The efforts were futile. His imagination, distorted by endless waiting, had become destructive. He was prey to wild forebodings of disaster. He might well be wrong about everything. He might have credited Gloria with intentions which she'd never even dreamed of, with desires that were so skin-deep as to dissipate the moment she expressed them. He saw her coming. She passed by him, dropped a cool, uncompromised Hello, entered her cabin, undressed, came out and went away. He sat looking after her, immobilised by her impassivity. Their encounter would probably be just like that —cool and uncommunicative. All his conjectures, all his abstruse inductions were nothing but the offspring of an inflated imagination, with no basis in reality. It was possibly truer to say that his egoism stopped him from sedimenting the truth out of his frothing fantasy. Francesca might be justified in jeering contemptuously at his ambitious plans. Was it all a fantasy? was he a lunatic? a nut? He was beginning to wonder if he'd really felt Gloria's hand on his back, if it hadn't all been hallucination, a product of these demented days, if reality were not precisely that anguish he'd thought he'd escaped from yesterday, just a few hours ago, when he heard someone stop beside him. He jumped, looked up. That's her. It was Fenzo—all decked out in blue, a tennis racket in hand. He suddenly felt uneasy, afraid that Fenzo would suspect something when he entered the cabin. He greeted Fenzo with effusive affability to compensate somehow for the abuses he'd decided to conceal. How are you? he grinned. What have you been up to? He could see that something was up. Fenzo answered with a nod, turned towards the cabin without so much as looking at him and quietly put down his racket on the table inside. He looked surly, irritated, exceptionally withdrawn. He got up from his chair and looked anxiously after Fenzo. What was the matter? was Fenzo angry with him? Did he mind his being there? God no, he thought squirming with revulsion, not you too. Not that I've ever had any illusions as to the limits of your friendship, but so far you've been an insignificant factor, a neutral entity, or at the very most, a slightly malignant presence. So I beg you.... But he realised that Fenzo's neutrality was over. Somehow Fenzo had joined the other camp. He had been metamorphosed into a new unforeseen source of uneasiness. He looked again. He was momentarily horrified by the prospect of Fenzo's turning on him and telling him to clear out, of having to exert himself to remain in Fenzo's good books in order to stay on. He pretended to admire Fenzo's tennis racket. Is it new? he asked. But it didn't work. Fenzo didn't answer. Inside the cabin he dropped one of his shoes and disappeared behind the curtain without turning round. Is it new? he asked more loudly. He was beginning to feel sick with shame. Is what new? Fenzo asked. The racket. New! He stirred uncomfortably. What had happened? why was he so bad-tempered? Through the doorway he caught a glimpse of Fenzo undressing behind the curtain that hung from the rafter. Fenzo couldn't see him, but he knew that Fenzo was aware of his proximity and was, for some obscure reason or other, deliberately spurning him. He wanted to speak, to take the chill out of the atmosphere, but he was afraid of making things worse, of provoking a retort which would inform him either bluntly or by implication just how things stood—Fenzo was tired of having him around. He tensed. No matter what it cost him, no matter what damage it did to his pride, he couldn't afford to take risks. If he walked out he'd be left empty-handed. So he would have to plead and writhe in shame and anger—anything to keep Fenzo from so much as suggesting that he was displeased with him. He tapped his fingers on the side of the cabin, picked up Fenzo's tennis racket again, whistled, leaned his knee on the chair. He was excruciatingly conscious of how clumsy his gestures were, but there was nothing he could do to alter them. Fenzo appeared on the doorstep in his bathing suit, with a cigarette hanging from his lips, and he moved back to let him past. He felt more and more humiliated, inferior, embarrassed, and something more: he'd been sunk half-asleep in the deck chair painfully waiting; he'd wandered like a vagabond in the night; he'd been tortured by a thousand worries, at the cinema, in front of Fenzo's house, as he'd spied upon Fenzo's games by the news-stand. Fenzo had been serene and gay meanwhile. Fenzo's comfortable detachment robbed him of the momentary peace he'd won for himself. There was something other than humiliation, then. He drew himself up behind his friend's red back, behind the smarmy, vulgar figure with its hair curling on its neck, and he exploded into a mute gesture of repugnance which immediately freed him of his discomfort and awkwardness and restored equilibrium. In spite of all the glaring evidence to the contrary, this is the way they'd always been to one another—he, indifferent or contemptuous of Fenzo; and Fenzo, servilely jealous of him. All right, he thought, he must stop worrying about every little nothing, about what others thought, or what they might think, and he really must stop wasting time on Fenzo. He knew what his target was even though it kept on moving in and out of range all the time. He couldn't afford to let anyone distract him, let alone Fenzo of all people, all togged up in his blue outfit sporting his damn silly air of outraged dignity. He left the cabin and looked out at the beach thinking, no nothing has happened, Fenzo hasn't even come, he doesn't exist, he means nothing. He felt curiously calmer now, eager to take the lead, as if the irritant had been a catalyst needed to pull him out of his depression. He looked at his watch; it was almost eleven. If Gloria didn't arrive in half an hour, he'd go and look for her in the hotel. In only half an hour, he thought, he'd be with her and could finally talk to her, unless she decided to do to-day what she hadn't done yesterday—go to Venice to collect her bikini from Pettinelli's. He was surprised that he'd overlooked this possibility till now. He hadn't a moment to lose. He must run to the hotel. He was sick to death of his perennially passive role and it was about time he did something about it. As he started resolutely towards the hotel, Fenzo, sprawling in the deck chair in the sun, called him. He stopped and glanced back irritably at Fenzo, without a word. Come here, Fenzo said. He stayed put and said, Wait, I'll be back in a moment. He set off again. Didn't you sleep at home last night? Fenzo asked quickly, before he could move away. He was bowled over by a swift, hurtling sensation of disaster. He looked at Fenzo, astonished. His eyes dilated into a look of idiotic bewilderment. What? he mumbled hoarsely, what was that? Surely he couldn't, he thought, he couldn't have noticed anything, he couldn't have guessed so soon. He choked back a kind of silent whimper and his heart palpitated wildly. Somehow he must have asked Fenzo to explain himself, because Fenzo sighed and muttered something about Francesca going to his house during the night. So that's what he wanted to tell me, he murmured. What a relief. He stepped forward towards Fenzo grateful that at least the cabin was still safe. But he didn't really feel relieved, because Fenzo's words hit him brutally, thrusting him hours back, setting him squarely in front of Francesca's actions after he'd turned his back on his besieged household. She'd come at one o'clock in the morning to ask if he, Mario, was there, Fenzo continued. She wanted to know if he was there or he'd seen him. Of course, he thought, he could just imagine the whole scene. She'd come out of the shadows in front of his house where they'd been waiting for him. She was the only one to realise that he wouldn't come back, the only one who'd dared look elsewhere for him. Where had he been anyway? Fenzo continued. She woke everyone up. She didn't come up. She rang the bell and stayed down in the street. Damn her. He could still see her there, still hear her voice: what do you mean you don't know? weren't you together all day? didn't he come back here? He didn't know whether she was terribly anxious or beside herself with rage. Before leaving she'd asked Fenzo to tell him, if Fenzo were to see him, to go straight home or to look for her in the shop. All right, what else could she say? Was anything wrong? she didn't want to say. Fenzo's father was furious, as was his mother. It was one o'clock after all and they'd been asleep for some time. It might even have been half past one when the bell woke them. At first, they had all assumed it was some kind of a prank and no one had got up. But the bell kept ringing relentlessly, maliciously. His mother went out onto the balcony, then his father went out and finally Fenzo did, too. What was up? Did he return later or had he slept out? He dropped onto the sand, kneeling, and combed his hair with his fingers to hide the pain. He felt exhausted and worn to a frazzle: all the effort he'd put into defending himself had been wasted. A few words alone had sufficed, a few words and a sneaky little incident in the middle of the night had been enough to shrink the distance between him and his family. They were there again, surrounding him, fencing him in, forcing him to wonder wearily why on earth he took them so seriously instead of forgetting them entirely, or at least restricting the sphere of their influence. Things simply can't go on like this, he thought. He cursed himself as well for having been so stupid as to hope he could make his decisions privately, entirely on his own. He knew that he had to confront them and tell them just how utterly futile it was, to wait for him on his doorstep or to go round looking for him in other people's houses. His body felt shrivelled up on the sand as he passed his hand nervously through his hair down to the back of his neck. Fenzo was staring at him, waiting for an answer. He had to reply immediately

101

to get rid of Fenzo and organise his thoughts. It was very hard, very hard indeed. With a great effort, he rose on his knees and began to speak in a wisp of a voice. He asked Fenzo to forgive his sister. He understood Fenzo's annoyance and was in complete sympathy with him. He would have reacted in exactly the same way, or even worse. He had had a row with his family, he added. He'd left home. He'd spent the night out, slinking round like a vagabond, from one corner of the city to another. He, too, had gone to find Fenzo to get some moral support, but then he'd changed his mind. Why should he burden Fenzo with all his troubles? He could imagine what it was all about : the same old business, that he found it impossible to have any relationship with them, that he couldn't see any sense in the institution of family, and least of all in a family like his. Fenzo listened silently, giving no sign that he was curious to probe further, that he wanted to know more about what had happened. Good, he thought wearily, just as well. I can do without him poking his nose into the matter. That's the way things are, he concluded. He got up. Fenzo did nothing to restrain him; instead he too got up from the deck chair, a cigarette between his lips, and made for the water. He still looked irritated, but the danger was over. He had other things to think about, other more immediate problems to solve. First of all, there was Gloria, then there was Francesca and all the mess that surrounded her. But Gloria was the most important; his plans for the day had been upset by Fenzo's story. It was absolutely clear that Francesca had been looking for him to take him to Luisa's; that was the only explanation for her shameless street performance in front of Fenzo's house, before Fenzo's parents on the balcony, and with Fenzo cursing her. She'd obviously offered to be the go-between, presuming to make herself answerable for him, making all sorts of promises and threats : don't you worry, I'll get hold of him, you'll see if I don't send him over. . . . Filthy little schemer. She would be in the shop now, looking pale,

102

troubled, ready to lose her temper, convinced that he'd capitulate. She'd soon think otherwise, as would the others in turn, no matter what they'd thought before. He found himself back on the beach again standing alone before Gloria's cabin. He was cooling down and putting a bit of sense into his thoughts. All right, he'd go now; he'd known all along that the time would come. He only regretted that it had to be precisely on the day he was expecting to meet Gloria. He went into the cabin. Beneath the surface of his expression, a bitter smile forced its way onto his lips. Was it merely by chance that crucial events occurred in both compartments of his life at once, or was the simultaneity a logical outcome of leading a double life? He'd have to go anyway, and until he did so he'd be subject to continuous bouts of fear, despair, doubt, uncertainty, like someone who has a huge problem to solve but procrastinates daily from doing so. He took his trousers off the hanger and began to dress, thinking of his oncoming encounter with Francesca. He foresaw an unpleasant row, but he couldn't say he was afraid. Rather he was rabidly looking forward to it all. The discussion would be useful. It would help him free himself once and for all from Luisa, Marco and Francesca. But first he must look for Gloria and talk to her. He didn't want to go back to Venice leaving a void behind him. The long, weary ordeal which his imagination had undergone had left him hopping with impatience. He couldn't wait. He'd ask for her at the hotel; he'd go up to her room even if it meant turning the whole hotel upside down. It was strange how at last he felt fully capable of doing this. And if Gloria rejected him, denying the previous day's, or the day before yesterday's, incidents—how much time had elapsed?—or if she preferred not to attribute to them the significance he'd attributed to them, fair enough. He still wouldn't give in. He'd still stand firm against Luisa, and still feel the same revulsion for her. He left the cabin, pulling his blue shirt down over his trousers, one of his rope-soled shoes on and the other in hand. Through the

103

sun that dazzled the beach, among the playing children and brightly coloured li-los and the umbrellas and the awnings, the first person he saw was Gloria. She stood a few yards from the cabin examining the sea-front as if she were looking for someone. Then he saw Matteo going into the cabin and Elena stretching out on her deck chair with a lazy groan. He let the shoe drop from his hand. He leaned against the table. At last, he said, three or four times, at last, at last, at last. In spite of his surprise, he didn't lose his presence of mind. He immediately asked himself what Gloria was looking for, who was she looking for. It seemed as though he'd caught her in a moment of disappointment, as if not having found him in front of the cabin, she was searching about with the hope of finding him by the water. Gloria seemed to intuit his presence and turned. She blushed momentarily when she saw him, greeted him with an uncertain smile, and moved towards the cabin bowing her head. Before entering, however, just as she was passing Elena, who was sitting in the deck chair lighting a cigarette, she turned towards him and gave him a quick, intense, and oddly pained look. Then she vanished into the cabin. He heard her sandals on the cabin floor, the jingle of her handbag as it dropped onto the table, her voice whispering and Matteo's deeper voice giving fragmented responses. Hearing her moving about, he repeated, at last, thank you for coming like that, in such an absolutely transparent way. He could see it all clearly now. He had no doubts about it. He hadn't been mistaken. Gloria loved him. She'd come because she loved him. He wasn't a delusionist, he wasn't a lunatic. All of his theories about her failure to appear, all his deductions about her evasive behaviour that had seemed momentarily over-subtle and neurotic—all of them had been well founded. Gloria's face had betrayed her. She had fought and now she had surrendered. He had only to touch her and she would melt. She had lost all resistance. He felt a kind of festive pride at his victory, waiting calmly to, securely for its confirmation. She was changing

104

now. In a moment she would emerge, leaving the space behind the curtain to Matteo, who was waiting half-dressed at the cabin door. Matteo had neither greeted him nor given the slightest sign of recognition. He stared blankly at the sea, hands on his hips, ignoring him. Who cared? For the first time since he'd met Matteo, he could laugh at his offensive indifference. He felt stronger than Matteo. He felt as if he'd finally alighted from dizzying heights after having been all too long in danger of falling. He felt fresh, lucid and satisfied, iconoclastically, blasphemously energetic. He insulted Matteo under his breath, selecting with relish the most offensive expressions he could muster from his plebeian vocabulary: son of a bitch, bastard, you've had it. He laughed inwardly, savouring the words like exquisite fruits. Then he decided that the best way to insult him was not to think of him. He started getting ready for Gloria. He had to hurry. In a few minutes they would start talking. It didn't really matter what he said now. He need only nod, he thought, and she would follow unresisting. My sweet, he thought. Their understanding of each other was so profound that any gesture he chose to adopt would be interpreted for its precise significance. She, too, would say, my love, at last you are here. Whatever gesture he chose to adopt, whatever word he chose to pronounce in reference to their unspoken relationship would elicit an immediate response. He would prove this right now, when Gloria got the hell out of that cabin. He dropped to his knees on the sand and bent his head so as to watch Gloria's cabin without betraying his impatience. He could feel Elena's eyes on him. She had shifted round in her deck chair. He felt Matteo looking at him too. He wasn't afraid of Matteo's judgment any more. He had been encouraged by Gloria's arrival. He felt sure of himself, kneeling there, his body arched in an elegant curve on the sand. He felt his body fitting him like a perfectly tailored garment, functional and unsurpassable. Let them stare, let them examine him, let them try to discover who he was, because their

105

curiosity could only give him pleasure now. He was no longer the tortured, anguished, doubt-ridden soul. He was a new, dangerous element on the scene, and the weight of his presence had been revealed both to him and to the others by the look Gloria had given him. He remained bowed over the sand as he began to smooth the ripples with his palm. Anyone would think that he was totally absorbed by the wavering patterns which he traced and erased, when he was in fact focusing all his attention on the comings and goings in the cabin next door. He saw Matteo go in and Gloria come out. Her body was tanned and he noticed that she was wearing a bathing suit he'd never seen before as she brushed past, grazing his body with her long, brown legs to kneel down on the sand beside Elena. So, he thought, she's actually wearing the blue-green bikini. He wondered when she'd gone to Venice to collect it. He heard her lean back on the sand. As she did so her arm entered his field of vision and he could see as far as her shoulder and her head resting on her arm. She moved restlessly, inclining first to her right where he was sitting, then to the left, then right again. Finally she rose on her arms, bravely lifting her face, framed by her hair, and boldly revealing her lovelorn eyes. He looked at her, preparing for the opening move. Without smiling, he swept away an armful of sand at her side to make way for that hard damp layer beneath. He kept his eyes on her. Then he wrote something—not I love you, or I like you, as he'd first intended—but, Please. This seemed to him much sweeter, much more revealing than anything else he could write. Gloria read the message and smiled. She buried her head in her arms and lay motionless for a moment. But she seemed to be fetching about for something to write an answer with. She propped herself up again and wrote with her finger beneath his message, all right. She sat up, resting her arms on her knees. She looked at him and smiled again. Meet me four o'clock at San Marco, right? she said softly. He nodded and said softly, Yes, of course. He brushed the messages over with sand. He'd done it. Joyful metaphors assembled in his mind. Life had stopped passing him by, the castaway had been rescued, the deserter had found a new homeland. He felt utterly fulfilled, satisfied, as if he stood before a finished masterpiece after years of labour. He examined his work with pride and amazement, wondering if it were really his, if it were really he who had created it with his own hands. Was it more pride than love? he wondered, more relief than joy and less the abandon of the rewarded lover and more the joy of the released prisoner? did any of his reactions have anything to do with love? He remained kneeling. He couldn't get up and leave Gloria, who was still smiling with a mixture of tenderness and amusement at his almost childish manifestations of pleasure. He didn't move until he heard Matteo come out of the cabin and saw him lie down on the other side of Elena, who seemed not to have noticed what had been going on beside her, but then she was wearing her dark glasses that concealed her eyes, which were probably closed, anyway. Or perhaps she had noticed and was now weighing the consequences. He got up unselfconsciously and whispered to Gloria that he had to go. He smiled at Gloria's expression of gloom and disappointment. I have to, he said. Matteo heard him and jerked his head round. Really I must. He couldn't move, though, and he couldn't take his eyes off hers. She held him back, asking why he was leaving, why didn't he stay with her. Stay, he thought, stay, don't go. He was tempted to undress again and forget about his trip to Venice. But he couldn't. He had to go. He had to speak to Francesca. It was his only remaining uncertainty, the very last problem. Then his freedom would be complete. He had to go now, when he felt stronger than ever before, strong enough to overcome the virulent opposition of his family. He smiled at Gloria. I really can't stay, my sweet. He backed away, picked up the shoe he'd dropped, and slipped it on. Gloria tucked her face between her arms which rested on her knees. She looked sad, locked within herself. Was she offended by his departure? was she mortified? He suddenly realised she was a stranger and that danger lurked in her curving, locked body, which unmistakably outlined the disappointment she felt just because he was leaving. He didn't know her at all and he had no way of knowing how intense her feelings were. Was she madly in love with him? or was she just a hypersensitive, vindictive, weak, vulnerable, jealous girl? He couldn't harm her now, unless it was absolutely necessary; so he stopped, sank into a deck chair and decided not to leave until Gloria had accepted his departure. He watched her and waited for her to look at him. She sat motionless, distant, as if he'd already left. What was the matter with her? Of course it was flattering that she should so long for his presence; her ruffled silence communicated better than any explicit gesture exactly what the days she'd spent without him had meant to her. But he had spent too much energy in getting here to let the thing slip through his fingers and vanish into thin air. He didn't want to lose his chance to say all he'd wanted to say, or the chance of meeting her later on, or even lose the hope that she might turn up. A little slip now could be fatal. Again he cursed Francesca, he cursed everything, even his own perennially vacillating nature—everything that prevented him from staying and from putting out of mind those who awaited him. Gloria didn't move. Perhaps she thought he'd already left. She hadn't so much as lifted her eyes to follow him; she'd just let him go without saying good-bye. He wanted to call her, but Elena and Matteo blocked communications; their very presence interfered with their dialogue. He buried his foot in the sand, dug around, and kicked some sand up towards Gloria. It fell on her ankle, but she still didn't move. He repeated the gesture and showered her again with sand. She stirred and looked up at him. She didn't look irritated or vindictive. Apparently their moment of estrangement hadn't had the effect of making her want to punish him for his somewhat rude, untimely motion of departure or desertion. She was only surprised,

or at worst, saddened, to see him leave. His sally retained
its aura of opportune advantage. She looked so inviting
that it took no little effort to stop himself lying down
beside her and to be satisfied instead with just smiling and
motioning her with his head to follow him; but then he
knew it couldn't be otherwise. He got up, walked between Fenzo's cabin and hers and headed slowly for the
beach entrance. Gloria caught up a moment later, stopping right in front of him and so close that her hair and
her breasts almost brushed against him. He took her hand
and she squeezed his with a strange nervous intensity,
then she rose up on her toes and kissed him quickly on
the mouth. Desire, which had lain dormant, sequestered
since he'd decided to leave Luisa, suppressed by these
past exhausting days, surged violently within him now
for the first time. He put his arm under Gloria's, almost
unaware of what he was doing, careless of who was watching. He drew her close to him, slipping his hand up to the
strip of cloth across her back, penetrating the soft, dry
cavity of her armpit, moving on towards her blue-green
bra. Then he drew away quickly and put his arm on her
shoulder and pushed her towards the entrance. Curiously
he didn't think of anything. That equivocal spectator that
he was wont to carry about within him was suddenly
struck dumb by the sureness of his movements. It was
so easy to speak now, so easy to explain how sorry he was
to have to go. Gloria put her arm round his waist and
knocked his shoulder twice with her head in a puppy's
gesture of ironic pique. She said she'd understood. He
could go where he liked to all his other lovers. He could
stay away all day, she said capriciously, she didn't care—
but adding illogically that she wouldn't follow him, and
that they wouldn't see each other ever again. She smiled
and her lips touched his arm, which he had round her
neck. Only a few minutes ago he'd written the magic words
on the sand, the plea that had opened the way to Gloria's
world, and already the abstract, spectral patterns of the
past days' vigil were fading to insignificance before the

109

thrusting immediacy of the present. He'd so longed for things to turn out like this; he'd longed deeply when, in moments of exultation, he'd had a foretaste of the relief he knew he'd feel once their clandestine relationship had come to light. But that exultation, that feeling of triumph and of defiance which he'd experienced a while ago was completely unforeseen, as was his present self-assured certainty compared with his previous nervousness, as was the unexpected docility with which Gloria, previously angular and elusive, allowed herself to be guided in silence towards the beach entrance. She didn't have to ask him where he was going, nor why he had to go so soon, the grip of her arm round his back was enough to tell him that she felt calm beneath his touch. She wasn't worried about that question which had just disturbed her and which now no longer awaited a reply. It would actually be wise, he thought, to enlarge upon his reasons for his departure, even if he couldn't reveal the real reasons why he had to leave her. Listen, he said, don't get me wrong, I have to see my sister and it's got to be some time this morning or in the early afternoon, and I can't get out of it. He added that if he'd known she was coming he'd have made a point of not committing himself otherwise. But how could he have guessed that she would reappear at the cabin after having waited uselessly for her for two days, after searching for her for days, after two whole days of her evasion? Gloria stopped and looked at him. Did you really search for me, my love? she said, I knew it, I knew it. Then she asked him seriously if he'd have preferred that she gave herself entirely without any resistance, at all, without a fight, without as much as a show of struggle for her benefit and for the others' after she'd behaved so shame-lessly with him in public; didn't he remember how she'd caressed his shoulders and his back during the boat ride? Alessandro, of course, had been hurt; not that she was at all committed to him; she really wasn't; there'd never been anything that serious between them; they'd just made love and he was in love with her, and, of

110

course, he was jealous; anyway, he hadn't made a fuss because he never lost his temper; no, she'd never known him to lose his temper; but he had given her a good talking to after the motorboat ride and had forced her to stay in her room, where Matteo had later come to demand an explanation of her behaviour; he had told her off, he'd even insulted her until she finally couldn't take it any longer and so she walked out and slammed the door behind her; when she had seen him with Fenzo at the bar opposite the Casino, the time she was with Elena, she'd mentioned him to her and discovered that she already liked him quite a lot, and next morning she'd found Alessandro gone. She laughed, and yet she seemed touched when he told her that he had waited sadly for her in front of Pettinelli's from ten until half-past eleven. He told her how disappointed and angry he'd been when he'd finally realised that she wasn't coming. My love, she said again even more sweetly than before, and she started to explain that she was suddenly, stupidly afraid to meet him so soon because she knew that he would be there waiting for her. You see, she said, we understood one another without exchanging a word. He thought of Francesca without even a hint of malice as if chatting affectionately with her, I told you, Francesca, I told you, you see, I'm not dreaming and I've never dreamt, oh, if only you were here to admit that you were wrong. In the meantime, they'd come to the beach entrance and it was time to part; before they'd begun to say everything their dialogue was abruptly interrupted. Both regretted it for different reasons, he because by going he was sacrificing his first few moments of freedom and she, probably because she was being denied him so soon after having waited for him and looked for him for so long. It made him light-headed to think about it. What time is it? she asked. It was eleven o'clock. It would be hours before they could meet again. We could meet earlier, he said. No, she answered, shaking her head mournfully, I'm afraid I can't. She'd already arranged to have lunch with Elena and a few

111

friends who'd just arrived last night, two men and a girl she'd not seen for some time, she couldn't possibly get away until three, but she'd be in San Marco at four or just before by the bell-tower, where during the last few days she'd somehow pictured meeting him when the moment finally came. The moment had finally come now, hadn't it? Now there'd be no more speculating as to what they were about, there'd be no more doubts, at least she no longer had any, and perhaps she'd never had; perhaps she'd only felt slightly uncertain and understandably hesitant. Did he really have to go now? They'd paused by the gate, just by the path he'd so furtively followed the night before when he'd been driven on madly by his angry challenge to climb the fence, his heart set on Fenzo's cabin. Now the frontier might never have existed; or he may have crossed ages and ages since. Did he really have to go now? Would he at least make sure that he kept the whole afternoon, and even the evening, free for her? God, he thought, as if overwhelmed by too much joy, is it really true? He was deeply moved and flattered. As he was making up his mind to go, he caressed her face, passing his fingers over her lips; and as he did so he became aware of twinges of uneasiness amid his emotional responses. He wondered how the hell would he manage on the money he had if he had to take her to a restaurant or what have you. He surprised himself stroking the nape of her neck, her hair, while feeling miles away and duty-bound to tear himself away and go in search of the money he needed, assuming for the moment that he wouldn't dare ask any-one, and he fetched about his memory for someone who could help him. He wasn't worried. Gloria was still there, her arm round his waist, stroking his side. She shifted her feet and turned and faced him. Who cared how much money he had? She put her hand on his face and before turning her back to leave him, she reminded him of the time and the place of their meeting, begging him not to keep her waiting. He stood watching her for a moment, then passed through the gate. The street was burning

112

hot and the sun beat on the back of his neck. The square before the Casino was a sea of sizzling asphalt. At that hour Venice would be an oven. In these miraculous days, he thought, lots of things were burning up: the hours of vigil, the deep wells of anxiety, the fears, the recent and past humiliations, the brambles of bitter regrets. They burned like logs on a great bonfire which would leave his life free. He felt like running and jumping and laughing, like giving vent savagely to his newly acquired strength: he was longing to get to Venice and deal the final blow to his painful old ties. He had to go immediately, before the miraculous vitality was spent, immediately because he would need time to find some money, some ten or fifteen thousand lire. He couldn't think of anyone to ask, but he was certain they were there waiting for him in someone's pocket. He almost started running. He followed the street past the Casino, reached the landing-stage, and again he was on the boat, returning once more to the place he'd forever abandoned the night before. His return, he reflected, was a chance occurrence, a brief non-committal interlude, a momentary reconsideration which didn't alter the established course of events. Essentially he was staying behind, even if the boat was now emerging from the canal and the city began to rise at the far end of the lagoon like some sinister memory. They'd be meeting in a few hours' time, but they hadn't in fact separated. They weren't even separated now, because what was happening now, and what was about to happen in the interlude before they were together again, couldn't touch them. Only a minute elapsed between separation and meeting. A minute? he thought, looking at his watch, yes a minute of three or four or five hours, from now till four o'clock, a long minute which he would live in a state of hypnosis as a sleepwalker who consumes the dark hours unconsciously. He was suddenly struck by an unwise, unexpected, and irritatingly acute question: how did he know? how could he tell? mayn't it be that the interim hours were temporarily concealing their treachery only to yawn and

113

stretch and multiply and envelop him, only to spring up before and behind and beside him monstrously growing before his eyes till they finally suffocated him? He felt weak. He realised that during the last few minutes the prospects of his trip to Venice had undergone a transformation. At first he had seemed to yield entirely to the blithe cruelty that Gloria's surrender had inspired in him, but now he was seduced by a curious drowsiness. He believed he could get through the meeting with his sister in a stupor of indifference in which all that happened would leave no mark on him. But wouldn't it be wiser to be alert more than ever, to be cruel and remember that his future would hang upon the outcome of the next few hours' events? He struggled angrily to regain his sense of reality, realising that he would have to prepare for the worst if he wasn't to be caught off guard. Perhaps cruelty wouldn't be sufficient armour to defend him against his encounter with Francesca, against the words she'd use, the generally clammy family atmosphere—not to mention the possibility that Luisa, Francesca's trump card, might well have been instructed to be present in the shop or might walk in on their discussion looking troubled and ghastly as an angry bat flaps crazily into a room. He must realise that the danger period wasn't over yet. If he persisted in evading the real reason for his trip to Venice, he would risk losing everything. They were waiting for him in Venice, with angry impatience. He would have to make a public declaration that would amount to an unfair renunciation, at least so it would appear to his audience. This was why he was going to Venice. The trip was not going to be that minute composed of four or five hours, or some foray in which he'd keep Gloria's image before him, or any of the other idiotic fantasies he'd played with a few minutes ago. He must be on the alert, he must prepare and arm himself, as if he were about to encounter his most formidable enemy. He looked out at the city and the pallid houses and landscape that changed as he travelled farther and farther away from the Lido.

114

He was no longer sure that he'd attained the necessary level of insensitivity. He was pretty certain that he could take Francesca's insults, but he didn't think he could stomach Luisa's desperation and her obscene, hysterical display of grovelling misery. He was tired. God, he thought, here we are all over again and again and again. Nothing I feel remains constant except this fear of losing hold over myself. His heart beat loudly as he fought back an impulse to slip into that shapeless zone of consciousness where he'd vegetated for so long. He tried to grasp his previous self-assurance, only to find it had gone. The only memory he had of it now was of some stupid, ludicrously miscalculated feeling, and that in spite of having consciously experienced it but a few minutes ago. The boat had only just left the wharf, and yet the Lido and Gloria seemed far away now, in the same way that, when he'd been near Gloria, Venice and Luisa had seemed far away. He could scarcely remember what Gloria had said. Her words sounded hollow and mutilated in the whirlpool of strident sounds from the approaching city. Aeons seemed to have passed since he'd seen her come running down towards the cabins. So soon, he mused bitterly, so soon. No, they'd never parted, they weren't apart even now, because all that was to happen didn't really matter; yes, he knew himself well enough now, he was sure he could rely fully on his instincts; he was totally self-assured, all man and completely ruthless. He realised he was repeating his previous reassurances in an ironic key and the irony was wearing him out. As if to shake it off, he got up from his place and went over to lean against the railings, vaguely aware that he was going through the process of disarming himself. He must be more careful, more alert, and why on earth couldn't he think a little more kindly of himself? If others hurt him, it was only to be expected, but if he spent so much energy on hurting himself it was really too much. He was so excruciatingly thin-skinned as to be totally pathetic. His vulnerability softened him, curving his lips into a gentle expression of glum self-pity. Were he

115

not so self-conscious he could have put this self-pity to good advantage, could even use it to arm himself in his fight for survival. It could be an invaluable implement of self-defence. Instead he decided to have a good laugh at himself, to make a mockery of his own emotions and deal himself the kind of acrimonious ridicule an enemy might have dealt him. He wearily breathed the fresh air of the lagoon. Enough's enough, he murmered for the umpteenth time. I must put an end to all this. The boat had arrived. The boatman was securing the hawsers to the wharf and he prepared to disembark. So he'd come back, after all. He started out towards Francesca's haberdashery, that dreary, cramped little shop that reeked of his family life, where his mother had worked until a year or two before, until the time came for the shop to throw her out. That also was a delightful story and one that typified his family to a T. His mother used to displace her immense body behind the counter at the expenditure of such gigantic quantities of energy and difficulty that even the customers winced with embarrassment. Her every movement was accompanied by plaintive expressions of self-pity : do you see what I'm reduced to? how can one be expected to work in these conditions? She would struggle to open drawers, to rummage around incapable of finding what she was looking for and this was her way of demonstrating that it was humanly impossible for her to find whatever goods were requested. A delectable story. Francesca had to give up her job to take her mother's place at the shop. Every time he'd had to go there, he'd gone with fists clenched, utterly depressed and ready to bolt, of course, at the drop of a hat, to put a good distance between him and it. Now as he approached the shop by way of the sweaty alleyways of the neighbourhood, which at this sweltering noon-day hour were endowed with an almost palpable density by the natural smells emanating from the fuming canals, the rotting, trampled left-overs from the market, the vegetables and empty crates, he started to feel the habitual revulsion overtaking and choking him, as it always did whenever

Fate set him down in his natural landscape. The courage he'd felt before embarking for Venice, which had inspired him to rush off to a showdown with Francesca, had vanished in the atmosphere of all-prevailing anxiety; his recent self-congratulations on the outcome of his miraculously propitious day, which had dominated his mood on the Lido and the reinforcing wave of the subsequent optimistic calculations, now seemed to be vainly exaggerated misconstructions before the present moment which was in fact his yesterday only slightly altered by place and manner. Everything was changing. His feelings of nausea and fear grew as he drew closer and closer to the real axis of his life. He experienced afresh last night's sense of having finally left this world forever, astonished that he'd ever hesitated to leave, that he'd ever succumbed to uncertainty and scruple. He was shocked to find that his uncertainties and his scruples were luring him into still another encounter, just like the one he'd had with Luisa. He ought never to have let himself be lured into the earlier one; and now he ought to turn back and reject this encounter with Francesca and all encounters with anyone he didn't want to see. He stopped and looked round. Before he got to Francesca's shop with its faded awning that shaded the window, and the dog from the next-door shop sprawling across the entrance, he turned off in another direction. But he realised that he wasn't very certain of his new direction, that he had left part of himself behind in that point where the street and the shop merged into one: Francesca's counter and the canal wall, the dog, a dusty old woman coming out of the shop, Francesca placing skeins of wool on the glass counter and staring up at him silently. What could she possibly have to tell him? what she'd said two nights ago? or was there something new? What could have happened since then? As he followed the same street back, he seemed to understand why she'd summoned him, what she wanted to say. Perhaps Luisa had committed suicide, or had tried anyway. Hadn't she implied that

117

in the threat she'd screamed just before she'd left him standing there on the bridge: there's only one thing left for me to do? No, she wouldn't, he muttered, not Luisa, not her, she'd never bring herself to do anything like that, not over something like this. He smiled bitterly as he realised how eager he was to let his imagination unleash the most hideous possibilities. Not Luisa, he repeated, not on your life. Nevertheless, he'd felt a painful spasm, that quick, icy sensation of death. What if Francesca really did want to tell him something like that. He shivered as the internal monologue doubled in ferocity. He could hear her talking flatly, softly, completely detached from what she said. He listened silently as the images of the previous night raced across his mind: that group of people silently clustered round his doorstep, the voices drifting over to him across the canal, the light in the dining-room window. They were charged now with the anguish and the pain that had previously evaded him. He felt what he'd been unable to feel last night: panic, fear, the certainty that something was about to crash down upon him. He could see himself walking next to his sister along the whitewashed *fondamenta*. He heard his own footsteps and the determined sound of her footsteps that were leading him to some remote spot where Luisa lay dying. She'd tried to commit suicide, she'd slashed her wrists, she'd thrown herself off the balcony, they'd carried her off to hospital, her brothers had gone after him, he'd fallen into the trap which both families had jointly laid for him. They were dragging him across the city now, a cohort ahead, another behind, cutting off all routes of escape, right up through an open door, perhaps the fetid maw of the hospital, and up to Luisa, who in the meantime had been turned into something horrible and inhuman by the devastating violence of her tragedy. For heaven's sake, he thought, why should I think such things? People didn't do such things nowadays. Luisa would never be able to muster up enough courage to solve her problems like that. She was dead only in his fantasy; the only place she would

118

even try to commit suicide was in his weary, tormented imagination that was so bewildered as to mistake a remote possibility for an irreversible fact. It was much more likely that Francesca wanted to see him for very different reasons, to drive home her message of two nights before, You'll do it, I tell you ... you see if you don't ... you've never done a decent thing in your life. Nothing this definitive and binding could have occurred since he'd left home. Nevertheless, he couldn't shake off his fantasy of a dead Luisa, a moribund Luisa, as if he'd actually seen Francesca and she'd told him that Luisa was dead or dying. When did it happen? he wondered. Last night. She'd been shut up in her room for two days. They kept talking to her through the door. Then they heard her groaning or screaming, they'd heard a shot or a crash, a body smashed onto the pavement or bloated with water in the canal, unknown faces gaping from the windows near by, excited voices, a sputtering motorboat carrying a body: possibilities, horrifying possibilities that swarmed like ants through his mind to cohabit with his hope and his certainty that nothing had happened, with his decision to leave, with the anguish he'd feel if he really saw her lying in a hospital bed, or when he ran out of the hospital to feel his sister's bewildered, impotent gaze upon his shoulders. Good God. He was at a news-stand, paper in hand, feverishly looking for a confirmation or a denial of the suicidal events he'd just witnessed in every gory detail. He couldn't find the slightest reference to Luisa, nothing to justify Francesca's horrifying summons, or the ambush they'd laid at his doorstep the night before. He felt calmer for not having found any confirmation in the paper; on the other hand, that wasn't necessarily proof that nothing had happened: it was too soon, the papers didn't always report such news, whereas he did know that the ambush had actually been laid and that Francesca had actually gone to Fenzo's in the dead of night to look for him and he did actually feel that sense of inevitability, of defeat. Luisa's tragic power prevailed. How

119

much longer would he have to allow his imagination to leap from one possibility to the next? How much longer would his feelings, troubled as they were, have to coexist with the confused emotional consequences of his refusal to see Francesca? He was calmed at least by the reflection that this discordant coexistence was preferable to any confirmation of his fears. As long as Luisa's hypothetical suicide appeared to him as impossible as it did possible, as long as his resistance counter-balanced her aggression, he would have enough freedom of motion to act within that no-man's-land that existed between himself and Luisa and to repel her all the way, so long as he didn't cross the point where his thrust could be parried by her overreaching him. Of course, Francesca might have something entirely different to say which would dispel all his fears. His fears, after all, were not well founded and not at all as binding as a confirmation of them would be—in which case he'd have to go to Luisa's and encounter her shattered parents. Best to know nothing at all, he thought. He walked slowly on, determined now to get away and stop succumbing to his malignant thoughts of Luisa. He would accept the discord, the remorse, and the resulting indignation as the price of the freedom he would be left with. He was now far away from Francesca's shop, threading his tired way through the streets and still in the state of shock which had been induced by his suspicions and his fears. He was a bit surprised that he had been capable, in spite of everything, of reaching a decision. He tried to imprison his fantasy and to keep it from revolving round the spot in his mind left empty by his refusal to encounter Francesca and the great stain that had replaced the host of possible events: what had happened? what might have happened? what would he have done if he'd gone to see Francesca? He tried to think of what he would do now, of who he could find to lend him money, of his rendezvous with Gloria, of Gloria's love for him, of everything beyond the edge of that dark smear of ignorance. His body meanwhile, unaffected by the thoughts which preoccupied him, continued to move across the city. Without realising that he had been following a definite path, he found himself before a canal across which the barracks of the Customs Guard rose massively grey in the sunlight. That's it, he said; he'd found the path which would lead him back to safety, back to Gloria, back to his hopes for the future, to his most distant goals. He felt as though he'd come out of a maze in which he'd wandered directionless for ages. He was calmer. A great expanse of time seemed to have passed. He had a task to perform and he plotted his strategy with eerie calm.

While he'd been on the *vaporetto* to Venice, his imminent meeting with Francesca looked like being a brief shadow across the sun, and he had not yet had time to clarify his fleeting sensation that it wouldn't be that hard to scare up some money. Here he was then as if he'd decided from the outset that he would ask his pupil, the Customs official, that small but substantial benefactor, who'd be easy to convince and towards whom he'd obviously been directing his steps. When had he actually conceived of borrowing from him? He couldn't recall. He may not have considered it at all, but his instincts had surmised that the official was the only person who could help him, the only one who would lend him the money he needed. Ten thousand, fifteen, maybe more, something to last him a few days, he thought. He could see him standing in the courtyard of the barracks where he'd go to meet him. He'd take out his wallet with his usual grave smile and ask him how long he would need it for. A few days, only a few days, Salvatore. We can count it as advance payment towards your lessons. He stepped onto the bridge and crossed over the canal. Nothing could have happened to Luisa, he thought. She might well be nearer now to some resolution of her difficulties than she'd been before when no one knew of her condition and when she'd been so terrified of the scandal it would cause. The news was out and everyone seemed to have rushed to her defence. Their two families had leagued together to protect her; perhaps they'd agreed upon some remedy for it all. Everything will sort itself out, he thought suddenly cheering up. Perhaps the baby won't be born after all, in which case everything will be forgotten after a few months or a few weeks. The afternoon shadows had begun to lengthen towards the canal. A launch was moored to the bank. The air round the barracks was sharp with cooking smells. He stopped on the threshold and peered into the shadows of the gateway, looking for the guard. The gateway was deserted, but he could hear someone whistling softly at the far end of a long corridor that opened into a hidden corner of the courtyard on the other side of the gateway. He went in and entered the corridor that led to the courtyard. He wondered if it might be Salvatore whistling. He gave a loud shout, the whistling stopped, a door slammed nearby and a guard appeared in his trousers and vest, his face soapy, a shaving brush in hand. The guard looked at him suspiciously as he asked for Bonucci, Salvatore Bonucci of Section 11, he had to speak to him, could he go to look for him? The guard made a face. He didn't know if he was in the barracks, he had a feeling he was out on duty. But he could go up to the first floor and look for the orderly, if he wasn't asleep. He pointed at a stairway that led to the upstairs offices and left. He leapt up the stairs. He was weighed down now by a confused sense of shame and alarm. He was vaguely afraid that his plan might go up in smoke. He'd never asked his pupil for an advance before. He pictured the moment when he'd be confronted with him and he felt irritatingly embarrassed. To hell with it, he thought; he needed the money and nothing else mattered. Ten or fifteen thousand to keep him going for a few days. The stairway led to a landing. At the far end was a closed door. He knocked softly and waited. After a moment he knocked again and opened the door. He was in a huge empty room. Its windows were gigantically open. There was a long bench against the wall and at the far end was another closed door. He cursed beneath his breath. Was there no one about? were the barracks deserted? He looked at his watch: a quarter past one. They're sleeping, he thought. He crossed over to the door and knocked discreetly. He hoped that some one would answer now, some guard slumped sleepily across a table would get up and answer his knock. But the door stayed closed. Silence reigned beyond it. He threw it open almost violently and walked into an empty, dusty room full of tables and shelves. He was painfully uncomfortable and angry. He felt like yelling till someone finally came. Hello, anyone here. He knew no one would answer. He went to the window and looked down onto the embankment. The moored launch was still there and so were the street he'd just crossed a few minutes before and that acrid smell of cooking. He retraced his steps, ran down the stairs and into the courtyard again, certain that something was slipping through his fingers, that if he didn't find someone immediately his anxiety would overwhelm him again. Guard! he called, Guard! His cry sounded like a desperate cry for help. The guard in the vest reappeared ten yards away. There's no one about, he said to the guard as he appeared. These bloody bastards, he fumed to himself. They're asleep, the guard said, it's early you know. Could you look for him? I must find him. His voice sounded strangely shrill. Go and call them, you silly ass, he raged inwardly, go and look for them and wake the blithering idiots up. I'll go and see, said the guard, as he strolled off. He waited on a marble bench and lit a cigarette. His throat was dry and his mouth felt pasty. He recalled that he hadn't eaten and he'd been living like a tramp for almost two days. He passed his hand over his face. It was rough and bristly. I must shave and eat something. But his thoughts circled back. Perhaps the image of the vagabond which had just flashed through his consciousness was not an idle metaphor but an unconscious definition of his condition. He imagined how others might see him—the guard who had just left him, for example. He passed his hand down his shirt, which felt

123

wet and sticky with sweat. He was ashamed, afraid of being dirty, smelly, ashamed of his face and clothing that showed the first signs of his vagrancy. It suddenly occurred to him—for the first time since he'd left home—that the future would mean more than just the next day, or the next few days that Bonucci's money would make possible; there was much more time to fill, a cold dizzying expanse which he'd have to cross carefully, clutching for support at each step so as not to fall. Suppose the man didn't give him the money, and even if he did get it, what would he do when it was gone? How would he live? would his relations with Gloria be strong enough to free him from want before the money ran out? would he allow himself to be kept by her? He shuddered with revulsion. That's not what he was after. He wanted other things from Gloria. Whatever confused significance he might attribute to her, its only bearing was on his emotional freedom and not on his economic survival. If he could narrow it all down to a single element, Gloria was no more than a pretext—a pretext for promoting himself to a world of better, easier relations. She was the first step towards a new way of life. He didn't expect any material assistance from her. He didn't want it. But how would he live? would he return home? how should I know? he sighed bitterly. A rustling at his side announced the guard's return. He turned without speaking, his heart thumping. He's out, he's not found anyone, no one knows anything. He's out on duty, the guard said, he'll be off at half-past one and back here before two. He looked at his watch: twenty past one. Things could be worse. He sighed with relief. You can wait here if you want to, the guard said, or come back later, as you like. He thanked him and offered him a cigarette, which he lit. It's hot, he said, by way of small-talk to lead into a conversation which he hoped would restore his dignity, would erase the impression of desperate dereliction he must have given the guard. How stupid of me, he thought, it probably hasn't crossed the fellow's mind to pass judgment on me. It

124

wasn't worth worrying about in any case. The guard exhaled smoke. A bit of lather still clung to his cheek among the tough dark roots of his beard. It reminded him that he should have a shave if he could find a barber still open at that hour. There was one near the barracks which he might find open if he left immediately. He decided to give it a try, and so he hurried off telling the guard that he'd be back. The barber was a few hundred yards down the pavement where it turned away from the canal into a cosy little square with a blocked well in the centre and grey windows in the surrounding shadows. The shop was still open, but the barber was just getting ready to leave and he scowled as he entered: it's late, I'm closing. He seemed friendly nonetheless and good-humoured, giving him to understand that he was open to persuasion. All right, the barber sighed when he offered to pay him double, all right. He was shocked by his own extravagance, but as he inspected the blue shadow of his beard in the mirror before him, the removal of all traces of disorder from his face seemed worth the money. While the barber was preparing to lather his face he stared into the mirror at his own deep grey eyes, at his tanned face, the gentle curve of his hair, the straight cut of his mouth. Contemplation of his face always restored his self-assurance and his heady pride, it was a confirmation of the rights which his refined looks afforded him. He always enjoyed searching for assurance in the mirror; so whenever he was offended, provoked, confronted by the permanence of his condition, whenever he lost faith in himself, he managed to find the comfort he needed by looking in a mirror, which always magically restored his true image and his courage, his vanity, his ambition, generously conceding to him all the stimuli he needed to resist humiliation. Not that, in the light of the shop, as the barber ran his brush left to right and right to left, spreading the white foam over his face, he would admit to gazing at himself with smug self-satisfaction. Of course not; on this score he had always been quite objective about himself. He did, of course, inspect himself, but serene and unconcerned, thinking the time had come for him to make full use of these resources. The razor scraped across his skin obliterating the traces of the vagrant hours, sweeping away the shadows that rose from beneath, closing the wounds, smoothing out the furrows like a magic wand. When he left the shop, he felt better and whole again, as if he'd regained a part of himself which he'd detached and temporarily lost. If he could take a bath before he met Gloria, he'd feel even better. But there wasn't time. He had to go back to the barracks. Perhaps Bonucci had already arrived. He had to see him before he had a chance to take a nap or go out again. He quickly doubled back along the *fondamenta* and soon stood before the barracks entrance again. It wasn't silent and deserted now but noisy and crowded with Customs men. He looked about him. The minute, orderly figure of Bonucci was drifting towards the courtyard. There he is, he thought, at last. He passed by the guards and ran to catch up with him. Bonucci looked at him with amazement and replied to his greeting with a slow, halting good afternoon. Listen, he began. But it was suddenly too difficult to go on. He'd noticed a slight diffidence, an instinctive shyness, as if the patrolman had not only been surprised to see him but also suspicious. He wondered if Bonucci had already guessed the purpose of his visit. He had to explain himself immediately, to tell him what he wanted before Bonucci had a chance to formulate some tremendous judgment against him. But as he spoke he became acutely aware that his words only confirmed Bonucci's suspicions, that the moment Bonucci had seen him he'd expected to hear how a sudden, pressing matter forced him to ask for an advance on the lessons, about ten or fifteen thousand lire, no more, how he was forced to cancel all lessons for at least a week. Bonucci had expected to hear exactly what he was saying.

He'd never been so embarrassed. Nevertheless he asked humbly for help. If he could be so kind he'd be very grateful. They'd always been on friendly terms, hadn't they? He might have said, we're friends, aren't we? even good friends, but he didn't want to force the other's hand, nor to debase himself too much by assuming a confidential tone which he'd never used before. On terms, he finally hazarded, which were such as to allow one of them to turn to the other for help. He studied the official as he quietly passed his hand over his face. He felt just what he'd felt at their last lesson—dismayed by this quiet, dignified being, irritated by his pupil's self-assurance. Bonucci hesitated. He's adding up the lessons, he thought, to see how many the advance corresponds to. At a thousand lire an hour, ten or fifteen thousand came to fifteen lessons or a little more than a month or a month and a half. Come on, he thought, please, please don't wait too long, don't take vengeance now if I've ill-treated you. All that I ask will be returned. But Bonucci could be hesitating for other reasons. He now told him, without embarrassment, something he hadn't expected to hear. He had decided, he said cruelly, to break off the lessons, not only because he wasn't very satisfied with him as a teacher —that wasn't the only reason—but largely because he felt he was now ready to start singing lessons and he couldn't afford two teachers at once. He was frozen to the spot. He looked at Bonucci almost without seeing him and started to stutter some conventional phrases of regret, adding with a slight touch of bitterness that he couldn't, shouldn't say such things and certainly not with such offhanded indifference. His bitterness lasted but a minute. A wave of resentment intervened: the fellow had let him down when he most needed him. How could he? He'd approached him cap in hand and heart aching, and now the man had the gall to insult him. What a nerve! For heaven's sake, why did he mutter apologies instead of simply seizing him by the neck and trampling him with all his blasted ambitions? Resentment choked him, but he continued to dawdle before the official, dismayed, confounded, rooted to the spot. Even Bonucci seemed

127

embarrassed; he passed his hand again slowly over his face. While casting round for some way out of this painfully embarrassing stalemate, he heard the man say that if he really needed the money, he would lend it to him, but as a loan, he said, giving a warning shake of his finger, not as an advance. In any case, he couldn't give him all he'd asked for, just eight, at the most ten thousand lire. Really? he could hear himself asking, can you really? He nodded almost happily and slipped his hand into his jacket. He closed his eyes so as not to be forced to witness the gesture which couldn't help but wound him. He moved into a position which would conceal Bonucci from view and cover his outstretched hand which proffered the banknote. He was about to assume an easy, cordial air when a sudden wave of shame reduced him to murmuring humbly, thanks, I'll return it soon.

Once out in the street, the strong smell of cooking participated in an ironic psychological mutation in which it was somehow identified with the shame he'd just felt, as if the odour rose from an intimate, decaying part of himself, a pungent evidence of what he knew he was— a homeless vagabond, a bitter little slob, practically a beggar. He hastened away from the barracks over the bridge and into the neighbouring alleyways. He thought despairingly of himself as someone whose ruin he was witnessing, and he kept telling himself, Mario, dear old Mario, always betrayed, always short-changed, why the hell can't you get used to being what you've decided to be? He cursed, as he was wont to do whenever self-pity and anger began to mingle with each other. He clutched the 10,000-lire note in his pocket and mused. Well didn't you get your money? you've got it, haven't you? so stop grumbling, what more do you want? what else matters? He crossed the Campo dei Frari and headed towards Santa Margherita. It was two o'clock by his watch. Two hours to go before his rendezvous. A distant bell sounded two distinct, staccato strokes. He couldn't tell if they were marking the time or announcing how many hours were

128

left before his meeting. There must have been some reason why the strokes reminded him of a week long ago, a whole week of playing truant from school and waiting in the streets till it was time to go home. Of course there was a reason: the street was the same, the bell was the same, the guilt which corroded his future was the same. He'd always been the same, always running away from something: school, people, things. His every relationship had been marked by a sudden characteristic parting of the ways, where the course he followed inevitably branched away from everyone else. If one left aside the variations in superficial appearances, his situation was always permanent. His situation now was as it had been before. What do I care? he thought on the defensive, what do I care? Didn't this simply prove that at an early age he had instinctively begun to reject his condition and hanker after another one? The unconscious tenacity which had upheld him for so long now surfaced and revealed itself in this last pitiless rejection. He'd probably felt guilty even then, but it was useless to puzzle over such impossible factors. In any case his condition had changed. Something new had occurred. The moment he'd decided to proceed on his own, his itinerary had ceased to trace a confused, tortuous spiral in a vacuum. For the first time his own obstinacy was leading him towards a definite goal. At this very moment, for example, there was nothing tragically precarious about his gait, about his gestures, even about the simple act of entering a café, as he was doing, nothing doubtful about the way he made his order, or about walking round in the sun for an hour or two, nothing he should feel particularly ashamed about. These actions, each and every one of them, participated in his plans, constituted a necessary phase in a perfectly ordered strategy. If he wanted to have a roll and a glass of milk at two in the afternoon, there was no reason why he should fear being taken for someone who couldn't afford a full meal, no reason to be frightened that he would reveal, for example, his variance with the rest of the world. Not

129

at all. He was there, at that time, in that bar, because his plan excluded the possibility of eating either before or after or elsewhere. This was the reason.

He didn't sit down at the bar. He ate standing, to let time slip by, gazing out through the window at the street and the passers-by. It took some efforts to avoid remembering the past few hours, to skirt round thoughts of Luisa, Francesca and the Customs man, his latest source of pain. He immersed himself in the peace of the objects round him, the cool external objects so totally foreign to his personal history: the cool glass that held his milk, the espresso machine, the neat rows of bottles on the shelves, the street, the passers-by. They were a diaphragm between the palpable present and his memories of past moments. His discomfort might jeopardise his future much more were it not that the future seemed so imminent, so certain, so free of unpredictables, with Gloria certainly coming to meet him and preparing herself now, perhaps, to set out, or at least thinking about setting out shortly. He needn't be surprised; it was Gloria, after all, whom he held in his heart as his inviolable refuge, his warm shelter into which he retired from the cold. If she disappeared occasionally, swept away by the tide, he invariably managed to retrieve her again, miraculously warm and intact and still eager to receive him. He imagined Gloria sitting in the *Excelsior* restaurant amongst the others of her class, and he wondered if she was restless and impatient to leave. She might be looking at her watch every two or three minutes, absent-mindedly participating in the conversation or totally remote from it, as someone teased, Gloria seems to be in an awful hurry, look at her, she's miles away, I bet someone's waiting for her, attributing some ulterior significance to her impatience. And so he was present in her quick glances at her watch, hovering in her restless eyes, insinuating himself into the conversation: who can it be? do we know him? what's he like? what does he look like? He left the bar with a flattered smile curling his lips. He was in the street again. It was

130

only ten past two and the streets were infernally hot. Perhaps he ought to look for a public bath. It would be hard to find anything open at this hour. The only thing for him to do was resume his aimless stroll, taking a random selection of turnings because the streets were all very much of a muchness at this hapless hour; even the shady ones weren't very inviting. Passing down them meant braving the clammy exudations from the adjacent houses: the smells of brick and mortar and the odour from the concentrated sludge of the canals. What a bore, he thought. Then, emerging from the rank exhalations of a long sewer-like alley, he was surprised by a cinema's festive, colourful posters, which came as a marvellous relief, as would the sea after an endless trudge in the dust. He stopped to study them. A grade-B movie. A certain Frank Millard leered at an unknown Yvonne Bennett; he was astride a garden wall in the moonlight, he leapt along a palace rooftop, sword in hand, hair blowing in the wind. The cinema was already open, but the film hadn't started yet. It looked like a second-rate film: just the kind to instil gentle torpor in mind and heart; perhaps it would daze him enough to allow him to isolate himself in time and sever himself sufficiently from his memory so as to feel refreshed and carefree when he emerged. He started to go in but then hesitated with indecision at the door. The deserted lobby, the heavy faded velvet curtains that concealed the entrance to the theatre, the dim yellow light, the cool silence in contrast to the dazzling sun on the square outside had the effect of making him feel disoriented and pained, as if going to the cinema were an error of judgment, a gesture of guilty isolation, something stealthy, shameful, like larceny. He felt frightened and almost started to back away, and yet he knew that what he really wanted to do was escape from the blasted heat. He couldn't bear another hour and a half's walking round, nor did the alternative of sitting it out on some beach have the slightest appeal. He didn't, however, walk straight in; he stood motionless at the door wondering what it

131

was that was so shameful, so painful, until it began to dawn on him that it was Luisa. That's where it had all started. When he left her he lost his bearings and upset his chronology. If he now found himself before a cinema at the odd hour of two in the afternoon and was about to go in by himself, having turned his back on the blazing hot sun and the empty square; and if he had to face solitude and another night in Fenzo's cabin, the beach and the fear of being caught, the unknown twists of his imagination, tomorrow's countless anxieties and his perennial fluctuations, it was only because everything had changed, because he had furtively migrated from one world to another only to end up looking over an unfamiliar landscape. Of course, of course, he mumbled wearily. He stepped towards the ticket window realising that for two days now, or however many days it was, he'd kept coming to the same conclusion a thousand times and every time it came as a thundering revelation whereupon it was promptly forgotten. He entered the cinema so as not to lose sight of the image he had of himself and so as to get used to being what he'd become, so as to identify himself with what he'd done, so as to learn how to be his own accomplice. He bought a balcony seat and climbed the stairs.

The lights were still on and there was no one around upstairs. A scattering of spectators dotted the empty rows of the stalls below. Cautiously leaning over the balcony, he counted them : fifteen in all—a few fellows, a couple of women, a soldier, a couple of middle-aged men. He shuddered at the thought that this rabble were his companions. He couldn't distinguish their features, their faces, but he recognised them. He could feel the terror they felt, imagine the horror on their faces and the way their hands desperately clutched the arms of their seats as if they were riding out some personal disaster. He was quite ready to believe that they'd come here bearing lonely-heart stories not unlike his own. Should they turn to look up at him and meet his gaze he knew how their

132

thoughts would read: oh look at him up there, he's here too, and they'd smile recognition. But hadn't he just decided that his every action belonged to a carefully preconceived plan? hadn't he just decided that his visit to the cinema was a necessary phase in his search for an accomplice? He sat in the centre of the balcony and settled down to wait for the lights to go out. He wound his watch to be sure of leaving in good time. He lit a cigarette and slowly savoured the smoke. The cigarette smouldered away the seconds leaving something more than ash behind. Somewhere within him a restless energy barbed his sensibilities and made its presence felt by hammering painfully. Why the hell don't they turn the lights off? why don't they get on with the film? A sound like the hiss of rain rent the auditorium. There was a buzzing in the void behind him. The lights went out and a blade of blue light cut across the cinema and clung to the screen. He stretched his legs and settled back in his chair. As the cigarette between his fingers continued to consume time and as the gigantic words paraded before his eyes, his growing discomfort splintered into a mood of giddy unreality. What's the matter with me? He read on the screen, Imperial. I'm sick, he thought, there's something wrong with me again, it's worse than before, something ghastly is happening; presents Yvonne Bennett, could she really have tried it? shall I ever be able to free myself? and Frank Millard, still, it's only natural that I shouldn't want to see her, anyone in my shoes would have done the same, even if perhaps in not quite the same way, in *The Flaming Sword*, I can't stand it any longer, even if I've tried to fool myself into believing I'd get used to it, I can't, it's just a hoax every time with the guest appearance, I'm drowning, I'm bursting, I'm going to pieces, as though I never will be what I want to be, I'll never get away without someone stopping me every time, I've had all I can take. He dropped his cigarette, ground it under his heel, and concentrated hard on trying to grasp what was happening to him, considering that it

133

was fatigue that had frayed his nerves and triggered off uncontrollable neurotic forces within him. He shivered and sweat poured down his spine. He could barely distinguish a blurred screen across which the first images of the film were passing: a working-class quarter of an eighteenth-century village, a rider picking his way through a crowd, a lady at a window. He leapt up from his seat and hurried across the empty balcony and into the lavatory. He turned on the taps and let the water run in the basin. Then he bent over the basin, cupped his hands to the water and doused his face and neck. Contact with the cold water brought a brief sense of well being. Water seeped into his skin and sent a cool undercurrent through his body, flooding the knotted mesh of his nerves. How glorious it was to feel the tension dissolve and the knots loosen and to breathe the fresh air again. This was a crisis, all right, but fortunately it was going to be short-lived as it had almost spent itself by now. He began to feel peaceful as if the nervous bile were slowly discharging. He straightened up from the basin to look at himself reflected in the mirror. His tanned face still bore the marks of the recent storm. He wondered if it mightn't be wiser to rest a while until he regained enough strength to control his facial expressions of anguish, and to suppress all cause for desperation. But for the first time his face provoked a sense of weariness and revulsion, and his eagerness to see himself reflected provoked shame. Every manifestation of himself, even an elementary physical one like this to which he'd always made recourse in his most troubled moments, was branded with the humiliation he'd just undergone. It was an isolated inert particle that had been liberated from its splintered nucleus. His image annoyed him. His face, which a moment before had possessed devastating power, now seemed wan and weary—proof of how difficult he found it to live with his immediate past, proof of the struggle he still had to face if he wanted to liberate himself completely from it. But the discovery caused no great discomfort now. If he couldn't rely on himself for the

time being, there was always someone to fall back on—
Gloria for example, who came to him to restore his lost
powers. He hoped that when he saw her presently she'd
be able to bind him to her so completely as to make him
one with herself, as to superimpose herself on his every
other thought. Come to me quickly, he murmured, quickly,
come to me now and be ever beside me. A woman's
metallic laughter and crowd noises drifted in from the
theatre: someone was pouring wine and drink my friends,
drink. The film went on, but he didn't feel like going
back yet. Propped up against the lavatory wall he stared
abstractedly at the water still running into the basin. On
the spur of a sudden impulse, he took off his shirt and
hung it on the door knob. I'll wash, he thought. He bent
over the basin and aimed a jet of water towards his chest.
There was no soap, but water alone would remove the
sweat. He bathed his arms and shoulders, his chest and
armpits. As his body temperature subsided, the intensity
of his emotions gradually faded and finally died out. He
felt better for having his chest and shoulders dripping.
The bracing contact of the water restored not only his
physical but even his mental equilibrium. That was better.
Perhaps in a moment now he'd be able to say that his
little crisis had been positively beneficial; it would be some
time before his anxieties began to rise again and between
now and then things would have started happening. Anyway, it was all decided, wasn't it? So why should he
torture himself with useless reconsiderations? He felt his
shirt. It was soaked with sweat. He decided to remain
half-naked until it dried. No one would see, even if he
did return to the empty gallery. He left the lavatory and
returned to his seat. He spread his shirt out on the seat
beside him and tried to iron out the wrinkles. His chest
and shoulders were still wet, but he found it pleasantly
refreshing. He was in the mood for watching the film
calmly. Coloured images passed across the screen. A rider,
the same one, stopped beside a garden wall and clung to
it without dismounting. It was night. The film must have

135

reeled off to the part that was illustrated on the poster outside. It's a pity, really, to have missed the beginning. He settled into his chair. A dog barked, and the horseman crouched low atop the wall. A guard passed between the bushes.

10

A DOG FOLLOWED HIM zig-zagging behind him down the street; it followed him across the bridge and into the shade; it followed him across the empty square and under the Portici di San Barnabà; it seemed to be following him deliberately, as if it had taken a liking to him from the moment it'd seen him and had decided spontaneously to offer its companionship. It was twenty to four; he decided that if the hound persisted for much longer, he'd be able to offer it to Gloria. I've brought a little gift along, would you like it? he's an old friend I've just made, you can have him if you want to. It wasn't a particularly handsome specimen, but Gloria would laugh and he would gracefully shift his weight from one leg to the other, one hand in his pocket, the other, with his beachbag, hanging free. He'd silently contemplate her stooping over the dog, her knee grazing the pavement. At last, he'd think, at last you're here. He'd sigh with relief. It was hot, but he hadn't started sweating yet. His body had cooled during his hour and a half at the cinema and had collected a good reserve of freshness. He felt good now. And as he approached the meeting place he felt better and better, as if the street he followed led beyond the narrow limits of his spirit. For a moment, when he was standing on the Ponte dell'Accademia, the dog lagged back with a look of indecision, as if it wondered whether it hadn't followed long enough now. He looked out at the distant San Marco basin, the slow curve of the city, a *vaporetto* approaching the shore, and he wondered if Gloria would come, if too many hours hadn't elapsed since their meeting, if his relations with her hadn't changed in the interim. However he remembered too well what had happened that morning to be worried now. He still heard Gloria's words,

137

at least we can spend the whole afternoon together. He felt the heat of their embrace. He recalled the other things she'd said and how she'd hoped to spend the evening with him as well, and the way he'd felt like shouting for joy. It was Gloria's cry of joy, too. No matter what happened, she couldn't forget that she had wanted to meet him as much as he'd wanted to meet her. The bridge sloped steeply beneath his feet, but he walked calmly wondering if it wouldn't be better to arrive slightly late and find her there waiting at the appointed place dressed, let's see, perhaps in blue, her hair loose on her shoulders, glancing round impatiently. Perhaps she was already there looking about her, trying to find him among the people streaming into the Piazza. Couldn't he even think of it without feeling utterly weak with his desire to hold her and to be held by her? He walked on at a lively pace, discarding any schemes of arriving late. He cut diagonally across Campo Santo Stefano and entered an alleyway that opened through the chairs and sun shades of a bar. This side of the square was already in the shadows, the bar's enclosure was deserted. The dog reappeared suddenly and scampered madly across the square and then, as he turned down an alley, he heard it barking in the distance and he felt sorry that he no longer had the dog familiarly at his heels, that he wouldn't be able to offer him to Gloria when they met. For he realised he was afraid their first encounter alone might easily turn into a confrontation, a chance for Gloria to find him out, to test his strength. He felt paradoxically that had the dog kept by him and had he successfully pulled off the gesture of offering it to her, he wouldn't be alone before her, he'd somehow have joined forces with the dog and with the gesture and he'd feel protected by them. Bloody hell, he raged almost aloud, cursing the frightened mouse within him. You want everything, don't you? don't want to run any risks, do you? you even want to use the poor dog to help you out, as if you were embarking on some perilous feat of great daring, you louse. He quickly covered the intervening distance; alleys and bridges ran beneath his feet, until the warm expanse of the Piazza surrounded him. She was there, dressed in blue, just as he'd pictured her, her hair loose on her shoulders. She glanced peacefully about in the shadow of the bell-tower, the very picture of serene self-assured expectation. He almost laughed. She'd actually come. She'd already arrived. How glorious it was to see her, under the bell-tower, waiting for him. No one had ever waited for him in that way; no woman like her had ever before waited for him beneath the bell-tower or anywhere else. Seeing her from a distance, spying upon her movements whose significance seemed so intimately familiar, was an utterly new experience and so delicious that he longed to protract it, to savour it all. He stopped. He felt her glance pass by him without detecting him. It slipped over the empty Piazza, lingering occasionally on a figure here, on another there, tracing the halting flight of a dove on the cobbles, then starting round again. She was so calm, her calmness made mockery of the intolerable anxiety with which he had waited for her the day before and of the time it had taken him to accept the fact that she was not coming. She knew very well he would come, she was absolutely certain that her eyes would light upon him any moment now. There, she'd just noticed him; she waved to him smiling as she came towards him. He suddenly felt like destroying her certainty, like revenging himself upon her. Instead he dashed, galloped across the Piazza. His fleeting irritation became fused with the relief her presence afforded him and the incredible certainty that she'd come, that all this was happening now at this very moment, to him, to the same man who a short while ago was choking with anxiety. An instant later they were embracing like lovers who'd been apart for ages, and she hugged him as he hugged her, and they were both overcome, as they had been that morning, by the urge to have each other there and then regardless of who might be looking. He recited a sort of confused, joyful prayer, may this be the end and the beginning, may there be nothing

139

else, may I be what I am now ever more and nevermore what I used to be, may everything always be as it is now. Arm in arm they began to walk along the basin. He felt weightless as if they weren't moving towards another place, but towards another time, towards that future moment when they would be unalterably together, when his memory would be so engaged in other things as to recall nothing prior to the era initiated by his meeting with Gloria below the bell-tower. How far away Luisa seemed now, how far Francesca's shop where she might still be waiting for him, how far the spectral hospital room where his hostile fantasy had situated Luisa's last breaths. That whole weary world where he'd dwelt for so many years flowed out of him and spilled into the sunlit street. God only knew what would happen now. Perhaps Gloria would tell him she loved him, perhaps she would reveal the significance of the looks she'd given him and her many puzzling gestures. Perhaps she would ask him if he were prepared to be with her forever, to follow her everywhere, perhaps even to marry her. He was overwhelmed by a sudden surge of tenderness: Gloria, I love you. She laughed softly and looked up at him, Really? He should have gone on: don't you know how important you've become to me, don't you know how I've had to struggle and suffer to survive till this moment, the effort I've had to make, the sleepless nights, the need to rest. Yes, he said, and in a tone of incongruous gaiety added, Oh lucky little fan that fans your cheeks and fans your breast. She laughed, where did you pick that up? He told her he'd heard her singing it when she was playing with a child on the beach and the sweet lyrics and tune that he'd never heard before had inflicted a mortal wound; her singing had caused a lingering malady, a yearning within him; she'd revealed herself to him in her song, a ditty he'd never heard before and which he suspected had no history and no author—it didn't have an author did it?— Revealed? how? she asked. Well; he shrugged knowing he was making a fool of himself and not caring, I don't

140

know how exactly but somehow you did, and it all started from there. And you, he added, do you love me? No, she said seriously, but tightening the grip of her arm as if to belie the brutality of her reply, as if to convey that it wasn't true, that she wasn't to be taken seriously, that it was all the same old teasing game, the usual prelude to love. They strolled along the basin towards the *Salute* ferry-station. Clouds of steam gathered in the sky far off on the horizon. How happy they looked, how marvellous it was to look at them together. People couldn't help staring at them as they passed. Someone turned to look at the pair of them strolling along, their arms round each other. Their happiness generated jealousy and sighs, nostalgia and even resentment. Their haughty stroll had begun perhaps at some sumptuous hotel in the centre or on the beach and led wherever such strolls lead, wherever those mysterious couples wind up. He'd seen them many times, as if appearing out of the blue, with their incredibly elegant gait, their fair hair or dark hair smoothed, their faces tanned, their peaceful eyes ready to accord gracious consideration to whatever they rested on, eyes that offended him when they brushed past him unseeing but which more frequently flattered him with their curiosity. These glances had been the first confirmation of his illuminating intui-tions about himself, as if they invited him to join their graceful, happy stroll. But he'd always had to return home to his mother's shapeless flaccid body, to the window at which he'd seen her picking her nose, to Francesca's spiteful intelligence, to Luisa's cloying love, all of which gripped him in an iron clamp. He felt a sudden sharp pain in his heart. His thoughts cunningly split away from the path he wished to travel. Careful, he murmured, careful. But he knew it was too late. The brief, involuntary time-gap in his memory had revived his consciousness and now his chest burned with the anxiety he'd forgotten. Some-thing always happened; whenever he went home after one of these illuminating confirmations about himself, he invariably discovered that some malevolent force had unleashed still greater violence from his family's obstinate collective soul: Francesca screeched poisonously, his mother mysteriously shaken out of her lethargy wept, doors slammed, the air hissed. Now that he was walking with Gloria, now that it was his turn to provoke envy, sighs, desires, he was accompanied by the dark blotch he hadn't wanted to obliterate, by the hidden hours he should have spent with Francesca, by the aura of scandal and by the presentiment that something terrible had occurred. He felt his face drop; his eyes, restful until now, took on a restless, furtive glint; his whole person was deprived of the light which Gloria shed on it to become a cowering creature who guarded guilty secrets within him. He realised that his compressed, eclipsed reality was gaining the upper hand. He wanted to shove it back, kick it away, clutch onto Gloria, sink into Gloria, soothe himself in Gloria. He wanted to ask her to help him, to talk to him, say anything, don't leave me alone, you can't leave me alone for a moment or I'll be lost. She walked silently beside him, her head slightly bowed. She looked preoccupied now beneath the hair that fell across her face, not as close as she'd been before, changed somehow from the passionate decisive girl he'd seen that morning. As he looked at her, he felt strangely alarmed. Had something happened during these few hours she'd been away from him? or had this meeting in Venice been right from the start more of a disappointment than she'd expected? He was casting restlessly about to find a reason for his puzzlement, when Gloria spoke almost as if she hadn't heard what he'd told her before. She spoke softly to herself, Maybe it's time for me to figure out how this all happened. So, he thought, so that's what it is, is it? But he wasn't really sure what it was about, or rather, he couldn't piece together her elusive references, nor the thoughts which had produced them. Perhaps its because we're in love, he said, just to be safe. He for his part might even be sincere. He thought he really did love her, or at least he was certain that at a certain

142

moment his seething, hidden desire for her had generated
something which was much more racking, much more
profound: a sense of real love now completely detached
from its initiating cause. The sensation was so strong that
if Gloria told him that it had all been a mistake, that she
didn't love him enough to stay with him, he would feel
like dying, not only because of the disastrous consequences
of a rejection, but because he would lose her. I love you,
he repeated, and he added with a touch of tranquil irony
provoked by his fear of sounding too sickly, it was love at
first sight. Gloria smiled and he felt her tighten her arm
round him. But he felt the same panic, and now he could
guess why: Gloria had expressed rather more than reasonable doubt, she had avowed a hesitation, an uncertainty,
perhaps even a full-blown suspicion that she was committing an error. I ought to try to figure out how this
happened, she had said. But why, in Heaven's name?
Didn't she know? Just wait a moment, wait, he thought
irritated, slow down, all in good time. Gloria should have
replied, Me, too, with the same ironical tone, that's how
it was for me. He stopped and caressed her face, brushed
a finger over her lips. Well, what's wrong? I really don't
know, she said. It was all so sudden, such a rush that
she probably hadn't even had time to breathe, to ask
who he was. Who was he? what did he do? how and
where did he live? what sort of family did he come from?
She'd asked herself for the first time while she'd been waiting under the bell-tower before he'd appeared on the other
side of the Piazza. She'd been waiting two or three minutes,
a very short while, just long enough to think over their
meeting that morning and the kind of subterranean
conspiracy that had held them together in the previous
days. She'd have had ample opportunity to ask herself
all this during those few minutes. Now she probably realised
that she herself preferred her ignorance, she'd rather accept
him as he appeared without probing farther, even if the
whole idea of it rather made her shudder. Makes you
shudder? he asked. Yes, she said, rather as if I were

143

about to make a first parachute jump; I've never done it, she added laughing now, but I imagine it must be good and scaring, one must really shiver. He laughed, but the truth was it wasn't funny, certainly nothing to remove his panic or keep him from groping to find the cause of her uncertainty. Was it simply a matter of basic timidity before an unknown factor? or did it express some specific reservation about him or her suspicions of the world he was trying to hide? or was she disappointed with him. Suddenly he had the unpleasant impression that he was exposed to her penetrating gaze; he was spied upon, observed by a blinkered eye reluctant to see beyond appearances for fear of discovering something that would repel. Something, he thought painfully, something that had inadvertently cast doubt upon his face, that same old business of his melancholy house, his mother, Francesca waiting uselessly in the shop, his fresh terror that Luisa had somehow annihilated herself. Was this why Gloria had posed her shattering question without expecting a reply? He sighed. The tribulations he had to bear. He'd never deluded himself into believing that he could have her just simply by meeting her alone without Alessandro's and Matteo's hostile presence; but he'd hoped that after so many hours of waiting, of doubting, of fearing, their first meeting would at least go smoothly without any sudden jolts, without unpleasant surprises. Instead things had turned out very differently: he'd started to realise that Gloria was not just a character in his speculations; she had a life of her own with her own problems to sort out; she was still bound by her social obligations, by the world from which she came, and stepping out of that world for a moment to come to meet him didn't mean a thing. It hardly mattered if she loved him. Perhaps she did love him, but her feelings were in a prison. He suspected that he couldn't explain it except in the most humiliating terms: Gloria felt him to be different. But who the hell was he if he was different from her too? He drew away from her embrace and leaned on a canal wall.

144

What's wrong? Gloria asked. She leaned softly against his back, circling his waist with her arms. He didn't know what to say. He could only think angrily of ironical, insane things which confirmed his incapacity to realise himself definitively : the motorboat proudly slipping through the Lido waters, Gloria's brother, who suddenly leaped out from her like a jack-in-the-box. He looked at her and thought : was it possible that he and Gloria had established the same kind of relationship as he'd established with Luisa? I ought really to ask myself how all this happened, but it really doesn't matter; not much has happened and certainly nothing which prevents me from turning back if necessary. At best this would be exactly what Gloria was thinking. It might take another form and still endorse substantially the same opinion, with the same limitations and uncertainties : don't say anything, I don't want to know anything, I'm not so sure whether I'd go through with it all even if you turned out to be all you seemed; in any case, I think I understand you pretty well, and I don't think there's much point in our expecting too much from each other. It did look as though Gloria took him up with the same sort of reservations as he'd applied to Luisa when he'd first decided to take up with her : she'd do for the time being, but only for so long as things remained unchanged. Gloria's resistance was clearly not a calculated move, but it did imply an intuitive grasp of the precariousness of their relations, a certainty that they would eventually separate, and she wasn't particularly perturbed by it. He thought of the bobbing jack-in-the-box again and the slick nimble lad who gave Gloria her certainty : her brother. It was he who had the discriminating hand which she used to keep him at bay : she might do as she pleased but try to think of him in another context; she'd do well to remember this tip; she doesn't care? oh but she does, though; take a good look at him, look a little closer, think of him in his more ordinary surroundings; there's something—let's see ... something slightly displeasing about him; she must have noticed; she

145

always knows what she's about. Yet he couldn't possibly claim that Gloria was cold with him or that her actions were inhibited by secret misgivings. On the contrary, she seemed to become sweeter and sweeter. She was a murmur at his shoulders, words breathed into his ear : what is it? what's the matter my love? If she had reservations, they seemed to be far away and buried under her sudden violent excitement. As it happened, he might well have hated her if he hadn't suddenly recalled that he'd never shown such warmth to Luisa, nor had he ever shown such demonstrative affection as Gloria was showing to him. He'd never so much as uttered words of longings. So the distance between him and Gloria was much smaller than between him and Luisa. He was thoroughly fed up with himself. He couldn't decide whether to make up a story that would soothe Gloria's suspicions or to give full weight to things she hadn't said and to her recalcitrant invitation to keep his silence. What questions; who d'you think? I'm a decent type; I'm not rich like you, of course, but neither am I a...a....I study, I'm a student, I teach, I live with my mother and my sister; my father is dead; my mother bought a shop with the money he left, but it was a silly investment; sure, I had a girl some time ago, but that's all over now. Maybe this would satisfy her, but he'd never manage to sweeten the facts about his family or about himself without looking a sham to himself and everyone else. If he bravely told all the truth, if he confessed that he was an unemployed teacher, that his mother weighed close on twenty stone, that she picked her nose, that Luisa belonged to an even sadder social stratum than his own and that he didn't even know what had become of her, that he had borrowed ten thousand lire from a Customs man—the true evidence in fact of his blatant inability to accept himself, it would be far too risky. Far wiser to lie low, for God's sake, than to embark on ill-judged confidences to someone whose positive response couldn't be guaranteed. Far wiser for the time being to be content with her physical presence, to live the hour and postpone

146

his life story until Gloria had reached the point of persuading herself to accept it all without misgivings. It's much too early for that now. He was determined to act in such a way as to avoid all manner of risk to himself. He turned and took her in his arms. He held her close, and in a curious way felt vindicated now by a sudden vision of Gloria's brother watching their embrace and listening to Gloria's breathless panting. Come on, have a good look, look at us together, witness your sister's treachery to her kind. They walked on as far as the ferry landing and got into a gondola that took them over to the *Salute*. They were both silent. He couldn't express to her the fury and grief which had just overtaken him; and she, perhaps, was waiting for him to answer her question. He soon realised that Gloria had given up asking him anything. She was physically restless. She held his hand and first she squeezed it, then she let it drop to put her arm round his waist, then she dropped her arm and took his hand again. He felt almost tempted to reconsider his decision in the light of her restlessness. If he had prepared her to know the truth, if he'd made an allusion to a sticky situation, he'd be able to estimate more accurately how important Gloria felt their relationship to be. It seemed a good time to act. For the moment he was, so to say, stronger than she, he dominated her. Perhaps he should take up the issue which Gloria had momentarily confronted and then had dropped, as if on second thoughts. He ran through the text they'd followed, spelling out each point in turn: you're wondering who I am and I find it hard to answer, I really don't know, I've not really found out myself. This might be a discreet, elegant way of starting, but it was a bit silly. How else could he start? He couldn't tell her everything about Luisa; he couldn't mention either his running away from home or the cabin he'd used as his nocturnal refuge. I suffer from a kind of vague, incomprehensible discontent, he might inform her, a kind of bitterness towards everyone, my mother, my sister; my solitude is evil and proud. It wasn't telling her much, but

147

he ought to say this much at least. He would be able to glean from her answer a fair indication of the degree to which she would accept him as he was. She'd already noticed this, of course, she would answer. Indeed his bitterness was what had first interested her because even she was sort of its victim, wasn't she? Perhaps now she would smile at him with a shade of tender irony. She couldn't fathom its source; it must have enormously deep origins. The conversation might shift to their future. He might stare at the ground as if he were searching for something while he glumly asked her if she would marry him, or if she would consider marrying him, if she'd be his, in short. How about you? she might answer. Yes, he'd reply without a moment's thought, even this very evening, if only he knew of a place to take her. And in the meantime he calculated, this is it, this is the beginning of our conversation. But was this really the way to begin? Now that we're both here, he heard himself ask her with a trace of anger as if he'd unconsciously decided to risk it, now that we're walking alone together, what do you think I could become in your life? Gloria laughed, half-tenderly and half-embarrassed. I don't know, I can't tell what will happen but isn't it a little early to ask? Good God, he thought as he was stabbed with shame, Good God, what an ass I am. Without knowing what he was doing, he'd finished up his fantastic internal monologue with a brusque question. He felt as if he'd exposed himself openly to her, he'd revealed the anguished nature of his feelings for her, the inflated one-sided significance he'd poured into their relationship from the very start, all the impossible hopes he'd attached to it. He was furious. Should he seriously be asking such questions? If only he'd taken care to use an ironical tone, to show some sign of intelligence that would make it sound playful. His question had been an ingenuous expression of his heart. It had been sincere, brutal, naked and embarrassing to a degree which nothing he'd said before had ever reached. Gloria was silent. He listened in his mind to her brief chuckle, to the reply she'd

148

given him : I can't tell what will happen. He wondered why on earth she claimed she didn't know what she, in fact, did know very well. Perhaps at that moment she'd been thinking that it was impossible, that it was doomed to end the moment she left the Lido. He hated her again. She seemed much more distant and distracted than he'd thought. Look here, though, he thought, you know damn well there's no choice, you really can't mistreat her or treat her as an enemy. What if she goes off in a huff, what will you do then? They walked along the wall of the Customs house towards the Zattere. At that hour, the street was almost deserted. On the Canoeing Club wharf two boys were swabbing a boat. He still felt the need to reaffirm his intimacy with Gloria. Cautioned by his experience of a moment before, however, he got a tighter hold on himself and decided for the time being to go on playing it by ear, to avoid taking the plunge until later, until the evening or the next day, or until he'd managed to have her, which might not be too far off. This, of course, had to be his main objective now that he'd finally managed to be alone with her and to walk by her in the street. It was the first step towards the security he knew she could give him. He had a feeling it was imminent and to be expected very soon but nevertheless it seemed remote. The beautiful American woman he'd had last year, during a sort of rupture in his relations with Luisa, had taught him that a woman might very well surrender just when insisting seemed to become useless. Her resistance suddenly breaks down and she gives way to desolate self-renunciation, to complete selfless submission. He had to be patient as he had been the last time, when he'd been rewarded with that painfully irrational feline surrender. It had made him feel so strong that he'd been almost ashamed. Then she'd gone away. She'd borne him off in her heart without judging him, without asking any of the perplexing questions that Gloria was undoubtedly asking. He'd let her go without feeling any sense of loss, because times were different then and he didn't need

149

help. I must wait, he murmured, wait. He stopped on a bridge under the walls of the seminary; unable to think of anything else to do, he pulled her close to him again. Gloria clung gently to him. She let his hands caress her hair, her shoulders, her hips, climb again over her breasts, rest on her cheeks. She looked at him. She became a present, tangible being again, a single entity together with him. She resembled an image he'd invented, a docile person without a personal past, without autonomy. He realised what it was that could take her from him and restore her in so short a time. The resistance he'd noticed before showed itself only when she could see things at a distance, in terms of her future, in terms of their relationship. Now, at this moment, and in every present moment they would ever have together, he could do with her as he liked. All right. He wouldn't mention the future to her again. They would construct a future together, a future which would secretly absorb her into his life. They would construct it out of moments like this one, gestures like these, caressing her breasts, gently feeling her groin. Gloria mumbled something feebly. He couldn't hear. She broke away and started up the steps of the bridge. What did you say? he asked, following her. Without looking round, she shook her head and continued up the steps. Let's sit down over there, she pointed at a bar on the far side of the bridge. Large umbrellas spread open on a wooden terrace by the waterside. As they sat next to each other she reached over to his hand and pressed it against her face. Tell me about yourself, she said. A few short words that made him shudder because he'd thought she didn't want to know any more about him than she already knew. Her question momentarily disoriented him. He shook his head as if he had nothing to say, as he thought confusedly that he'd best watch out. He'd best be careful what he said. Gloria was still undecided about his deceptive manner. She wasn't really interested in who he was; she only wanted him to reject her suspicions that he was other than he seemed. By what self-indulgence had he allowed himself to ask her these questions before? How could he have deceived himself into thinking that he could trust her straight off, that he could tell her about himself on their very first meeting? Maybe it was his anxiety and all the hopes he had placed in her that had misled him into treating a nascent relationship like a mature liaison. Gloria judged him diffidently by her aristocratic standards, and he had to confine himself to convincing her that she wasn't really taking much of a risk if she yielded herself up to him. Yes, that's it; he was emboldened by pulling the whole situation into sharp focus. He began to speak without telling her a thing, tracing an empty image of himself which she could fill in as she liked. He added ironically that he could say nothing of his past because his life had begun when he met her. And furthermore he honestly didn't think that there was anything to tell, anything that would be interesting or moving, that was really worth revealing or that she'd miss if he withheld it. He spoke quickly, almost jovially, always attentive to her reactions, however. As he continued his empty dissertation, he realised that every lie, every shady omission, sprang shut round her like a trap into which she entered with sweet abandon. She almost seemed to be thanking him for sitting there on the terrace of the bar under the umbrella and cutting himself away from that other self, the one that was always on the point of showing its face, peeping out of his eye like the frightened spasm of some animal. I'm free of all ties, the order of my life is completely unperturbed, everything is fine; of course things would be better if my father were still alive, if my personality were more open, more accessible, not so touchy, not so ready to stick out its spines to prick anyone who wanted to hurt me; but what could he do? he'd grown up that way, the distant sound of danger in his ears, his hand constantly poised to strike a defensive blow; she wasn't to think he was actually in danger; not at all; rarely had life ever seemed as easy as it did at that moment; the world was at his fingertips; perhaps it was because he'd met

151

her. She drew closer laughing and encircled his neck with her arm. He felt a sudden wave of futility. Nothing had changed. He was still a fugitive. The whirlpool in his life still gaped before him a few steps ahead. His hope that Gloria could save him suddenly seemed as remote as Luisa's hopes that he'd come back to her. He felt powerless and frustrated as never before. His mind froze with the certainty that not even Gloria could soothe him. As things stood now, Gloria couldn't possibly stay with him. He'd been foolish even to hope that she would. He'd approached her bearing a burden of pain and anxiety, hoping she'd help carry it. She hadn't even let him come clean about himself, or even touch anything that vaguely resembled the truth. She'd excluded past and future from their relations, exactly the parts of himself which most needed her understanding. How could he have believed she could ever be his ally and accept all of him—his past life and his present anguish? He was far away from her. He wondered if her long fair hair, her long, tanned hands, her opaque bracelet, her brown knees beneath her blue dress, her foot, had any purpose. Whose were they? Somehow they were petrified: the warmth had frozen to taciturn hostility. He felt Gloria's hand caress him gently. It dawned on him with sudden clarity that his agitation might very well have been provoked not only by Gloria, but by the psychological fragility emanating from his resolution to ignore what had happened to Luisa, from his decision to ignore the mess he'd left at home, Francesca's attempts to track him down and even the persistent anguish within him that muddled time and made present events seem unreal and remote and past ones vital. He'd been forced to live as if things which had probably not happened actually had happened. What must he do to make Gloria real and present, to make a tangible event out of her? What must he do to impose himself on Luisa and Francesca and all the emotions that issued from them? He got to his feet wearily and started to weave through the deserted tables to the end of the terrace. He stared into the canal while imagining that Gloria must be really petrified as she looked at his back, really surprised by his mysterious suffering. What if I went off? he mused, what if I put on an act for once and left her here wondering if I'm really mad or just unhappy, or if she hadn't let me down somehow? He didn't seriously consider walking off even if he could see her turning her head towards him and getting up to follow him. She might call him by name for the first time; Mario, she might say, and as she caught up with him she would tug at his hand to make him stop. In any case, he wasn't really that upset. Her tug at his hand restored to Gloria the immediacy she'd lost. Once again she represented the tangible vehicle for realising his potential. Stop, he thought, don't waste time on abstracted conjectures, one thing at a time. He recalled his posture in other moments of uncertainty to stimulate a new optimism, a gentle gust of wind that soothed him. He recalled that he had no proof of not being able to count on Gloria; it was their first meeting after all. There would be other meetings. Gloria could give him all the reassurance he needed, but later; yes, all the reassurance he'd not yet had. He turned to meet her eyes, and realised suddenly that there was another solution to his problems. It was strange how the same fact could assume such entirely different significance from one person to the next. The solution was to aim for more than just getting her into bed : to aim at getting her into bed and getting her pregnant. He felt a muddled sense of excitement. This wouldn't be the best way of securing her. He'd prefer that she accepted him unconditionally. But he might achieve this later on when ineluctable external circumstances dealt the final blow to her hesitations. All right, so it was a humiliating device, a trick, an expedient which wouldn't close up the distance between them : but it was too useful to overlook. Desperate situations require desperate remedies. If Gloria continued to offer her obscure resistance to him it was because he'd done nothing to secure her future. But if he deliberately induced now what he'd

153

accidentally induced with Luisa, he'd force her to stay with
him even after she'd left the Lido. She herself would try
to preserve their tie to each other, to tighten it, to conse-
crate it, he thought with bitter irony, just as Luisa had
tried. The inflated tum of the one would deliver him
from the inflated tum of the other. Good God, he shuddered, why didn't I think of this before? He went back to
her and kneeled beside her, placing his hand in her lap.
Gloria kept her head lowered; she looked perplexed. He
tried to catch her eye and smiled when he saw her
troubled, slightly surprised expression. Sorry, he said, it's
nothing. Again he was overwhelmed by the need to hurry.
Now, he thought, this must happen now, maybe in a boat
out on the lagoon, or in a shack among the brushwood.
Gloria didn't react, she asked no questions. She only stared
at him as if she didn't recognise him for a moment and
now she found it hard to see him as she had before. She
wasn't annoyed. His outburst, the way he'd brusquely
withdrawn and left her alone had disturbed her a bit.
It had disoriented her, but it hadn't hurt her pride. It
was as if she resisted asking anything of him not because
she wanted to separate her life from his, but because she
was afraid she would betray her weakness, she would
confess the power he had over her. You defend yourself
with silence, he thought. Maybe you think I'm mad,
and certainly that I'm difficult to make out. You have no
idea how simple it all is: I'm here; you're there, but you
are only partially present, another part of your life is far
away, hidden from view, safe from the assault of thieves
like me. And it's that part I want. Still, her body was so
close to him and so inviting. Perhaps if he took her body
he would also capture all of her mysterious unknown past
years and all her future. He would imprison her entire
life, like a wild animal, until she was tamed. Let's go,
he said. Gloria followed him docilely. He led her past the
tables, out onto the street and towards the Zattere at a
determined pace as if to a definite goal. He thought he'd
hire a boat and take her way out on the lagoon. He

154

felt that she would come. She held his hand tightly. Her
hand seemed strangely aware and naked, as if Gloria
knew that in a short while they'd be close together in
a more naked embrace and her heart beat fast with sudden
excitement. They were certainly both thinking of the same
thing. They were united, superimposed upon each other;
he was located in a precise place on the floor of a boat
with the water lapping round him, with the distant
train whistles, the sun still hot on his back. She was probably located in no specific surrounding, in no precise
embodiment, but in a place of similar isolation where their
shouts rose in the silence. There might be a lamp on as the
waning sun filtered through some window. Suddenly a
distant clock struck five. Gloria's hand contracted in his
own; she stiffened and said softly, no, not now, I can't
now. A voice from a radio above him began singing a
song: Oh, my love, bury me in roses. He stood still feeling
desolate. Why not? he asked. She shook her head. I can't,
she insisted. She said the same words with more resolution
now, as if it were really true that she couldn't. And again,
pick me the thorniest roses, the voice continued. Would
I hurt her, he thought involuntarily, as she hurts me?
Why not? he asked again. I don't know, she said looking
at him. He realised that something had stopped her. The
spell was broken. The desire and the train of fantasies had
ceased: What's happened? tell me. He wondered if she
hadn't been halted by the same doubts that had previously
prevented her from thinking about a future with him.
Nothing, she said, shrugging her shoulders. The empty
word lingered before him and he felt he had to fill it.
He was alone, frightened before a blank wall, before a
barrier more sturdy than any reasonable refusal Gloria
might have offered him. But still deep down he felt he
couldn't give up, he had to fight to persuade her to come
with him. For there could be no question but that the
moment to clinch their relationship had passed within their
reach. Oh, my love bury me in roses. Rebellious thoughts
clustered in his mind. Enough of this, I must have results.

I must feel something definite in my hands, something tangible. Tonight I want to go to sleep without being afraid, without remorse, with the certainty that the day has not been wasted. He looked at Gloria. She stood motionless beside him, gazing at the ground. He looked for some sign of hesitation, a trace of uncertainty, but she looked determined. After a moment of docility, she no longer wanted to follow him. God damn her, he thought. He felt like pushing and dragging her, forcing her to come with him, because her refusal had shaken his whole being. The invitation to wait patiently which he'd made to himself a moment before had been forgotten. It whirled into his dizzy certainty that it would take very little to have her.

They were both motionless the one next to the other. She couldn't follow him where he wanted to take her. He couldn't persuade her to follow him. There seemed to be very little else to say. There was nothing left for them to do but go their separate ways. He was afraid that this was just what would happen if he didn't find some way of taking up their conversation. As you like, he said without conviction just to say something. He took her arm and guided her on, dropping the recent frantic pace, now ambling aimlessly so as to indicate to her that he had given up. He wondered why on earth he'd not been able to understand a thing about her since they'd met, or very little, whereas before, when he'd looked at her from a distance and waited for her, he'd managed to interpret even her most minute gestures and looks. I wanted to take something of you away with me, he mused bitterly after a pause, today, not tomorrow or the day after. And he added with angry sincerity that it was because he was sick and tired of being alone, of going home alone and thinking about her. She nodded once or twice as if she knew very well what he meant and it was really she, not he, who'd had enough of only thinking about him. Then why not? Mario asked. Because, because ... said Gloria; she seemed to be collecting herself: he always asked questions like a little boy. It was important, wasn't it? It couldn't be decided in a flash, as if it were a trifle that didn't matter; she, too, wanted him; a great deal; sometimes the extent of her desire made her ashamed; this is why she had to control herself. She was silent, but he listened intently wondering if another more obscure significance lurked behind the surface of her words. He felt a spasm of gratitude and relief because Gloria's words seemed to have reopened the dialogue which she'd so brusquely cut short. That wasn't the only reason, she said. She couldn't today because of other things; she couldn't go with him because she had to go back to her hotel early; she had to spend the evening with some friends, the same friends she'd lunched with; she'd left them abruptly on some pretext which no one had taken seriously, she couldn't even remember what she'd said; she felt she really ought to see them again before they left. What do you mean? he thought, confused again, remembering the anxious questions she asked that very morning, what ever do you mean? wasn't it you who asked me to spend the evening with you, the two of us alone together, united? wasn't it you who left me with such a miraculous sensation of incredulity, with the certainty of possessing you, of never having cause to fear anything ever again? what has happened? what has made you change your mind? why is it so difficult to stop your world from getting in our way? Matteo and a fair girl he'd never seen, or perhaps she was dark, or perhaps they were two girls and two fellows he'd never seen, but whose voices and gestures he could easily imagine to be just like Matteo's, called her, begged her to return: don't be late, come on, they said, what time will you be back? There was a trace of sophisticated irony to their words, which were totally free of the agony he might feel. After she'd left, they stretched out on the beach near Fenzo's cabin, or they stayed in the cool lounge of the hotel to wait for her. O.K., he would have liked to say, let them wait. Didn't they have all they needed to make their evening enjoyable? did they also

157

have to have Gloria? why couldn't they take him into consideration. But maybe it was she who wanted to go back. Good, he said. He couldn't see why Gloria betrayed him, but he decided not to hurt her: all the same, won't you give me something to take away with me. Gloria was finally freed from her discomfort and began to laugh. She threw her arms round his neck and kissed his lips. She bit them with provocative vigour. He cried out, half-playing, half because her bite had hurt. No, he said, that's not enough. And he pushed her towards the opening of an alleyway. In the shadows, far from the light that lingered on the *fondamenta,* he slipped his hand into the neck of her dress, he unclipped her bra and slowly pulled it out. This'll do, he said. Gloria looked at him, perhaps undecided whether to feel offended or amused. For once his action had been guided entirely by his instinct, without taking time to consider, to fear interfering with their relationship. He wondered if taking her bra from her in the middle of the street were not a scandalous, vulgar act. With one hand he stuffed it into his pocket while the other returned beneath Gloria's dress to find her naked breasts, to caress them, to squeeze them gently, possessively. Regardless of her first reaction, Gloria seemed, upon this new contact, to give up trying to evaluate his gesture. She threw her arms round his neck again, perhaps because earlier on, it had cost her an effort to stop before they'd gone any further. For the remaining time they slipped furtively from one alley to another; she would stand with her back and her hair against the damp walls, while he stood beside her, caught up in the game which lacerated him, but alert to recover himself every time there was a sound in the street, every time someone passed. He didn't want to give Gloria the chance to accuse him of compromising her. Evening came. Gloria had to go. They were sitting on a canal bank. The air was suffocating and quick flashes of lightning shot across the cloudy sky. I must go, she said. She rose and gave him her hand to help him up. They returned to the Punta della Dogana,

158

recrossed the canal and made for the wharf where the crowds were returning from the Lido in the light of the freshly lit street-lamps. He felt strangely calm. He had actually managed to have something. What Gloria had given him was no slight matter. It was a gift, a small gift, but one which she'd give again tomorrow, perhaps many times during the day. It was the first of a long series of gifts which he would seize from her every day until, without noticing it, she had given herself entirely. He would still have to wait, but he wasn't simply waiting now. It was as if he'd noticed that in fact he hadn't lost whatever he'd thought he'd lost. He couldn't help laughing every time he thought of the bra he'd filched from her. What a clever idea it had been. What an inspiration. He thanked heaven that he'd obeyed his instinct, he'd not been calculating for once. He'd traced the first gesture of his new freedom, a gesture without calculation, born of spontaneous impulse. And she'd accepted it. He could have faith in himself, he could yield to his inspiration more than he had done until now. He put his hand in his pocket to touch the cups of the bra. He recalled her naked breasts beneath her dress. His desire overtook him again. Tomorrow, perhaps, tomorrow. Gloria walked beside him holding his hand. She quickened her pace. A *vaporetto* at the wharf was just about to leave. They sat next to each other on the upper deck while the boat began to move, leaving behind the illuminated wharf, the cafés, the bustle of the crowds along the quayside. He felt free, almost happy. Something followed him of course, a memory that was still alive, the smell of squalor and death that wracked his whole body : Francesca waiting in her shop, the confused image of Luisa, his flight. It was far away now, choked in what the day had brought him. He was surprised, however, to find himself trying to imagine what his mother was doing just then and what his flight had meant for her. Gloria sat close by, leaning her head on his shoulders. She was there, her presence exorcising evil spirits. She smiled. He need not

159

worry about tonight. He might take a room in a hotel. He considered it for a moment, but gave up the idea. True, Gloria had cost him nothing today, but this was not enough for him to waste the money that Bonucci had given him. He'd return to Fenzo's cabin across the same course he'd discovered the night before: the dark cabin beneath the illuminated walls of the *Excelsior*. He would take another midnight swim to get to it. It was worth it. The cabin was his new home now, his clandestine refuge. The hot, odorous, wooden walls would protect him again tonight.

=====

HE'D KILLED TIME walking round the lighted streets, exchanging one bar for another, mingling with the evening crowds that filled the pavements. He'd eaten hurriedly in a cheap *rosticceria*. On his way out, he'd bumped into the same two smarmy types of the day before, the ones of the tight T-shirts and the insults that had exploded behind him as he'd dashed onto the beach. They hadn't seen him, but the encounter aroused a kind of superstitious discomfort in him. They had nothing whatever to do with him. They knew nothing about him. But coming upon them had been a little like picking out the same card from a pack too many times for it to be a mere coincidence. He felt trapped by an evil eye which would continue to haunt him wherever he went. Now, as he dried his frozen body in Fenzo's cabin, he heard the wind blow across the cloudy sea and his mood threatened to become unmanageable again. They refused to leave him, they were all excited, they shouted, and they seized at every opportunity to remind him of their presence. They broadcast their messages to him over loudspeakers. He cursed those two little buggers for cropping up like bad pennies, swore at himself for having read almost comic significance into their sudden reappearance; boy, aren't we superstitious? he thought. He forced himself to relegate the meeting to oblivion and recover his previous mood of satisfaction. Let them shout to their hearts' content, and let them look for him and send him messages; for as far as he was concerned the world didn't exist outside the rigidly personal sphere he'd constructed at such cost and with such pains. He drew the bathing wrap round him as he'd done the night before, then lit a cigarette and lay down on the stretcher. The anxiety, which had started

161

to stir once more, began to make itself felt, but only to a limited degree. He fought it with mute stubbornness. He would put Luisa out tonight, out and away from him. Why the hell was she still nagging him? Hadn't she realised yet she'd hadn't a hope? It was all so obvious. No one could possibly misinterpret his actions, or expect anything from him other than what he'd done. Yet she kept on thrusting herself before him, poking her tear-lined face into his, grimacing in that sickly way, he honestly felt tempted to slap her: hopeless, irremediable, eternally so; eternally, continuously the same, impossible, intolerable. He suddenly realised that his very resistance had led him straight into the insidious territory where Luisa lay lurking. He leaped to his feet, groped for his trousers, fished out Gloria's bra and threw it onto the stretcher. He lay down and squeezed it as one would an amulet, hoping that the excitement from their contact would placate his insistent memory. He lulled himself to sleep in the shadow of his fetish. Then suddenly he woke to a violent gust of wind that drove across the beach to hurl itself against the cabins. He propped himself up on his elbow and listened excitedly. The sea breathed loudly and scattered cries travelled wildly on the wind. A distant band was playing, and the beach seemed to come alive as if touched by a magic spell. His first reaction was one of terror : someone would burst in on the cabin. He shrank into a dark corner like a frightened beast. But the voices were distant, they were laughing down by the shore. He cautiously opened the door, careful not to upset the chair, and peered out. The silhouettes of several men and women ran dancing against the lowering background of the sea; linking hands, they snaked to and fro dipping and rising, the women's evening dresses fluttering like pennants in the wind. Hotel guests, no doubt, he thought as his heart contracted. He stared into the darkness, worried and fearful. Docile Gloria, who had become his image of reassurance after a long day of doubt and conflicts, Gloria, whose existence he'd captured and whose destiny was at his

162

disposal, now re-emerged as a problem still unresolved. She became the burning disappointment of a broken promise. When they'd parted only a few hours ago, she'd made no allusion to a party at the hotel that evening, and yet she was more than likely out there capering along the seashore with those people. There she was, he was certain he'd detected her nimble figure in the crowd. She broke out of the chain and began to dance alone, raising her arms and twisting her torso above her legs, which she'd firmly anchored in the sand. His heart beat faster. Was it really she? The girl rose on her toes and leapt into the air with outstretched arms, then dropped and leapt again, as the other black and white figures clapped rhythmically in a circle about her. They enclosed her, closing in on her and then expanding to give her room for her dance. Was it really she? He strained his eyes as he died a hundred little deaths. She hadn't mentioned a party, and yet here she was dancing alone. She had made vague allusions to spending an evening with friends, but here she was: she dropped down before her audience and writhed in the sand. Someone helped her up laughing. Then a gust of wind lifted a whirl of sand and skirts. Her voice rose shrilly among the others', laughing and embarrassed. Was it really she? If it was, she had withheld a hell of a lot from him—not only her party, but also all that was going on now, all this serpentine dancing, those skirts flapping in the wind, and the laughter and what had led up to all this and what would happen before the night was through. Yes, she'd kept all this dark. He felt paralysed by the suspicion that she had deliberately excluded him; this and the painful realisation that he could mean so little to her sent shivers up his spine while also goading him to violence; he wheeled round to face the enemy. He threw open the cabin door and stepped out. Frigid, distant woman, he intoned glumly. A destructive urge goaded him to dash across the sand as far as the circle of dancers, but he stood motionless. It might not be she after all; she might not be the

163

one that was dancing but the one standing alone, apart, as if reluctant to participate. He strained to recognise Gloria in that solitary figure, hoping it was she, for that far-away look, that reserve suggestive of secret, distant thoughts were just the attitude he thought Gloria should adopt when she was without him. Surely it was she. But there was to be no answer to the question, for a sudden tremor shook the shore. The sand whirled up again and the cabin awnings flapped madly above him as a downpour of rain fell upon the scene. The serpent dancing in the dark disintegrated into a thousand fragments. Black and white shadows tore off shouting and colliding. In a trice the beach was empty. He stood still for a moment listening to the voices fading out, oblivious of the hissing rain and the sudden cold. When he was certain that no one would come back and that he would never know if Gloria had been but a few yards away, he turned back into the cabin and closed the door behind him. That sudden mirage on the dark sands had disturbed him thoroughly. Uncertainty prevailed again. Had he been deliberately excluded? Had she not mentioned the party so that she wouldn't have to invite him? Was she ashamed of him? or was it that she hadn't known there would be a party and had only excluded him accidentally? If only he hadn't woken up. His questions would needle him all night and irritate all the old wounds. She'd be with friends, would she, he thought angrily, with friends. When Gloria had first mentioned them he'd managed to make them seem innocuous, imagining them to be whatever best suited him. Just a few short hours ago he hadn't felt a bit threatened by the knowledge that Gloria would be meeting them. Now they were a hostile army that withheld Gloria and joined forces dangerously and unexpectedly with Luisa. It didn't really matter whether or not Gloria had been there on the beach. What did matter was that every night, every evening, every minute she was away from him she was stolen from him, she entered another orbit, from which he was excluded. He could no longer control his anxieties which now unleashed, ran riot through his mind. Now there was nothing he could possibly do, he felt it essential that he start moving quickly to waste no time. Had time itself joined the ranks against him in systematic persecution, revealing its urgency only when he couldn't move? He struck a match and looked at his watch. It wasn't even two yet. It would be hours before he could see Gloria, possibly even longer than usual because of that damned midnight party. Now she'd get up late tomorrow. She might even sleep until lunchtime, as I suppose one's bound to do, he thought disconsolately, if one stays up all night. He cursed her and the dark beach and the howling wind that had wakened him to such misery. He could of course get dressed and go up to the hotel, find her and bring her back to the cabin. She would be so amazed to see him that she might come without requesting or being given a single explanation. He knew the temptation to be quite futile, because even if it were the only thing to do, he knew he would never go to the hotel at that hour. The hotel terrorised him; it was an enemy citadel, a foreign state requiring a passport. He might enter with relative ease during the daytime, but at night, when everything bore its own exact weight—the burning lights, the icy, reticent bell boys, the rooms he'd never seen, the carpets and the guests, above all the guests in their evening dress, their soft leather suitcases, the whispering in the corners and their air of quiet self-sufficiency—all confined him to his station. He might invade the place if desperation drove him to it, but he wasn't desperate yet. Perhaps he was still in control despite the pain his awakening had caused, perhaps he could vanquish his impatience. He was tired, that's all, weary of his obsessive plunges out of calm into anxiety, out of the certainty of being able to wait peacefully into the fear that time was running out. A few hours ago, when he was swimming in the icy water, Fenzo's cabin had appeared like the end of his day, the last spurt before rest: he was going to lie down and sink into warm oblivion. He swam

165

on against the rough sea and the chill of the water, but he was already home and dry, lying on the stretcher, snug in the bathing wrap, and he slept in attendance of morning. But it wasn't like that at all, everything within him was awake and alight. He wasn't desperate, but he saw it all too lucidly now: Gloria's dangerous elusiveness, Luisa's hospital bed, his own precariousness, and above all, this blasted sense of urgency that kept cutting his breath. He felt Gloria's bra and the contact was remote, as it is with an object reconstructed from memory, bereft of physical tangibility; even its very origin eluded him. It no longer had the qualities of a garment wrested from Gloria, its intimate connection was severed to the extent that it had nothing whatever to do with Gloria; and this because she'd been taken away from him, because she had, in the interim, become someone else—that girl writhing on the beach, who might now be laughing in the hotel lounge, laughing in her quiet self-sufficiency amongst the soft leather suit-cases. Now was the time when he should snatch off her bra if he wanted to regain his self-confidence and his confidence in her. Now was the time when he should clasp the dancing girl in his arms until he felt her autonomy drain from her and merge into his. At every moment that passed, she fled farther away from him, she danced farther and farther into the heart of the hotel where he couldn't follow her. And where was he meanwhile? where had she left him? Maybe she'd dropped him into oblivion at the door of the hotel, maybe in Venice when she'd said she had to get back. He remembered that on the way back Gloria had seemed preoccupied as if she were thinking of something else, of her transformation when she left him. Her distraction had begun many hours before. He had been left behind there, lost in the crowds that returned from the Lido. He ought to make a dash at recovering his identity before she was too far away. It was pouring outside and the wind scalloped puddles in the sand as the sea rose to the cabin. Frigid, distant woman. Before he fell asleep again, the black and

166

white serpent fixed upon his vision for a long while, coiling and unwinding on the shore. He felt weary. He wanted to be rid of it all and flow once for all into the sleep that approached.

THE RAIN BEAT upon the slate roofs and a grey spoke of light filtered through the cracks between the boards, accompanied by a cold sliver of wind that shook the curtain. It was day. The bathing wrap was damp and his bones ached. What time was it? He lifted his arm and looked at his watch: almost nine. He sat bolt upright on the stretcher. He was completely awake. He must get up and dress before anyone came. He shivered as he pulled on his trousers and his shirt. He ought to have considered the risk he'd run by sleeping so late, but the silence, the cold air, and the even patter of the rain guaranteed an empty beach. The rain was a mixed blessing, though, because even if it had saved him from being discovered, it threw him up against the problem of time again. He wouldn't be able to do anything, he would have to wait passively for hours and hours. He carefully pushed open the door and the wind broke into the cabin. The beach was blackened by the rain and the sea was stormy and there wasn't a single sign of life from the hotel behind him. Would the day be a total loss? He suddenly thought of that invitation of Fenzo's about which he'd forgotten as he had about Fenzo himself: come any time, it's O.K. by me, what super weather! there's a marvellous girl next door. He'd gone; he'd met the girl and had made out famously with her. But she wasn't there now and the weather had changed. He shivered. His shirt wouldn't be enough; he'd be cold all day long, unless the wind fell. How many hours would he have to stand at the cabin door without being at all certain she'd turn up? It was barely nine o'clock and she couldn't have gone to bed much before three. Were six hours' sleep too little or enough for her? He'd also slept six hours but he didn't feel rested. His whole body ached as if he'd been trampled on or beaten up. It didn't really matter, except for the cold. Was she still asleep? What about Luisa? Was she dead? Was she alive? Were they still looking for him? If only the weather would brighten. The sky was dense and heavy and hopeless. The rain was like an unfettered fury relentlessly determined to smother the beach. He really didn't feel like braving the rain without a clue as to why he should do so or where he was going. His hair, his clothing, his shoes would be immediately drenched, and even if he were to explore the beach quickly, he'd deprive himself of his only set of clothes for the day. Why the hell do I have such rotten luck? Why the hell does the world have to stop today of all days? He would fidget all day and be impatient about every-thing he did, whether it were closing the door, or putting on one of Fenzo's sweaters and wondering if Fenzo would be annoyed if he found out, but it was too cold to resist. Everything would be seen through an eye rabid with impatience, with the awareness that time was passing uselessly and he couldn't do a thing to stop it. He lay down wearily on the soggy stretcher. Luckily he had to wash and eat. Here were a few things he had to do which he might have worried over or not done at all had he been in a hurry. He got up, opened the cupboard door and took out a cup, the coffeepot, the spirit-stove and a pitcher of water. He poured water into a plastic basin and washed his face as best he could. Then he made breakfast. He tried to move slowly and to concentrate exclusively on little tribulations that helped while away the time: the damp matches that wouldn't light, the cup that had to be washed, the stove with a wick that was almost burnt out. But by the time he'd drunk his coffee, only a few minutes had elapsed. Again he stood impotently before empty time, before the rain that prevented him from leaving, and before his need for acting as soon as he could. He opened the door again and looked out. The beachscape hadn't altered significantly; there were the same layers of shape-less clouds, the same fomenting sea, the same wind. The

rain, however, gave signs of diminishing. It's going, it was
drumming less insistently on the roofs. It's moving off.
Maybe today wouldn't be a dead loss, after all. Perhaps
hopes and possibilities could be harboured again. He
leaned against the door jamb and stood motionless,
scrutinising the sky for some hint of blue between the
clouds. As the minutes passed, his hopes for improvement
were dogged by a growing disquiet. The source of his
disquiet was no great mystery, nor was he surprised that
he wasn't jumping for joy now that the weather gave
signs of changing. He knew what it was about. When
the rain stopped he knew that if Gloria didn't come out
right away he'd have to go and look for her; he'd have
to go into the hotel and find her. He couldn't wait any
longer, and he wasn't prepared to chance anything and
lie around hopefully as he had done for so long. If his
timidity and his pride, with which he was generally so
content, masqueraded as prudent counsellors to remind
him that, rain or no rain, it was more polite to wait for
the lady than to seek her out, he'd just discredit their
feeble attempts. It would be even worse if he compromised
by saying that he'd wait an hour before deciding what to
do: even if the sun emerged immediately, it would take
more than an hour, more than two hours, for the beach
to dry. He would be proven right were he to predict that
nothing would happen that morning unless he took the
initiative. He was alone before the execution of some
decisive action. His heart beat heavily. Go, stop, wait,
cross now—it all depended on him. By now he could
emerge from his shelter and run over to the hotel: a mere
drizzle was no deterrent. All he needed was to take himself
in hand rather ruthlessly and forbid any dallying over
his petty weaknesses. He would defy his inertia and
recover—if he'd ever possessed them in the first place—the
springs of action. The hell with it, he said. He was running
across the open space as if shot from a catapult. He
jumped from one puddle to the next, reached the
concrete path, and raced on towards the hotel. As he ran,

he wondered what he'd say, whom he'd meet. He vaguely anticipated the discomfort he'd experience in a few minutes' time. He continued to run with a vengeance which lent strength to his resolution to see the matter through to the end this time, no matter who tried to stand in his way. He climbed the steps as the rain still pelted down on him. He caught a fleeting glimpse of his own reflection in the entrance windows, running like someone else with long, determined strides, pushing open the door and vanishing. He was in the empty lounge, isolated in the morning silence. The excitement and the run made his heart beat fast and his breath rasp. He was inside. He'd overcome his greatest obstacle. If someone would only come up to him, everything would be taken care of in a minute or two—just enough time to leave a message or ring her on the phone. In a couple of minutes he'd be back in the cabin, delivered from the worry of useless expectation and certain that Gloria would have been informed. He crossed the lounge without knowing where to go. He saw a waiter in a white jacket dart between the chairs and the archways like a flash of lightning and he hurriedly called, Excuse me, please. He almost ran, so that the minutes would pass more quickly and the mild, dishevelled little waiter would tell Gloria all the sooner that he was there and she would come down that much sooner to meet him. He told him he was a friend of Gloria's and he wanted to talk to her, but the waiter shook his head and politely waved him on to an invisible corner of the lounge, explaining that he didn't know about these things and that he should go to the Reception Desk. The minutes, which should have disappeared from the short familiar round of his watch's dial, began to multiply and swarm before his eyes. Wherever he looked he stood before a hostile, occupied space. The hotel, he thought absurdly, is raising the alarm to throw me out. But he was completely determined. He need take no notice of the alarm even if the demeanour of the clerk, in a dark suit and with the hotel insignia on his lapel, changed from impersonal to disdainful to positively distrustful as he looked up from the desk on the other side of the lounge and watched him approach. May I help you? Some help you are! he muttered as his anxiety turned into a sudden hatred for the hotel insignia, a fat lot of help. Without greeting him, he blurted out what he wanted as if assaulting or shaking the fellow with his angry impatience. They stared silently into each other's eyes for a moment of mutual hostility. Of the two of them, he was obviously the beast of prey poised for attack because the clerk, as if somehow dominated, lowered his head and ran through the register that was open on the counter. He mumbled something—Gloria's room number, perhaps— and lifted the telephone. His heart beat painfully as he leaned on the counter visualising the phone ringing in her room, Gloria stretching out her hand: in a moment she'll know I'm here and I can go happily back to the cabin. The telephone was ringing, but Gloria wasn't answering. The clerk held the receiver in his hand, but bluntly shook his head, as if to say she's asleep, she can't hear it, she's not answering, she's out. He felt momentarily at the clerk's mercy: all he had to do was hang up and he'd have to leave. Then, as the clerk was lowering the receiver and he was desperately raising his hand to stop him, his mouth dry, his chest aching, he heard a distant metallic click. A voice, Gloria's sleepy voice, was answering the phone. Gloria, he murmured, grasping the phone. The answer arrived after a momentary pause with the muffled sounds of waking, Mario? Her voice was warm and attentive, Darling, she said, what a time to call; where are you? what's it like outside? He told her while staring at the clerk across the counter with malicious irony, it's marvellous out, it's raining cats and dogs, the sky's competely overcast and the sea is rough. He was fully self-possessed now, happy to have found her again. They had everything they could possibly need, he said. All that was missing was her; please come down. She laughed, all right, I'll get up. He returned the phone to the clerk.

This time he politely bid him thank you and good day before he walked off as if his conversation with Gloria had taught him a new language. In a few minutes, the curve of his whole day had changed. A bit of courage, a single self-assured gesture, that hadn't been all that daring after all, had been enough to make him deliriously happy as he returned to the cabin and the beach and the tempestuous sea and his rainy solitude—which had a little earlier been a source of anxiety and annoyance. He could not imagine better weather or more ideal landscape than this. Let it pour all day long, let the sea swell and flood the beach. He wouldn't even mind if the playful sea merrily swallowed him whole; a kick or two and he'd surface at will. A kick, a hop and a spring like the one he was doing now and he'd be safe and sound inside the cabin again. He gurgled with laughter as he heard the rain on the roof and recalled how tender Gloria's voice had sounded. She'd realised why he'd phoned and she knew what would happen. She was probably coming down now thinking of the request he'd murmured—please come down, come quickly—and thinking of what he hadn't been able to say and would say when she arrived. What progress he'd made in such a short while: the waiter had looked completely unsurprised, and when he'd indicated in a mild and curiously familiar tone the whereabouts of the hotel desk on the far side of the hall, he'd been knocked sideways because he'd expected to be shown the door. He must have been quite mad to take them all so seriously. It had been so terribly easy and everything had gone so smoothly that now the recent anxiety and fear seemed quite ridiculous. It was odd that even the clerk behind the desk had let himself be dominated, in spite of his hostility, and that Gloria had answered the phone so easily. A breach had been opened in the citadel. He could come and go as he pleased now and no one would stop him. He had free access. He'd broken the magic spell that made it so difficult for him to approach Gloria—or better still, he'd

173

discovered that there was no spell to isolate her and that he only needed to call for her to come.

Gloria appeared noiselessly beside him. Her hair was caught in a scarf and she wore a raincoat buttoned to the neck. Less than twenty minutes had elapsed since he'd called her. She looked at him silently, half-smiling and slightly shy. He looked at her calmly, still surprised at how easy it had been to persuade her to come: a few words in her ear, and she'd leapt out of bed. Her presence distorted his memory of his previous fears and gave him a sense of malicious triumph. There was something hilarious about their affair; they were both ridiculous—he because of all the prestige games he'd had to play to get her, and she . . . he wasn't quite sure why but it was her devoted availability that somehow made her ridiculous. Mario? Gloria? He took her arm and drew her to him as he moved towards the cabin door. As he kissed her and she tightened her arms round his neck, he reflected that he probably didn't love her at all and that consequently, once he'd had her he would have quite an advantage over her. Gloria broke away from their kiss, leant on his shoulder and turned to look up at him arching her body. She was in the perfect position to be swung off her feet. He carried her over the threshold to the stretcher. But he felt a bit out of character. This sort of thing really didn't suit him. Surely he ought to be doing something else, like kneeling at her side or going over to close the door and lean against it looking at her intently for a good long while to give her the first cue. There were thousands of things he could be doing, but what really worried him was that he could feel that something had gone wrong: here she was snuggled up in his arms, all warm from bed, and yet his desire for her was not as vigorous as he would have liked it to be. He suddenly realised that desire hadn't come into it much up to now. His desires had been suppressed by other more urgent stimuli, checked by other problems so that it had only made itself manifest on rare occasions such as yesterday when they

174

were walking about Venice. Now that they were alone and free to love each other, his desire was still bridled by his calculations and mislaid in the labyrinth of his thoughts. Could it fail him now just at the crucial moment? Gloria's tongue licked his mouth, then sweetly and provocatively slipped between his lips. He felt oddly remote and cool. He could see himself as if in a mirror, plying into her lips in response to her playful call to action. Yet he wasn't beside himself with passion. He might well be unable to take her now, and wondered if it wouldn't be better to put it all off. Gloria was blissfully unaware of his condition. She reacted to him as from another world. Their embrace drew her into a warm, moist isolation where no one could follow her; as she drifted, her eyes closed and she breathed heavily. She was alone as his hands discovered her, drew her slacks off her legs until she was naked inside her open raincoat and unbuttoned cardigan. His impotence gave way not to the sight of her breasts and belly but to the significance that finally seeing them held for him, and to the accumulation of resentment and anxiety, the cumulative effect of days of misery and cold, of his mother and Luisa, of Francesca's sarcasms, of the hotel's mystique, of the insults undergone and his self-derision for having feared failure, and to the sudden glorious realisation that he'd succeeded—to everything he was and everything he had been all those tortured days that had culminated in the offering of this body before him. He penetrated her murmuring words of anger and joy, so you're here, at last you're mine. He loved her and assailed her; his was an act of love and a declaration of war. Bursts of laughter and of triumph accompanied his thoughts, darling, you didn't think twice, you knew all along, damn you. Finally her cries and the twitching of her body lifted a great wave that swallowed him and flooded that small recess of his mind where all that laughter and resentment had taken refuge. Even then he managed to retain an iota of lucidity: God, may she become pregnant. They lay a while trembling motionless

175

one upon the other. He remained inside her and she made no attempt to push him out. In fact she drew him closer and held him tightly inside her to keep him there. Well he'd had her and he still wasn't satisfied. It hadn't been the soul-shattering experience he'd expected. Yielding to Gloria's timing, he'd come too soon, which had only freed him from desire and left so much undisturbed. The clot of bitterness persisted and so had his remote uncertainties, whose corrosive energies remained stubbornly intact and active. He slowly raised his head to look at her. Her eyes were closed and her lips slightly parted. Her face showed not a single trace of the recent tempest. It was utterly peaceful and composed. He suddenly recalled how it had been with Luisa the first time, her damp wide-open eyes in the half-light, her noisy breathing, and his feeling of self-satisfaction at his easy victory. She'd run out of the cinema. Something had broken in her and her world had come tumbling down. She'd rushed off to wash herself all frightened and ashamed. Gloria lay perfectly composed beneath him in her open raincoat. She seemed to be sleeping peacefully, blissfully unaware of her nakedness and of what might be happening inside her. He needed no expert's opinion to tell him that giving herself to him had meant very little to her; it was an innocent, habitual operation that might free her from an itch. Her arm had loosened its grip round him and the contractions round him had ceased. Was she asleep? He was about to call her name, but something stopped him. There she was, so quiet, so free, whereas she should be quaking with fear and asking, Now what? what shall we do? what'll you do if I'm pregnant? Leaning on his elbows, his head in his hands just above Gloria's, he wondered if her silence were not the expression of a world structurally different from his own, a mode of being which excluded fear, a rule by which each action should be self-contained and without consequences. But he could not convince himself that this was so. He'd come inside her; he'd stayed inside her; his sperm trickled in to irrigate her just as it

176

had into Luisa. The same dangers prevailed. How could she be so calm? Had she given herself so completely as to accept all the consequences of her submission? He was all at sea, in spite of his valiant efforts to anchor himself to the cabin, to the stretcher, to Gloria's body beneath him. His queries pulled him towards a desolate island where his every thought would be a torment. He was still inside her, but if he yielded to these insidious conjectures he'd soon come out willy-nilly, and then he'd have to stretch out alongside her and study her enigmatic repose. He began to move slowly caressing her face and feeling her breasts until he roused her from slumber if not from sleep.

He'd retraced his steps back from the point where he'd risked getting lost. Somewhere at the back of his mind he felt that some survival instinct should prevail upon him not to submit this time round, but to preserve and hold out as long as he possibly could. If he couldn't take her even by fear, the only alternative open to him was to fuddle her senses and force her to the conviction that no other man could ever give her such exclusive pleasure. The storm was beginning to well up through Gloria's repose. Something was exploding inside her and her world also was tumbling down. He made an enormous effort to resist being drawn into it and so to hold out until she lay quivering and shattered. He wondered vaguely whether this round would yield the desired effect or if Gloria would quickly regain her composure as she'd done before without, in fact, imploring him never to leave her—stay by me forever, marry me—without ever uttering all he hoped to hear and all he knew she'd never actually say. He lay breathless beside her and all she did was to look at him, sweet and satisfied, smiling as she'd never done before, her lips barely quivering. Gosh, she exclaimed, that was good, I feel great. What she said concerned only herself rather than him. But he wasn't disappointed; for somehow his love for her had begun to function like a corrosive agent, a solvent whose action would gradually change her nature

177

and accustom her to accepting not only the pleasure he gave but also his very self and all of him, with all his needs to escape from his own world and be with her and follow her when she left. He sat up and looked proudly at her naked body, her slacks at the foot of the stretcher and her raincoat that she hadn't taken off. It was as if he were examining the mortal remains of a defeated enemy strewn beneath his billowing victory banner. But Gloria, he considered, immediately refuting the image, behaves far too calmly and self-sufficiently to be the defeated enemy. He'd had other women besides her and Luisa, but no one had ever submitted with such calm, such disconcerting indifference. After all the other times he'd made love, after the cooling down from the usual frenzy, the significance of the act always began to graze the surface of his partners' consciousnesses through their physical calm, and they'd grown uneasy, even when he'd been quick to withdraw from them. Gloria was miles away from any such apprehension. She calmly sat up on the stretcher, her raincoat and cardigan slipping off her shoulders. Was the girl sterile? Couldn't she have children? He realised that she was still capable of eluding him and that the smallest, most unexpected circumstance might intervene to upset all his plans. He wanted to interrogate her, to ask her how she could be so self-assured, why she wasn't worried as all the others had been, and why, for heaven's sake, she couldn't forget herself for a second and devote a little time to soothing him and thus recognising the importance of what had just happened. But he couldn't bring himself to say a thing because he feared she might suddenly recall something that had not so far crossed her mind and go dashing off to the hotel before it was too late. Better let her linger in the languid memory of her pleasure. She was still there in flesh and blood. Perhaps this self-sufficiency which seemed to sustain her was but a front. It was so painful, though, to have no explicit reassurance, to have to continue waiting for a long, problematical flowering of which there was no guarantee anyway, and to be left with the prospect that their relationship might never be defined now, or that it might even change into something else or fizzle out completely. On the other hand, she had cried out; she had been his accomplice until that painful cry of love and even after that, as she'd murmured contentedly before lying back exhausted. Then that equivocal calm had reappeared, that obscure well-being that seemed to issue from some exclusive source of indifference. It had superimposed itself upon her previous excitement and now banished her to isolation. He had to realise that Gloria was insulated by a conscience completely different from his own, an enigmatic, foreign conscience that was totally invulnerable. It seemed that she could forget at the snap of her fingers all her love cries, all her clawing of his back, and the utter abandon which he'd induced in her. She could dismiss them as if they'd never happened. Was what had happened so very insignificant? Gloria was dressing. She pulled her slacks over her naked body and buttoned up her cardigan. She looked unsmilingly at him through the curtains of hair that fell over her face. Her eyes were still dilated and moist. She was beautiful. She was all the women he'd seen fleetingly from afar and all the women he'd ever imagined or wanted. Being with her now, watching her slowly dress, zip up her slacks and pull down her cardigan over the belt, and knowing that she'd just been his had the power to estrange him from himself and push him finally into a new dimension. What if you do have to go on waiting? He was determined to shake off his recent doubts. What if you're not certain of anything, not certain of her, not certain of how long it will last? This is just the beginning. There's plenty of time. So lay off. Be satisfied for now just to be with her in this beautiful deodorised world where you can at least breathe without suffocating. Suddenly Francesca began to laugh inside him; her scorn cut him to the quick. But, he pondered, I've settled my accounts with myself and I am what I am and I can't escape that. I have faults, I'm vile, I have warped ambitions, I know all this. I've heard it all before and you can't imagine how little I care. Gloria was beside him. She put her arms round his neck. She smiled and told him that she'd had a marvellous time and that he was good in bed. He wasn't her first man, she said, but never had she felt what she'd felt with him. There you are, he said to Francesca, don't you see how different it all is here, how it belies all you can say? He almost smiled with amusement, hearing her screech and clack about futilely in her slippers. Malicious bitch, he thought, but he couldn't get so worked up over her. He was just taking stock of the facts. Shall we go? Gloria asked. He opened the door and saw the sun, the rain-rinsed sky, and way off, the slowly pulverising clouds. The weather had changed but the beach was still deserted. The white figure of a life-guard stood out on the windy jetty. They crossed the wet sand over to the water's edge. Gloria had her arm round his waist and leaned her head on his shoulder. The life-guard greeted them as they passed. Mario looked at him and wondered what he would have said had he known that Mario had spent the night in the cabin and that she had joined him later. He chuckled and savoured the adventurous angles of the situation in spite of the tragic undertones. He might even tell Gloria that he'd been living in the cabin for the past two days without saying why; and if she asked why, he could always say because he wanted to be near her. Then he might find out if Gloria had been on the beach the night before. No, he couldn't do it. A kind of cautious reticence prevented him from revealing his secret to her. Fenzo might find out or might suspect if she made any allusion to it in his presence. But he could ask her what she'd done last night after he'd left her, without having to refer to the midnight party. Oh, nothing really, she answered. They'd danced, as usual, and then they'd gone to bed. He couldn't tell if she was hiding the episode of the beach from him or if such episodes were so habitual that they weren't worth mentioning. He didn't probe

180

further because it hardly mattered if she'd come out in the middle of the night to dance before everyone because he had, after all, had her afterwards and they were together now. Without realising what he was saying, he asked where her brother and his friends were now. They're probably asleep, she said, they couldn't have gone to bed much before three. Nor, she added mischievously, was anyone to wake them at dawn to make love. She was exaggerating, he said, it had been almost ten o'clock. Exactly! she said, at dawn. It was no chance reference he'd made to her brother; he was actually curious to find out how far Matteo's hostility had progressed. He had no illusions about it; he knew Matteo detested him as Alessandro had done. But now that the situation had come to a head and he'd drawn fresh strength from Gloria, he almost felt like a confrontation, like offering himself to Matteo's provocation and responding with malicious vigour. Gloria hadn't taken up his invitation to talk about her brother. She wasn't thinking about him, nor was she worried about explaining what he'd been doing. What marvellous weather, she said, and she drew closer to him as they walked into the wind. He was a bit dazed by this fresh proof of Gloria's freedom. The truth was that Gloria had done absolutely nothing that she need worry about. Giving herself to him meant nothing to her—it was perfectly all right, anyway, and at all events it was entirely her own affair. How different it all is, he thought, recalling Luisa. How much easier it is. He felt almost enviously resentful of Gloria as he observed his previous fears were slowly being confirmed. This carefree attitude and this way of being free and easy, unfettered by what could be regarded as a commitment, was proof of the moral imperturbability of Gloria's class. The diversity that divided them seemed to strike a new key. They have everything, he thought, even different laws, even different moral standards. What's bad for us is good for them, or insignificant. What tortures us amuses them. They speak the same words with entirely different meanings. Their

181

relations are governed by different rules. He was jealous and resentful. Devious thoughts assembled in his consciousness. He could intuit the infinite possibilities of Gloria's world and he realised that if he could manage to become part of that world he would become another man. If only he could manage. . . . It seemed so easy, but the requisite conditions, the essential qualities for psychological freedom were wealth, a long habit of ease, and above all, a tradition of having intercourse with people who measured life with the same yardstick. The same yardstick, he thought again. He looked for the right word, but couldn't find it. Illegal, he concluded, because Gloria, Matteo, and all the others resembled a clique of happy-go-lucky bandits. Envy and foreboding mingled with a sense of discomfort and joy. Gloria was his way out. Her wealth could sponsor him. The hotel was the entrance hall. He had to hold onto them tight and not let go. He had to preserve contact with them, pursue them, observe their every move, never let them out of sight and conquer them bit by bit even at the cost of stifling with the resentment he felt towards them. What about the others? Would they let him go about his business in peace? Certainly not. While he was sleeping in the cabin or continuing to withdraw from his home in search of greater security, while he was walking as he was now along the seashore with Gloria, all sorts of things were bound to be conspiring against him. Someone was trying to bind up his broken ties with Luisa; someone was patiently reweaving the web he'd seared. Francesca went to see Marco. Marco went to Fenzo's. And Fenzo, without realising what he was doing, or perhaps realising all too well, and maliciously determined to interfere in his relations with Gloria, told them where he was. A shiver swept down his spine. God, he thought, Marco might arrive on the scene any moment. He might be striding over the beach right now. Soon he might face him there where the first morning bathers were appearing on the beach while the air was still heavy from the rain. And when Marco, the unexpected hostile element, hurled himself upon him, he would close his eyes screaming inwardly, No, for God's sake, no, not here in front of her. He felt the old anxieties torment him again. Why didn't he forestall Marco's arrival by going out to meet him before fury made Marco track him down? Why hadn't he been on guard? Couldn't he have protected himself more carefully by somehow securing Fenzo's silence, or by isolating Gloria in some inaccessible place? It wasn't guilt or the need for expiation, but the law of his jungle. Until Gloria's world welcomed him into its sphere, he knew he would have to go on expiating the wrong he'd committed against Luisa. He'd known this all along. He could count on Marco coming after him—and it would be soon, today or tomorrow Marco would come or Francesca or someone in a position to demand an explanation. At this stage, after persistently evading all encounters with the slighted characters of his little drama, he could reasonably predict that the explanations would be demanded at the least opportune moment—when he was alone with Gloria, for instance. The law by which he lived was ruthless. Whosoever enforced it would follow a geometrically exact formula of obscure origin and bring disaster at the least foreseeable moment. If Gloria's world was permissive, indeterminate, autonomous, evasive, and lawless, his own was rational, petrified, confined by immoveable laws. His was a world without accidents in which even chance happenings were transformed into requisite consequences which in their turn were inevitably linked to a host of other events by an ironical, immutable, crazy chain of logic. Hadn't he already had more than sufficient proof of the negative, mock logic that governed his life? Didn't Luisa become pregnant just as he was about to meet Gloria? Hadn't he confronted Luisa at her most unprepossessing the very day of his first outing with Gloria? He wouldn't be at all surprised if Gloria's self-offering weren't countered the very same day with the most viciously cunning move dreamed up by that obscure negative power from which he was trying to flee. He looked anxiously about as the arm he had round Gloria's shoulders contracted in a nervous spasm. What's the matter? she asked, but he scarcely heard her. He'd shifted back to the moment before, when Marco had jumped him and he was falling now as Gloria shrieked his name and Marco's breath, words, and tears announced Luisa's death to him. He raised his head more out of entreaty than in defence, thinking, God, What am I doing? His knees dug into the wet sand, his heart ached, a heavy weight on his shoulder held him down. He sensed the absurdity and the unreality of it all, and the wind that carried weird sounds and the icy desperate certainty that Gloria was there. Gloria, he murmured to himself, Gloria. Oh, it's eleven, she said, I must get back. They'd gone quite far, he realised, coming down to earth. Time moved in a different orbit for them. They turned back towards the hotel. Gloria maintained her light-hearted pace, while he staggered out of the trauma which had just occurred in his mind and which might well really happen to him any moment. Unless Francesca had given up plotting his downfall, he wouldn't even be safe on the Lido, inside the hotel, or even in Gloria's arms. Any moment now Marco might be landing his forces on the Lido from one of the *vaporetti,* from an enemy man-o'war; he might mingle with the innocent crowds that flowed towards the beach, then slowly creep up on him and pounce upon him from behind. What would he do? How would he react to Marco's assault in Gloria's presence? But it was eleven and Marco would be on his boat laden with fruit for the market. He, too, had to reckon every day with that impersonal, mundane law that chose to ignore that his sister was in the hospital, that his heart was swollen with hatred, and he longed to head his boat out for the Lido. Perhaps Marco actually knew where he was and had decided that all he could do for the time being was to insult him from afar. Francesca wouldn't be able to do much either, unless she closed the shop to come after him. Francesca could do this, of course, but she wouldn't just yet, not to-day, anyway, not so soon; she was no doubt still hoping he'd return of his own accord, and she was willing to give him time, yes, please give him a few days to come round, after all, he's not that bad, you know, he'll come, don't you worry. He would too; he'd go and see Marco that evening just to anticipate his moves and avoid being discovered in his refuge. He'd tell him it was all quite futile and that would be the end of that. Now that he'd had Gloria, he would find it easier to measure up to him. He stroked her head grateful for the strength and the courage she gave him. He heard her laugh. It was a short, jarring, puzzling little laugh. He looked at her amazed as he always was when he discovered that Gloria's train of thought diverged from his own. Then he realised that she hadn't just laughed to herself, but at the approach of a young man, on the short side, all in grey with a bright fluttering tie whom he'd never seen. Gloria steered him towards the newcomer whom he heard announce as he approached that everyone was looking for her at the hotel. The man turned round as someone called, and waved at a girl a little way off in sweater and slacks; she stood between two cabins shouting something impatiently, something like hurry up, or what are you waiting for? And he heard Gloria shout back, I'm coming, hang on. His heart contracted with disbelief and surprise and visions of what might happen now. He felt Gloria's arms round his neck and her lips brush his cheek as she whispered sweet loving words in his ear, I must go now, my love, don't keep me, sweet terrible words, sweet faithless, incomprehensible words which left him speechless. Gloria was leaving him just to go off with her friends. She wouldn't take him with her. All that had gone on between them had come to nothing because she still kept him at arm's length. She would make him wait for her again as she'd done so often now; and this while just a second ago he'd been fool enough to think he'd never again be parted from her for so much as a minute. Don't go, he said hoarsely, stay with me. I can't, she said, they're waiting

185

for me. She broke away and joined the short man. When she was a little way off she turned as if to say something, but she simply smiled at him. He felt his strength drain at her sudden, unexpected departure. He didn't smile back, but shook his head sadly as if to say, what's happened? where are you going? Don't worry, she said with a fresh smile, don't worry, where do you think I'm going, wait a bit, I'll be right back. She might just as well have said nothing at all or have uttered other, incomprehensible words that didn't explain why she was leaving. She could have been saying just one word. She could have been saying something else, something plain and cruel and hard to believe, like for example, good-bye. Good-bye? What rubbish. She wouldn't have said good-bye like that—with a hurried embrace and a few whispered words and a smile. And she wouldn't be turning round once again before she disappeared beyond the cabins. He forced a smile over the panic she'd stirred. Just a few minutes, he thought, just enough to greet her friends, it wouldn't be long. It was odd how the beachscape and his heart seemed drained of something vitally necessary, as if they'd sprung a leak and a bit of their life leaked hissing away. A few moments before they'd been together, her arms fastened round his back in a close knot and here she was suddenly a mile off, discrediting all those past moments, as if they'd never happened, as if all the time they'd been in the cabin or walking along the beach the only effective reality was one he hadn't reckoned with, an obscure private anecdote at a certain point in which this unknown lad with a bright fluttering tie was to appear on the beach and she'd make off with him. Rubbish. She'd be right back and they'd walk on together or they'd sit down near the cabins, which were all one single cabin. Her private tale would be forgotten and they'd pick up their joint tale where they'd left off. He sat on the jetty, his legs dangling and his arms propping his torso from behind. A light wind still blew and up above the clouds were still dismantling. She'd be right back. Whether he liked it or not, though, he felt uprooted again, at the mercy of infinite possibilities regardless of the memories fresh in his mind and the recent sensation of possession and his hope of moving onto solid ground. Did he have a good grip on the life he wanted or could it still elude him? had he managed to obliterate one reality and submerge into another to be changed out of recognition, a man totally new to all who'd known him before? Not at all. As long as Gloria could leave him like this, he knew that nothing had changed, no conclusive event had come to uproot his existence, which remained the same as it had always been despite all his contact and involvement with Gloria. But even this wasn't true. His absurd resistance to her momentary abandonment and his sudden, reluctant solitude were responsible for returning him to his part and for the fragmentation of his future into the infinite variety of shapes offered by that speculative kaleidoscope that was his mind: Gloria would never come back; or, she'd return to say good-bye; or, perhaps she'd already said good-bye; or, she'd return to stay with him; but, if she came back, something would happen and she'd have to leave him; or he'd never see her again; or, if he did see her she'd be unapproachable; or, if she was approachable he wouldn't recognise her because she was actually someone else. Well then, he murmured, trying to dam the spate of his fantasy with an objective reconstruction of recent events, she's gone off for a moment with a friend, a totally innocuous fellow, and there's nothing so grave about that, she's probably on her way back already. He looked towards the hotel whose steps and glass entrance were visible from his position on the jetty. The entrance had swallowed her up, but the revolving doors would soon restore her to him. Time was passing, though, and there was nothing he could do if the moment when Gloria had been in his arms was receding into the distance, or if everyone, everyone in the world but Gloria came out of the hotel entrance, all sorts of people, unknown and well-known, flashing colours and gesticulations. It wasn't his

187

fault if terrible memories and an anguished wind that darkened the beach blew out of that hotel entrance as from some cavern in his consciousness. It was still too early to be alarmed. No one else would have tormented himself to such an extent over so short a separation. Yet he couldn't help suspecting that even if she were involved in his personal reality she nevertheless judged it in an entirely different way and might well be back in two hours or not at all, not all day, nor ever. This suspicion justified his disquiet, keeping it active despite the tranquilising replies of his wristwatch, which weren't so very comforting anyway. An hour had quickly passed; even if Gloria did return and explain her absence with mollifying arguments, she would never eradicate the painful, unalterable fact that she'd found it easy to go off at a certain point in their relations, at the very tensest moment perhaps—she'd gone off to rejoin her own kind and had had no difficulty staying away for an hour, two hours, three hours, forgetting him all that time and leaving him at the mercy of terrible memories, new gloomy presentiments which entered his heart through that whirling glass door of the hotel. Presentiments and memories, shapeless possibilities, possible events, contradictory and conflicting intuitions accumulated within him like a tree latticed with a million boughs. Had Gloria remained with him, there would have been only the one branch to follow, the one offshoot in a single direction, a single fate. Gloria was with me, she loves me, he repeated, trying to return to the objective order of events. We left the cabin and strolled for a while. Then her friends came after her and she went away for a moment after saying good-bye so sweetly. And now I'm waiting for her. But his efforts to keep his hands on the moment she'd left him were useless; as the minutes passed, time became confused. The curve of his day, which had seemed assured and predictable from its basic premises, was obscured like a rainbow lopped off by clouds. He couldn't be sure of anything, until he saw her again. He jumped up and headed towards the

188

hotel. Gloria alone could tell him where he stood, where he would go from there, which way his life would move, because his life now depended on her.

He walked towards the hotel, retracing Gloria's footsteps. In a rapid, painful process of identification and in spite of himself, he became Gloria—Gloria, who was leaving him at the side of that fellow dressed in grey, entering the hotel, going up to her room, or stopping in the lounge where her friends were waiting for her. What then? He was back at the starting point again, a little nearer the hotel, because he couldn't imagine what had delayed her for so long. He couldn't see her any more and he'd lost track of her mental process. He was inside the hotel now, in the lounge. He asked a waiter if he'd seen Gloria, and the waiter, maybe the same one as before, invited him to step through the variegated crowd to the hotel desk. As he threaded his way to the point indicated, he confirmed that she wasn't about. He approached the mahogany counter, cluttered with registers, bells, shuffling hands, naked arms, tanned, ringed fingers, and heard himself ask for Gloria; he noted the clerk's grin behind the counter and the hand that lifted the receiver then lowered it after a long useless ring. He left the hotel cursing her. He floundered once more in the dark shapeless sea of possibilities to which Gloria had relegated him. God, what can she be doing? where has she got to? Suddenly, as he approached the cabin, his one reliable point of reference, he noticed that two attendants had opened its doors and were sweeping out the surprisingly empty, cavernous interior, obliterating all traces of Gloria's and her brother's presence, as if preparing the cabin for other occupants. His heart began to beat furiously. Are they leaving? he stammered. They must have left by now, one of them replied. And the other voice sounded vague and muffled in his ear, as though it came from outer space. But they were still at the hotel a little while ago. He stared at them blankly. It can't be, this couldn't happen. When they said, in answer to another stammering question, that the hiring of the cabin had been cancelled today or yesterday, one or the other, he felt a foretaste of defeat, of finality, mingled with disbelief and dismay. Good God, he thought, it can't be. He was incredulous more than shocked, because somewhere at the back of his mind he'd already begun to fear that she might abandon him; he'd had inklings of disaster the moment he saw her walk off with that young man in grey. There was something about the way Gloria had said good-bye—something ambiguous. I must go, please don't keep me. It had been a good-bye that was both temporary and final. Now that he'd discovered its essence, he was more incredulous than shocked. He couldn't believe it was possible. Good God, had that really been good-bye? had she all along been planning to leave? he could understand that she might be away from him for a good while after the man in grey came to fetch her; he could even conceive of her forgetting about him for an hour or two; but he just couldn't believe that she'd planned to leave without saying anything, or that she'd given herself to him in the tacit knowledge that she was about to leave. Hadn't it been an effort to break away without a word? was he so unimportant to her? were the mysterious, unknown circumstances of her departure and the even more mysterious unknown reasons which had provoked it the only considerations worthy of her attention? He remembered how she'd been after making love, totally self-composed, totally unapprehensive. He once more found himself faced with a world that eluded his grasp, with a conscience diametrically opposed to his. Gloria could drop him without a wince because she'd come to him without any need for him. What did it matter if they'd gone to bed together? He'd never got anywhere near her intimacy. She'd remained sealed within herself. If now she was able to evade him, as though he'd never existed, then he truly hadn't existed for her. He'd meant nothing to her and all the loving words, all her love had had no object. Even that last embrace, which he'd felt through the length of his body, had been a vacant gesture.

190

She'd embraced the nonentity that he was. He felt the
disparaging blow of her departure and the offence it
implied. Accidental or deliberate, planned or decided at
the last moment, her departure amounted to a rejection.
She was immediately deprived of all the qualities which
had made her attractive to him and she joined the ranks
of Matteo, Alessandro, Luisa, his mother, and anyone else
who denied him his freedom. She was reduced to being
another hateful face of the enemy. He just hated her now.
As he stood staring at the two men at work, he howled
inwardly with the same intensity with which he'd longed
for her, you bitch, you filthy whore, damn your eyes. He
had nothing now on which his hatred could get a
purchase; he had nothing beyond himself, nothing with
which to ward off his enemies. It had been easier to fight
them off before, with Gloria at his side, but now that she'd
abandoned him, now that she'd crossed over into the
enemy camp to join in the general plot against him, his
inimical conspirators had become infinitely powerful. He
was drowning in his solitude. He grasped desperately at
the hope that she hadn't left yet; he had to see her again,
to talk to her, to make an attempt, at least, to stop her
leaving. No explanation she might have offered, he thought
distractedly, could be as cruel as this silent desertion. He
had to see her, to talk to her. He left the cabin and ran
over the moist sand. He was determined to do something
about it. He wouldn't go to the hotel; he'd phone from
the nearest bar. The beach was beginning to come alive as
it did every morning. A girl in a bikini, a restful sight
he'd seen a thousand times before, unfolded a deck chair
and stretched out in the sun. Someone ran shouting down
to the shore. For a moment as he approached the bar, he
seemed to be functioning in another time zone, where
nothing had happened yet, where Gloria was with him
and the day had not yet begun. Perhaps everything would
revert back to its previous form, perhaps she'd smile with
amusement at his suspicions or gaze at him serenely saying, you're out of your mind, darling. I love you. But her

191

cabin behind him was growing more and more empty. Everything that had been carried out from it started to pile up willy nilly on some other part of the beach, in some other area of his heart. The fact was he'd come to the bar to phone out of sheer desperation. Answer me, Gloria, he implored, you can't leave without seeing me, your departure doesn't make sense. He could hear himself asking for her. A brittle clack, a buzz, then a throaty trill like that of a distant cricket that began to sing in her room. The trill rose to the ceiling, reverberated round the walls, rolled over the bed, which was probably still unmade, and sizzled venomously throughout the deserted room. There's no reply, a voice said. She hasn't gone, has she? he bellowed, is she still staying there? A pause followed at the other end of the line, while a distant, spasmodic buzz of information was exchanged, oh, yes, and the young lady? . . . ahah . . . then the voice drew into the foreground again, they've left the hotel, yes, just a little while ago. Before he could formulate another question a gloomy, inert silence blacked him out. She'd left, she'd gone. The sun caught him in the eye through the plate glass windows of the bar and blinded him. A group, two men, two women, passed by outside, strolling along the cement paving. Everything seemed so familiar, so peaceful, so habitual. The image the world held up remained the same; only he'd changed and Gloria, who was lost in the mystery of her departure. Unless of course she hadn't really left, he thought with a start, unless she's only left the hotel and returned to the beach by Fenzo's cabin. He tore out of the bar and retraced his steps. He wondered if the decision to leave the beach hadn't been Gloria's but her brother's, and if she hadn't hurried back to tell him not to worry, that she would never leave him. But she wasn't there. The cabin was shut, there was no escaping the conclusions at which he'd previously arrived and which he'd refused to accept at the time: she'd left him, he'd never see her again. Were he to see her now, he would crush her with all his pain, with all the fury and bitterness he'd felt when he'd seen the cabin cleared out. How could she have left him? What had escaped his notice? What aspects of her character had he ignored? How could he not have foreseen her departure? What crucial indications had he overlooked? If there had been any logic or at least an inertial continuity to the things she'd done and to the words she'd whispered before leaving, she would by rights be with him now, a bit uncertain perhaps, a bit diffident, but nevertheless she'd be beside him and not totally lost and gone forever. What could have happened? Had her brother put his foot down? or was it she who'd decided to leave him after reaching the conclusion that she wouldn't be able to sustain a lasting relationship with him? But then why the hell had she given herself to him in the first place? Suddenly the cabin incident in the grey hours of the morning lost all the significance he'd attributed to it, lost the only meaning that had plausibility up to now and began to take on a thousand different meanings equally plausible: Gloria went to bed with him without loving him; she'd done it to gratify a passing fancy and had immediately put him out of her mind; or, Gloria went to bed with him, had loved him to a point, but not beyond the point where she felt tied or in danger of losing her freedom, which she intended keeping anyway; or, Gloria hadn't gone to bed with him at all, but had taken him to bed with her so she could dispense with him at will; or, she'd jumped into bed with complete equality of rights and responsibilities, and as she asked nothing of him and needed no one, she could act under the assumption that he didn't need her and she could opt out whenever it suited her; or, she went to bed with him by way of a conclusion to their romance, knowing that she'd never see him again; or . . . As he wandered back to the hotel like a zombie, still hoping unconsciously he'd run into her, he tried to retrace the course she'd followed after leaving him, and with a jolt he came first upon Matteo; Matteo, who had seen them from the hotel lounge or from his room as they'd walked along the shore; he'd been waiting

193

for her and when he saw her he'd rained a torrent of abuse and insult upon her, or he'd coldly informed her that he'd decided to leave and that she was going with him. His posture may have reminded her of the lecture he'd read her a couple of days earlier and she answered, all right, you needn't go on, I'll come, it's all over. She'd been his but a few minutes ago, true enough, but their relationship was too tenuous to have continued. She didn't even feel obliged to tell him she was going; she didn't even have to worry about what would happen inside her violated womb. There's always a remedy for such things, for Christ's sake. Saying good-bye would have been too awkward and embarrassing; better be gone without more ado. Nothing had happened that couldn't be remedied by avoiding any further contact with him, by going back home, in fact. What about him?—oh he would soon be forgotten, all she'd need do now was avoid exposure to his entreaties, hide when he looked for her and refuse to answer the phone if he called. Besides, it was all over and done with, finito. Was this all she'd been then? Only this? Or was she crying her heart out wherever she was, calling him softly, or fighting her brother to let her return to him? Some hope!—Gloria had known full well that she was leaving him when her friends came to fetch her. No one had forced her. She'd already known when she'd come down from her room to join him in the cabin. Perhaps she'd known from the very start, when they'd met in Venice, or even earlier, when she'd stretched out her arm to stroke his back on the boat. How ridiculous it all seemed now. His conjectures on his fascination, his presumption of being able to free himself from his past all seemed quite insane, utterly irrelevant now. What was he going to do? go back home? would he resume the life he'd interrupted a few days before? He felt himself yielding, surrendering, sliding back into the wreckage of his hopes. He couldn't even discard the old contentions which he'd thought he'd long since resolved; extinct possibilities revived and ironically returned for redefinition.

He was still waiting for Luisa on the bridge. She came along the *fondamenta* bearing the secret in her stomach. He couldn't breathe : his mouth was stuffed with swabs of cotton wool, his nostrils were choked with camphor. He was in Francesca's shop and at the hospital and in Luisa's room, pregnant with Luisa. He was assuring her relations, Here I am, you see, I've come to stay with her now. Everything was changed. Time was in a tangle as though some monstrous finger had mischievously muddled all the threads. He needed desperately to tether himself to something certain; he sought to retrieve the man who'd been walking securely along the sands with his woman. But time was irretrievable, centuries had passed, confused centuries of horror. What shall I do? he wondered. His specular image faded out in wavering distortions as if a flood of water washed over it intermittently and he was powerless to halt the process. An infinite sense of angry frustration and his own ridiculousness fogged his mind.

He stood on the steps of the *Excelsior* again. They were quite dry and swarming with the holiday crowd. He looked out for Gloria but, those moments when he felt he still might see her, and he pictured her coming towards him, he saw her pass by without looking at him, or look at him from a great distance, from where she'd been when she'd left him. Now he seemed to understand her thoughts and he felt furious, impotently furious. What about us then? he wanted to yell at her, what about you and me? what about this morning? didn't we give all we had? so isn't parting insane? She shook her head; Why? she smiled with that same cool serenity that had frightened him so often, what we shared wasn't that important. An indefinite, horrifying image began to take shape in his mind, something like a mongrel, some creature scratching whining on a shut door; he recognised it before he could distinguish it clearly, it was the image of his failure, of his solitude which would soon erupt within him. Gloria had left him. He had to convince himself. He didn't have to see her and hear her say he'd lost her. The beach atten-

dants had given him sufficient evidence; they'd been the
unconscious instruments of his destruction, obliterating all
trace of her from the cabin, the lilos, the clothing, the
blue-green bikini, her very thoughts of him. She'd wished
that destruction. She'd witnessed it with serene approval,
damn her. He knew he'd lost her, and yet he kept on
talking to her. You can't, he faltered, after all that's
happened, you can't leave without a word, were we never
even friends? was there nothing between us? was there no
communication? nothing then? nothing but the dermal
contact of our bodies? don't you remember? I went inside
you, your body now carries a part of me, your body is like
the bodies of all the other women I've had, they've
remained attached to me ages after, even now they're close
to me. She didn't answer, she was miles away from the
world to which she'd so imprudently and so briefly lent
herself. She'd lent herself, a loan, a momentary shift of
axis, not long enough to induce the merest loss of balance,
a short-lived, abstracted exploration of another world.
Then her own past reclaimed her. A man in grey with a
flapping tie had come to fetch her. She'd gone off with
him and painlessly concluded her sortie into alien territory.
She'd gone to resume the course of her life, which she'd
never really interrupted—a life which had never lost its
integrity even when it had momentarily fused itself with
his. My life, he thought emotionally, my permanent miserable condition. There was something he could salvage,
something to be proud of : he'd stirred a deep love within
her. Consciously or unconsciously, he'd mythicised his
relations with Gloria all out of proportion with reality, and
he'd never once tried to control it. All that remained was
the exertion of a long and fruitless exercise. What triumphant laughter would erupt from Francesca, I told you
so, it's always the same, can't you be original for a change?
it's happened so often, and down you flop every time you
try to rise above yourself. The distorting lens of his desperation had projected an image of Gloria which had nothing
to do with reality. In spite of all the danger signals, she'd

become his salvation, a plot of promised land to be pursued rabidly and at any cost. No, she was really something quite different. His hopes of remaking himself through her had nothing to do with her at all, nor did the breadth of emotions he'd conveniently attributed to her, nor the positive motives he'd read into everything she'd done. The application of a faultless lens to the reality of Gloria had pulled her into sharp focus, producing her true likeness from the blurred images he'd had of her, revealing a fleeing prey. Had she suffered at all in leaving him? had she felt any of the pain or the alarm or the regret he'd undergone when he'd felt obliged to abandon Luisa? Not at all. In some mysterious way she seemed to be naturally cruel, to be able to rid herself of him without any anguish or melodrama, as if the same power that guarded her class from all intruders also defended it from the interferences of conscience. He felt her last embrace again. I must go now, my love, don't keep me. He remembered the strange fears he'd felt, the presentiment that she'd never return. He had rolled back a few hours; he was down by the sea with the wind still blowing and the smell of recent rain and the short young man in grey appeared. Gloria broke away from him. He watched her move away from him beside the newcomer, turning to wave, passing the row of cabins, walking up the steps to the hotel entrance. He followed her up the steps as if trying to catch up with her to ask if she wasn't sorry, just a little sorry. As she prepared to step out of his life, he suddenly stepped out of his consciousness into the real, tangible presence of two tall female figures leaning against the door of the hotel, that very same glass door. He met the gaze of two dark eyes that studied him, smiling beneath a curtain of wavering hair. The memory of Gloria returned and the smile waned. But as he tried to resume his mute dialogue with Gloria, his head downcast, his back to the balustrade, and asked her, doesn't it matter to you at all? not even a tiny bit? and as he felt only the bitter residue of her departure, he caught himself

197

wondering what that smile had meant, what had instigated it and what had caused that lock of hair to stir. He wanted to express his pain, his frustration at their abortive meeting, but beneath this he felt an old emotion : his heart beat faster somehow stimulated by the inquisitive presence of the two tall female figures. It wasn't quite an awareness of them, but a sudden, illuminating intuition, akin to a faint, distant tremor of relief. He looked up again towards the glass door, and the smile that flickered through the dark cascade of hair lit up and died in a flash like a flutter of wings. As the girl turned her head, as if to hide her embarrassment, he felt as though something new had happened. He was telling Gloria to go then, because if she found it that easy to leave him, he'd just as soon leave her and have nothing more to do with her. He felt vaguely that he'd already lived this moment when he'd first encountered Gloria's smile through the indifference and the hostility of Alessandro and Matteo. Gloria sank in his heart, oblivious of the grimace that accompanied his last effort to wound her by brandishing the inert weapon of memory, recalling to her all that had gone on in the cabin a short while ago, her cries, her nakedness, her avid body spread-eagled. Simultaneous with this mental progress the two tall female figures beside him began to move towards the door just as he lifted his gaze to catch sight of that head again and its dark eyes that darted towards him with the faint smile on its lips—a fleeting, sweet, overpowering smile which miraculously absorbed his gaze. Who could it be? he asked, who is it? And before the hotel engulfed her, he caught another glimpse of her through the revolving glass door, a gleam in her smiling dark eyes, perhaps the hint of a wave.

HE WAS ALONE, drained and weary as if he'd just
returned from a long hike. He sat down before Fenzo's
empty cabin, next to the cabin Gloria had occupied. It,
too, was deserted, abandoned. He was still fully conscious
of the absurd and incredible angle of this precipitous
disaster which had served as epilogue to his affair with
Gloria. He wanted to cry, to swear, to entreat someone,
anyone, and find out why life had it in for him. He
returned to his previous considerations. All of his deal-
ings with Gloria, from the very beginning, had to be
reviewed in the light of her departure. He'd barely scraped
the surface of her life. He'd never really had her; even
when he thought he was really possessing her, she'd been
far away and safe in that remote natural habitat that
was hers. He'd been left outside, as something different,
alone outside her door, outside a slippery blank wall. Her
essence had remained alien to him. His doubts and his
suspicions of her non-committal participation had been
forced down whenever she'd been a physically immediate
reality; when they had walked to the beach entrance together, his arm round her shoulders, when they'd met in
Venice, when she'd given herself to him in Fenzo's cabin,
how could he have been suspicious before such seductive
distractions? He would have had to be impossibly cool
and level-headed to have calculated his every move in
the light of his suspicions and to have been a monster
of equanimity to consider the physical side of their
relationship as merely deceptive. He'd never possessed
this sort of self-control; he'd never been able to exert it to
banish Luisa's haunting intrusions. That was it—it was
she who'd chased Gloria away, he thought with the excitement of someone who is about to see the light, which was

still tantalisingly out of sight. When Gloria had embraced him, she hadn't only embraced him, but also Luisa, who'd been with him all along. Gloria had sensed her sick, swollen stomach and her whining voice whispering desperately. Maybe he had meant something to Gloria after all. She may have loved him to the extent of realising that she couldn't love Luisa and Francesca and his mother as well. His painful intuitions of Gloria's secret reservations, of her panic that she might discover a world too alien from her own if she were to get more involved hadn't been so far out then. He was almost convinced now. Her presentiment of that world had induced her to hold back and cling to those precepts which excluded him, to that safe and familiar world she couldn't possibly share with him. She'd always been afraid of what lurked behind his façade. She'd given herself to the façade and fled before having to witness its collapse under the crashing blow of the reality that stirred behind it. Had he had more time he might have insinuated himself into her so many times as to feel her stomach swell, puff up, befoul and deform itself irremediably; but he hadn't had the time. Luisa had interceded—or rather, Gloria had intuited her dull wounding presence within him. He couldn't rule out the possibility of Luisa's direct interference either. It was easy to reconstruct Gloria's movements after leaving him in the light of this new painful realisation. He could see them as predestined by distant powers radiating from that axis of his predestination : She doesn't know me, but I know about her relations with Mario and I'm going to warn her, he's a cad, his woman is expecting a child and she tried to kill herself because he was going to leave her. Gloria listened to the voice on the phone; she tried to break off but the voice on the other end rose to a hoarse, stuttering, desperately sincere and authoritative pitch. She listened stiffly to the exposition that laid him bare and defenceless. It was all so possible, so very probable, especially if Fenzo had told Francesca Gloria's name. He could just imagine Francesca's sadistic pleasure in destroying him, and he could visualise Gloria's steely cold compliance, It's very kind of you, I'm sure, but this really doesn't concern me, there's absolutely nothing between me and. . . . She wouldn't even mention his name. Good-bye. Then Gloria would quickly size up the situation and decide to get out of it by leaving. Is this what had happened? just like this? or had Gloria simply left without external intervention but rather of her own free will, having coolly decided to be rid of him as quickly as possible? He realised sadly that he would never know what had happened; it was too late to know what had happened. The only alternative was to choose the most plausible explanation for her departure. He would be destined to suspect ever more that he had deceived himself into choosing the least painful explanation, but he might be able to dispel this suspicion by recalling that she had really been with him, she had really given herself, she had actually revealed. . . . On the other hand, he thought as his frenzy revived, why should he believe in this particular group of causes of destruction which drained every moment of any significance and blasted every episode, even the cabin one, to bits? why, for heaven's sake, should he give up so easily and accept her flight as a natural consequence of their relationship when he knew he'd never been alone with her, never for a minute, that he'd always been haunted by Luisa? His head was bursting with the incessant recirculation of the same ideas. But something new was rising within him, a new, active form of resistance, a violently angry desire to send everyone to hell which brought with it a bizarre sensation of appeasement. Apart from his recent failure, he had the sensation that things had changed somewhat during the last few days and that the situation was looking up a little. Luisa's terrible retaliation and the long-awaited counter-attack had already taken place. The world he'd betrayed had mysteriously revealed itself to Gloria, had provoked her flight, thus wreaking its vengeance upon him. No one could claim he hadn't paid his dues. He didn't feel obliged to Luisa. She had cannibalistically devoured enough of him to compensate both for her wounds and for her child. Something positive was emerging from the asphyxiating circumstances of these days: we're quits, he thought, ever more convinced of having unearthed the true reasons for Gloria's flight. I don't owe you anything any more and I am no longer going to be remorseful or anxious or frightened. Never more would he be afraid of the protagonists of his world. Gloria may be gone, but it didn't necessarily follow that he had to be stuck with Luisa. Gloria's departure, which still hurt him, had the effect of thrusting Luisa away from him, of consigning her to the category of problems solved in an indifferent memory zone. Had he been capable of foreseeing that Gloria's departure could actually have a stabilising effect, he would have spared himself the tormenting experience of exposing himself in Luisa's room to the mercy of her relations, but this experience, along with Gloria's incredibly swift metamorphosis, the pain he'd felt on hearing her phone ring uselessly through her room, and the insulting haste of her departure all belonged on his score with Luisa. He was reasonably convinced that even if he'd hurt Luisa, so had she him—differently, perhaps, certainly less conspicuously and with less fuss and remorse, but nevertheless just as cripplingly. She'd been the cause of acute pain and sorrow which had disturbed him mentally and emotionally. How he hated her. How he hated her tenacity, her voracious determination to destroy him. Now that she had learned of the outcome, she was probably putting her feet up for the first time feeling satisfied and spent, as if she'd just been to a banquet. It was all her fault. If it hadn't been for her, he could easily have managed to hide his situation by pretending either to care not a damn, or even to be positively proud of it. He would at least have had time to lay waste the last bastions of Gloria's resistance. But no, she'd gone to all lengths to make herself noticed: Look I'm here, he's not so fancy-free and free of cares, I'm here too, look at me. Eventually Gloria had heard her voice and then seen her break in

202

triumphantly upon his life. It was therefore logical to conclude that none of this would have happened had it not been for Luisa. Gloria's flight wasn't his fault but Luisa's fault and the fault of all those who'd helped her, Marco's fault, Francesca's fault and his mother's fault, too. Gloria had run from them, not him. He'd had nothing whatever to do with this disastrous epilogue. He, the tall, agile, bronzed youth whom Gloria had known and loved a while, would have triumphed but for their intervention. Now they'd gone, disappeared into thin air, evaporated, banished by Gloria's departure. He was alone, without past, with nothing to conceal, no one to put a spoke in his wheel. He was simply a tanned, tall, dark and handsome young man getting up from a deck chair to walk along the sand, not quite sure of his destination but sure that he wasn't returning home to his mother that evening, because quite simply he had no home and he had no mother. He didn't need to plan his immediate future whose hours and days were still covered by the patrolman's money; nor would he worry now over the many unpredictable hazards that could still arise. He was there at the *Excelsior,* the nerve centre of his aspirations, willing and able as ever to participate in anything which might happen. He was even more ready and willing than before, for he was free without a care in the world. Francesca, the lunatic crystal-gazer, had read his fortune and read it wrong. Even if he had to admit to an unwitting propensity to distort reality, he must not underestimate himself; for if Gloria had ultimately felt contaminated, through no fault of his own, the fact remained that he'd first possessed her—proof that there were some grounds for his presumption that he might actually belong to her race. And further confirmation had been offered by that pair of dark appraising eyes and by that fleeting smile which had renominated him to Gloria's world after her departure had temporarily disqualified him. This thrilled him. Out of his previous bitterness emerged that fleeting smile, that ironical but promising and naughty laughter-bearing smile and that wink of complicity and encouragement. He revoked his last meeting with Gloria between the two waiting female figures and he realised that perhaps nothing had finished, that he could take up where he'd left off living, perhaps at a slight and insignificant handicap. He had only to fill the gap left by one who'd been too weak to accept him. This was within the realm of probability as Gloria's departure coincided with the other's arrival— excelling Gloria's calibre and easier to conquer. He could easily put Gloria aside and pick up where he'd left off with this smiling girl who may also have waved at him. He could ask her to take him back into the territory from which he'd just been expelled. Gloria wasn't the only girl on the far side of that invisible frontier : there was this girl, there was Elena, there were a thousand girls who would want him as much as Gloria had. There were a thousand cabins next to Fenzo's, a thousand hands eager to caress his back, a thousand hotels by the sea. The lump in his throat was melting, as he realised he could still forge ahead, persevere, cling to the old certainties, never say die. Or was it not at him at all that she'd been smiling? He looked round. The beach was quite oblivious of his restless presence. It swarmed with a thousand possibilities which lay indifferently at his disposal. It could all begin again in the shadow of the *Excelsior,* amid the browned bodies stretched out by the sea and the gaily coloured cabins. Above all, he must meet that girl again, catch her eye, strut and preen himself before her. If he saw the same light in her eye, he might whisper darling to her. He didn't know her name. He could pursue her as he'd pursued Gloria. He would trace the pattern of her movements. He would overtake her and take refuge in her. From that time forward he would live only through the eyes of those admirers who wouldn't devour him or hurt him, in eyes such as hers in which he caught a glimpse of his own image as if reflected in a mirror, a delicate, loving accomplice who would protect him from the treachery and the offensive indifference of all other eyes.

He started running towards the *Excelsior*. The movement
on the steps was as before: colourful figures going up and
down and the glass door revolved upon its axis, winking
blindingly in the sun. He had to find her; he had to see
her; he had to look in her eyes to see if he could trust her,
Where are you? where did you go? please come back,
don't stay away too long, don't keep me waiting. He ran
up the steps, glancing feverishly round the terrace for that
tall, curved, female silhouette. He pushed almost auto-
matically through the door round which she'd disappeared.
He zigzagged between the tables and the armchairs in the
lounge, round the archways and round the cool whispering corners without a thought of what he'd do if he
found her, thinking of nothing but the eyes that would
smile at him and say so many things—you're right, you
haven't made a mistake, I do really like you, follow me,
don't be afraid, I'll never find out about you, there's nothing to find out, and even if Marco or Francesca or Luisa
come after you—because you know they'll come, don't
you?—it doesn't matter. I do like you, it will be easy to
love you. Darling, darling, he thought, convinced that no
matter where she went, she would bear his image with
her. She would see his graceful bronzed figure on the steps
of the *Excelsior*; she would try to recall the precise moment
when their eyes had met. She was coming back for him
from wherever she was, she was opening the door which
Gloria had just shut. He began to move towards her,
leaping over the intervening hours, climbing the fence
between the street and the dark beach, entering the sea,
living another night in the warm silence of the cabin, and
returning the next day to where she'd first set eyes on
him—that graceful bronzed figure on the steps of the
Excelsior.

1ˢᵗ n⁵

4

ACE OF DIAMONDS

MARK SCHORR

Author OF
Red Diamond: Private Eye

St. Martin's Press
New York

ACE OF DIAMONDS. Copyright © 1984 by Mark Schorr. All rights reserved. Printed in the United States of America. No part of this book may be used or reproduced in any manner whatsoever without written permission except in the case of brief quotations embodied in critical articles or reviews. For information, address St. Martin's Press, 175 Fifth Avenue, New York, N.Y. 10010.

Library of Congress Cataloging in Publication Data
Schorr, Mark.
  Ace of diamonds.
I. Title.
PS3537.C598A64 1984   813'.52   83-23119
ISBN 0-312-00260-2

First Edition
10 9 8 7 6 5 4 3 2 1

To black dogs and
the woman of many names

ACE OF DIAMONDS

1

"I don't feel that we're making any progress," the portly psychiatrist said, gnawing the stem of his pipe.

"Why is that, doc?" the man on the leather couch asked.

"I'm not sure, perhaps it's because . . . " The psychiatrist paused. "There you go again, asking the questions. I ask the questions. You probe your psyche for the answers."

"I don't probe my psyche. The last time I had my psyche probed was in the service, and the guy was wearing a rubber on his finger."

The frustrated doctor got up and took fresh tobacco out of an ornate cut glass jar on his desk. He tamped the tobacco into the pipe, dribbling a few bits on the carpeted floor.

"I've been doing this for fifteen years," the psychiatrist said. "Everyone has responded to some form of treatment. Gestalt. Jungian. Primal. Even Freudian. Your psychosis is deeper than anything I've ever encountered."

"Is something else bothering you, doc? You're acting like a guy expecting his first kid."

"Mr. Jaffe. We must come to an understanding. We're here to discuss your problems, not mine."

"I got two problems, and I told you about them already," the man on the couch said patiently. "I need to find my gal, Fifi La Roche. And I need to get my hands on a mug named Rocco Rico. Fifi I'm gonna marry. Rocco I'm gonna kill. Simple enough?"

"Mr. Jaffe, you must realize—"

"I realize all I gotta realize. And my name's not Jaffe. It's Red Diamond."

"That is your problem. You are not Red Diamond. You are Simon Jaffe. You are not a private eye. You are a cab driver."

Diamond sat up, lit himself a cigarette, and stared skeptically at the doctor. He snorted, lifted his six-foot, 200-plus-pound body up, and headed toward the door.

"Where are you going?" the psychiatrist demanded.

"I got better things to do than listen to the same old story out of you. I been coming to you a dozen times and we always go running around the same track."

"Do I need to remind you that the District Attorney dropped the charges on those homicides in return for your getting counseling?"

"It was only a recommendation. The charges had already been dropped. And I was just coming to you to make it easier for me to get my ticket back."

"Ticket?"

"My license. Those bureaucrats up in Sacramento said they couldn't find any record of a license under my name. And shooting all those people didn't make me popular with the pencil pushers."

"What about the homicides? Do you feel any remorse?"

"The bums deserved to die. And I don't like the D.A. sending me to get my head shrunk after I was cleared on the beef."

"Whether you like it or not doesn't matter. You and your attorneys agreed to it. And I'm sure the District

2

Attorney will be very displeased if I have to notify him that you've ended treatment."

"I wouldn't want to make the D.A. upset," Diamond said sarcastically. "He might be so broken up he couldn't run for the Senate."

"It doesn't seem so tough, your coming in and talking to me," the psychiatrist said. He pointed to the couch with his pipe. "Please have a seat. You have fifteen more minutes."

Diamond returned to the couch. He grumbled and sat down.

"Let's confront the facts head on," the doctor said. "You are forty-three years old, you agree?"

"And feeling every day of it."

"Very well. Now you claim you began your chase of this Rocco Rico person in 1938?"

"Yeah. And I met Fifi the same year. It was a helluva time. Rocco was wearing a black silk suit, a white tie and a scowl. The suit was nice. His face wasn't. Especially after I busted up his fruit cart extortion racket pretty good. He wanted his boys to bust me up even better. I showed them. They tried—"

"I've heard this story several times. Now the point is—"

"And Fifi. She was working in that club he owned. Called herself a chanteuse. A voice like a warm summer night. A body that sent the mercury right out of the thermometer. All the guys wanted her. Rocco thought he owned her. But then . . . "

"The point is, if you're forty-three, you were born in 1941. Therefore this supposed adventure took place three years before you were born."

Diamond felt the throbbing begin. "Don't try and trick me," he said, pressing his hands against his temples.

3

"I'm not trying to trick you. I'm trying to help you. We must break through these barriers you've erected. Does your head hurt?"

"Just a migraine. Comes from going to a head-shrinker."

"I want to help you but you keep resisting."

The pounding was growing worse. Native drums beating while elephants jitterbugged on his skull. Get Johnny Weismuller to call them off. Diamond felt dizzy.

"I . . . am . . . Red . . . Diamond."

The psychiatrist hesitated as Diamond grew pale.

"We'll slow down a bit," the doctor said. "Let's assume you are Red Diamond. Let's try some word associations."

The pounding was still fierce, but it had stopped getting worse. Diamond tried focusing on the plaques and diplomas that covered the doctor's wood-paneled walls.

"Shoot," Diamond said.

The doctor took out a small notepad. "Green?"

"Money."

"Black?"

"Mail."

"Male?"

"Mail. Blackmail."

"Red?"

"Blood."

"Wife?"

"Beater."

"Home?"

Diamond paused and lit a cigarette.

"Home?" the psychiatrist repeated.

"Most accidents occur there."

"Family?"

"Feud."

"Car?"

4

"Crash."

"Love?"

"Death."

The psychiatrist sighed. "Your responses are extremely violence-oriented. Let's explore that."

Diamond had regained his composure. "No surprise. I deal in murder, mayhem. I do people's dirty laundry for them. Make sure it doesn't get hung out for the world to see. I'm a shamus. If I was a gardener I could tell you about petunias. Because I'm a dick I can tell you about twists on a bullet or how to kill someone so the coroner don't know it's murder."

"You call yourself a dick. Is your masculine identity tied up in your role?"

"If I call myself a private eye, you gonna think I'm a Peeping Tom?"

"You're asking questions again."

"They're better than the questions you ask. That's what I do for a living. I ask questions until I get the answers no one wants to hear. A great job if you like seeing people at their worst."

"Then why do you do it? Do you feel a need to prove you're better than everyone else?"

"I do it because it's the right thing to do. Half the time I don't even get paid. I'm there to make sure the system works. When the cops screw up and the bad guy gets away, someone's got to clean up the mess. I'm the guy that follows the horses in the parade and cleans up the stuff they leave behind."

"Do you see the people you deal with as feces?"

"You mean shit?"

"If you prefer."

"Some, yeah. Some are just decent people who stepped into it. And one of these days I'm going to catch up with the horse that's making the biggest mess. Rocco. Then I'm going to stop him."

"How?"

"It depends what's handy. If it's a gun, I'll shoot him. A knife, I'll stab him. A club, I'll beat him. If there's nothing else, I'll strangle him with my bare hands."

Diamond's voice was low, but the vehemence made it sound like a scream. He held up his hands for the doctor to see. They were tensed and looked quite capable of the job.

The doctor failed to hide his distaste. "You're talking about murder."

"Do you call it murder when you step on a roach?"

"But you're talking about a man."

"A man who laughs when women and children die, a man who listens to screams like they was the best bebop. Anyway, you once said he was a figment of my imagination."

The psychiatrist fumbled with his pipe. "Yes, but still, I mean you—"

"Pull yourself together, doc," Diamond said, grinding out his cigarette in an ashtray while a smile played about his lips.

"You are not Red Diamond," the doctor said after a long pause. "Red Diamond was a character in cheap detective novels. Like Philip Marlowe or Sam Spade or Mike Hammer."

"They're all right Joes. They ever been in to see you? That Hammer guy could definitely use a little help. That Manning broad was in the same racket as you, so I guess Hammer might not be too trusting. Turned out she was the killer. I helped Mike out on that case back in 1947. He gets that book *I, the Jury* and I get left out in the rain."

"No. No. No. No. They don't exist. You don't exist."

"What do you mean I don't exist? Who are you hav-

6

ing a conversation with? Are you talking to yourself, doc? That's a bad sign."

"No. No. I mean these fictional private eyes are not real. They're fantasies."

"I wish they were. Sometimes the competition's tough in this racket. And they get more ink than I do."

The doctor's chair squeaked as he jumped up. "Stop it! Right now! You are Simon Jaffe. You developed an obsession with this Diamond character. You had a traumatic experience and you became your fantasy character."

The throbbing began again.

"Your wife is named Milly," the doctor continued, waving his pipe and spilling smoldering tobacco. "You live on Long Island. You've got two children. A boy and a girl. You abandoned them and took off on—"

"Doc, they say I killed a bunch of people," Diamond said slowly through clenched teeth.

"Yes. In California and New York."

"Some real tough characters."

"Yes."

"Then how come some dumb cabbie took on these bad eggs and came out in one piece?"

"You were lucky. You were nearly killed. I'm trying to help you."

Diamond got up and walked to where the doctor stood. The P.I. ground the glowing tobacco embers underfoot.

"I know. You're here from the government and you're here to help me."

"I'm an accredited, court-appointed psychiatrist."

"You know what goes with that?"

"What? Court-appointed?"

"No, the saying is the biggest lies are 'I'm here from the government to help you,' 'your check is in the mail,'

7

'this won't hurt,' and 'I promise I won't come in your mouth.'"

The small digital timer on the psychiatrist's desk made a few beeps and Diamond moved toward the door.

"Time to go," Diamond said happily.

"Mr. Jaffe, we haven't made any progress," the doctor said petulantly. "I'm going to recommend we discontinue treatment. Perhaps someone else can be of more help."

"Don't bother unless you know someone who might be able to clue me in to where Rocco is."

"There is no Rocco. There is no Fifi. There is no Diamond," the psychiatrist insisted.

"If there's no Red Diamond then there's no point in wasting fifty minutes of your time," Diamond said as he reached for the brass doorknob.

"Don't you understand, you believe this so you can escape—"

"Speaking of escape," Diamond said, opening the door.

A fidgety middle-aged woman, nibbling on silvered nails that matched her hair, sat in the waiting room.

"A nice-looking doll like you shouldn't have too many problems," Diamond said to the woman.

She blushed and bowed her head.

"Listen, go easy on the doc. He's had a hard afternoon."

"Mr. Jaffe, I don't need you to tell my other—"

Diamond handed the woman one of his business cards.

"You see, my name is Diamond. The doctor has a fixation. Delusions. Reminds me of this case I had once. Guy going around saying he was the king of France. Tried to have me guillotined."

"What happened?" the woman asked.

"I crowned him," Diamond said with a wink.

8

She tittered. Diamond smiled. The doctor frowned.

"Go in and talk to the doc," Diamond said to the woman. "Maybe it will help him."

Diamond took his rumpled gray snap-brim fedora off the wall rack, placed it jauntily on his head, and walked out.

He tipped the Mexican kid who got his car a buck. The kid pocketed the money without acknowledging it.

Beverly Hills, bah, Red thought. He got in his Plymouth and drove back to Hollywood.

2

Diamond leaned back in his chair, resting his size elevens on the chipped paint of the windowsill. He sipped cheap Scotch from a heavy tumbler. The sweet sounds of Benny Goodman's band flowed from the radio perched on the lone file cabinet. Blue smoke from his cigarette drifted up to the water-stained ceiling. The smoggy skies on the other side of the venetian blinds were dark.

It was quiet now. The building noises had surged at five P.M. as hundreds of workers were disgorged from the twelve-story structure near the corner of Ivar and Hollywood. A couple of cleaning ladies and the arthritic night watchman would be the only ones going through the corridors.

It wasn't the kind of building where ambitious

9

executives worked long into the night. If they had any ambition, they wouldn't be working for any of the companies in the Carlin Building.

Diamond had unwound after his session with the Beverly Hills psychiatrist. Seeing the shrink always keyed him up. It took a few belts of Scotch and some toots from Goodman's clarinet to get him back in the groove.

Not that the groove was so great. Diamond had been back in the business for eight months and had barely that many cases. He'd helped a woman find her long lost sister, cleared a guy falsely accused of a robbery, helped a storeowner catch an embezzling employee. Nothing to write home to the folks about. He'd already forgotten the details of the cases. The fees had been small, when he'd been able to collect. He wasn't good at squeezing his clients for bucks.

The phone rang. Diamond let it jangle a couple of times. Chances were it was a wrong number. He got a lot of wrong numbers. Especially when he stayed late on Saturday nights. His number was two digits away from Grauman's Chinese Theater's. Tourists who wanted to see if their feet were as big as Clark Gable's often called Diamond for directions. Most times he obliged them.

He set his drink down and wearily picked up the phone. "Diamond Detective Agency," he grumbled.

"Howdy. I'd like to chew the fat with Red Diamond."

"There ain't much fat. Just gristle."

"You Red Diamond?" The voice had an exaggerated Western twang. Red tried to picture the owner. A middle-aged-salesman type, probably drove a pick-up truck and lived in Fontana.

"I'm Diamond and I'm not buying any debuggers, new holsters, skip-tracing manuals, correspondence courses, or walkie-talkies."

10

"I'm not selling any, partner. My name's Edward Evans and I'd like to hire you."

"The Edward Evans?"

"Sure enough."

"Is your refrigerator running?"

"What? I guess it is."

"Well tell it to slow down," Diamond said, crushing out his cigarette. "I'm not in the mood for jokers."

"Neither am I, Mr. Diamond." The aw-shucks Texas twang was gone. It was a hard voice, used to giving commands that were obeyed. "Look out your window."

Diamond plopped the phone down on his booze-stained blotter, got up slowly, and walked to the window. He parted the blinds. Ten stories below him a long black limo was parked at the curb.

Tourists stood off to the side, trying to peer into the windows. The street people ignored the car, knowing that the days of catching a celeb on Hollywood Boulevard were long gone. These days, the fancy cars belonged to pimps and dope dealers.

"Do you see the limousine?" Evans said when Diamond retrieved the phone.

"Yeah."

"That's for you. My driver will take you to the airport. My jet will fly you here and we'll talk. This is the type of matter best handled face-to-face. At worst you'll get a free trip to Las Vegas."

"And at best?"

The line went dead.

The broad-shouldered chauffeur wore a dark blue uniform with a diamond-shaped yellow patch on his right arm and a matching patch on his peaked cap. When Diamond tried to question him, the driver said, "I have to concentrate on my driving," and clammed up.

The Lear 35A was parked on the tarmac at Burbank Airport. The driver walked Diamond to the plane, where two crew members wearing uniforms similar to the chauffeur's nodded to their passengers and climbed into the cockpit. Diamond and the driver entered the passenger compartment.

There were four seats around a diamond-shaped folding table and a divan at the rear of the cabin. The driver walked to the back, stretched out on the couch, and pulled his cap down over his eyes.

"Fasten your seatbelts and extinguish all cigarettes during takeoff," a voice said through the intercom.

Diamond lit a smoke and walked around the compartment as the plane took off. It was so smooth he only had to grab a chair for balance briefly.

He glanced in the diamond-studded mirror that covered the galley. A little baggy under the eyes, a little jowly under the chin, but not bad for a private eye who hadn't had a paying client for more than a month, Red thought.

Business had been good when he'd first gotten out of jail. Because of the publicity, he even needed a secretary to fend off the wacky clients.

He'd turned down the divorce cases. Tracking pudgy businessmen to seedy hotels where they'd make their secretaries work for a bonus was not for Red Diamond. When a marriage turned sour, it was uglier than year-old cottage cheese. And Diamond had no desire for a taste.

He'd turned down the industrial-espionage cases. Who cared if Amalgamated Grommet was stealing trade secrets from United Tang? Tang got it by screwing some inventor anyway. Diamond couldn't play the corporate kiss-ass games needed to make it with the large companies.

Bugging and debugging was a job for someone who liked feeling under toilet seats for wires. And skip-tracing usually meant collection work; finding out-of-work

12

guys whose wives didn't know when to stop using the charge cards.

Marlowe or Spade wouldn't dirty their hands with those kinds of cases. Shell Scott or Chet Drum would just laugh. Race Williams or Mike Hammer would start busting heads.

Red Diamond was as good as any of them. Better. Half the cases those guys took credit for, he had solved.

The Garrett Turbofan engines roared quietly as the plane climbed to thirty thousand feet. Diamond swung open the galley door, retrieved a bottle of Chivas Regal, and took it back to one of the suede-upholstered seats.

There was a diamond design embossed into the chair. The wallpaper had a similar pattern. The six windows on either side of the plane were diamond-shaped. Through them he could see the wings of the Learjet cutting the cotton candy clouds.

Diamond took a swig of Scotch and set the bottle down on the table. There was a stack of papers on the flat surface. Whoever was running the show was too sharp an operator to leave them around carelessly. Red decided to play along and began leafing through them.

The top one was a full color brochure, the kind a travel agent would use to convince a customer that he or she couldn't live without going somewhere. The somewhere was the Ace of Diamonds Hotel and Casino. Twenty-one hundred rooms covering a hundred acres by the Strip. Five restaurants. Four cocktail lounges. Saunas, Jacuzzis, tennis courts, waterbeds, cable TV. The two-thousand-dollar-a-night Diamond Suite, home to celebrities and moguls. A casino big enough to park a 747 in.

The slick brochure had photos of dazzling women in bikinis lounging by the six swimming pools, and suave studs in tuxedos gaming at the four baccarat tables. Everyone looked sexy, wealthy, and content.

Red remembered his cases in Vegas. The fat men in

13

polyester blowing their savings as they looked down the flimsy dresses of the waitresses. The junkets of blowsy blond broads and the gigolos who convinced them they were as desirable as the chorus girls who were young enough to be their daughters.

Mobster Bugsy Siegel, who should've been honored with a plaque that said "Our Founder," instead was memorialized with Bugsy's Rose Garden at the Flamingo Hotel. The joke was that associates and enemies who earned his wrath wound up as fertilizer for the roses. Real funny.

The whole town had the splendor and tackiness of a movie set. Caesar's Palace could boast it spent $2.9 million on its swimming pool, using marble from the same quarry as Michelangelo.

Vegas was built on money and sex. Disneyland for adults. The big fantasy was that some worthless piece of desert real estate would become a multi-billion dollar boomtown based on making people winners.

Diamond took another gulp from the bottle. It seeped down his gullet like smooth fire.

Vegas was the kind of town Rocco Rico thrived in. A born corrupter. A Sicilian Fu Manchu. Responsible for more deaths than Smith and Wesson. Red could see the lights of the Strip flickering in Rocco's cash-register eyes.

And Fifi, what about her? The town would draw her like a beautiful blond moth to a flame. He'd found her there once, during what he thought of as the "Killer Casino Case." The dealer was equally adept at cutting a deck of cards or a P.I. like Diamond.

He was cornered and he knew it. He had the kind of face only a mother weasel could love. His predatory teeth nibbled his lower lip.

14

I could've wasted him right there. Give him the same treatment he'd given the two nuns who'd seen his last murder. He deserved to die, or my name isn't Red Diamond.

He'd left bodies across the town. All I had to do was follow the corpses. It hadn't been a pretty trail, but no one ever said pleasant sights went with the job of being a dick. He'd spilled enough blood to fill the pool at the Sands.

And now I had him.

"It's time to talk," I said, keeping the .38 in my hand lined up with his gut.

"I got nothing to say," he whined.

I smiled and dropped the roscoe on the floor. He dove for it like an Olympic swimmer, and my gumshoe caught him right in the puss. A shiv appeared in his hand and he lunged for me.

I waltzed him around a bit. Arthur Murray would've been proud. The dance ended when I kissed his jaw with an uppercut.

"You feel like making with the words now?" I asked. "Like telling me where Rocco is?"

He got cute. It was almost as ugly as the last victim he'd carved up.

"What's in it for me?" he asked.

"You don't tell me and I give you a set of false teeth. How's that?"

He smirked and dove for my .38. I was getting slow. The punk got his hands on the gun. He started squeezing the trigger as I hit him. A bullet creased my arm.

I grabbed the .38 and began twisting as he kept pulling the trigger. Shots were going off like popcorn. He ate the last one.

Too bad. Life is tough. Death is tougher, unless you're an undertaker.

That's the way Scott Marks had written it up, Red recalled, taking another belt of the Scotch. Marks was as good with the words as Red was with his fists. He forced the memories from his mind and shuffled through the papers.

Six of them were travel brochures for other casinos, similar to the first. Lush, colorful, promising more fun than a night at El Morocco. Gambler's Gulch. The Diamond Mine. The Lucky Cowpoke. Trail's End. Rugged Rock. The Mother Lode.

What they had in common was the small print at the bottom of the back pages, where they read "Owned and Operated by the 4E Corp."

Edward Evans Entertainment Enterprises.

A few sheets of typing on plain white paper gave Diamond an idea what the suckers had donated to 4E. The statements were public record, nothing that someone checking Nevada Gaming Commission and SEC records couldn't find out.

Evans was worth more than most millionaires dared dream about. He could buy a mansion the way Diamond picked up a pack of cigarettes.

Underneath the papers was a bunch of newspaper clippings. None of them were more than six months old. There was an analysis piece from the *Wall Street Journal* reporting that Las Vegas business was down sixty-five percent. It blamed the economy and Atlantic City, which was wooing away East Coast gamblers. Four stories were about fires of suspicious origin, including a disaster that killed eighty-five. The rest were about classic mob hits: men found in expensive cars with bullets parked behind their ears; cars that blew up like Lupe Velez; a couple found hanging with picture-wire around their necks. The victims' names were unfamiliar.

The roar of the Turbofans changed and Red's ears

16

popped as the plane began descending. He peered through the diamond-shaped window. The lights of Vegas glittered in the dark desert night. The landing lights at McCarran Airport had to blink hard to stand out.

"This place has better security than Jack Benny's vault," Diamond said as the chauffeur led him down interminable corridors lined with motion detectors and video cameras. They were buzzed through three sets of thick security doors with monitored sallyports, and Diamond was frisked twice by unsmiling, firm-handed guards.

The driver stepped up to a panel next to a knotty oak door and pressed his thumb against a metal plate. A red-eyed video camera winked down on them, a muted electromagnet hummed, and the door swung open.

The chauffeur waited outside as Diamond entered the inner sanctum.

"Welcome to my spread," a voice boomed. "The name's Ed Evans, but my buddies call me Tex." A giant figure unlimbered itself from behind an equally massive desk and thrust forward a hand that wasn't as big as a catcher's mitt. Evans was easily six feet six inches. He had a lean body and a leathery face under a beige Stetson. He wore a Ralph Lauren cowboy shirt, with a cowboy lassoing a calf embroidered on the yoke. He had a leather vest and chaps on. His dungarees were held up by a broad belt with a plate-sized silver buckle. There were six-shooters on both hips. Diamond didn't need to look at Evan's feet to guess the kind of boots he was wearing.

"I see why they call you Tex," the P.I. said.

"Just a brand they hung on me out on the range," Evans said. There was a boyishly happy look on his weathered features. "Hope you enjoyed your flight in."

17

They pumped hands. Evans's grip was as strong and dry as a Santa Ana wind. Red decided he liked the oversized billionaire.

Tex moved back behind his desk and sat on the saddle—mounted on a wooden block—that served as his chair. "Take a load off your feet," he said, gesturing to a chair in front of his desk.

Diamond removed his fedora and sat.

The walls were covered with Western memorabilia: branding irons, spurs, barbed wire, Winchesters and Colts. There were original prints by Frederic Remington and Charles Russell.

While Diamond took in the scene, Evans got out a can of Bull Durham tobacco and some rolling paper. He nimbly tucked and twisted until two cigarettes were produced.

"Effie used to do that for Spade," Diamond said as Evans handed him one.

"They call 'em quirlys where I come from," Evans responded.

Diamond lit both of their smokes and the two men sat back and puffed contentedly.

"I figured this was some sort of joke when you first called," Diamond said. "It looks like the real thing, but I still don't understand. You've got a small army of guards. I bet there's no shortage of shamuses who'd jump through hoops for a retainer from you. And I don't believe you just picked my name out of the Yellow Pages."

"You're right about the Yellow Pages, but it was the name that did it," Tex said with a grin. "I got a thing about diamonds. I won my first cow in a poker game. A diamond flush, king high. Since then, I've played my cards right. And relied on diamonds whenever possible. Do you know there are eight detectives in the U.S. named Diamond."

18

"I know a Richard Diamond," Red responded. "Ex-New York cop, had an office in Hollywood."

"I don't recall his name from my list."

"Makes sense. I heard he retired a few years back. Married his secretary. A doll named Sam with thoroughbred legs."

"Whatever. The other investigators were unacceptable for a variety of reasons. And I liked your background."

"What do you mean?"

"Some people seem to think you're crazy. Living in a dream world."

Diamond felt himself tightening up.

"It don't bother me none. Lots of folks think I'm plumb loco. But I'm rich enough so they got to call me eccentric. When I insisted on buying two thousand acres by Blue Diamond mountain and setting up the Diamond Bar ranch, my financial advisors did everything but have me committed. So I fired them.

"Anyway, Mr. Diamond, I've got more money than Tom Mix had hats. I can hire anyone I want. And I want you."

"I guess your problem's got something to do with those papers you left for me to read on the plane."

Evans nodded. "Red, the mob is trying to take over Las Vegas," the millionaire said solemnly.

Diamond couldn't suppress a smirk. "That's like saying the Commies are trying to take over Russia."

Evans tongue darted around his mouth searching for a piece of tobacco that had gotten caught in his teeth. He juggled it on the tip of his tongue for a second, then spit it out to his left. It landed dead center in a diamond-studded brass spittoon.

"This town was built up by some outlaws that would've made Wyatt Earp break leather. Bugsy and Meyer and the Ma-fie-ah turned it into a boomtown and

19

then tried to rob it blind. But we cleaned it up pretty good."

Diamond snorted and dropped his hat back on his head.

Evans flicked his cigarette into the spittoon. It made a sizzling noise.

"By the early 1960s I was worth a half-billion greenbacks," Evans said, "give or take a few. I been a gambler all my life. Oil wells, cattle ranches, real estate, and, of course, diamond mines."

Diamond yawned and ground out his cigarette in an ashtray in the shape of, and nearly the size of, Texas.

"I became interested in Nevada. I wanted a state where I could expand, where the government bureaucrats wouldn't be buzzing around like flies on a fresh cowflop. I saw the quote from Governor Sawyer about things being relaxed, tolerant, and mindful about folks going their way unmolested with a minimum of irritation. So I began moving my business out here.

"There was all kinds of varmints, men bad enough to make a preacher cuss. The local law was as crooked as a sidewinder with a bellyache. So I got the Kennedy brothers to put the squeeze on. At the same time I was offering the boys in silk suits good money to sell out. They did.

"It took more'n a dozen years but we pretty much cleaned up this town," Evans continued. "Got some honest cops, judges that couldn't be bought too cheap. Even a couple of legislators who could be trusted not to clean out the till at the orphan's home."

Evans paused and fingered the brim of his Stetson. "So what do the lowdown cusses do but open up Atlantic City."

Diamond tilted back his fedora in a reciprocal gesture. "Tex, it sounds to me like you're beating around the sagebrush. What kind of job do you have in mind?

You want me to blow up Atlantic City or start bringing tour groups to this town?"

"Red, I don't mind the competition. There's no way they can hurt Las Vegas legitimately. We're still known around the world as the best gambling town. You want to get gussied up like in some high falutin' European casino, we got the place for you. If you're just a regular cowhand and want to let off a little steam, you can do that too. Or if you want to go up against the one-armed bandits, we can make you happy. And our weather's great."

"I read the travel brochures, Tex. I'm impressed. Vegas is like a hooker. She'll take your money and screw you good no matter who you are."

Evans didn't appreciate the humor. "You know about the problems we've been having. The fires, the murders. That's just part of it. There's more street crime, more hotel burglaries, more cheating at the tables."

"Times are tough all over," Diamond said. "Go to any big city and you'll find more cockroaches crawling out of the woodwork."

"But this is organized," Tex said. "What I want you to do is find out who's behind it. Who had two of my key employees killed and ran off a half-dozen others? Who's bringing in the low-class hookers, the burglars, stick-up men, card cheats, con men, car thieves?"

"Vegas is just the kind of sweetheart of a town to attract them," Diamond said. "You got a large transient population and cops as used to getting taken care of as a baby at its mother's teat."

"No!" Evans shouted, slamming a ham-sized fist down on his desktop. "This is different. It's a conspiracy."

I spent enough time trying to talk this guy out of hiring me, Red thought. It wouldn't hurt to nose around

21

Vegas a couple of days at Evans's expense. He could afford it. And the millionaire might have a point.

"If it's a conspiracy, there's only one man who could pull it off," Diamond said slowly.

Evans leaned forward. "Who?"

"Rocco Rico."

"I read in your file about him. Do you really think he exists?"

"As sure as Jesse James robbed banks."

Evans leaned back. "So you'll snoop around and see if you find him here? I'm asking for your help, Red."

"You got it."

"Whooie," Tex yelled, jumping up. He took out both six-guns, twirled them, and then let off a couple of shots into the ceiling.

Diamond looked up, expecting to hear the sound of bodies falling. The ceiling was pocked with bullet holes.

"Don't worry partner," Tex said. "It's my way of letting off a little steam. The office is soundproofed and the ceiling is lined with batting like they use at target ranges."

"Glad you're happy," Diamond said, trying to remain nonchalant.

Evans glanced at the diamond-encrusted Rolex on his wrist. "I've arranged for you to stay overnight in our Diamond Suite. The staff thinks you're a high roller from back East. Only me and Norris know who you are."

"Norris?"

"My driver and Man Friday."

"Ordinarily I'd say you should hire me through your attorney. That way I'm acting as his agent and get the benefit of the attorney-client privilege. But if the scam involves Rocco, I don't know if there's a lawyer you can trust."

"I trust them as far as I can throw a Brahma bull. You got as many honest lawyers here as you got clocks

22

in casinos. Let's keep it just between ourselves. This is a gossipy town. You'll be amazed at how many people know all about you before too long. Or at least about this high roller you're going to be. You got a moniker you want to use?"

"How about John Dalmas. My friend Marlowe used that name a couple of times and it seemed to work."

"Dalmas it is then. Norris will take you to your room and give you any background you need."

"Yeah. He was bending my ear all the way from Los Angeles."

"He had orders not to talk," Evans said. "Now that you're on board, you'll find he's a straight shooter. He's my eyes and ears. Now if you don't mind, I'd like to celebrate. Do you want to join me? I've got a Cisco Kid film set to unwind in the screening room."

"I'll pass. One last thing. I'll be wanting a thousand a day plus expenses." Diamond waited. The figure was five times his usual rate. But Evans was worth five thousand times as much as any previous client.

"Norris will arrange payment. I don't bother with petty cash."

"Sure. I feel the same way," Diamond said.

Evans pressed a concealed button on his desk and the driver entered.

"This is John Dalmas," Evans said. "Take him to the Diamond Suite. And give him full cooperation."

Norris nodded.

"*Adios, amigo*," Evans said.

"Hasty banana," Diamond answered as he walked out with the driver.

The guards' scrutiny was lighter as they left Evans's quarters.

"Do these guys know who I am?" Diamond asked, waving a thumb back as they passed the final checkpoint.

"They know you're a valued customer who wanted to speak with Mr. Evans about extending your one-million-dollar credit line."

"Did he?"

"Of course, for a high roller like you," Norris said without any mirth.

"Not bad for a guy who can't play strip poker without winding up a nudist."

Norris didn't respond.

"Okay chuckles, tell me, who are the movers and shakers in this burg?"

"There's only a few casino owners who really have juice in this town," Norris said. "Eddie Mars owns a couple of places. Dave Palermo, Adam Dawson, and Mega Corporation own a bunch of others. But they're running scared. The only other real power is Moe Greenberg."

Norris said the name like a priest forced to utter a four-letter word.

"What about him?"

"He owns the Lion's Den, the Trojan Horse, the Ramses, the Sheik, and the Tahiti. The last two are downtown. Very lower class. Just like him."

"You don't like the guy?"

"I used to work for him. I despise him. He's a ruthless conniving ex-bookie who'd slit a blind beggar's throat for bus fare."

"No wonder he's a success. Tex said you could arrange things for me. I need a local contact. Is there a cop I can trust?"

"I believe so. I'll check."

"Also I don't have a piece with me."

"We frown on prostitution in the hotel, but I suppose something could be arranged."

"Not that kind of piece. A roscoe. A thirty-eight and some ammo."

"That shouldn't be a problem."

It seemed like they'd been walking for a week when

they finally reached the private elevator that lifted them soundlessly to the penthouse.

"There's only one other guest on this floor," Norris said as the elevator doors opened. "A Mr. Vincent Van Houton. From South Africa. His family is almost as important in diamonds as DeBeers."

"His mother must be proud."

Norris took out a diamond-shaped key and opened the door to the suite at the right end of the corridor. "The suite is completely stocked. Everything you need should be there. If not, just ring double zero and I'll arrange it."

The door to Van Houton's room opened and two gaudily dressed black women stepped out, laughing as they counted a sheaf of $100 bills.

There was no reaction on Norris's face.

"I see you run a real respectable joint," Diamond said. "Good night, Norris."

"Good night, Mr. Dalmas."

3

There were seven white-shag-carpeted rooms in the Diamond Suite. The living room of the duplex had a bar to serve ten without anyone rubbing his neighbor's elbow. There was a giant television set with video game hookup that would have made an arcade owner jealous, a quad stereo system with recessed speakers, and a wireless telephone in every room.

Diamond knew from his past adventures that guests in the plush hotel suites stayed rent free. Either they were high rollers with six-digit credit lines or celebrities. Gold-framed, autographed photos of some of the hot shot previous guests covered one hallway wall. Sinatra, Wayne Newton, Danelia Wild, Tom Jones, Cher, Ann Margaret.

An inset Jacuzzi, big enough to float a submarine, was near the two-story window looking out on the bright lights of the Strip.

Diamond peeled off his clothes and plunged into the whirlpool. After a couple of minutes soaking with his eyes closed, he got up, dripped his way across the room, and retrieved a bottle of Scotch and his cigarettes. He flipped on the stereo and plugged in a cassette. Artie Shaw's trumpet tooted "Stardust." Diamond returned to the tub.

The lights blinked at him through the window, reminding him of the hundreds of cities he'd been in, the lonely nights spent in hotel rooms looking out at Times Square, Wanchai, the Tenderloin, the Sunset Strip, the Ginza, the French Quarter, the Combat Zone. He was destined to roam the underbellies of the tough towns searching for the lice that clung to the bottom.

He'd been shot at more times than Audie Murphy and hit in the head more than Jake La Motta. He'd helped Travis McGee when dope runners had tried to blow the *Busted Flush* out of the Florida water, and Spenser when the Massachusetts mobsters tried to run him out of town. When Johnny Milano and Miles Jacoby were jammed up in the Big Apple, they turned to Diamond. And Lew Archer and Phil Marlowe would admit he'd saved their lives from California crazies.

And what had it gotten him? A run-down office on Hollywood Boulevard that hadn't been painted since Grover Cleveland was president, an apartment in Los

Feliz that was as homey as a bus station bench, a two-pack-a-day habit, and an empty feeling in his gut.

Fifi. It always came back to her. The blond bombshell with the mischievous blue eyes.

The candlelight flickered off irises as blue as the Colorado sky. Her hair was the color of freshly harvested Iowa hay. The curves under her clinging sequined gown were as smooth as the Appalachian hills.

But underneath, her heart was as solid as New York bedrock.

Fifi La Roche had paid her dues. Her father had been killed when he refused to pay tribute to a small-time mobster with big-time ambitions. Fifi had been the sole support of her sister after their mother ran off with a trombone player from Glenn Miller's band.

Fifi had worked as a cocktail waitress in some of the most dangerous dives in the country. It was at the Dew Drop Inn that she'd caught the evil eye of Rocco Rico.

He owned the inn, as well as a hundred other gin joints, topless bars, whorehouses, opium dens, bookie parlors, and porno theaters. He could pick and choose from any of the hapless dames that fell into his clutches.

But he made a mistake when he chose Fifi. She had spirit. Even after he gunned down her sister, Fifi wouldn't give in to him.

Her heart belonged to one man. And that man was me. Which made me number one on Rocco's hit parade.

It didn't make him too popular with me either. We'd swapped shots around the world. I'd taken my lumps and dished them out pretty good too.

But Rocco was still around. And so was I. Fifi was out there somewhere, scared that if we came together, Rocco would take us apart. Permanently.

I wasn't about to let that happen.

27

Rocco had to pay for what he'd done. And Red Dia-
mond was the guy who'd tally up the bill.

That was the way Scott Marks described it, Red recalled. So it went in the P.I. racket. The dick dodged
bullets and a guy at a typewriter got rich.

All the shamuses from Pat Abbott to Sidney Zoom.
The famous names like Marlowe or Hammer or Spade.
None of them got rich. Just the wordsmiths. Half the
writers didn't even use their real names. Erle Stanley
Gardner and John Creasey had more aliases between
them than a pack of bunco artists.

Sometimes the eye don't even get his name in the
book, like that guy that Pronzini writes about. People in
the biz know his name but John Q. Public thinks of him
as the "nameless detective."

So Dash Hammett worked as a Pinkerton for a
while. Big deal. Why didn't he use the Continental Op's
name, give credit where credit was due?

What the hell. Diamond lay back in the tub enjoying the heat and the alcohol and nicotine in his blood.

The scream woke him up.

He jumped out of the tub, wrapped a towel around
his thick waist, and opened the door. There was another
scream. It came from Van Houton's suite.

Barefoot and still dripping, Diamond hurried down
the hall. A woman ran out of the South African's room
as Diamond neared and she staggered toward him.

She was a well-built brunette in her mid-twenties.
Diamond didn't have a chance to really look at her. A
gorilla hard on her heels was less pleasant to look at,
but a more immediate concern.

He was six feet four inches tall and nearly as broad
at the shoulders, barechested in black leather pants.
The rippling muscles of his upper torso bore bullet and
knife scars.

28

The gorilla grabbed the girl's long brown hair as a gaunt man in satin bikini briefs came out of the room. "VVH" was embroidered on the blue satin. Pale and just over five feet tall, he carried himself like the King of Siam. He had long straight hair and a mustache the color of gold. A riding crop in his hand matched a welt on the girl's overly made up cheek.

"Let go of the broad," Diamond growled.

The gorilla looked back at his boss.

"Mind your own business," Van Houton told Diamond. He turned to his aide. "Bring her back in, Mike."

Mike tugged at the girl's hair. Her dark eyes were wide with fear but she talked tough. "Get your paws off me, you ape!"

Mike jerked and she yelped.

"You heard the lady," Diamond said.

As he stepped in, Mike let go of the woman and took a roundhouse swing at Red. The punch would've knocked him to Arizona if it hadn't been telegraphed from Reno.

Diamond ducked under the punch and caught Mike twice with short jabs to the abdomen that had little effect.

"Hit him! Hit him!" Van Houton screamed petulantly.

"Shut up, you little creep," the girl said, catching Van Houton with a blow that sent him staggering back into his room. The South African slammed the door, leaving the trio out in the hall.

Diamond turned at the noise and the slow-moving behemoth caught him by the neck and slammed him against the wall. He began choking Diamond. The P.I. landed a few punches that Mike didn't bother to notice. Things began to get hazy.

The girl reached from behind Mike and grabbed his testicles. She wrung them like a dishrag and the gorilla yowled.

29

With Mike folded over in pain, Red delivered a half-dozen knockout punches. It was a knee to the jaw that finally got Mike's attention and put him to sleep on the diamond-patterned carpet.

"Look what that asshole did to my dress," the woman said as Diamond leaned against the wall and enjoyed the clear passage of air into his lungs.

Her sea-green outfit had about as much fabric as a large handkerchief. Low cut on top and high on the thigh, the torn garment left nothing to the imagination about the slightly plump body underneath.

"Damn! This was my best trick dress," she complained. "Now I look like shit. Can I come in your room and freshen up?"

Without waiting for a response she marched past Diamond and down to his room.

He realized he was naked. No one had said anything when his towel fell off during the scuffle. He pulled it out from underneath Mike and followed the girl into his room.

She was helping herself to a slug of Scotch as he shut the door behind himself.

"What's your name?" she asked.

"Red. I mean John Dalmas."

"Don't worry. What's the matter? You got a wife or something?"

"No wife. My name's John Dalmas. Red's my nickname."

"How come? You're obviously not a natural redhead."

She looked down at Diamond's clump of brown pubic hair, then smiled as he hurriedly wrapped the towel around himself.

"Don't be embarassed. You look like you got the right equipment. Want to try it out?"

"You don't miss a trick."

30

She broke out laughing and he joined her with a smile at his unintentional pun. They were standing near the living room bar and she reached out and squeezed his arm.

"I owe you one," she said. "Would you like a free ride? On the house. And I'm good. That creep down the hall was supposed to pay me five hundred bucks for an hour."

"That's more than most politicians make."

"Yeah. And it's a lot more fun when I fuck you."

"I've had a hard day."

"I can make it a hard night." Her long nails doodled on his arm.

"I'll pass."

"That's your loss," she said in the same cheerful, professional tone. She stopped touching him. "Can I stay here tonight?"

"Don't you have business to take care of?"

"Taking care of business is my middle name."

"That's a pretty long name. What else do they call you?"

"I like your style. My trick name is Patty Cakes. My real name is Teri Lennox. No circle above the *i*. Call me what you want, as long as you call me."

"That line was old when Mae West used it. What do you like to be called?"

"Teri."

"Okay, Teri. You can stay the night. But I got to get something in return."

"A quick trip around the world?" she asked with a knowing smile.

"No. Just talk."

"You want me to talk dirty to you or are you one of those guys who get off hearing how I got into the sporting life and what's a nice girl like me doing in a business like this?"

31

"Neither. Why don't you freshen up and we'll have a nice long chat. Have you eaten?"

"You mean food?"

"You gonna make everything I say sound dirty?"

"No to both questions. I'm starving."

While Teri showered, Diamond phoned down for room service. He ordered the best the kitchen had to offer and a wine to match.

She was in the bathroom long enough to wash away a ward heeler's sins. By the time she came out, wrapped in a diamond-shaped towel the size of a Persian rug, a big surf-and-turf extravaganza was being brought in on a silver cart.

The bellhop smirked at her while Diamond signed for the meal. He gave the kid a $20 tip.

"You're not famous, so you must be quite a high roller to get comped like this," Teri said as they sat down to eat.

"How do you know I'm not famous?"

"I read *People* magazine."

Diamond grunted and dipped a piece of lobster into the drawn butter sauce. It had exactly the right texture and taste. Soft but firm, with the barest hint of the sea in the glossy white flesh.

They ate in silence, washing down hearty mouthfuls with sips from the $100 bottle of Puilly Fusse. He could tell she was sizing him up and trying to figure out how she could get a chunk of his cash.

Diamond knew the $20 tip, one fifth of all the money he had on him, was a good move. He had to keep the front up, ask the right questions without blowing his cover.

After dinner they sat on a couch that faced the window and polished off a second bottle of wine. Teri's eyes were lightly glazed. The tension around her mouth

32

seeped away with each sip. They sat for a long while in silence.

"I came here about five years ago to work in one of the shows," she began. "Sweet and innocent. Fresh off the farm in Manhattan."

Diamond's eyebrows lifted.

"Manhattan, Kansas," she said. "I had this guy promoting me. He made a whole bunch of promises. I had had the lead part in my high school play. Thought I was going to be a real star, you know, Barbara Mandrell look out. What a chump."

Diamond nodded, encouraging her to spill her story.

"I was in the chorus line at the Treasury for a while. I really wasn't very good. Then my boyfriend split, taking the little we'd managed to set aside. I was hanging around a casino all down in the mouth when a guy offered me fifty bucks for a date. It was easy after that." She peeled her towel off. "I've got a great body, don't I?"

"Yeah."

She rose from the davenport with exaggerated sensuality, walked to the Jacuzzi, and bounced in. She beckoned him with an index finger.

Diamond dropped his towel and joined her. They leaned against opposite sides of the tub. She bobbed around, managing to brush against him several times. He grew hard and she winked at him.

"I guess you're not queer. Would you like me to take care of that?" she asked, indicating his erection and slithering her tongue across her lips.

"Maybe later. Have another drink."

"I'm not some high school cutie you have to get drunk to screw."

She was a lot younger and less experienced than she made out to be, Red decided. Her gestures designed

33

to turn him on were overdone, like she'd gotten them from watching movies or looking at men's magazines. He took a swig from the bottle he'd left next to the tub. She took it from him and swallowed an equal gulp. The hot water bubbled around them.

"What do you want to know?" she said with a slight slur.

"Tell me about Vegas."

"Vegas sucks. Business is terrible. Low-life tramps on the street. Spreading syph and the clap. Rolling tourists. The johns are going to the ranches out of town. Some nights I barely make enough to pay for rubbers."

"When did it start?"

"About four, five months ago. Right around the time the Ultimo burned. That wasn't too great for business either. They busted some bellboy for it, said he set the drapes on fire with a cigarette. Those damn things are fire resistant. The whole thing stinks."

A ripple of fear rolled across her face, then disappeared as quickly as a two-digit tip in a maitre d's hand.

"I heard a bunch of guys got knocked off."

"Are you a cop?" she asked abruptly.

"You know many cops can afford a room like this?"

"Plenty in Vegas. You can't get a safe-deposit box in this town. They got them stuffed with cash."

"What about Evans?"

"He's a nut, but an honest one. Nuts about cowboys and diamonds. He's supposed to run a pretty legit outfit. Doesn't gyp the suckers and doesn't skim. But I hear he's getting squeezed."

"By who?"

She froze up again.

More wine, coupled with the soothing warmth of the tub and Diamond's gentle, insistent questioning, loosened her up. He had to lean in close to understand her

34

slurred words. She rested her head on his shoulder and spoke slowly.

The street people believed the same theory Evans had voiced. The mob was up to its old tricks, using terror to eliminate the competition as they made their move to the Jersey shores.

Teri closed her eyes as she recited the evils that were befalling Las Vegas. The owners of four clubs on the Strip and three in the downtown area had already sold out to mysterious corporations. Evans was the last major holdout. If he gave in, the other independents would turn the town over to the wiseguys.

Teri passed out and Diamond carried her to the couch. He put a blanket over her and tucked her in. The makeup washed from her face, the muscles relaxed by sleep, Red could imagine the kind of girl who gulped a triumphant chocolate shake at the malt shop after a couple of curtain calls in the high school play. That probably was no more than a couple of years ago.

The alcohol had taken its toll on him but he couldn't sleep. Cleaning up Vegas might be the toughest job he had ever tackled. Bigger than smashing Rocco's multi-million dollar heroin ring or the white slavery operation that nearly trapped Fifi into a life of sin in British Columbia.

It would take time, time away from Los Angeles. That was the last place he'd seen Fifi. Though he wouldn't admit it, even to himself, every time the phone rang in his Hollywood office, he'd prayed it would be Fifi's raspy-honey voice on the line.

But she never called. She must be hiding somewhere, or else held captive, Red figured. The thought of her in Rocco's clutches made him gnash his teeth.

Who else but Rocco could call out an army of

torches, hit men, hookers, scamsters and assorted mugs, pugs and lugs?

Diamond could feel Rocco's menace looming over the town like a satanic Goliath.

It was time for Diamond to play David.

4

Slightly groggy, Red peered out the two-story window. The gaudy splendor of the night before had been bleached out in the hot desert sun. The only sign the girl had been there was the scent of her perfume, which clung to the sofa.

After ordering up breakfast and using the toiletries in the bathroom, he rang up Norris, who escorted him to Evans's office.

"Why the tight security, Tex?" Diamond asked after passing inspection by a new crew of guards. "You been getting any threats?"

"A man can't be too careful nowadays," Evans said. "Some coyote took a couple of potshots at me a few months ago."

"You see the guy or got any idea who he was?"

Evans shook his head and changed the subject. "Norris said you wanted a shooting iron and a cop you could talk to."

"I got a question about Norris. He said he worked

for Greenberg. Are you sure he can be trusted?"

"Did he tell you what happened?"

"No, but I guess there's no great love lost."

"That's for sure. Norris worked for him for three years. Got to the point where he was managing the dining room. The all-you-can-eat buffet."

"Yeah?"

"Norris used to let the old folks come in and sneak food out. Made like he didn't see them packing their feed bags. They were poor people and it kept them going. He told his staff not to stop them.

"One of the busboys snitched. Norris was fired, the busboy got his job. Greenberg had Norris blackballed and nobody would hire him. He was out of work for nearly a year when I took him on. He's been my top hand for five years now and I haven't regretted it one day."

"Sounds fair."

"So what are you going to do?"

"Drift around a bit, get the lay of the land."

"That Lennox girl last night wasn't enough?" Evans said with a smile.

"I don't like my business being broadcast."

"You're among friends. I told you word gets around. I don't reckon there's many people don't know about John Dalmas by now."

"That reminds me, if I'm going to be a high roller I've got to have some cash to flash."

Evans walked to his desk and took out a stack of hundred-dollar bills.

"That's fifteen thousand dollars. Just make sure if you go dropping it, you do it at one of my casinos," Evans said, reaching into another drawer and fishing out a .38, leather belly holster, and three boxes of ammo.

"The cop you'll be wanting to talk to is Lieutenant

Frank Saint," Evans said. "He's so honest I'd shoot dice with him over the phone. Not that he's a gambling man. Meet him at four-thirty out where Paradise Road hits Flamingo. Don't want to get the tongues in town wagging about your setdown. There's a leased car waiting downstairs in the garage. Any questions?"

Diamond shook his head.

"Ride 'em cowboy," Evans shouted.

He was halfway out of the room when Evans let off a couple of rounds into the ceiling.

Diamond exited I-95 north and picked up scrap wood from an abandoned filling station. He pulled off a few hundred yards into the desert and put together a crude target.

For the next two hours he practiced firing. He never bothered to go more than ten yards from the target since virtually every shootout he'd been in was at close range.

He fired standing, crouching in police combat stance, and with arm extended. By the time he was done his hand was blackened with powder and sore from the effort of squeezing and the .38's polite recoil. But as he holstered the weapon he knew it was a friend he could count on.

He took a leisurely drive toward his meeting place. It was easy to enjoy the desert from inside an air-conditioned car.

As he neared the city, the Joshua trees were replaced by billboards. Murals of giant women, their skimpy bikinis bigger than his car; blowups of hotels as sleek as the women, but with fewer curves. Gargantuan head shots of Sinatra, Wayne Newton, Liberace.

Paris has the Louvre, Madrid the Prado, Washington, D.C. the Smithsonian. Las Vegas has the Liberace Museum, Red thought. He was no culture vulture, but a good investigator has to know about that sort of thing.

Like in the case of the Gibraltar Tercel. The dame had come to him with this story about the statuette and he'd checked with Herb Barber, the expert at the Museum of Natural History.

Barber had given him the history. Too bad Rocco had gotten to the smart little guy before Diamond had a chance to warn him. A museum guard had found Barber the next day, stuffed into the mouth of a Tyranosaurus Rex. One more item on the bill Rocco owed.

A beat-up 1978 Chevy was parked near the intersection of Paradise and Flamingo. Walking about a hundred feet away was a man who couldn't be anything but a cop.

He was about five-eleven and two hundred and twenty pounds. The weight hung on a broad frame, but a lot of his girth was in his gut. He was wearing a loud green-plaid jacket that didn't quite match his green trousers. His eyes and hair were a steely gray.

As Diamond slowed the car near him, the man's hand scratched at his chest, his fingers brushing the butt of a barely visible 9mm in a shoulder holster. Diamond kept both hands on the wheel and a friendly smile on his face as he pulled up near the cop.

He tapped the button to lower the window. The cop's hand stayed on his gun.

"Saint?"

"Diamond?"

"Hop in," Diamond said, and Saint did. Red made a U-turn and drove away from the city. After ten minutes, they found a quiet spot, and Diamond pulled off and shut the engine.

"Tex said you're working for him," Saint said tersely. "That makes you okay in my book. I find out differently, I'll be all over you. I don't like P.I.s."

"I don't much like cops," Diamond responded. "But I play straight. Tex said you could give me the lowdown."

"Lowdown is right. He said he told you already. The mob is coming back into town."

"Hard to believe they ever left."

"They figured straight guys couldn't make it work and they could take it back whenever they wanted. It didn't turn out that way. The wiseguys missed the skim and the money-laundering opportunities. You got more than twelve million people a year coming through here."

"And lots of cash changing hands."

"Right. When the mob wanted back in, they found Tex and a few others had more balls than they reckoned on. So they're trying to drive them out. Even if the straight players stay, so much business will be swung to Atlantic City it'll never be the same here."

"So why don't you do something about it?"

"I'm one guy. There's about a dozen guys on the job I'd trust not to steal gold teeth from a dead man. The Law Enforcement Intelligence Network won't even share information with our department. There's two detectives who do nothing but tail me."

Diamond checked his rearview mirror.

"Don't worry. I've gotten used to ditching them."

"Anything solid from your snitches or wiretaps?" Diamond asked.

"Forget about taps. As soon as we go to a judge, his clerk is dropping a dime to the wiseguys. The snitches come up with a half-dozen different stories. Mafia. Mysterious foreign interests. Martians. We're not getting anything worth diddly squat. No names to pin it on."

"Ever hear of a guy named Rocco Rico?"

Saint thought for a moment. "The name's familiar but I can't place it. What's he into?"

"Everything. I'm sure he's behind it. Who's the local hotshot?"

"Moe Greenberg. Also known as Iceberg. He's got a bunch of front men and corporations but they say he's involved. One of his casinos had a fire, but it only did a couple thousand dollars damage."

"Just to look good?"

"I think so."

"I've heard his name," Diamond said. "Where do I find him?"

"Under the slimiest rock," Saint said, reaching into his jacket pocket and pulling out a half-dozen mug shots. "Here's some players I thought you'd be interested in."

Diamond thumbed through the stack, committing each face to memory. The names would be etched in later.

"The guy on top is Greenberg," Saint said. "The photo's from a 1966 arrest. Conspiracy to commit murder. He beat the rap after two witnesses had car trouble. Their cars exploded."

The black-and-white picture showed a middle-aged man with slicked-down graying hair and a Mona Lisa smile.

"The next two are the ones that do his dirty work. Washington Rogers, also known as Silky, and Vito Falanges, also known as Fingers. Both got rap sheets thicker than the Chicago phone book. They were thrown out of the Windy City mob for being too vicious."

Silky was a good-looking black man with high cheekbones and an arrogant expression. Diamond studied his mug while Saint continued talking.

"Silky did something nasty to a young girl. He'd done the same kind of stuff before, but this one was an alderman's daughter. Fingers set a fire that killed a priest and five kids at a home for crippled orphans."

Diamond flipped to the next picture. Fingers was a sharp-featured white man who looked like a cornered ferret.

"Real cute," Diamond said.

41

"The others are flunkies that handle different dirty work. I wrote the details on the back of the photos. If you need more info, here's my card."

"Thanks."

"Let's head back."

Diamond started the car and pulled onto the road.

As they neared his car, Saint warned, "Be careful with your snooping around. These are real bad boys you're playing with. I don't need any more customers."

"What do you mean?"

"I work homicide," the cop said. The deadpan expression locked onto his face briefly flashed into a tight smile.

A few minutes after he dropped off the cop, Red's stomach began sending messages to his brain. When he saw the classic diner, looking like a railroad car parked at the side of the road, he knew it was time to give in.

HOME MADE PIES EVERY DAY promised a sign in the window. The heat hit him with a blast as he hurried by the four cars and two red-and-gray cabs in the lot.

The air-conditioned cool inside was as soothing as a chilled beer. The stainless steel furnishings gleamed. From the shell-patterned wall behind the grill, to the dozen stools, the metal looked hard and clean. The dwarf-jukeboxes found in diners across the country were perched on the counter and at the eight booths. But you could tell it was Las Vegas. There were almost as many one-armed bandits, their handles greasy from players trying their luck in between french fries.

Diamond sat at the counter. A napkin and silverware were set before him by a blonde who might've been a chorus girl fifty pounds ago. She took his order and relayed it to the sweaty Hispanic man working in the hot kitchen.

"Excuse me buddy," a man said, tapping Diamond on the shoulder.

His swarthy, pocked face was topped with curly hair as black and shiny as a colonel's boots. The man had a silver dollar on a pendant brushing his hairy chest. He nervously rubbed the silver dollar.

"Could you do me favor please and put quarter in slot machine?" The man held out a coin.

As Diamond reached for it, the man pressed the coin to his forehead, so hard it left an imprint of George Washington on the skin. He mumbled a few phrases in what Diamond guessed was Greek, then handed Diamond the quarter.

The Greek's overweight buddy was sitting at the far end of the counter chuckling. Diamond figured he was being set up for a practical joke but he couldn't guess what it was and decided to play along. He dropped the coin in a nearby bandit and reached for the arm.

"No. No. I do it," the Greek said. He wiped his hands on his trousers, mumbled again, and gently eased the arm down.

Click. The figures spun by. Apple. Lemon. Bell. Bar. Cherry. The machine flashed "Win! Win! Win!" as three cherries turned up through the glass. It noisily spit up a mound of quarters.

"Shit," the man at the other end of the counter said. "It finally worked."

The Greek threw his arms around Diamond and collected his money from the mouth at the bottom of the machine.

"Come, you must join us. You bring me luck. My name is Nicholas Papadokadis." He pulled Diamond down the counter with the feverish strength of a winner.

"I told you. I told you. See," Papadokadis said to his friend.

43

"My name's Bob Kincaid," said the fat man whose haunches hung over the stool. Diamond shook the fleshy hand he proffered.

"Papa's been stopping strangers for years," Kincaid explained. "He kept saying he'd meet a stranger who'd change his luck. It can't get much worse. How much you owe?" he asked the Greek.

"But no more. Now I have luck. I win it back, bring my family over. Buy a restaurant. Two restaurants. What is your name?"

"Simon Jaffe." It slipped out before Diamond had a chance to think, coming from a part of him he didn't know existed. As he wondered what it meant he got dizzy and grabbed the counter for support.

"Are you okay? You look sick," Kincaid said.

Red sagged on his stool and gulped a glass of water.

"I heard of people getting sick after eating one of Ginny's meals, but never before."

"Aw, shut up," the waitress said, setting a cheeseburger, coffee, and slice of pie in front of Diamond.

"I'm fine," Diamond said.

Kincaid tried to grab the waitress's hand. "You love me, don't you Ginny?"

She shrugged his grasp off easily. "If you were ten years younger, one hundred pounds thinner, and had as much money as Onassis, I might let you kiss my hand."

"It isn't your hand I'd like to kiss," Kincaid said with a leer.

"Slob," she snapped and walked away.

Diamond dug into his food, trying to put thoughts of Jaffe out of his mind.

"We both drive for Speedy Cab," Kincaid said. "What do you do?"

"I'm between jobs right now," Diamond said. "I'm looking around."

"I get you job," Papa volunteered. "I am good friends with the boss. You can be driving for us right away."

"What's the deal?" Diamond asked. "Owner operated, lease, fleet?"

"It sounds like you know your way around," Kincaid said.

Diamond gagged on a slice of pie. He was disoriented, a medium in touch with an unexpected ghost.

Kincaid studied him as he began speaking. "We're fleet here. Total of four hundred cabs spread out in a dozen operations. There's thirty-five at Speedy. You make fifty percent."

Diamond had lost his appetite. He pushed the plate away and lit a cigarette.

"Some radio dispatch, not much hail business," Kincaid continued, eying the leftover pie greedily. "Guys pick up extra bucks referring tourists to sociable girls. And you can work out a deal with the Marrying Sams."

"The what?"

"Marrying Sams. The preachers got these storefronts for quickie weddings. They kick back if you refer people to them and sometimes the happy couple hires you as a witness. That's the business here in a nutshell."

"How is business?"

"Terrible," Kincaid said. "You make more selling hot plates to Gila monsters."

"Jaffe change that," Papa said. "He bring luck."

"You don't know the half of it," Diamond said.

5

After promising to stop by the garage the next morning and exchanging farewells with his newfound friends, Red headed back to the Ace of Diamonds.

On the way, he checked into the Last Chance Motel under the name of Simon Jaffe. The dingy one-story complex, with two dozen rooms around an over-chlorinated pool, was a more plausible home for a job hunter than the Diamond Suite. He stopped at a K-Mart and bought work pants and a sport shirt.

He returned to the Diamond Suite and sent his suit out to be cleaned and pressed. He showered away the sweat and sand and called Evans on the house phone, arranging an interview with the chief of security, Ron Braun.

Braun had the build and warmth of a fireplug. He crushed Diamond's hand and made it clear he was a busy man.

"What can I do for you, Dalmas?" he demanded. "Tex told me you're going to be carrying a gun around here. I don't like it, but I gave my boys instructions not to hassle you. And I know what a tough guy you are."

"How's that?"

"I heard about your run-in with Mike Gregory."

"Who?"

46

"Van Houton's bodyguard. The ex-mercenary you laid out in the hall last night. We frown on that sort of activity. If I had my way, you'd be gone too."

"He's gone?"

"Him and Van Houton checked out this morning."

"I'm terribly sorry I hurt his feelings," Diamond said sarcastically.

"You should be. He makes a bad enemy. So do I."

"I'll remember that."

"So what do you want?"

"I carry large sums of money," Diamond said. "I've already seen what a great job you do keeping hookers out of this place. I wanted to make sure it was safe. I've heard about the trouble a lot of places have been having."

Diamond noticed a slight stress quiver in Braun's eyes.

"What have you heard?"

"Just rumors."

"Listen Dalmas, I was a cop for twenty-four years in New York. There isn't anything I haven't seen. I've got a hand-picked force of five hundred men under my command. I can take care of things."

"Good. I feel much better now." As the P.I. moved toward the door he said, "Say hello to Moe."

"What? What?" Braun asked, the stress tremor again crinkling his deepset eyes.

Diamond exited without answering.

He took the elevator down to the main floor. The noise of chips clicking, slots jangling, roulette wheels spinning, and cards snapping, overlaid with the moans of losers and shouts of winners, hit Red as he stepped out into the main casino. It was about one-third full and decorated with the same diamond motif as the rest of the hotel. Diamond-shaped fixtures, diamond patterns on the wall, diamond designs in the carpet. The usual

47

Las Vegas gaudy overkill. It was enough to make Diamond wish his name was Smith.

The casino was dimly lit, with each table bathed in a soft spotlight and every slot machine its own little glowing temptation. White-gloved old ladies sat at the slots, oblivious to their surroundings as they plunked quarter after quarter into the one-armed bandits. At the craps tables, men in conventioneer's fezzes shouted "Six the hard way" and "Be good to daddy" as they nuzzled the dice and bounced them down the green felt. The well-dressed men and women around the baccarat tables were quieter, pretending they were princes and princesses looking grand at Monte Carlo.

As Diamond sauntered past, he could feel questioning eyes on him. John Dalmas, high roller with a .38 on his hip, was making a grand entrance. The pit bosses' antennae vibrated.

"I think I'll start small," he said to the man behind the cashier's window. "Give me ten chips."

"Very good, sir," the cashier said, accepting ten thousand dollars in cash and giving back ten brown chips with white diamonds embossed on them.

Red toyed with his chips as he passed by the row of crescent-shaped, green felt-topped blackjack tables. Small plaques at each one announced the minimum bet. The seven seats at each of the half-dozen $2, $5, and $25 minimum tables were filled.

The hard-boiled detective could never go for baccarat. Get dressed up, bet before you see your cards, and hope to get as close to nine as possible. About as much fun as watching a one-armed mechanic rotate the tires on a sixteen-wheeler. Roulette and the slots were too mechanical. Keno was jazzed-up bingo. He'd never gotten along with dice. And poker was more fun to play with a few buddies and a case of beer.

Besides, Diamond had been sapped enough that the name blackjack had a certain appeal.

The dealer at the $1,000 minimum table stood alone, arms akimbo, a slight challenging smile on his face. He had stern features and thinning hair. Four decks of cards were fanned out on the baize before him.

Diamond sat down casually and put his ten chips on the table.

With long thin fingers, the dealer collected the fanned out cards into a stack. He shuffled without looking at his hands, keeping his appraising eyes locked on Diamond's. After nearly a minute, he offered the P.I. the pile and a green plastic card. Diamond sliced the card into the middle of the deck. The dealer cut where Diamond had indicated and put the cards into the shoe at his left. Diamond put two chips into the circle painted in front of him and the game began.

Diamond was no card counter. He had no system. All he did was draw another card whenever he had a diamond in his hand. He played with a casual boredom, his mind barely on the game.

He scraped the table, indicating he wanted a card, even though he had seventeen in his hand. The dealer hesitated, but flipped Diamond his card. It was a four.

Rocco was running around loose, Fifi was missing, and here I am playing cards, Red thought. It's part of the role, he knew, but he still felt rotten. Wasting valuable time. Playing with house money. A shamus acting like a shill.

Making it through the day was a gamble, Red figured. He didn't need to play games. The deck was stacked enough in the real world.

A cocktail waitress in a zircon spangled mini-dress brought him a drink. He tipped her ten dollars. She had bleached blond hair, a nose that bore a plastic surgeon's

49

touch, and pushed-up breasts. But nice legs that appeared to be the original issue.

The legs reminded him of Fifi. Legs that went from here to there and back again. Legs that could wrap around him and shut off the rest of the world.

The game continued. Diamond didn't bother splitting pairs, doubling down, or getting insurance. Simple, straightforward. He won most, lost some. He noticed a bead of sweat on the dealer's brow.

Fifi could be anywhere. Dealing cards, waitressing, running Keno cards, operating a switchboard in some back office where he'd never see her again.

But she was talented and loved men's eyes on her. A mutual pleasure. She'd want to be in the public eye. On the stage. In the chorus line.

Las Vegas was a city of two hundred thousand, but Red had found smaller needles in bigger haystacks. The total population was deceiving. In any city there are hundreds of communities. Not geographic areas, but occupational, socio-economic, sport, enclaves.

To find a missing stamp collector, go to a philately society. A doctor, call the medical association. A jockey, the race track. Even if a fugitive gave up his or her profession, they'd return to familiar stomping grounds. Like the lawyer Diamond had found working in a gas station in Milwaukee. The ex-attorney had blown his cover by becoming a court buff.

What better place to look for a raving beauty like Fifi than in the Las Vegas floor shows? And chorus girls were as chummy and gossipy as any other people. If anyone would know where his beloved Fifi was, it would be the women who danced and sang for their supper.

Diamond pocketed a dozen of his chips, and flipped the dealer his thirteenth.

"For good luck," he said and slid away from the table.

50

Without a glance back, he headed to the cashier's cage. As he cashed in his chips, a man standing at the back of the cage let himself out and came over. Balding, with tufts of brown hair and a thin brown mustache, he extended his hand.

"My name's Slim Vogel," he said with an artificially sincere smile. "I'm the hotel's courtesy officer. You're John Dalmas."

"That's what my driver's license says."

"Are you enjoying your stay? Is there anything I can do?"

"Yeah, come to think of it. I wonder if I could get a tour of this place?"

"No problem. What would you like to see?"

"How about backstage at the show?" Diamond said with a properly lecherous tone. "I've heard you have some of the best-looking dames in the world."

"An excellent choice," Vogel said, throwing his arm across Diamond's shoulder. "Come with me."

They walked out through the casino and Vogel launched into a well-practiced spiel.

"We get more than one hundred thousand people a week coming through here. More foot traffic than the busiest railroad station. Our casino's bigger than a football field. And it has a lot more action. We have more currency transactions than the Bank of America. And we burn enough bulbs here and in the display outside to light up the city of Des Moines."

Diamond put on a suitably impressed expression. They edged through the milling crowds to a metal service door marked EMPLOYEES ONLY.

Vogel opened the door with a key and they entered.

"Not many outsiders get to see this. Only staff and our most favored guests. This corridor here leads to our 'Eye in the Sky' monitoring rooms," Vogel said, gesturing to a hallway.

51

"How many people have access to it?"

"The 'Eye in the Sky' allows us to monitor dealers and . . . What did you ask?"

"How many people can get back there?"

"That's a strange question."

"I'm a strange guy."

Vogel stopped and plucked at his mustache as he thought. "Oh, I guess a couple hundred. Why do you ask?"

"Just curious."

They continued down the hall, passing workers wheeling carts loaded with food, linens, and assorted hotel supplies.

"Our kitchen is down here," Vogel said, gesturing off in another direction as food smells drifted to them. "We serve over twelve thousand eggs a day and ten thousand pounds of shrimp. Besides our five restaurants, we have room service available in all twenty-one hundred rooms and snacks in our four cocktail lounges."

"You're full of facts and figures, aren't you?"

"Thank you," Vogel said. "If you like figures, wait 'til you see our showgirls. Anyway, the hotel cost a hundred fifty million dollars to build and that was back in . . . "

As Vogel babbled on, they passed a man in a bellhop's jacket wheeling a handtruck laden with metal cans. The ferret-faced bellboy looked familiar but Diamond couldn't recall where he'd seen him. The man showed no sign of recognizing Diamond.

" . . . One hundred thousand square feet in our shopping arcade," Vogel was saying as they came to the end of the cinderblock corridor. Diamond dismissed the bellboy as someone he'd seen around as Vogel swung open another metal door.

The purified air smell of the corridor was replaced by a wave of perfume, sweat, and female odors. They stepped into the showgirls' lounge. It was a brightly lit, mirrored room with a half-dozen couches and women in various states of undress. None of them made any move to cover up as the men entered.

Vogel was clearly enjoying the view and Diamond's embarassed expression. Red felt like a lion in a herd of wildebeest, not sure how to react to the appealing flesh circulating around him. The mirrors multiplied the effect of the breasts, buttocks, and thighs. Sequins, spangles, bangles, feathers, and generous lengths of female skin were everywhere.

"These are the Diamondaires, the most talented group of females in Las Vegas," Vogel said. "And some of them can dance too."

A redhead with small breasts and taut legs gave Vogel a punch in the shoulder. "Introduce your friend," she said.

"This is John Dalmas, a guest in our Diamond Suite," Vogel said.

The women made cooing noises.

"Are you as good with the ladies as you are with the cards?" Vogel asked Diamond.

"Only if I can cut the cards first," Diamond said.

He was rewarded with a few giggles.

A tall black woman with mahogany-colored skin entered and frowned at Diamond and Vogel. She had short cut hair and a muscular, but womanly, body. At her side was one hundred pounds of muscle disguised as a Samoyed. The dog stalked over to Diamond, sat down in front of him, and bared his fangs.

"Cute puppy," Diamond said, standing motionless. "Has he killed anyone today?"

The black woman strode over and stood behind her dog. "Bart don't like strangers."

"He's not going to make many friends like that," Diamond said as the dog continued to sneer.

"It's okay, Rosie," Vogel interjected. "John is a friend of the house. Don't be so protective." The courtesy officer turned to Diamond. "I've got to get back to the cage. I'll leave you in these ladies' capable hands."

"I'll take good care of him," the redhead said.

"Just don't keep him away from the tables too long," Vogel said with a wink. He opened the service door and disappeared into the hallway.

"What you want?" Rosie demanded of Diamond.

"How about giving Fido a bone so he stops eyeing my leg like he wants to take it out and bury it?"

"Bart! Place!" Rosie said, and the dog regretfully moved to a small rug on the far side of the room. He kept a hungry eye on Diamond.

"The girls go onstage in a few minutes," Rosie said. "They don't got time to be flapping their lips."

"Are you the house mother?" Diamond asked.

"She's just a mutha," one of the showgirls said.

Rosie swiveled her head quickly but didn't catch the one who'd said it.

"My job is keeping lowlifes from bothering the ladies. Me and Bart keep these sweet young things safe."

"They look like they can handle themselves," Diamond said.

The redhead looped her arm through Diamond's. "I'm Angie. And you can handle me however you want."

"Are you ready to go on?" Rosie asked Angie.

"You think I dress like this to do the laundry," Angie snapped. She was wearing a sequined G-string and pasties with tassles hanging from them. She had blue plumes coming off her rump and head. "I'm not on until the third number anyhow."

"Rosie, I need a hand with this strap," one of the women at the other side of the room said.

With a glare at Diamond as hostile as her Samoyed's, Rosie stormed away.

"That's my friend," Angie said, indicating the woman who'd asked for help with the strap. "She knows when to get Rosie out of my hair."

Women drifted out of the room toward the stage area. The band began to play. Soon Diamond, Angie, and two other women were in the lounge. The other women sat on a sofa gossiping while filing their painted toenails.

Red knew he could get more from one-on-one questioning than he would if he asked the roomful of women. He put his arm around Angie, squeezed her shoulder, and led her to a corner away from the toenail trimmers.

"You got a powerful grip there," Angie said. "I bet you could crush a little gal like me."

"Angie, you're cuter than a pet shop full of puppies, but I'm looking for a particular lady."

"Oh." She stiffened.

"But I'd be real grateful to whoever told me where she was. Her name's Fifi La Roche."

"How grateful?" she asked, her flirtatious manner replaced by a cagey tone.

"A C-spot grateful."

"We're talking a cecil? A hundred bucks?"

"Crisp and green."

"You must really love her," Angie said. "I don't know the name. What's she look like?"

"She's a blonde. Early thirties. About five and a half feet tall. Hundred and twenty pounds. Blue eyes."

"If you want you can order girls like that by the dozen."

"But Fifi's different. Her hair is like gold, her eyes so blue you want to swim in them. And she's got the kind of body men kill for."

"I bet music plays when she enters the room," Angie said. "You're a real poet but your description doesn't help. Every time they have a cattle call here, you get a couple hundred girls that could fit the bill. I'd like the money, but I can't finger her for you. If you'd like a redhead, however . . ."

Finger. Fingers. Diamond plunged his hand into his pocket and grabbed the mug shots. Fingers. Vito Falanges, ex-Chicago hood. That's who the bellboy had been.

"Hey. What gives?" Angie asked.

Diamond spun and jerked at the locked service door. It didn't budge. A quick look at the hardware and he knew he couldn't batter it down or open it without a pick set.

"Quick, how can I get back in the hall?" he asked, grabbing the bewildered Angie.

"The only way out is through that door," she said, pointing to the door to the stage. "But you can't go—"

Diamond was barreling toward the stage before she finished her sentence. He ran into the wings. A thickset man wheeling a prop chest tried to stop him but he shoved the man aside.

"Hey, you can't go out th—" a security man shouted. But he didn't move quick enough. Diamond pushed through a heavy curtain.

Several thousand watts of light hit him, freezing him momentarily in place. The security man grabbed for his arm and Diamond began moving again.

The band was playing "Raindrops Keep Falling On My Head." The chorus girls, wearing translucent droplet costumes, were kicking. Diamond ran between their flying legs. Three women fell over trying to avoid kicking him. He stumbled over one well-shaped leg and got kicked by two others. The band kept on playing and the audience roared with laughter.

But when he made it through the gauntlet Rosie was waiting with anything but a smile on her face.

"You stupid bastard! You ruined the—"

"Listen and listen good. I've got to talk to Tex. It's an emergency."

Rosie hesitated.

Diamond took out his gun. "If you don't hurry, I'm going back on stage and start shooting this thing in the air."

"There's a house phone on the post," she said, backing toward it. She walked to the wall box and lifted the phone. "What's going on?"

"No time to explain. Just get me Tex."

"He don't answer the phone for no one," she said, handing the receiver to Diamond.

It took thirty seconds for Evans to get on the line.

"This is Red. I saw one of Moe Greenberg's boys in the service corridor a few minutes ago. Does he have any business being here?"

"Who?" Tex asked.

"Vito Falanges. Fingers."

"Hot damn no! That polecat makes Billy the Kid—"

"No time. He was heading to the casino area from the corridor backstage. What's there that he could hurt?"

"Everything. There are doors to the basement, the spotting rooms, kitchen, storage rooms. It's like a maze."

Diamond glanced over at Rosie. She was staring at him wide-eyed. He covered the mouthpiece of the phone.

"Do you have a key to the service corridor?" he asked her.

"Yes."

"How's Bart on tracking?"

"He can do it."

Diamond put the phone back up to his mouth.

"I'm going to hunt for him with Rosie and her dog,"

57

he said. "If you don't hear from me within fifteen minutes, you start evacuating the place. Got it?"

"Sure do," Tex said.

Diamond hung up. "Let's go."

"But we got a full house," she said. "I can't just leave."

"You've got to trust me. There's no time to argue. Fingers is a torch. I saw him with a bunch of fluid cans. Do you understand what that means?"

She nodded.

"What's the quickest way to the corridor?"

"The audience seemed to like your act last time," she said with a grim smile.

Diamond and the woman ran back across the stage. This time he only got kicked once. And Rosie deftly avoided the fast moving feet of the thoroughly confused chorus line. The crowd loved it.

As the P.I. ran into the girls' lounge, Bart put the snarl back on his face. But he kept his distance. Rosie hurried to the service door and opened it.

"Come," she yelled, and the dog ran to her side.

Stepping into the hall, Diamond offered his .38 to Rosie. "You know how to use this?"

She shook her head.

"Aim it at the center of the target. Keep both arms out in front and point. Don't lock your arms. Squeeze the trigger slow, don't jerk it. It's simple to shoot. Once you decide to do it, empty the gun. Stay calm. And make sure it's not me in the sights."

She took the gun awkwardly and Diamond ran to the stairwell. "Anybody up there?" he shouted. His voice echoed off the hard walls. There was no response.

"Send Bart up," Diamond said.

"Bart, search!" Rosie commanded, and the white Samoyed took off up the stairs. They counted him

58

bounding up three flights before Diamond had Rosie call him back.

"I've handled a few arson cases," Diamond said as the dog ran to them. "Heat rises. The pros usually go for the stairs or the basement."

"The basement is this way," she said, and they ran further down the hall.

Red opened the cellar door. The smell of fresh linen and a variety of stored foodstuffs came to his nostrils. But the scent that got to him was the pungent odor of gasoline.

"No smoke yet," Diamond said, breathing heavily from the exertion. "Are you ready?"

She nodded.

"Don't shoot unless it's necessary. If a slug sparks off the metal, we could do Fingers's job for him."

"Okay. Be careful," she said reflexively.

He smiled, and they descended the metal stairs. The only sound was the click-click of the Samoyed's nails on the metal tread. When they reached bottom, Diamond whispered, "You hide over here. If he gets past me, shoot him. He's a killer."

"I understand."

"Will Bart obey me? We haven't exactly hit it off."

Rosie knelt and put her face by the dog's. "Give me your hand," she said to Diamond.

The P.I. extended it reluctantly. The dog still looked hungry.

"Bart, friend," she said, putting Diamond's hand to the Samoyed's nose.

The dog opened his mouth and licked Diamond. The canine's fluffy tail wagged.

"Let's go Bart," Diamond said, and they moved to the far wall where a half-dozen metal conduits were blocked by a stack of cartons.

Diamond spotted a crowbar lying on a wooden crate. He picked it up, hefted it, and moved on. The dog looked at him like they were about to play fetch.

They moved cautiously around the warehouse-size basement. The gasoline smell grew stronger. The dog sneezed.

They came to a stack of cartons. FLAMMABLE was stamped on each box. They could hear movement on the other side of the eight-foot-high, and twice as wide, stack. The Samoyed's white fur seemed to stand on end as his hackles went up. He looked at Diamond for direction.

"Search," Diamond said. Bart seemed to be smiling as he set off in a stealthy, hunter's prowl.

Diamond waited, the crowbar poised above his head. He breathed in and out. The stench of gas filled the air.

A man screamed, and Fingers came staggering around the corner of the cartons. He was trying to pull his gun out with his left hand while one hundred pounds of Samoyed was turning his right into chopped meat. He drew his gun and was shoving it into Bart's rock-hard belly when Diamond brought the crowbar down on his head. Fingers fell to the floor and Bart let go. The dog walked over to Diamond and licked his hand.

6

The cops came and took statements from Diamond and Rosie. The only statement Fingers made was a sad moan. Bart looked pleased with himself.

As firefighters vacuumed up gasoline and spread foam, Norris materialized and escorted Diamond to Evans, who was waiting in a locked broom closet.

"I don't like crowds," Evans explained as he and Diamond huddled amid mops and cleaning gear. Norris stood guard outside.

"I heard what happened," Evans said. "Partner, you already earned your keep. And then some. The Fire Department boys said there was enough to make us go up like a Comanche fire arrow. I'm mighty pleased you're on my side."

"The dog did most of the work. And Rosie's a pretty ballsy lady."

"I reckon so."

"I met your security chief. I wasn't very impressed. This shows I was right. I think you should give Braun another job, or the boot."

"Would you take over?" Evans asked, chomping enthusiastically on a chaw of tobacco.

"I've got too much to do," Diamond said, thinking of

61

Fifi. "But I bet Rosie could handle it. I know she'll run a tight ship."

Evans thought for a moment, punctuating the silence by spitting into one of the pails. As his shot pinged off the side, he said, "I bet you hit on something there, fella. The sun's coming up on Las Vegas. With Fingers in the hoosegow, there's bound to be a whole lot of pressure on the guys in black hats."

"I got a feeling you're seeing the opening shots in a range war," Diamond said.

He slipped out of the closet and took the elevator to his suite. He relaxed with a Scotch and a cigarette while reviewing the mugshots.

Fingers should be a guest of the government, at least for a while, Red thought. If the cops were able to get anything out of him, it could crack the case wide open. Fingers drops a dime on Greenberg, Greenberg gives up Rocco, and Diamond gets Fifi.

Red didn't believe in the Easter bunny and he didn't believe it would go that easy. Greenberg's money and muscle gave him more juice than Sunkist. Fingers would keep his mouth shut.

Diamond skipped the pictures of Greenberg and Silky. He had them committed to memory. Fingers's photo he put off to one side. That left Babe McCloor and Freddie DeFilippo, also known as Flip.

Babe was a three-hundred-pound mountain with a thick black eyebrow that stretched from temple to temple. He looked like he could slip into a Neanderthal cave and mingle unnoticed. *Seventeen arrests, mainly assault, and as dumb as he looks*, Saint had pencilled on the back.

Flip was a greasy-haired lounge lizard with a sensual, mean mouth. The type who thought himself a real lady-killer. On the back of the mugshot, Saint noted that he was indeed a lady-killer, having married a heiress and then running her down with her down with her own Rolls Royce. The cops had gotten wise, and instead of an inheritance, Flip got ten years in the slammer.

Flip and Babe were a two-man team. Flip managed Greenberg's prostitution rings and Babe kept order.

There was a knock at the door. Diamond walked over and swung it open.

"I came to return this," Rosie said, holding out his .38. "Thank God I didn't have to use it. Can I come in?"

Diamond stepped aside and the woman and the dog entered. Bart marched over to the couch, jumped up, and promptly went to sleep.

"It's been a long day," Diamond said, holstering his gun.

"You're telling me. Tex offered me the job as head of security," Rosie said sadly. "He said it was your recommendation. Thanks."

"You don't sound too thrilled."

"I'm not taking it," she said, lowering herself into one of the chairs. "I've got a few hundred saved up. I'm leaving."

"Why?"

"You don't know this place the way I do. It's a different world. There's hundreds of dudes who will off me just so Moe will give them a nod. I don't know where you're from, but you ought to take my advice and go back there."

"I never backed down since the doctor slapped my butt as a baby."

"You ain't seen what I have, John. You may be a big gambler, but you don't know the game you're playing in. I'm clearing out."

"It's your decision. Is there anything I can do?"

"Can I stay here tonight? I'd feel safer."

"Sure."

"Don't get me wrong. I sleep alone," she said with

some of her old spark. "I don't shack up with a dude 'less I really know him."

"I don't shack up with guys even after I know 'em for years," he said with a smile. "I'll take the couch, if Bart will share it."

They both looked at the dreaming dog, who was flicking his paws and making little whining noises. It was the only sound in the room.

"I'll take the couch," Rosie said. "I'm used to sleeping with Bart."

"Lucky dog."

She gave him a weak smile. "I'm really tired," she said, droopy eyed. She pointed at his crotch. "Do you mind leaving that with me?"

He looked down at his fly.

"The gun," she said.

"Oh." He thought of the Army chant, "This is my rifle, this is my gun. One is for shooting, the other for fun," but said nothing. He took the .38 in the belly holster out and put it on the end table next to the divan.

"Thanks," Rosie said. She walked to the couch and shoved in behind Bart. The dog grumbled and barely opened his eyes. She was asleep before Diamond shut the light.

Diamond went to the bedroom with a bemused expression on his face. The second night in a row he had a woman sleeping in his suite and the relationship was platonic.

It hadn't always been that way. In his prime, he could outdo Shell Scott, Mike Shayne, Timothy Dane, or any Don Juan dick in the sack. During his cases, he'd picked up secretaries, waitresses, embittered divorcees, women lawyers, switchboard operators, gal reporters, gun molls, and nurses. A dirty job, but someone had to do it. He'd broken dozens of cases by taking advantage

64

of pillow talk. But then he'd gotten involved with Fifi and it just wasn't the same.

Fifi and me checked into the small motel on the outskirts of the dry Texas town. Our clothes were torn from the car crash, after Rocco's thugs had tried running us off the road.

With a couple of slugs from my gat, I sent them on the highway to Hell.

The palsied gent behind the motel desk grinned at our shabby look, but Andrew Jackson convinced him we were all right. We signed in as Mr. and Mrs. Chandler Raymond. Most of the other entries were from the Smith family.

We went to our room and locked the door. Fifi's perfume mingled with the stuffy, mildewed odor of the sparsely furnished room.

"Listen dollface, maybe I should . . . "

"Not now, you fool, kiss me," she said and gave me her lipstick to taste.

I pressed hard on her lush lips and they opened. She ground into me until the throbbing of my lust felt like a balloon about to bust.

I picked her up and carried her to the swaybacked bed. Our clothes disappeared and I was on her and in her and with her. It was like never before. And even better a half hour later when I entered heaven again.

The night was a blur of passion, building to crescendos, peaking, and then building again. It only got better.

By the time the sun came up, I decided I never wanted to leave the motel room.

How the heck did Scott Marks know every intimate detail, Red wondered. It was like he had the room bugged; he even knew what Red was thinking.

Diamond didn't believe in psychics. He'd busted up too many scams—like the time Gabrielle Leggett got mixed up with those wackos in Frisco—to fall for that hokum. But Marks did seem to be a mind reader.

The Ameche rang three times before Diamond slipped out of his reverie.

"Dalmas?" a smarmy voice said when he picked up.

"Who's this?"

"I got someone wants to talk to you."

Diamond heard a scuffling sound and then a terrified woman's voice.

"John. This is Teri Lennox. Please help me. They—"

More scuffling and the smarmy voice was back on the line.

"I want to see you," the man said. "Take Tropicana out past Jimmy Durante Drive. Make a left when you see the dirt road. Get over here right away or the girl dies."

"Who is this?"

"Just so you know we're not kidding around," the voice said. There was a woman's scream through the phone, so strong it made Diamond's ear hurt. There was no question it was real. It sounded more like a hurt animal than a human.

"You harm the girl and you'll pay."

"Tough talk," the man said smugly. "You're in no position to make threats. The sooner you get here, the less time we'll have for fun with her."

Click. The line was dead.

Rosie was standing in the bedroom doorway.

"I heard the phone," she said. "What happened?"

"I got to go get someone I know."

"It's trouble. I can tell by your face."

"She's being held."

"I'll go with you."

"No. Besides, I thought you didn't want to get involved."

"I'm already in this up to my ass," Rosie said. "I got nothing to lose. And I'd rather be where the action is than sitting back here worrying about you."

"I don't have time to argue."

"Then get the safari going, *bwana*. And you try anything from the movies like knocking me out so I miss the party and Bart gonna take a piece of your hide."

The dog looked like he would.

The three of them ran to the elevator. Diamond cursed at its slowness as it descended to the garage. They jumped in his car and screeched out.

"Do you know the area where Tropicana meets Jimmy Durante Drive?"

"I knew you'd need me," she said. "It's out on the east side. It shouldn't be more than fifteen minutes. The area's being developed. They got a lot of vacant lots over there." She acted as navigator as they sped through the streets.

It was 3:00 A.M. and the hard-core gamblers were either in the casinos or their rooms, dreaming of how much money they'd win their next time at the tables.

The Strip was far from deserted, though. Hookers offering a different kind of roll waved at cars, doing everything but throwing themselves under the wheels to get attention. Cars filled with losers, who thought their luck would change if they tried their own kind of table-hopping, drove from casino to casino in search of Lady Luck. A few drunk conventioneers cruised, yelling out of their car windows like teenage boys with their first car.

Diamond swerved in and out among them, drawing beeps and curses. Rosie bit her lips.

"Do you have to go this fast?" she asked.

"Don't worry," he said, banging the curb as he took a corner sharply. "I've always been a pro behind the

67

wheel. There's something about being in a car that makes me comfortable."

He made a left onto Paradise Road, nearly hitting a slow-moving Cadillac. Traffic was lighter and he leaned on the gas pedal.

"I feel like I spent my life in a car. Must come from the surveillances I been on. I must've tailed a couple hundred people. Did I tell you about the case that got some ink as 'Race to Death?' I was following this race car driver, a real hot rodder—"

Brakes screeched and a Toyota driver leaned on his horn.

"Please don't talk, just watch the road."

"Don't worry, babe. You're in good hands."

"Famous last words."

He immersed himself in the task of driving, moving the steering wheel like an artist stroking a canvas.

They passed malls with the usual franchises, and developments with cinderblock walls shielding identical houses from the roadway. The houses got cheaper-looking, Spanish-style quickies put up by developers who didn't come to Vegas to gamble. It was strange seeing regular homes in Las Vegas, like finding a normal household in the middle of an amusement park.

The houses thinned out. There were more sandy vacant lots with sparse scrub grass eking out a dry existence. Wherever man didn't irrigate, the harsh environment took over.

There was no one on the street.

"You're not what you seem, are you?" Rosie asked.

"Huh?"

"This talk about surveillances, cases. The way you got Evans on the phone. Who are you?"

They passed Jimmy Durante Drive before he had to come up with an answer. "Get down," he ordered, and she squeezed below the dashboard.

He drove another quarter of a mile. The ground was flat, with dry arroyos carved into its harsh face.

He saw no one as he pulled the car a dozen yards up the dirt road.

"Stay inside," he whispered to Rosie. He pulled the dome light cap off, and took out the bulb. No point in giving his caller an easy target.

Diamond stepped out into the cold night air. A dry wind blew an ominous silence across his ears. Torn sofas, car fragments, and rusted refrigerators were strewn near a NO DUMPING sign. The city lights in the distance gave a faint glow to the sky.

He walked a few yards into the brush, carefully watching where he stepped. He was an urban tough guy but he knew the snakes came out at night. And if there was one thing Red Diamond was scared of, it was snakes. Goons with guns, double-crossing dames, sharp knives, bomb blasts, windy heights. None of them bothered him as much as the slithering reptiles.

He heard a cry and began moving in the direction it was coming from. He reached for his .38.

It was gone. He stiffened. Then he remembered where it was. On the small table. Where he'd left it for Rosie.

Diamond was alone in the snake-infested desert, looking for a ruthless kidnapper, without his trusty roscoe.

He felt a quiver of fear, an urge to run back to the car. But he was Red Diamond, and Red Diamond didn't back out of a jam. He pushed on.

The night wind felt colder. The whimpering was louder. It was the sound of a woman in pain.

He nearly stumbled over her. She was staked out naked, spread-eagled on the ground. It took a moment for him to recognize her. Someone had done cruel things to Teri Lennox. Burn marks and freshly crusted blood.

He thought back to the night before, her young body. Was it only twenty-four hours earlier? Now only a doctor could view her without feeling sick.

"It's Red. I'll get you out of here," he promised, kneeling and tugging at the ropes that bound her wrists to pegs set in the ground. She moaned.

A shot whistled over his head. He threw himself flat and cursed the weapon that lay useless in his room.

"John?" the girl said in a sickly croak.

"We're going to be okay," Diamond said, trying to express confidence he didn't feel.

Another shot singed by, kicking up sand as it burrowed into the ground nearby.

"Who did this?" he asked.

"Babe picked me up on the Strip. I should've known," she said. Every word was an effort. "Him and Flip took me here." She moaned again and there was another shot.

It was closer. Diamond saw the muzzle flash. Near the ground. The gunman must be hunched down in one of the arroyos.

"They left me with . . . " she coughed, and made a gurgling sound. Blood, redder than the reddest lipstick, burbled out of her mouth. Diamond wiped it with his hand.

"Take it easy," he said, feeling helpless as the rage built within him.

"They left when Silky came. He did this. I hurt, I hurt real bad. Please help me."

Diamond grabbed a stake and the adrenaline surged. He ripped it out of the ground. Wooden splinters stuck to his hands. He tore at the other stakes until the girl was free. His hands were a bloody mess.

She curled into a fetal ball.

"Who knew that you'd been with me?" he asked.

"I didn't tell anyone."

70

Another shot kicked up sand barely a foot away. They were pinned down like butterflies on a bug collector's board.

"Please! Get me to a doctor," Teri wailed.

Diamond rose and another shot went off. It was too low to hit him. But not her. Teri Lennox's pain was over. Forever.

Diamond crouched down and moved toward the gully as shots went whizzing by. He yelped in pain and fell on his belly. The sand felt cold and gritty against his face.

A half-dozen more rounds were fired. After the final crack there was a long silence.

Diamond saw the lone figure rising out of the arroyo. Silky. The P.I. struggled to lie still as every muscle in his body cried out for vengeance.

Silky moved cautiously forward, his gun trained on Diamond's body. He was about fifteen feet away when he lifted his gun for the coup de grace.

The headlights from the Plymouth froze Silky like a deer on a country road.

Diamond stopped playing possum and charged as Silky fired at the oncoming car. He saw the windshield shatter, the car swerve out of control and crash into a gully.

Silky turned and aimed at Diamond. The P.I. hurled himself through the air and caught the hood in the gut with his head. Diamond's fists were pumping like jackhammers before the two men hit the ground.

"Don't hurt me. Don't hurt me," Silky whined. He was clumsy with his fists when a helpless girl wasn't involved. The P.I.'s punches sent Silky to thug dreamland.

Red's hands felt like tenderized beef as he got up and ran to the car. It rested at a forty-five-degree angle with its nose at the bottom of the slope. Rosie looked like a boxer who'd gone one round too many. Bart was licking her face.

"Are you okay?" Diamond asked, regretting the dumb question as soon as it was out of his mouth.

"I guess," she said weakly.

"Damn women drivers. Can't get behind the wheel without wrecking a car."

"I must look a mess," she said.

Little bits of glass stuck to her hair and clothes. Diamond leaned in and kissed her forehead, damp with dog saliva. He took some rags out of the trunk and began cleaning her up.

"Can you walk?" he asked.

"I think so."

"Good. We got a long walk home. I don't want a cab picking us up anywhere near here."

"Was that Silky?" she asked.

"Yes."

"Is he dead?"

"I doubt it."

She looked sad. And scared.

"You stay here," Diamond said. "I've got to go talk to him."

He walked back to where the thug lay. Diamond was five feet from the man when he saw the movement. Silky had his handgun pointed at Diamond.

The private eye kicked sand in the punk's face. Silky fired. Diamond dove on top of him. Again they struggled. But Silky was weak from his beating. Diamond twisted the gun as Silky fired and the hood caught his own bullet.

"Who sent you?" Diamond demanded of the dying man.

"Help me."

"Who sent you?"

"Moe."

72

"What about Rocco? Where is he?"

"Who?"

"Don't try and cover up. Rocco Rico."

"I don't know no Rocco Rico. Help me."

"Don't try and cover up."

"I'm telling the truth," Silky said desperately. "Help me and I'll tell you about them. I don't like that bastard anyway. He called me a—"

He coughed blood. The life fluid didn't show as clearly on his dark skin as it had on Teri's, but it reminded Diamond of her just the same.

"I know about it. About Atlantic City and the mob."

"It's more than that. The lands. They looking to—"

Silky began choking. It was the last sound he ever made.

Rosie staggered over. "What happened?"

"Silky wasn't smooth enough," Diamond said. "Scratch one punk."

"Thank God," Rosie said as she collapsed into the desert sand.

7

The eastern sky was glowing as they neared the Ace of Diamonds. For most of the walk, Rosie leaned heavily on Red. But by the time they reached his suite, she didn't look much worse than a gambler on a losing streak.

Bart curled up on the couch while Diamond soaked in the hot tub and Rosie cleaned herself up in the bathroom. She came out rejuvenated and promptly got motherly, plucking splinters from Diamond's palms as she swabbed his hands with antiseptic.

Diamond put on the work clothes he'd bought, stuffed his money and rumpled suit into a laundry bag, tucked his gun into his belt, and they were off.

In the garage he made a fuss about his car being stolen. The P.I. said he was in a hurry to get to the airport. The valet coming on duty said he'd handle reporting the crime to the police after Diamond greased him with twenty dollars from the seventeen thousand in his laundry bag.

They took a cab to Rosie's apartment. It cost another ten dollars to convince the driver that Bart was an acceptable passenger. Rosie took fifteen minutes to pack.

At McCarran, Rosie stood off to one side while Diamond went to the counter and bought two tickets to her hometown—Washington, D.C. One ticket was in her name; the other in John Dalmas's.

Rosie was supervising two freight handlers who were nervously loading the Samoyed's sky kennel onto a conveyor belt as Diamond returned. Bart peered out of the wire bars like a hardened con.

"You set?" Diamond asked Rosie as Bart rolled off on the conveyor belt.

"I s'pose. I wish you were coming with me. You're someone special."

"So are you."

"I really like you."

Diamond took her in his arms and gave her a big squeeze. As he embraced her, she felt his hands pressing her buttocks. She pulled away.

"Don't spoil it, John."

74

"You're right," he said. "My name's not John though. It's Red Diamond. I'm a private eye Tex hired to clean up the problems here. After what we been through, I ought to tell you that much."

"I figured you weren't just another gambler," she said, nodding her head. "I knew there was more to it. Please be careful, Red."

"The long good-bye has never been my style," he said.

They locked eyes, and she touched his cheek. She pecked at his lips.

Diamond smiled as she disappeared. He wondered when she'd feel in her back pocket and realize why he'd pretended to play grabass. He knew she could use the three thousand dollars he'd slipped her.

The flight had twenty minutes to take-off. Diamond scanned the terminal. The major difference from the hundreds of airports he'd been in was that at most, the only machine you could gamble on provided flight insurance. At McCarran, banks of one-armed bandits tempted the traveler as soon as he or she deplaned.

Flights were announced, passengers were paged. People moved in and out of the restaurants, which served food one notch above the in-flight fare.

Diamond spotted a middle-aged man who looked roughly like himself. The same size and weight, but with thinning hair and coarser features. He'd have to do.

The man had a forlorn look as he slipped silver dollars into a slot machine. Diamond put on an unctuous grin and sauntered over.

"Hi, my name's Alex Kendall. Las Vegas Board of Trade. Why so glum, chum?"

The man had a limp handshake. "I thought I had a winning system for craps. It cost me thirty-five hundred dollars to find out I didn't. I have no luck."

"Not true," Diamond said, pumping the man's hand furiously. "As part of a special no-hard-feelings deal the Board of Trade will give you this free airline ticket." Diamond held up the second ticket. His other hand held the laundry bag like an attaché case. The man looked at him suspiciously, but took the ticket.

"But it says 'Dalmas' here. And it's for Washington. I live in Pennsylvania."

"Mr. Dalmas was so happy about winning, he decided to stay," Diamond said glibly. "And as long as you travel to our nation's capital, we throw in five hundred dollars. Stay in the hotel of your choice and fly home whenever you wish. May I recommend the Jefferson Memorial as a particularly rewarding experience."

Diamond took five hundred dollars out of his bag. The man grabbed the money. Diamond took his arm and escorted him as far as the metal detector.

"Give me your ticket to Pennsylvania. I'll handle getting this exchanged and baggage transfer. Think of us fondly here in the luckiest city in the world. And come back real soon."

"I don't understand. Why can't I—"

"The flight is leaving. Would you prefer I find somebody else?"

"No . . . No."

"Have a nice flight," Diamond said, nudging the man through the detector, careful that his gun didn't set it off.

Diamond cashed in the man's ticket and had the baggage shipped to Dulles. He explained to the clerk that the man was a congressional aide rushing back to his office on an emergency legislative matter. It took quick work by the baggage handlers but the flight took off only ten minutes late.

Diamond went to the coffee shop and got a seat facing the runway. Vehicles of bizarre shapes and sizes scurried about outside, tending the big silver birds.

John Dalmas was gone, Red thought as the waitress brought him the bacon and eggs he ordered. It was time for cabbie Simon Jaffe to begin snooping.

He felt a twinge every time he thought of that name, but forced himself to concentrate on Silky's final words as he wolfed down his food. The Lands.

After the meal, he checked the phone book for any casino named The Lands, or anything similar. The closest entry was The Sands, but he was sure Silky hadn't said that. There were two people with the last name Land in the phone book.

Diamond called Saint and asked him to check out the listed Lands, as well as any others Saint could get from the Department of Motor Vehicles.

"Anything else?" Saint asked. "Maybe you want me to collect fingerprints off every cactus in a twenty-mile radius?"

"While you're at it, could you find out who swiped my car?"

"It happens all the time," Saint said unsympathetically. "What's your angle on this Lands deal?"

"Just a few leads I'm running down."

"You're running down? It sounds like I'm doing all the work."

The cop continued to complain for a few minutes, with Diamond making agreeable grunts in the right places. After venting his spleen, Saint didn't press very hard when Diamond double-talked about what he was up to.

"Remember, you get any solid leads, I want to hear about them."

"You will," Diamond promised. Saint would hear about it, even if it was a day after Diamond got the lead.

They hung up, Diamond went to the cab stand at the south end of the building, and headed to the Speedy Cab Company garage.

It was a little after 8:30 A.M. The only other lands

77

he could think of were the real estate kind. Too early to check the assessor's office. Besides, he couldn't casually walk in and say, "Tell me about the lands."

The cab company was housed in what had once been a gas station. The pumps were still used to tank up the thirty-five red-and-gray Dodges in the Speedy fleet. Where mechanics had worked the office now was set up. A carpet as worn as a taxi dancer's shoes covered the oil-stained floor. Some of the oil had seeped through.

The room where the cash register and counter had been was now the cabbies' lounge. It had a few metal folding chairs around a folding table, a coffee and a cigarette machine, and a half-dozen pinups on the walls. The pinups had been doodled on by an artist with a crude wit and an exaggerated idea of male anatomy.

"Mr. Lucky. Mr. Lucky," Papa shouted and threw his arms around Diamond.

"Hey, Sy, what do you know," Kincaid said. The fat man was eating a Twinkie.

Two other drivers were sitting at the table playing poker with Papa and Kincaid. They glanced at Diamond and returned their attention to the pasteboards.

"Hey you bums, say hello to Sy Jaffe," Kincaid said.

The two men looked up. One was middle-aged, with birdlike features and thick glasses. He fiddled with his glasses, sliding them up and down his long nose. Kincaid introduced him as "the Professor." The other was a powerfully built Mexican with a bull neck and black hair in a crew cut. Diamond didn't catch his name.

"The Professor is as smart as you are lucky," Papa said. "Ask a question."

"Your name is familiar to me," the Professor said. He played with his spectacles, easing them against his brow as he studied Diamond's face.

"The Professor's a speed-reader," Kincaid said

proudly. "He goes through twenty newspapers a day. You ever been in the papers?"

"No," Diamond snapped. The Professor's steady gaze was making him nervous. Red racked his brain for a tough question to throw the speed-reader off his scent.

"Who's Vee Brown?" Diamond fired out.

"A fictional private investigator who appeared in pulp magazines in the 1930s," the Professor said as he leaned back confidently in his chair. "His real name was Vivian Brown and he was purportedly a popular song-writer when not going after the criminal element.

"Brown was the creation of Carroll John Daly who is probably better known for another hardboiled private detective, Race Williams," the Professor continued. "Daly wrote for the pulps, which survived from the 1930s to the 1950s. With authors such as Dashiell Hammett and Raymond Chandler, they glorified tough language and tougher men, producing a distinctive anti-hero portrayed by actors such as Humphrey—"

"Is he right?" Kincaid interrupted.

"Sort of," Diamond said, knowing that Brown and Williams were as fictional as Franklin Roosevelt. But he couldn't blow his cover and clarify things. "Yeah, he's right."

"The hardest part is shutting him off once he gets started," Kincaid said with a grin.

"We gonna play cards?" the Mexican asked.

"I got an open spot by the airport," a gravelly voice shouted from the office. "Any of you not too busy flapping your gums?"

The Mexican said, "My turn," dropped his cards on the table, and walked out.

Papa flipped the Mexican's cards. He had a pair of threes. The Professor dropped his hand, a full house, on the table without comment.

"No cab for me until noon," Papa said. "Since I see

79

you Sy, I feel lucky. I play craps. I have sure way a ride told me about. You bet on the pass line, since odds say every third roll will—"

"Tell us about it after you win," Kincaid broke in. "I hear about a new system every day. I'm going to the can, then I'll introduce Sy to the boss."

Papa and Kincaid each left for their important destinations. The Professor kept staring at Diamond.

All Red could think of were questions from his trade. What's the muzzle velocity on a .38 slug when it leaves a Ruger? What was Vivian Rutledge's secret? How can you tell if a body's been drowned in fresh water?

The Professor had a bemused, challenging expression. Diamond had seen that look before, on Oliver Quade, better known as the Human Encyclopedia.

"Who won the 1947 World Series?" Diamond said suddenly.

"I don't clutter my cerebrum with sports trivia," the Professor said.

"What year did Lionel Hampton do 'How High the Moon?'"

"It was nineteen—I got it. You're an ex-New York cabbie. Simon Jaffe. I should've known from the Vee Brown inquiry. You're Red Diamond, private eye."

Diamond put a finger to his lips in a shush gesture. He sat down at the folding card table. "You're right," Diamond said, knowing he couldn't bluff his way out. "But it's hush-hush. I'm on a case. Can you keep a secret?"

"Are you investigating Speedy Cab?" the Professor asked conspiratorially.

Diamond shook his head. "It's bigger than that."

"My conjecture would be that perhaps you are probing the recent rash of crimes in this city. Am I correct in that assumption, Mr. Diamond?"

80

"Call me Sy. And yes, you are. How'd you guess?"

"I am a member in good standing of the Baker Street Irregulars. As Mr. Holmes would say, 'Elementary, my dear Diamond.'"

"Not Diamond. Sy, Sy Jaffe, remember?"

"Yes, of course, Sy. Statistically, Las Vegas has always had a large crime problem. But as Disraeli said, 'There are three kinds of lies. Lies, damned lies, and statistics.' Because of our large transient population, compared to a year-round residential population of—"

"Okay, I get the message. Will you help me?"

The Professor fiddled excitedly with his glasses. "Most definitely. Will I get to meet gun molls?"

"I was thinking of something more up your alley. I got a tip the lands are involved. I can run down a quitclaim deed as good as the next dick. But this might require a couple of days pouring over records. I'll pay for your time, say, ten bucks an hour."

"When do I start?"

"The sooner the better," Diamond said. "Here's a hundred-dollar advance to get you going."

The Professor had just pocketed the money when Kincaid returned.

"That's easy," the Professor said with a secretive wink at Diamond. "The Tibetan name for Mount Everest is *Chomolungma*."

"Glad to see you two getting along," Kincaid said. "Hey Sy, bet you thought you could stump him?"

"He's got a lot on the ball," Diamond acknowledged.

"I'm feeling a trifle under the weather," the Professor said. "Probably a smattering of wayward bacteria, but I think I'll go home and avoid stressing my system."

"Sure, Einstein," Kincaid said, slapping the Professor on the back. "Got to keep that gray matter in tip-top shape. It's a lucky break for Sy. The boss will need someone."

As the Professor left, Kincaid slapped Diamond on the shoulder. "Great bunch of guys work here. You'll fit right in. C'mon, let's go meet the boss. His name's Bill Crane. Don't worry, his bark is as bad as his bite."

They stepped through the doorway onto the worn carpet. The office held a couple of file cabinets, four desks, and an antique radio-dispatching console. The decorator must've spent at least fifty dollars furnishing the place, Red thought.

It wasn't hard to guess who Crane was. The other, smaller desks were occupied by officious middle-aged women. Two were answering phones, the others shuffled paperwork. They didn't look up as Kincaid and Diamond entered.

A woman at the radio console gave Diamond a cool stare. She was younger than the other women and took great pride in her appearance. Her neckline plunged lower than a German U-boat. She was not unattractive, but not as beautiful as she thought, Red figured. A phone answerer handed her a slip of paper and she languidly picked up the microphone.

"This is Speedy base with a fare at the Paradise Valley Country Club," she said in a sultry voice that made Lauren Bacall sound like a squeaky teen-ager.

"What do you want?" Crane bellowed at Kincaid and Diamond. "And get your eyes off Velma. She's my squeeze. You got that?"

Crane rose from his desk. He looked like a third-rate lounge entertainer from a fourth-rate hotel; a leisure suit covering a lean body, hair a shade too blond to be natural, and gold chains the color of his hair around his neck.

"The Professor felt under the weather. This is Sy, Simon Jaffe. I'll vouch for him," Kincaid said as he threw his arm over Diamond's shoulder.

"Stop acting like a homo," Crane said. "I'll give

82

your friend the job, 'cause I'm such a nice guy. If he screws up, I'll take it out of both of your hides. Got me?"

Kincaid and Diamond nodded.

Crane stepped in close to Diamond. His breath smelled of mouthwash, antiseptic as a hospital floor.

"I got a few rules," Crane said to Diamond. "You get half what you take in. I catch you riding off the meter, you never work Vegas again. Got me?"

"Got you," Diamond said.

"You go out with a full tank, you come back with a full tank. You mess up the car, you pay for the body-work. No excuses. And you mess with Velma, I do body work on you. Got me?"

"Got you." Most of Crane's muscles were clearly in his mouth, but Diamond remained properly deferential.

"You ever been in an accident? Any arrests?"

"No."

"You're probably full of shit, like all these bastards that tear my heart out. I'm too nice a guy for my own good. You got number thirty-one. It's parked out front. It better be back by nine P.M. or your ass is grass. Got me?"

"Got you."

"And don't spend your time fucking off at Little Caesar's," Crane said, returning to his desk. "Now go out and earn your keep."

"Boy, he was in a good mood," Kincaid said as they walked out.

Diamond thanked him for the reference and went to the 1980 Dodge numbered 31. It had 98,000 miles on the odometer, the suspension was shot, and it made a sick clunking noise when he shifted it into gear.

He felt right at home behind the wheel of the clunker. There was a map lying on the front seat and he studied it for a few minutes. The main streets memorized, he stepped on the gas and began to cruise.

His first fare, picked up after they hailed him at the corner of East Fremont and Tenth Street, was a young couple from Dubuque who had just used a bunch of coupons in the downtown casinos. They had made a free phone call home, gotten free popcorn, drinks, and a keychain. They were boasting of how they'd shrewdly beaten the casinos. It slipped out during the ride that they'd blown sixty dollars at the slots while waiting to pick up their various rewards.

Diamond cruised for an hour, getting the feel of the streets. No one hailed him. He stopped at his room at the Last Chance Motel, dropped off his laundry bag of clothes. He took his cash with him. He drove to the Ramses and joined the line.

The casino was done up in the shape of a sphinx. The drivers clustered near one of the gigantic concrete paws shooting the breeze.

Diamond strolled over and stood with the half-dozen hackies. They were bemoaning the heat, the run-down cars, the economy, and how tough it was to make a living. At the proper lull, Diamond echoed their complaints, and was promptly welcomed into the circle.

The drivers offered advice on specific customers to avoid. Most were drunks who lost their money at the casinos and would throw up in the cab as they tried to deadbeat their way home.

Diamond kept the conversation casual as he asked about the Ramses. All he learned was tour-book information. The most interesting fact to the cabbies was that the hotel had a one-thousand-person auditorium where the shows let out at 10 P.M. and 1 A.M.

Diamond mentioned Moe Greenberg. Despite the ninety-degree temperature, they froze up. Diamond shifted the conversation back to problem fares and the talk resumed. But some of the men regarded him suspiciously.

When it was Diamond's turn, he drew a middle-aged couple from Arizona. Losers. At least that's what he figured from the amount of nagging the taciturn husband was getting from his sharp-tongued wife.

He dropped them off and joined the line at the Flamingo. He made chit-chat with the drivers and avoided mentioning Greenberg. It was easy to ruin an undercover role by pushing too hard.

The fare he caught was a white-haired gent who didn't say much but seemed quite pleased with himself. He gave Diamond a generous tip after being dropped off at the Desert Inn Golf Course.

Red didn't have the patience for more gossiping with other drivers, so he cruised down the Strip. A Chinese guy was standing in front of the Stardust. He signaled for a ride. There was so little hail business in Vegas that a couple of cabbies drove by without spotting him. Diamond caught the classic wave and pulled over.

"Take me to the Tropicana," the Oriental said.

Red switched on the meter as the voice stabbed into him like fingernails on a blackboard. It struck a chord deep in Diamond's brain, the spot where his headaches came from. He forced himself to look in the mirror. The face he saw set off a killer migraine. He drove on instinct as the man talked.

"Boy, oh boy, what a town this is. My kind of place. I won over three hundred dollars. I'm only down about five hundred now," the thin man said. "And eat all you want at the buffets."

Diamond gritted his teeth against the pain in his head. His vision was fuzzy, his ears were ringing, and his tongue swelled to fill his mouth. He gasped for air.

"You know I'm in the same racket. I drive a hack in

New York. The name's Fong, Eddie Fong."

They came to a light and Diamond hit the brakes. Too hard. The car bucked.

"Whoa," Fong said, leaning forward. "What's your name?"

He glanced at Diamond and did a theatrical double take.

"Holy cow! Sy, I don't believe it."

Fong was shouting but Diamond could hardly hear him over the ringing bells.

"We heard about you back in New York. Some of the guys wanted to go to the trial, but no one could make it. You know how it is. You miss a day, the bills start to pile up. But we read everything in the *Daily News*. What are you doing driving again? I thought you were a private eye!"

Diamond made an inaudible whimper. He drove at ten miles an hour. Horns honked behind him as he fought for control.

"You always used to talk about those private eyes. The guys thought you were full of it. When they read about you calling yourself Red Diamond and killing those people, they sure ate their words. You got talked about more than the Mets for weeks."

"Eddie?" Diamond's hands were crushing the wheel.

"Yeah."

"Eddie Fong?"

"Sure. Your old buddy. What's the matter, you forget your old friends?" he said with a smile.

They stopped at another light and Diamond struggled to squeeze his head back into shape.

"I've been—I've been—I've—I don't know what's going on," Diamond stuttered.

"Are you okay?"

"Mmmmmmmmmnnn."

"Maybe you better pull over, Sy. You don't look so hot. Like the time Pedro found out his new girlfriend was a transvestite. You want me to drive?"

"No. I can handle it. Where did you say you were going?"

"The Tropicana."

"Where's that? Midtown?"

"Midtown? Just keep driving straight."

The man who was born Simon Jaffe, was living as Red Diamond, and calling himself Simon Jaffe, kept his foot on the gas and jockeyed through traffic. "Why don't you have your cab?" he asked Fong.

"Sy, this is Las Vegas. My cab's a couple thousand miles away."

"Las Vegas. How'd I get to Las Vegas? I don't even go to Jersey."

"You better pull over."

"I can't. I gotta make my nut or Milly will be really mad. We're falling behind on the mortgage."

"Sy, Milly filed for divorce. After the murder trial. Don't you remember?"

"Divorce? Murder? What the hell are you talking about? Simon Jaffe wasn't born yesterday. You can't go pulling my leg like that."

"They said you went crazy. Thought you were this private eye named Red Diamond."

"Sure I read about Red Diamond. He's so tough he's got balls he hasn't used yet. I heard lots of stuff about him." He wrinkled his brow in concentration. "But Milly threw them out. And then—and then—then things get kind of blurry."

"That was close to a year ago, Sy. You been out of the picture for a year. The guys have been wondering where you been."

He thought for a minute or so. "Damned if I know.

It seems like only yesterday I was talking to the kids."

"Why don't we go to a doctor?" Fong asked solicitously.

"Can't. You know how it is. Got to keep the payments up. Never seem to get out from under."

"We were pulling for you. Being a celebrity and all that. Every cabbie in the city claimed he was your best buddy. Are you coming back now?"

"Back where?"

"New York, where else?"

"This isn't New York?"

"Sy, let's get you some help," Fong said.

"I'm okay. Really. I feel a little fuzzy. I'll go home and take a few Alka Seltzer and be fine."

He pulled up to the Tropicana and Fong reached into his pocket.

"Not for an old buddy," Jaffe said. "See you at the Balmoral and you can buy me lunch."

"They closed the Balmoral."

"No kidding. I was there a week ago. Where's everybody going?"

Fong got out. "Sy, wait here a minute. I'm gonna go inside and see if I can get some help."

A portly couple shoved past Fong and into the cab. "Downtown," the man ordered.

"Wait! He needs help," Fong yelled. He tried to hold onto the door but the woman grabbed it from his hands and pulled it shut.

"We saw him first," she said. "It's our cab. You people have no manners."

"Sy, you need a doctor. Wait here and I'll—"

"Downtown," the man repeated.

"Doctors cost money and I got money to make," Jaffe said. "See you later, Eddie."

"We're in a hurry," the woman said. "Let's go."

"Wait Sy, you need—"

88

"To make money," Jaffe said, tapping the accelerator and moving back into traffic as Fong shouted from the curb.

"Where you folks from?"

"Hartford. Connecticut," the man said. "This is our first vacation here."

"Your first? Jeez, I don't know how anyone could live near this town and not come sooner."

"This near?" the woman said shrewishly. "It took us more than four hours to get here."

"I tell you, train service is really terrible. You shoulda drove into town."

"Train? Drive? It's a couple of thousand miles," the man piped up.

Jaffe shook his head and made a clucking noise. "Some sharpie really gave you a bum steer. It's only about a hundred and ten miles to New York. Must've charged you an arm and a leg. I've heard of taking the long way—"

"Not to New York, you idiot. To Las Vegas," the woman interrupted.

"Las Vegas. Why the hell you want to go there? Atlantic City is much closer."

"I know it's much closer," the woman said, exchanging an exasperated look with her husband. "But we're in Las Vegas."

The cabbie smirked. "Lady, you got sold a bill of goods. If this is Las Vegas, my name isn't Simon Jaffe. Las Vegas. Hah, that's hilarious. Wait 'til I tell the guys at the garage."

"What should we do?" the woman whispered to her husband. He shrugged. "Just take us downtown," he said authoritatively.

"Sure. Where downtown? The Village? Wall Street? Chinatown?"

"Chinatown? No. The Lady Luck Casino."

89

"Must be some new restaurant. Never heard of it," Jaffe said as he continued south.

"You're heading the wrong way," the man said.

"Buddy, I been driving this burg for years. I know my way around. And I know the difference between Las Vegas and New York." He laughed.

The man looked nervously at his wife, who rolled her eyes.

"Look at these Nevada license plates on the cars," Jaffe said. "Must be a damn convention in town. I tell you, I don't blame you for getting lost. Things are always changing in the Big Apple. I hardly recognize the place, so much new construction. You got any idea where this Lady Luck joint is?"

"On Third Street."

"Oh sure, the Village. They're always opening up new places down there. Used to be all kinds of coffee houses. Beatniks. That was when you could walk around the city at night without some creep banging in your head. Now it's a nice area, if you don't mind junkies and other weirdos."

"You're one to talk," the woman said.

"What?"

"Nothing," her husband said. "We changed our mind. We'd like to get out here."

"Suit yourselves." Jaffe shut the meter, the man paid him, and the couple jumped out of the cab.

He continued south. The area was unfamiliar. No skyscrapers in sight. Just vacant lots and dry earth. Must be the Bronx, he guessed. He couldn't believe it. Simon Jaffe, veteran New York cabdriver, in an area he didn't know.

Maybe Eddie was right. He should see a doctor. His mind seemed to be slipping. What about Milly and this talk about a divorce? Must be a dumb rumor some bored cabbie got started. She'd never leave their Long Island home.

And the kids? Sean and Melonie. Sean was so perfect nothing could ruffle his feathers. Melonie was another story. Quite a handful. What would happen if her parents split up? It was ridiculous. He loved Milly and she knew it. Sure, he didn't make as much money as she would've liked, but they'd managed for years.

He made a U-turn and headed back. Still nothing looked familiar. There were only a few yellow cabs around. The rest were all different colors. The gypsy drivers were taking over, he thought angrily. And nobody seemed to be hailing cabs.

Finally a man with two large suitcases, standing outside a motel, hailed him. The man got out a mile later after an argument over whether it was called McCarran or LaGuardia Airport and where it was located.

What a day, Jaffe thought. Screwy neighborhood, screwy fares. He had to get back to midtown.

A sign advertised FREE MAPS—NEVADA TOURIST BUREAU.

Must cater only to tourists from Nevada, he decided. He pulled in anyway and asked the dumpy brunette behind the counter for a map. She gave him a map of Las Vegas.

"What kind of crazy place is this?" Jaffe shouted, slamming his fist down on the counter. A clock with dice for numerals fell over. "I want a map of New York. N-E-W-space-Y-O-R-K. This is the goddamn Twilight Zone."

"This is Las Vegas," the woman said timidly.

Jaffe threw the map down. "Nuts. I walked into the world's largest nuthouse."

He stormed over to a rack of brochures and pamphlets along one wall. He rummaged through them, dropping dozens to the floor as he fumbled with rage. The booklets were all for hotels. Las Vegas hotels.

The woman picked up the phone. "Hello, police," she whispered.

Jaffe was mumbling under his breath as he contin-

91

ued his search. A brochure for the Ace of Diamonds Hotel and Casino captured his attention. He picked it up.

" . . . out of his mind," the woman was saying. "He came in and started yelling and . . . "

One of the showgirls caught Jaffe's eye. Blond. A knockout. Third from the left, she held center stage for him.

" . . . yes, he's violent. Making a mess. He . . . "

Jaffe knew the girl's name. Fifi. Fifi La Roche.

He dropped the brochure as his head began to pound. He pressed hard at his temples but it didn't relieve the ache. "Ahhhhrrrggh."

" . . . him in the background. Hurry. Yes, the tourist bureau office. I'm getting . . . "

He fell to the floor and began writhing.

The woman hung up the phone, ran to a door behind the counter, stepped through, and shut it. Three locks clicked into place.

He lay on the floor moaning and panting.

Help me Milly. This is New York. No one else will. Fifi help me. It's Red Jaffe. Simon Diamond. Rocco. Cabs. Scabs. Stabs. Slabs. Fifi. Melonie. Sean. Kids. Skids.

"Uhhhhhhhn!"

Fifi. Needs me. Rocco. Get him. Save Fifi. New York. Los Angeles. Las Vegas. Lost wages.

A scruffly young man with a greasy red bandana circling his pimpled forehead entered.

"What's going on?" he said as he looked around. He took in the scene, vaulted the counter and opened the cash register. He began filling his pockets.

Diamond rose weakly to his feet. The pounding in his head lessened. He heard sirens approaching. He grabbed a couple of Ace of Diamonds brochures.

The man stuffing his pockets ignored him. Diamond

tottered to the door and out into the hot Nevada sun. The glare reminded him of the lights the cops used to grill prisoners. He could take it. He'd stood up to the toughest bulls. He was Red Diamond.

Police cars screeched into the lot. Officers jumped out with guns drawn. They paid no attention to Red as he calmly got back into his cab.

With the picture of Fifi burning a hole in his pocket, Diamond called Evans. The billionaire was watching a Cisco Kid film in his private screening room, Norris said after Diamond's insistent questioning. The door had a time lock on it. Evans could not be disturbed for several hours.

None of the chorus girls were in yet, Diamond learned after another phone call. Frustrated, he drove to the cab stand at McCarran.

More than two dozen drivers were waiting around. He showed the brochure with Fifi's face circled and offered one hundred dollars to the first man to spot her. He said she was his wife and had run off with a craps dealer. Lots of sympathy, but no leads.

After forty-five minutes, it was Diamond's turn to catch a fare. His customer was a scrawny young man, barely out of his teens, in tee-shirt and worn jeans. He had a pink complexion and a big nose. He stood with one leg bent and braced against the other as Diamond pulled up.

"Lemme guess, you're going to the Flamingo," Diamond said.

"What's that supposed to mean?" the young man asked as he got in.

"Nothing. It's been a hard day. Where you going?"

"To Sassy Sally's. On East Fremont."

Diamond hit the flag and the meter began ticking. Flamingo picked his nose industriously.

"Hey, wipe your hands and take a look at this picture," Diamond said, passing him the photo with Fifi in it. "You seen this broad around?"

"Maybe. Who is she?"

"My ex-wife. Ran off with the kids and my money."

"Nah. I ain't seen her," Flamingo said. A cunning look came over his face and he lowered his voice. "You looking to make some quick cash? Take your mind off your troubles?"

"You got an oil well for sale?"

"You a comedian?"

"Just a guy who takes his jokes where he can get 'em."

"Listen smart guy, you want to make some money, go to this address at nine P.M. tonight," Flamingo said, handing Diamond a business card that read *Advanced School of Dealing*.

"It ain't what it seems," Flamingo said cryptically.

"What's that mean?"

Flamingo returned his attention to probing his ample nose. He didn't give Diamond a tip. Red was not surprised.

His next fare was a couple of noisy conventioneers. Drunk and happy, they sat in the back and gave each other secret handshakes. Neither of them had seen Fifi.

94

Diamond went to the Sheik, an imposing casino-hotel done up like an Arab tent. A couple of valets in burnooses stood outside gossiping with the drivers.

No luck with the Fifi photo.

Diamond's fare looked like a fat, prosperous banker. He was more formally dressed than anyone Red had seen in Vegas, wearing a gray three-piece pinstriped suit. He had gold-rimmed glasses and the suave polish of a world traveler. The only signs of Vegas flash were the pinkie rings glittering on both hands.

"Quite a fascinating town," he said after instructing Diamond to take him to the Ramses. "A place where fortunes are made and lost every day. Do you enjoy it?"

"It's a living," Diamond said.

"That it is, that it is." The man had a British accent that sounded affected. "My name is James Thursby the third. What's yours?"

"Simon Jaffe."

"Mr. Jaffe, I've been all over the world. And I've always found taxicab drivers to be particularly savvy individuals. Men who appreciate the merits of a cash business."

Diamond drove while the man lit a Turkish cigarette.

"I wonder if you have managed to put your tips aside in a worthwhile venture? Something with enough risk to pay handsomely and yet not unduly gambling with your nest egg." He puffed and waited for an answer.

"I got a couple bucks put away."

"Would it be improper for me to ask how much?"

"You with the IRS?"

Thursby chuckled. "Far from it. To many of my clients, IRS is a four-letter word."

"So what's your pitch?"

"Very good. I like a man who gets right to the point.

My pitch, as you put it, is that I can invest your money in extremely profitable mining stocks. With an effective yield of thirty-five percent. And we work through Hong Kong banks. Wire transfers. The international money market is a thrilling place to be, Mr. Jaffe."

"I bet."

"In a few years no doubt you will own your own cab company. Think of it, Mr. Jaffe, your own boss, commanding a fleet. Make your own hours. Hire a beautiful secretary. A harem of beautiful secretaries. Vacation in Acapulco. Drive your own Cadillac. Better yet, have a chauffeur. What do you say, Mr. Jaffe?"

Thursby was too smooth, his spiel too professional. Diamond had met enough con men to know the routine. Advance fee schemes, Ponzi scams, faked inventory deals. And always at the front, a cunning salesman who came across like a respectable businessman. Play on the greed and ego the way Benny Goodman played on the clarinet. Call the sucker "Mister." Talk about beating the IRS.

Thursby misread Diamond's smile. "I see you are interested," he said. "I need a small good faith deposit to get the pump primed. A trifling, a thousand dollars. Cash."

"I'll get a receipt?"

"Of course. What kind of businessman do you think I am?"

Diamond didn't answer. He pulled into the Ramses.

"Thursby, you won't mind if I bring in a partner on the deal?"

"Not one bit. Another driver?"

Diamond turned and watched Thursby's face as he said, "No. A cop friend. He works bunco."

The fat man was good. Aside from pursing his lips and blinking rapidly a couple of times, there was no reaction. "Very good. I've dealt with many law enforcement officers during my career."

96

"I bet you have. That's five ninety-five," Diamond said, looking at the meter.

Thursby made a big show of rooting through his pockets. "My goodness, I must've left my wallet in my room. Would you mind waiting here while I run up and fetch it."

"Since you talked about good faith, why don't you leave me some collateral?"

"Surely my good man you don't think I would cheat you out of a pittance like five ninety-five," Thursby said haughtily.

Diamond smiled again and waited.

"Well! I don't think we shall do business after all. You are penny wise and pound foolish," Thursby said. He slid one of his pinkie rings off and contemptuously tossed it to Diamond. "This ring is worth several thousand dollars. Probably more than you will ever hold in your life again. I trust it is acceptable?" Without waiting for an answer, Thursby hopped quickly out of the cab. "I'll be right back."

Diamond took the ring and scratched the diamond along the windshield. It made no mark on the glass. Phony, just like the rest of Thursby.

The P.I. waited twenty minutes, listening to a radio show devoted to hits by Tommy and Jimmy Dorsey. No sign of the fat man. He dismissed Thursby as one of the imported con men, dropped the zircon in his pocket, and drove off.

He stopped at a pay phone and called Saint.

"I met this guy went by the name James Thursby," Diamond said. "Have you ever heard of him?"

The cop blew up. "What am I, an information operator?"

"Your voice isn't sweet enough," Diamond said.

"What are you, a comedian?"

"You know, you're the second guy to—"

97

"I got bad news for you Diamond."

"You don't love me anymore?"

"Shut up and listen. First, I ran down the Lands. The two you gave me and another one I got from DMV. They came up clean. One works at Nellis, another is a janitor at Frontier. The third is retired. The only trouble any of them have had is speeding tickets."

"Oh well, it was a long shot."

"Sure. Give good old Saint the busy work. Anyway, that's just the beginning. Fingers is dead."

"How?"

"The chief is putting out he killed himself."

"I got a hunch that's not the full story."

Saint hesitated. "Between you, me, and the lamppost, no. We're saying he cut himself and bled to death. But the way he cut himself. He lopped off his fingers."

"I never heard of anyone playing the Dutch act that way."

"Neither have I. And I been on the job nineteen years."

"What about this Thursby I told you about?"

"Before we get to him, one more little bit of business. They found your car."

"Great. What kind of shape is it in?"

"Not bad. A lot better condition than the bodies we found next to it."

"Bodies?" Diamond asked innocently.

"Teri Lennox. A pross. Someone had tortured her before she died. And a guy whose mug I gave you. Silky. Somebody shot him with his own gun."

"The girl?"

"She was in no shape. He had been worked over. Not a professional beating but a thorough one. What do you know about it?"

"Just what you told me."

"Any idea how your car got there?"

98

"It was stolen."

"I know you reported it stolen. Very convenient. We got better things to do than devote our time to a case like this. But if we did, you can bet you'd be answering a few questions."

"I'm always pleased to cooperate with the authorities."

"Just be available. I heard John Dalmas left town."

"He did. But Red Diamond is still around. I thought the Dalmas name was getting too hot."

"After killing Silky?"

"Nice weather we've been having. At least you don't think I tortured the girl."

"I don't want anyone taking justice into their own hands. That's what we have courts for."

"And they do such a wonderful job," Diamond said. "What about Thursby?"

"Also known as Sidney Green, Vince Moreno, Dr. Felix Goode, Krikor Armadjian, Sheik Abu Ben Diba, and a couple dozen other names. Fat guy, looks like he's worth a million?"

"That's him. What's his real moniker?"

"No one really knows. He's changed it legally a couple of times."

"Where's he from?"

"A local boy made good. Where'd you meet him?"

"In a cab."

Saint grumbled.

"Gotta go," Diamond said.

"Watch your step."

"Thanks for the free advice."

Evans was still unavailable when Red called and it was nearing 6:00 P.M. He drove back to the Speedy Cab garage.

Velma was waiting outside. "I tried raising you on the radio all day," she said.

"Damn, I forgot to turn up the volume. This is my first time in a radio group or a fleet." He felt a quick twinge of dizziness, the words coming from a part of him he didn't understand.

"Crane is pissed off, but that's not what I wanted to tell you, Red." She emphasized his name.

"What do you mean Red?"

"Red Diamond, hotshot gumshoe."

"Who told you that?"

"The Professor called. He wanted me to give you his number. He told me about the project you were working on."

Diamond said nothing.

"You come by my place in an hour and we talk," she said. It wasn't a request.

"And if I don't?"

"Tomorrow I go into the office and let everybody know who you are. Over the radio. My own little talk show."

"What do you want from me?"

"Come by my place in an hour," she said, handing him a slip of paper with her address and the Professor's phone number written on it. She flounced away.

Diamond entered the office. Crane was as happy as a flagpole sitter with hemorrhoids.

"I been getting calls from people about some madman driving cab thirty-one. They're going to complain to the state authority. What the fuck did you do out there?"

"I was—"

"And I saw you talking to Velma. She slipped you a note. What did it say?"

"She was giving me—"

"How much did you take in?"

100

Diamond tallied up his proceeds. "About a hundred twenty-five bucks."

"That's it? I'm going to check the meter. If I find out you're keeping anything, I'm calling the cops. Got me?"

Diamond nodded.

The hens in the office were clucking while Crane went out to Diamond's cab.

Crane stormed back in. "You should've made at least two hundred dollars with that kind of mileage," he fumed. "I'm not calling the cops 'cause I'm such a nice guy, but you're through. Got me?"

"Yeah." Diamond tossed sixty-five dollars on Crane's desk.

"You never answered my question about Velma. What did her note say?"

"That you were a loudmouthed jerk who couldn't get it up with a hydraulic jack."

"What?"

"You heard me."

Crane pretended to turn away, then came back at Diamond's face with a wide swing. Diamond turned his head and the blow grazed his face.

"You touch me and I file an assault charge," Crane said when Diamond grabbed his lapel. "It's my word against yours, and my girls will back me up. I got juice. You're just a two-bit cabbie. An out-of-work cabbie. Got me?"

Diamond smiled and hit Crane with an uppercut that knocked the man off his feet. Crane lay on the floor clutching his jaw.

"Got you," Red said as he walked out.

9

Diamond tried calling the Professor from his room at the Last Chance Motel. He got no answer. The P.I. did fifteen minutes of push-ups, sit-ups, jumping jacks, and shadow boxing, then took a steamy shower.

Evans was unavailable when Red called again, but Norris arranged for Diamond to get another leased car. The car was left on a street near, but not at, the Last Chance Motel. He watched as a casino employee got out and into a car driven by another employee.

Diamond waited until he was sure they were gone before climbing into the car, turning the keys that had been left in the ignition, and heading to meet Velma.

"What did you do at Speedy?" Velma asked as a greeting.

"Crane pushed me. He's used to pushing people who don't push back. He made a mistake."

"A couple of the women from the office called. They said you hit him."

"Just once."

He walked over to a divan and sat. She poured glasses of white wine, gave him one, and sat next to him. Any closer and she would've been on his lap.

She was wearing dime store perfume. Her face had a lot more lines than he'd first noticed. She flicked her tongue into the wine like a cat lapping milk.

They sipped in silence.

Velma lived in a seedy garden apartment, with a sunbleached carpet and stains on the frayed curtains. The room was cluttered with furniture that was more Salvation Army than W. J. Sloan. The only bright colors came from travel posters of Europe that were stapled to the cracked plaster walls.

"I've never been out of the country," she said when she saw Diamond looking at them. He felt her predatory gaze boring into him.

She was wearing a top that was not quite see-through but implied it was. Her ample breasts rolled with every breath. Skintight jeans tapered down to painted toenails and slingbacks. Her hair was freshly washed, her face carefully made-up. He was getting the deluxe treatment.

She kept her eyes seductively half-opened. Coupled with her natural hardness, it came across as dangerously cunning.

Diamond got out a cigarette. Velma reached into his pocket, took one for herself, and lit both.

"That Crane is a real creep. I'm sure he deserved what you gave him. He's got two other girlfriends. That I know of. And a wife and three kids. But he gets bent out of shape if I talk to another guy."

"Why don't you dump him?"

"The pay's pretty good," she said. "How old do you think I am?"

He debated whether to knock a couple of years off his estimate, but decided against it. "Around fifty."

"I guess it's starting to show," she said sadly. "I'm forty-nine."

Diamond decided to let her speak her piece. He puffed his cigarette.

"I been getting a raw deal my whole life. I used to be on the floor show at the Riviera. Then at the Lion's Den. You didn't know that, did you?"

He shook his head.

"That's right. Then I got involved with a half-smart guy. My ex. That's what I draw. Guys too smart to see how they're screwing up. He's in the slammer now. I hope the bum never gets out."

She rose and retrieved an ashtray.

"My father ran out on my mother the day I was born," she said. "And men been letting me down ever since."

"Not someone as sweet as you."

"Go ahead and make cracks." She stood up abruptly. "I want what's coming to me. I ain't ashamed I'm looking out for number one. It's a sure thing nobody else in the world will."

"How'd you get the Professor to talk?" Diamond asked.

"Easy. He's about as hard to read as the comic pages. Asked me out a couple of times. I heard he was real excited when he called in. I thought they'd gotten a new book at the library. I teased him a bit and he began showing off."

She smirked, an evil expression that fit her face too well. "The Professor showed me where the gravy train is and I'm climbing aboard," she said.

"What do you want and what are you selling?"

"Ten grand. A big time private dick can spare that. Then I keep my mouth shut. I want out of Vegas for good. Otherwise everyone finds out that Red Diamond is in town, and what he's up to."

"What am I up to?" he challenged.

"Something about the lands."

"You know you could get me killed?"

"It's your decision."

Diamond didn't tell her he was ready to shuck the Jaffe identity. Until he could get the Professor to safety, Velma could still hurt him.

"Yes or no?" she demanded.

"I've got to think about it."

"So think."

"I need time. Even if I decide yes, I'll need a bit to raise the money."

"You got twenty-four hours. Call me with your answer. I get paid, that's the last you hear of me."

"That's what blackmailers always say."

"Blackmail's such an ugly word," she said coyly as she sat down next to him again. "I rather think I'm selling information."

"Call it what you want," he said, getting up and moving toward the door.

She followed. "It doesn't have to be like that." She leaned against him, her voice the velvet rasp that drove cabbies wild. "I could use a real man. I'll take your mind off your problems."

"Baby, you are my problem," he said, pushing her away and walking out.

She yelled an obscenity at his back.

The murder of Teri Lennox weighed heavily on Red's mind as he tried calling the Professor again. No answer.

He drove over and tried the door to the Professor's apartment. Locked and solidly set in its frame. The Professor didn't seem to be the kind to be out enjoying Vegas nightlife. He was more the type who'd curl up with a good book than a showgirl.

He walked around back, carefully stepping over a vegetable garden. The windows were locked, as was the sliding glass door.

Diamond picked up a garden trowel, edged it between the sliding doors, and pried them apart. He slid them open and entered.

The apartment was a mess. Diamond assumed the

105

place had been ransacked. But the chaos was too casual. Underwear on the living room floor, dishes on every table, newspapers scattered. There were none of the signs of a determined search: torn couch cushions, opened drawers, bookcases dumped out. It was just a bachelor in his natural habitat.

The only neat room was the den: an overstuffed chair, reading lamp, and four walls of bookcases. The shelves held two full encyclopedia sets, Greek and Roman classics, and textbooks. Science, history, psychology, medicine, law, art. *Ontogeny Recapitulates Phylogeny. The Existential Dilemma in the Heisenberg Uncertainty Principle. Thermonuclear Ramifications of Mitochondrial Development.* Even the titles were hard to read.

Diamond felt the lightbulbs and the back of the television set. No sign of warmth. No signs of blood anywhere. And if Diamond was reading the debris properly, no evidence of a struggle.

He took a pen from the cluttered desk and wrote: *Dear Prof, Get out right away. Go to a motel. And don't tell anyone. Especially Velma. Red.* He taped the note to the refrigerator.

As he left he wedged a small piece of paper between the front door and its frame. He went to his car, which he'd parked up the block.

He sat in the seat next to the driver's. The car was facing away from the Professor's apartment. He adjusted the rearview mirror so he could watch where he'd just been.

He remembered the time he'd taught the trick to Jim Rockford, when Jimbo had been starting out in L.A. Competition was fierce, but Diamond didn't mind sharing his knowledge.

There were more good Angeleno dicks than stars on Hollywood Boulevard. Brock Callahan, Toby Peters, Fergus O'Breen, Archer, Stu Bailey, Fred Bennett, Lam and Cool, Marlowe, Shell Scott, J. J. Gittes, Jack LeVine, Ace Carpenter, Tom Kyd, Pete Schofield, Joe Puma.

Scratch Puma. He wound up with a .32 slug in the face. Word on the street was that he'd sold out. The temptations were great, but there could be no remorse for a good guy gone bad.

It's the P.I.'s heart that separates the good dicks from the ham-fisted yo-yos who spend their time gathering evidence to break up marriages, Red thought. Sure the gimmicks were nice, like Mike Hammer's move with the rubber wedge to trap a tail in a revolving door or Gittes's cheap watch under the tires to record the time a car moved. But it was heart, the willingness to bang your head against a door until it opened, that made a dick great.

So he sat in the passenger's seat, looking like someone waiting for a driver to come out. He fought to keep his eyes opened and focused, his lack of sleep tempting him with a persuasive lullaby. He kept awake by sorting through what he knew.

Not much. The only thing that intrigued him was Silky and Greenberg's role in the Teri Lennox murder. What was the connection between the Lennox incident, the South African, and Greenberg?

Despite his best efforts, after a half hour of sitting motionless, Diamond was getting drowsy. He remembered the invitation Flamingo had given him.

The Professor would see the note and hopefully clear right out. There was little he could do baby-sitting the apartment. And Velma hadn't begun to spread the news. Yet.

He fished Flamingo's card out of his pocket, read it, and headed out to the address in Henderson.

It was a run-down warehouse in an industrial part of town where asphalted, barbed-wire-fringed compounds held fleets of trucks and mammoth crates. The streets were deserted but around the warehouse a couple of dozen cars were parked.

Diamond leaned on the buzzer at the entrance, a panel in the metal door slid aside, and he held up the card for a suspicious eye.

"This place reminds me of a speakeasy," Diamond said to the unsmiling fireplug who opened the door. The man grunted and indicated Diamond should follow.

They walked down a long hall, past vile green walls lit by bare incandescent bulbs hanging by wire from the ceiling.

"Really spent a lot fixing this place up," Diamond said.

His host didn't answer.

The murmur of voices grew louder and then they were in a cavernous main room. Exposed beams crisscrossed the ceiling, which was thirty feet above the concrete floor.

Roulette wheels spun, dice rolled, and cards were slapped down. But it was no glitzy casino. The wooden tables were chipped and scarred. The green felt tops were mangy. And the characters operating the games looked like a bunch of outcasts from a circus sideshow.

A fat lady in an apron as big as a tablecloth spun a roulette wheel. Card dealers included a thin man, a woman with more stubble than Diamond, and a couple of dwarves. A pudgy man whose dark mustache glistened with beads of sweat stood on an overturned carton. "Welcome! Welcome!" he boomed at Diamond. "School is about to begin. The road to riches stretches before you and we're here to give you a lift."

The man turned his attention to the thirty-five other people in the room. They were a mixed bag of men and women, ranging in age from their early twenties to late fifties, white, black, Hispanic, Oriental. The only thing they had in common was a shabby, hungry look.

"Ladies and gentlemen," the huckster said in a voice that echoed off the hard warehouse walls, "step right up. Don't be shy. My name is Bob and I welcome you to the Advanced School of Dealing."

He shined a beatific smile on the group.

"I see a few new faces here tonight," Bob continued. "I trust our oldtimers won't mind a quick review. Las Vegas is a town built on luck. Great gushing fountains of luck. And tonight I'm going to tell you how to dip into those fountains. Through no fault of your own, you have been cheated out of your just deserts. But you listen carefully to what your friend Bob and our guest speakers have to say and soon you'll have so much money you won't know what to do with it."

He went on mouthing generalities and working the crowd up like a preacher at a Holy Roller tabernacle.

"I will teach you to beat the odds," Bob said. "The casinos don't like that. They have some nasty names for it. I say God helps them that helps themselves. I like to think of myself as Robin Hood. And I invite you to be my merry men. And women."

The crowd cheered like a bunch of bobby-soxers at a Sinatra concert.

"Enough from me," Bob said with false humility. "In past nights we've discussed card counting, magnets and working the slots, and techniques for making the pasteboards your friends. Who remembers some of those techniques?"

"Crimping," an elderly black man shouted.

"Riffle stacks," a white woman said.

"Palming," an Oriental man said.

"Very, very good," Bob said like a pleased teacher. "Now how about different ways of marking cards?"

A bespectacled Mexican raised his hand and Bob pointed to him.

"Edge work, line work, cut out, block out, shading, trims, and sorts," the man recited.

"Go to the head of the class," Bob said. "A quick reminder to practice your mechanic's grip. There will be a test next week. And now, let me turn the floor over to a gent we'll call Joe. Joe is a virtuoso with the devil's dominoes, a man who can make dice do everything but sit up and talk. Please give him a warm welcome."

A bald man with a head as white as a set of virgin dice and eyes as cold as snake eyes nervously got up on the carton as the crowd applauded and Bob stepped down.

Joe stuttered and stumbled over his words but relaxed as he warmed to his subject.

"There are four basic kinds of die that can help you get an edge," he said. "Flats, tops, loads, or edge work dice. Flats, as you might guess, are flattened on one side. Tops have ones, threes, and fives, or twos, fours, and sixes on their face. Loads are weighted. Thus the phrase 'loaded dice.' Edge work die are beveled so they tend to roll a certain way."

Joe got down and strode to a table. The crowd surged around him. He began demonstrating with different dice, keeping up a running explanation of craps. He told how the house can use the dice to cheat a gambler and how they could be turned around to work in the player's favor.

When Joe began lecturing on sleight of hand tricks for palming and switching the dice, Diamond walked away.

He couldn't stop thinking about the Professor. If he had told Velma, who else had he spoken to? Diamond didn't want the genius to wind up like Teri Lennox.

Bob stopped him as he was halfway down the corridor.

"My friend, where are you going?" Bob demanded.

"I remembered I left the gas on."

"The people that run this show don't appreciate anyone leaving early," Bob said, the huckster warmth replaced by a menacing tone.

"That's too bad. Who runs this show anyway?"

"None of your business."

"What's the tuition here?"

"First two classes are free. Then you sign a contract. After a month in the business you can pay the thousand dollar tuition with no sweat," Bob said, taking Diamond's arm. "Now c'mon back in."

The P.I. pulled away. "Mrs. Diamond didn't raise her baby boy to be a card sharp. Good-bye."

"Buddy, something's not right with you."

"You a doctor?"

"No."

"Then don't go practicing medicine without a license," Diamond snapped. "The docs are sensitive about that sort of thing."

"Are you a comedian?"

"I've heard that line before. I don't have all night to exchange witty repartee," Diamond said, turning and taking three steps toward the door.

"Hey, Rube," Bob yelled.

Two gorillas appeared faster than a bill collector on payday. They had forearms the size of sewer mains. They grabbed him.

"Dis guy giving you trouble?" Gorilla One asked. Gorilla Two licked his lips.

"Tell King Kong and his sidekick to back off. I'm not making half the ruckus I will if they get strong with me."

"We'll go outside and you can tell my friends a few of your jokes," Bob said. "If they don't laugh, they can do something funny to your face."

Diamond's arms were pinned to his side. There was

111

no way he could reach his .38 as he was quickstepped down the hall.

"You guys get those muscles playing with yourself?" Diamond asked.

Bob answered for the men, who only squeezed Diamond harder. "They used to pound bigtop stakes for a living. They still like pounding things, smart guy."

"I heard guys with big muscles are making up for having little dicks," Red said. "Not that it matters much, since most of them are queer."

Gorilla One gave an enraged snort, let go of Diamond's arm, and swung. Diamond spun, reaching for his gun. The blow caught his shoulder. It wasn't as painful as getting hit by a cement mixer. It took all of Diamond's willpower to keep from dropping his weapon. He shoved it into Bob's stomach.

"How'd you like another belly button?" Diamond asked. "Tell the goon squad to go play mumblety-peg or I waste some lead."

Bob nodded and Gorilla Two let go. They eyed Diamond like hungry sharks.

He cocked the .38. "They better back off or you won't be here to hear about it," Diamond said to Bob.

"Go. It's okay," Bob said, and the two gorillas reluctantly lumbered off.

Diamond stepped behind Bob, nudged the huckster's back, and walked him outside.

"Now what's the story?" Diamond asked.

"You a cop?"

"I ask the questions. Answer me. Who's behind this?"

"I don't know."

Diamond put the gun to Bob's head.

"I don't know. Honest."

"This set-up hasn't impressed me with your honesty."

"But it's true. We were a carnie group working the boonies. Business ain't what it used to be. This guy offered us a few grand to take over this place."

"What's the guy look like?"

"Flashy dresser. Slick hair. Slick all over. Too sharp an operator for Winnemucca," Bob said. "That's where we met him."

"Was he alone?"

"No. With a real big guy. Three hundred pounder. Had one bushy eyebrow running across his whole face. He didn't say nothing. I don't know if he spoke English."

Keeping the gun on Bob, Diamond dug out the pictures of Flip and Babe. "These two?"

"Yeah. Those are the guys. Who are they?"

"I ask the questions. How do you get paid?"

"A money order is sent to me. From banks around Las Vegas. I never see anyone. First couple of weeks I got paid in Krugerrands, then they switched to the money orders. The guy delivering them is just a messenger."

"How long you been doing this?"

"Three months."

"Tonight's your last night. Pack your tent and split."

"But—"

"No buts. Anyone contacts you, tell them Red Diamond is on the case." The P.I. stepped back, keeping the .38 pointed at Bob's middle.

"We could make a deal. I'll cut you in for—"

"No deals. Get going. I'll be back in a couple hours. If you're lucky only the cops will be with me. If I'm in a bad mood I'll bring a bunch of ass-kickers from the casinos. Catch my drift?"

Bob nodded glumly.

"I don't think the broken nose boys would be very happy with your show," Diamond said.

Bob yelled the same obscenity at Diamond's back as Velma had.

It's a good thing I don't have an inferiority complex, Red mused as he hopped into his car, and sped back to the Professor's.

10

The paper he'd left tucked in the door was lying on the Professor's doorstep. It could mean the Professor had returned or that someone else was waiting in the apartment. It definitely meant Diamond would not go barreling in like a country lawyer late for a hearing at the Supreme Court.

He'd first used the trick in "The Hard Time Killer" case. After tracking the man to a cheap boarding house in Kansas City, Diamond had taken the room down the hall from his quarry. The killer found out who he was and waited in Diamond's room with his well-used heater. The paper-in-the-door gimmick had tipped Diamond he was inside and . . .

No time for happy memories of shootouts. He cautiously crawled to a partially open window. He could hear two voices. The Professor had company.

"You said you had a message for me from Mr. Diamond," the Professor was saying. "But then you enter and insist that I imbibe. Rather strange behavior."

114

"Drink!" the visitor said. It was a cold, commanding voice.

"I repeat. I am not in the mood for liquid refreshment," the Professor said. "And I must ask that you give me the message and depart. I have work to do."

Diamond peered over the windowsill. The Professor was seated, the man towering over him with a tumbler in his hand. He was about sixty, with graying hair and nondescript features.

"This is good stuff," the man said. "Drink!"

Diamond took his gun out and aimed. "If the Professor don't want to drink, he don't have to," he said.

The Professor was still looking to see where Diamond's voice had come from while the man was reacting. Moving with the grace of a professional athlete, he dropped the glass and reached under his jacket.

Red knew he wasn't grabbing for his American Express card. The P.I. snapped off two shots as his suspicions were confirmed and the man produced a .22 Colt Woodsman.

The cigar-long silencer on the .22's end kept things quiet as three shots whistled through the air. One hit the glass near Diamond's head. The pane shattered. A sharp shard brushed Diamond's forehead.

The gunman kept moving and Red couldn't get a clear shot without winging the Professor.

Blood was running down Diamond's face as the killer took off to the back of the house. The Professor was watching the action open-mouthed.

"Open the door," Diamond yelled.

The befuddled genius obeyed and Diamond raced to the rear of the apartment. The man was gone.

When he was sure they were alone, Diamond went to the bathroom and washed the blood and glass fragments from his face.

"The lacerations appear to be superficial," the Pro-

115

fessor said after inspecting Diamond. "There should be no danger of infection, though I'd recommend consulting a licensed medical practitioner. As Jean-Paul Sartre once said—"

"I don't need no sawbones," Diamond cut in. "Just tell me what happened."

"Isn't this exciting?"

"Yeah. It's more fun than a brain surgeon with hiccups. Now what happened?"

"I borrowed several volumes from an associate I encountered at the library. We began chatting and soon were engrossed in the Sicilian defense."

"Mafia?"

The Professor chuckled. "No. A classic chess gambit. Tempus fugit and I only returned a scant fifteen minutes ago. That gentleman was waiting. He wanted me to drink and I was suspicious."

"A smart move."

"There may be veritas in vino but I believe spirits effect the cerebrum adversely by causing the death of brain cells. The neurons depend upon—"

"So you don't booze it up?"

"In a word, no. But I would've refused his offer anyway. The liquid smelled like a volatile alkaloid."

"Any idea what it is?"

The Professor walked out to where the fluid was puddling. He knelt, rubbed the spill between his fingers, and gingerly sniffed it.

"A complete spectrographic analysis would be invaluable but I think a safe guess would be conium maculatum."

"That don't tell me a lot."

"I suspect this is processed conium maculatum or perhaps circuta maculata. Coniine is the volatile alkaloid, the active ingredient. It causes depression of the motor nerves, a slow process beginning with the extremities. The corpus falls asleep. Irrevocably."

116

"The big sleep. This stuff got a name that's not a jawbreaker?"

"Hemlock."

"Wasn't there some famous Greek guy they made take that junk when he stepped on government tootsies?"

"Very good, though I've never quite heard it described like that. Socrates. In Athens. 399 B.C. Prior to his encouraging me to consume the toxic beverage, my visitor and I were discussing famous poisonings. The Borgias, Locusta, La Voisin. Women predominated, but there were—"

"You're not very shook up for a guy that nearly had poison shoved down his gullet and a shootout in his living room."

"This is quite exciting. Do you think I'll meet sensual but treacherous women who will try to seduce confidential information from me? Perhaps a vehicular pursuit with tires squealing and firearms spattering?"

The Professor's voice had risen with excitement. He made an effort to calm down.

"Perhaps the shock will set in later," he continued. "That is quite normal. But for now these are the sort of situations I had only read about."

"You're a strange bird but I can understand what you're feeling," Diamond said. "Anyway, you already met your beautiful treacherous doll. Velma."

"Surely you jest."

"She tried shaking me down for ten Gs. But she promised to hold off spilling the beans until tomorrow. Did you tell anyone else?"

The Professor thought for a moment. "Only my chess buddy. And the clerk in the real estate records office."

"A secret's a secret when two people know it and one of them's dead."

"And my landlady. And the clerk in the corporate

117

records office. Oh yes, my mailman too."

"Why didn't you take an ad in the papers?"

"You told me to keep it quiet," the Professor said. "I only told people I trust."

"Well you blew it with Velma. And who knows who else."

The Professor looked crushed. "You mean someone violated my confidence?"

"I don't think that guy with the poison and the twenty-two was here because you got library books overdue," Diamond said. "Did you get a good look at him?"

"He was a white male. Late fifties. Gray hair, brown eyes. About five feet ten inches tall. No more than a hundred and seventy pounds. Wearing a custom suit, expensive shoes. Scar on his left hand. At least partially ambidextrous. Thin lips and a broad nose."

"That's not a bad description. Sherlock Holmes would be proud."

The Professor grinned. "Also he wasn't wearing a wedding band and he had dandruff."

"I'll find him a broad and buy him shampoo," Diamond said. "But first we get you to safety. How's your investigation going?"

"No conclusions yet, but there are some interesting trends. I'd rather study the matter further before commenting."

"How much more time you need?"

"Another day. But I want to be in the thick of things. To smell cordite and cheap perfume, the thrill of the hunt, chasing villains down dark alleys while—"

"I don't have time to teach you the facts of life. Street life, that is." Diamond said. "Is there any city you'd want to go to?"

"I've never been to Los Angeles. I know it has a reputation as a cultural wasteland but they do have the Huntington Library, the Norton Simon, some fair universities, the Jet Propulsion Lab, Rand Corporation . . . "

The Professor continued his list while Diamond mulled over the pros and cons. L.A. was less than an hour flight from Las Vegas. A lot of the Vegas crowd hung out in "El Lay" and vice versa. There were plenty of wiseguys who'd snitch out the Professor or handle whacking him themselves. But Los Angeles was a good city to get lost in. Sprawling, with tangled jurisdictions, people who knew to mind their own business. If a guy kept his nose clean, he could easily get lost in the crowd.

" . . . C. Page Museum, Getty Museum," the Professor was saying.

"Fine. Could you stay out of trouble if I gave you a thousand bucks?"

"I expect I wouldn't need anywhere near that. My needs are quite modest."

"Grab your gear," Diamond said, pointing toward the bedroom. "We move you into a motel around here tonight. Tomorrow you do the research you have to, then fly to Los Angeles. Write up your report and give me a call. You can reach me at the Last Chance Motel or the Ace of Diamonds."

"I comprehend fully," the Professor said from the bedroom where he was emptying drawers.

It took the genius a half hour to pack, with most of the time devoted to deliberating over which books he should take.

They drove to the outskirts of town and found a motel that appeared to cater to tourist families. On the ride over, Diamond followed the Professor's car, and kept watch for any tails.

The Professor registered in the motel under the name Augie Dupin. Diamond gave him a grand and cautioned him to speak to no one about what he was up to.

The P.I. could barely keep his eyes open as he

headed back to the Last Chance Motel. He hit the pillow like a truck without brakes.

He was dreaming of a casino where one-armed bandits paid off in bullets. Rocco was the pit boss. A couple of strong arms were shoving Diamond toward Rocco's bottomless pit.

The dream shifted back to his room but the hands were still on him. He grabbed for the gun under his pillow. It was gone.

He was wide awake and thrashing, struggling with two gray-suited men. Faceless in the darkened room. A needle gleamed and was shoved into his arm. He felt the pinprick.

Seconds later his head seemed detached from his body. He had as much control of his limbs as a Raggedy Ann doll. The men dressed him like a mother preparing her child for school.

With a man on either side he was led to a car. The men had bland, expressionless faces. Midwestern WASPish, with thinning blond hair. The only difference between these men and pork-belly speculators from Topeka were their eyes. Hard eyes. The kind of eyes that watched people die without blinking.

They eased Diamond into the back seat. Not gently, not roughly. Efficiently. Like they'd been propping up doped private eyes in the back of Buicks all their lives.

During the half-hour car ride, Diamond kept sending signals to his limbs. The messages came back stamped "Moved—Left No Address." Even his vocal cords were numbed.

They arrived at a complex on the outskirts of town. It was the kind of building favored by insurance companies and budding computer firms—new, clean, with recessed lighting, brightly colored panels, industrial carpeting, and Muzak in the halls.

General Consulting Services read the modest plaque on the door of the third-floor suite. Diamond was lugged in.

It wasn't a good sign that the kidnappers had let him see their faces and destination, Red knew. It probably meant they didn't count on him being around to tell anyone about the excursion. But his body was unable to respond to his concerns.

"Have a seat, Mr. Diamond," a third man said as they entered the office. "Or do you prefer being called Simon Jaffe? John Dalmas?"

He was in his mid-sixties, dapper in a blue blazer and tan slacks. He had a perfect tan and neatly coiffed silver hair. His voice was cultured, as well-modulated as a radio announcer's. He oozed congenial confidence.

Red was lowered onto a leather davenport that probably cost as much as a new car. The warm patina of the antiques gleamed under subdued lighting.

The dapper gent took out a silver cigarette case, crossed his legs, and lit a cigarette with a Dunhill lighter.

"The muscle paralyzer you were given should wear off enough for you to talk," the gent said, consulting a Patek-Philippe on his wrist. "I hope you won't do anything embarassing like screaming. It's not even six o'clock and there's no one around to appreciate it."

Diamond tried speaking. He sounded like a frog with laryngitis.

"While we're waiting, my name is Stan Stanley," the gent said. "My associates are the Lee brothers."

"Gurgh-uh-gruh."

"Try swallowing and then speaking," Stanley said.

"Gruh. They look . . . grugh . . . like feebs."

One of the Lee brothers snorted.

"Not FBI. CIA. Retired," Stanley said pleasantly. "They came to work for our organization after serving their country for many years. Our cash is a nice supplement to their pensions. Do you have any idea which organization I represent?"

"The Welcome Wagon?"

"I see the curare compound hasn't dulled your wit," Stanley said. "Care to guess again?"

"If it's about my taxes, I can explain."

"We don't have all morning, Mr. Diamond. We are both men of the world. My client, quite simply, is the Mafia."

Diamond moistened his parched lips with his tongue.

"Surprised?"

"I'm trying to imagine your press releases. 'Narcotics up, prostitution down. The chairman sadly announces the departure of Vinnie the Blade who was found in a dumpster—'"

"Let's kill the chit chat," Stanley said, uncrossing his legs and extinguishing his cigarette. He leaned forward with his hands on his knees. "You are investigating the crime wave in Las Vegas. Your client is Edward Evans. You believe our organization is behind it. I can assure you we are not."

"Well I feel a whole lot better. Soon as I can move I'll pack my bags."

"I doubt that you believe me. To demonstrate our sincerity we will pay you double whatever Evans's fee is."

"I can't be bought. At least, no one's ever met my price."

"Not a buy-off. Continue your investigation. Take our money plus Evans's. Find out who is behind the campaign. But know it isn't us."

"Why do you care what I do if you're not involved in the trouble?"

"You have earned somewhat of a reputation for

122

blundering into things. In New York and Los Angeles. We don't want problems. We still own large portions of this town and don't want any disturbances. You find the troublemakers and we'll handle it from there."

"So I bird-dog for you and then they get whacked?" Stanley was silent.

"You're so efficient in bringing me here," Diamond said. "You know my background. Why can't you put your own skullcrackers on the case?"

"I apologize for having you transported so abruptly but we wanted to demonstrate how easy it would be to, uh, neutralize you. If that was what we wanted. As for sending some of our own people, we have. Two were killed. Another neutralized one of the saboteurs before we got any useful information. Unfortunately, this only added to the general mayhem. The last thing we want is open warfare. We're much more discreet nowadays. There also are certain politics I'm not at liberty to explain. We'll provide you any assistance you might need."

"Thanks but no thanks. Red Diamond works alone."

"A pity. How are you feeling?"

"Like Samson. With a crewcut. How long do I sit here like a potted plant?"

"You'll be fine within an hour," Stanley said. "The Lee brothers will take you back."

Diamond tried standing up. He got as far as a puppet with tangled strings.

"While we wait maybe you can help me," the P.I. said.

"Just ask."

"A guy named Fingers was killed in the jail. Were you behind that?"

Stanley shook his head. "I understand he cut off his fingers and bled to death."

"Your information is good. Another question. I'm interested in a button man. Late fifties, gray hair, brown eyes, snappy dresser. Five ten, about a hundred and seventy pounds."

"I'm afraid quite a few people fit that description."

"Ambidextrous. Scar on his left hand. Thin lips and a broad nose. And he's got dandruff."

"Gulo," Stanley said.

The Lee brothers looked impressed.

"Gulo?" Diamond asked.

"Very few people see him and live. You are to be congratulated. He was one of our best people."

"Was?"

"He got bored with the usual techniques of enforcement."

"A bullet behind the ear or a bomb under the hood?"

"Whatever. He billed himself as a lethal artist. Insisted on exotic methods custom-fit to each assignment. For example, Irish Kelly. He beat him to death with a shillelagh. You believe Fingers was his handiwork?"

"Yeah. And the attempt on the Professor."

"Who?"

"Never mind. You said 'was.' Gulo doesn't strike me as the kind to open a hot dog stand."

"True. He's now a freelancer, hiring out to the highest bidder. He's quite adept at disguises and extremely dangerous."

"Thanks for the warning," Diamond said. "One other thing. What do you know about Rocco Rico?"

Stanley thought for a moment. "The name isn't familiar."

"I didn't expect it would be. You have to cover up for the top cheese."

Stanley made a gesture and the Lee brothers lifted Diamond effortlessly. They carried him out to the car. During the ride home Diamond practiced wiggling his toes. By the time the brothers laid him back in his bed, he was as graceful as a drunken hippo.

11

There were no side effects from the drug when Diamond awoke at eleven. He called Evans, who at last was available. He hurried to the Ace of Diamonds. The guards were lackadaisical as he was hustled through security.

Diamond walked past the bank vault door into Tex's cozy little screening room that could've seated fifty. Only Tex and Norris were in the theater.

Tex had a glum expression as he watched a Lone Ranger film and mouted the words as Clayton Moore and Jay Silverheels spoke them. Norris sat next to the billionaire, dropping popcorn into his mouth like a slave girl feeding grapes to a Roman emperor. As the images flickered on the screen Diamond could make out posters of Hopalong Cassidy, Tom Mix, Roy Rogers, and a half-dozen other cowboy greats on the walls.

"Hi Yo Silver," Diamond said.

Evans looked up bleakly. *"Melody Ranch* is on next. It's got Gene Autry in it."

"What's the matter, Tex? You look like your prize bull got his dingus caught in a wringer."

Evans sulked. Norris got up quietly and whispered in Diamond's ear. "He's been this way since yesterday. He's subject to terrible depressions when things don't go right. Usually the old movies cheer him up. It's best to leave him alone."

"I can't. I need his help."

"Nobody disturbs him. I had hoped he'd be better by the time you arrived. I was mistaken."

"Hey, Tex," Diamond said.

The billionaire glanced up.

"Where does Tonto take the garbage?"

"You mustn't bother him," Norris said while Tex regarded Diamond blankly.

"To the dump, to the dump, to the dump dump dump."

The Lone Ranger film was ending and the only sound in the acoustically engineered room was the William Tell Overture.

"I get it. To the dump, to the dump, to the dump dump dump," Evans said. He let out a shattering whoop that made Norris jump. Evans unfolded his lanky body from the soft chair and bobbed around the room repeating the punchline. "That's great. I'll remember that one."

He slapped Diamond on the shoulder. "Red, you're my kind of fella." He bounced down the aisle and let out a near maniacal laugh. "I was letting these varmints in black hats get me down. I couldn't find a straight shooter to head security. We had a bunch of bomb scares and I was thinkin' of packin' it in. But not now. Whoooeie! When we going to send these desperados off with their tails between their legs?"

"Let me tell you what happened," Diamond said, launching into a recital of the past twenty-four hours.

"The Lands don't mean nothing special to me. How about you Norris?"

"No, sir."

"Do you reckon he was talking about the lands, you know, the wide open spaces?" Evans asked Diamond. "I know during the range wars folks got mighty touchy about that. And during the mining days claim jumping was as common as garters in a dance hall."

126

"Maybe. I've got an associate looking into it," Diamond said.

Tex began twirling a six-gun he took from his hip. "What's your next step?"

"I'm going to look for a woman."

Tex was annoyed. "I can understand a healthy young fella wanting to kick up his heels a mite but we don't have the time for that."

"This girl is the key to everything," Diamond responded. "Her name is Fifi La Roche and once I get her, Rocco will have to come to me."

"And you're sure this Rocco is behind the problems?"

Diamond nodded.

"Well then how can I help?"

Diamond took out the brochure with his long lost love's picture circled. "This," he said with a flourish, "is Fifi."

Evans took the brochure and studied it. "She's a purty gal. No question about that. We can do it two ways. I can show this to my personnel director and see if she recognizes her. Or we can go through a photo album I have in the library. It's got pictures of everyone who has ever worked here."

"Let's go for the album," Diamond said. "The less people that know the better."

Diamond had seen more books. Once. In the Library of Congress. The walls were filled with shelves and every shelf was packed with titles. Freestanding stacks held the overflow.

"How many books you got?" Diamond asked.

"I stopped counting a long time ago," Tex said. "Norris and me will mosey down a piece and find the volume for gals working here in the past five years. You jes' make yourself at home."

Every western author was represented. Louis

127

L'Amour, Zane Grey, Max Brand, Ernest Haycox, Luke Short, and hundreds Diamond had never heard of: Powder River Bill, Frank Richardson Pierce, J.E. Grinstead, Wayne Overholser and his son Stephen, Eugene Manlove Rhodes.

A smell came to his nostrils, a scent as alluring as Fifi's perfume. He sniffed his way to the section where the pulps were housed.

Real Western, Lariat Story Magazine, Two Gun Western, Complete Western, Famous Western, Smashing Western, Sure Fire Western, The Western Raider, Wild West Weekly, Western Story, Nickel Western, Western Tales, Western Round-Up, West.

He sucked in the woody, musty odor that gave him a thrill he couldn't understand. He was like a hophead in a poppy field. He gently took a magazine and gazed at the cover.

A stubbly, stern-jawed sheriff was blazing away at a half-dozen villainous outlaws. The cover was gaudy and garish with lots of yellow and orange.

Diamond was transfixed. It was like seeing the face of an old friend, only the face was slightly different, and it wasn't the friend you thought.

"Mr. Diamond! Mr.Diamond!" Norris said, hurrying down the aisle. "What happened? We've been calling you."

"Uh, huh, I've been thinking."

"Careful with that," Norris said as he took the pulp magazine and put it back. "These are very fragile. And precious."

"I know. I used to have quite a collection. *Black Mask, Spicy Detective, Ten Story Gang*, until, until. . . "

The words came from a place Diamond didn't know and the throbbing began.

"Do you want to sit down?" a concerned Norris asked. "You've had a difficult time."

"No."

"Well then, Mr. Evans is waiting with the pictures."

It took Diamond an hour of looking at photos before he found Fifi. She had been using the name Gayle Collins. The book said she'd worked in the show for seven months, then quit.

Diamond called the phone number on file for her. The number had been disconnected with no new number referral. He got a copy of her personnel photo, jotted down her address, thanked Tex, and headed out.

Fifi's trail was heating up.

It got cold quicker than a skinny-dipping Eskimo. Fifi had moved out of her East Las Vegas apartment two months earlier. Diamond plunged into the tedious chore of canvassing the area. He used the story that he was her long-lost relative trying to contact her to give her an inheritance. He offered a hundred dollar finder's fee to anyone who knew where she was.

No one did. He learned that she played the stereo too loud, had several male visitors who stayed overnight, and was a physical fitness fanatic. She had a blue Toyota with a bad muffler. And she had left suddenly, with no forwarding address.

Saint complained when Diamond called, but he checked Gayle Collins in the Motor Vehicle's computer. She had not updated her address since moving.

Diamond phoned Evans and asked for the home address of Angie, the redheaded showgirl. It took five minutes to get her last name, but then her address came easily. He drove to the house she shared with three other women from the chorus line.

She came to the door with curlers in her hair and a pink floral houserobe draping her body. "What do you want?" she asked angrily. He took out a hundred dollars and she invited him in.

He showed her the picture of Fifi.

"Her. Gayle what's her name. She left the show a few months ago."

"I know that. I need to know where she is now."

"She wasn't exactly Miss Popularity. Thought she was better than the rest of us," Angie said. "Red, I'll give you some advice. Stay away from her."

"I'm going to find her. With your help," Diamond said, waving the hundred-dollar bill. "Or without it."

"It's your life. She caught Moe Greenberg's eye. Lots of girls do. He goes through them like cheap cigars. He's got them stashed in pads all over the city."

Red felt a shudder at the base of his spine. If only Angie knew. Moe was no doubt fronting for Rocco.

"Any idea where he's got her?"

"I think one of the girls saw her a few weeks ago. He's got a couple he keeps in the Lion's Den. But I think someone saw her on the street. She jogs five miles a day."

"Jogs?"

"Runs. She's a health-food nut. Always kept yogurt in the refrigerator at work. The stuff would get old and stink to high heaven."

"Who saw her?" he asked.

"I don't know."

"Can you find out?"

"Tonight. At the show," Angie said. "I'll ask around."

Diamond pulled two twenties and a ten-dollar bill out of his wallet. "Here's half. You get me that information, the rest is yours. With my undying gratitude."

"You may regret it," she said, taking the money.

He went back to the Last Chance Motel and gathered his belongings. Simon Jaffe was history. Red Diamond was back in action.

He couldn't look like a rumpled bum when he met

his Fifi. He stopped at a dry cleaning store, dropped off his laundry bag, and paid for rush service.

While he was waiting he went out for a quick meal and called Velma.

"I ain't playing and I ain't paying," he told her.

"How about five thousand?"

"How about taking a hike?"

"A thousand?"

"I'll give you a tip. Don't go over twenty-one when you play blackjack."

"Bastard."

"And give up the blackmail racket. You're too sweet and innocent for it."

"I'll get you. Everyone will know who you are and what you're up to. There won't be a cocktail lounge in town you can go into without everyone knowing. I'll—"

He hung up on the fuming woman. Too many people already knew who he was. It was time to take a new tack. Red Diamond, bait. Set himself out like a bowl of sugar and wait for the roaches to come calling.

And maybe, if he was lucky, Fifi would hear he was around.

He called Saint and asked what the cop knew about Stan Stanley.

"Believe it or not he's a PR man for the wiseguys," Saint said.

"I believe it. Now I got a tip for you. I got word that Fingers was whacked by a mug named Gulo. Freelance killer and all-around nice guy."

Diamond gave Saint Gulo's description. He was rewarded with a begrudging thanks.

Back in the store, the P.I. sat and waited. How many precious years of his life were spent waiting; for clients, on surveillances, while clerks shuffled through records, for Fifi.

It was January and the rain was coming. The wind chimes on the redwood deck outside the Malibu restaurant jingled in the moist breeze. The sea outside the restaurant window was flexing its great green-and-white muscles.

It was the kind of night a guy should be curled up in front of a fireplace with a leggy broad and a bottle of hooch.

But Michael David Rankin had called me and told me to meet him at the restaurant perched on the ocean's edge. Rankin better show. I couldn't afford a Ritz cracker in this joint. I'd been sitting for a half hour trying to figure out what the dozen pieces of silverware in front of me did when he walked through the door, a harried man in a tuxedo as black as midnight on the high seas.

The maitre d' who had treated me like a steerage refugee would've kissed Rankin's feet if the man had wanted it.

Rankin's orbs glommed me and he hurried to my table like a Muslim to Mecca. My stock with the staff jumped 1,000 percent.

"Mr. Diamond, I need your help," Rankin said as he pulled up a chair.

How can you say no to a guy worth $35 million? Especially when you're a private dick whose socks have more holes than a field full of gophers.

Rankin shooed away the attentive staff that had been working hard at ignoring me. He laid out his tale of woe.

His closest living relative, a niece, had run off with a Lebanese tango dancer. He loved her and wanted to make sure her departure was entirely voluntary. The cops said it was. He wasn't so sure.

No rough stuff, he told me.

I said yes. But by the time the caper was through, there'd be nine jokers pushing up daisies.

Scott Marks had gotten most of it right, Red recalled. The Lebanese dancer had turned out to be making a little extra on the side by smuggling hashish into the good old U.S. of A. And selling American girls into white slavery in his native country. The kind of guy who liked dancing on people's graves. The trail had led back to Rocco. On the freighter. Red thought his ticket had been punched when the deck hand with the baling hook—

"Your order is ready," the teenager behind the counter in the dry cleaning store said.

Diamond retrieved his freshly pressed suit and neatly blocked hat. He got back into his car and headed toward the Strip.

His mind drifted back to Rankin's problem as he drove. He could almost smell the exotic odors of the Casbah, the spices, the sweat, the backed up or non-existent sewers. The way he'd stormed into the heavily guarded building where the women had been held.

And there was Fifi. About to be brutalized by a towering hulk with a scar like the San Andreas fault across his forehead.

Red hadn't spoken. His .38 had done all the talking. Four shots. Four dead. And Fifi was back in his arms.

The reinforcements had come storming in. They thought they were going to break up a squabble among the slave girls. They hadn't counted on the pitiless fists of Red Diamond.

He couldn't kick them in the balls. Most were eunuchs. But Algerian doctors must've had a field day patching up the busted jaws and noses he handed out.

With Fifi and Rankin's niece in tow, they'd traveled to Morocco, staying one step ahead of the pursuing thugs. Then Fifi had saved his life, when . . .

Fifi. God how he missed her. He thought of her held

133

captive in Greenberg's casino. He couldn't search every room. But he could make Moe talk.

Red knew he could get mean when he had to. And with Fifi held captive, he had to. He couldn't wait for the bedbugs to come to him.

He pulled his snap-brim down lower and leaned on the accelerator.

Five minutes later, he ventured into the Lion's Den.

12

A couple of big stuffed lions, looking bedraggled after being handled by millions of tourists, were set just inside the entrance.

A man in a Hawaiian print shirt was posing astride one of the forlorn beasts. His wife took out a camera and two bush jacket-clad security people hustled them away. The guards looked a lot fiercer than the lions.

Murals on the walls depicted herds of zebras, giraffes, and gazelles. Male employees dressed like safari guides; female employees dressed "native" in skimpy loincloths. Archways were framed by crossed spears and the concessions had names like "The Rhino Restaurant" and "The Watering Hole."

The noise of the human jungle was strictly Las Vegas, with chips clicking, wheels spinning, and cries of victory and defeat. Red moved through the crowds, longing to scream Fifi's name. Fortune-obsessed humanity swirled around him. His game was for keeps.

He stopped a bored brunette who was circulating with a tray of cigarettes. She was wearing a couple of slivers of fake leopard skin and a frown. The frown was bigger than her skimpy drapery.

"Where's Moe's office?" he asked.

"No one gets to see him," she said.

"He'll see me."

"Suit yourself. It's on the thirteenth floor. Private elevator behind the regular elevator bank."

"Thanks." He dropped a buck on her tray. She barely suppressed a yawn as she swivel-hipped away.

Diamond strode to where five stainless steel doors opened and shut, swallowing and disgorging those on the way up or down. Next to the bank was a door marked KEEP OUT: AUTHORIZED PERSONNEL ONLY. It wasn't locked.

The mock jungle decor was replaced by bare cinderblock and hard fluorescent lighting. His footsteps echoed on tile floors. He rounded the corner and came face to chest with a human mountain that could've been a linebacker if he had been six inches shorter.

"Who are you?" the mountain demanded.

"Phineas H. Thorndike," Diamond said. "That's 'H' as in hurry. I'm here to see Moe."

"Yeah?" The mountain was not impressed. He took out a notebook and scanned it. He moved his lips as he read through the names.

With the guard's attention diverted, Diamond took out his .38 and smashed the butt down on the mountain's crest.

The guard staggered back, then reached out and enveloped Diamond's gun hand in his paw. Red threw a half-dozen punches that weren't good enough. The man-mountain looked amused as he tucked the notebook

135

away. He gave Diamond a backhanded slap that sent the P.I. bouncing off the wall like an overinflated tennis ball.

Two men came running down the corridor with guns drawn.

"What's the trouble Lou?" one of them asked.

"No trouble Frank. This guy wants to see Moe. I didn't get a chance to tell him Moe's out of town before he gets smart."

"You want to handle it?" Frank's thin lips barely moved when he talked. He had an unhealthy complexion and spider tattoos on the back of his pale hands.

"You guys do it," Lou said. "I got to stay here."

The third man, shorter, with arched black eyebrows and a black goatee that gave him a devilish look, waved a .45 at Diamond. "Let's go for a walk," he said pleasantly.

Frank took Diamond's .38 from Lou, dropped it in his bush jacket pocket, and gestured with his 9 mm. "Move it."

"You're making a mistake," Diamond said, still shaking the blurriness from his head.

"That's what they all say," Frank answered. "Move it."

Diamond stepped forward and sized up the distance to the men.

"Don't even think about it," Devil said.

Diamond and the gun-toting duo moved down the corridor. Their footsteps had an eerie finality. The guards were pros. They stood just out of reach.

"Where'd you do time?" Diamond asked Frank.

"What makes you say that, captain?"

"The way you move your lips. Jailhouse style so the screws can't see. Either that or you're practicing to be a ventriloquist."

"Leavenworth, Marion, and Nevada State," Frank said as they continued to walk.

"I'm the ventriloquist," Devil said to Diamond. "And you're the dummy."

It was the last thing Diamond heard before the lights went out.

He woke tied to a heavy chair in a dimly lit room that had the dank feel of a castle basement. Power lawnmowers, shovels, and other gardening supplies leaned against the walls.

Devil was standing in front of him puffing on a cigar. He blew the smoke in Diamond's face and the P.I. coughed.

"He's up," Devil said, and Frank came out of the gloom.

"Let's make this short and simple, captain," Frank said. "What are you up to?"

Diamond rolled his head around. Aside from the sore spot where he'd been hit, everything seemed in place.

Devil blew another cloud in his face. "Frank, I can tell this guy thinks he's tough. We're gonna have to waste a couple hours loosening him up."

"But he'll talk. They always do," Frank said. "Remember that guy we had to break about twenty-five bones before he spilled his guts?"

"I liked the one where we used the acid," Devil said.

"Yeah. That was good. I heard he got a job in a freak show."

"What are you gonna do, talk me to death?" Diamond asked.

"I told you. A tough guy," Devil said.

Frank dumped the bullets out of Diamond's gun then made a big show of putting one back in. He handed the weapon to Devil who spun the cylinder and shoved the muzzle against Diamond's temple.

"Frank, I bet you a buck this goes off first time I squeeze."

"Deal."

Devil very slowly began to ease down on the trigger.

Red remembered a few tricks about Russian Roulette from his "Mayhem in Moscow" investigation. One was that if the gun faced you, you could see if the fatal cylinder was lined up. Diamond couldn't see.

But the other fact was equally reassuring. Gravity would pull the heaviest chamber to the bottom. Away from the hammer. Sometimes it didn't work but Red wouldn't be around to complain.

Click. Devil lost the bet.

"See. A tough guy," Devil repeated.

"Okay, tough guy," Frank said. "Let me tell you what we know. Your name's Red Diamond. You're a peeper out of L.A. You had a picture of Moe and a few of the guys in your wallet. And a shot of one of Moe's girls. Now you tell us who you work for and what you want from Moe and we can go on our way."

"Simple as that?" Diamond asked.

"Simple as that."

"I'm no hero," Diamond said after pretending to mull the offer over. "You know that South African guy that Moe's been dealing with?"

"Van Houton?"

"Yeah. Well I work for him. He wanted Moe checked out before they got any deeper on the deal."

"What deal?" Devil asked.

"The big deal. The lands."

"What do you know about that?" Frank demanded.

"They didn't tell me. I'm just hired help. Like you. You probably know more than I do."

Red hoped they'd take the bait and fill in some details. Instead Frank slugged the P.I. in the gut. Then it was Devil's turn, then Frank's again. They took turns pounding him for a couple of minutes without asking any more questions.

"You got a better story?" Devil asked after the beating. His cigar was nearly gone.

"That's the truth. Van Houton," Diamond said. It hurt to talk.

"Maybe it is," Frank said. "You needed to be taught a lesson anyway. Don't go snooping around where you shouldn't. I'm going up to check the story. If it isn't true I'll be back. And then we get nasty."

"I can use his puss for an ashtray," Devil said, gesturing with his cigar stub.

"Save it 'til I get back," Frank said, walking away.

Devil flicked his ashes in Diamond's hat, which lay on a table with the rest of his belongings. Diamond wriggled against his bonds.

"Struggle all you want," Devil said without looking up. "Frank was in the Navy. He ties a mean knot."

"Maybe we can make a deal."

"What kind?" Devil asked without real interest.

"Van Houton's got lots of bucks. He'd pay better than Moe."

"Probably. That cheap Jew don't pay much. But I don't have enough life insurance to switch bosses."

Despite Red's best salesmanship, Devil kept slamming the door in the P.I.'s face.

"Frank'll be back in a few minutes, shamus," Devil said. "I think you're full of it. Just shaddup."

Devil produced another cigar, lit it, and puffed more smoke in Diamond's face. "I want this nice and hot when we start round two."

The door at the far end of the basement opened and shut. Footfalls on the stairs. Devil grinned sadistically at Diamond, got up, and walked toward his partner.

"So what's the verdict?" he asked.

A few more footsteps.

"Frank?" Devil asked.

There was a thud and a choked scream.

139

Diamond strained to see what had happened. The man took his time walking to him.

A figure stepped out of the darkness. A stout forty-year-old with wavy blond hair. Diamond had never seen him before, but the way he moved was familiar.

He pulled off his wig, exposing gray hair. He took cotton balls out of his cheeks, knocking twenty pounds off his apparent weight.

"Do you know who I am?"

Diamond recognized the voice. "Gulo."

"Not my real name but that is what I am called. Do you know what I do?"

"Sell magazine subscriptions?"

"You are no better with jokes than you are as a detective," Gulo said.

"I been told I was a comedian."

"Don't believe what you hear. I don't go for working people over, like these amateurs," Gulo said, waving in the direction where Devil lay. "Again, do you know what I do?"

"You kill people."

"Very good," Gulo said condescendingly.

Gulo took a pearl-handed stiletto out of his pocket. He pressed a button and a five-inch blade appeared. Diamond sat very still as the killer moved to him.

"I do not see fear in your eyes," Gulo said. "You are either very crazy or very brave. Maybe a little of both. I approve. You will make a worthy kill."

Diamond could smell the killer's cologne. If the P.I. was free he could've lunged. But the ropes were too secure and he didn't bother to try.

"You are like a great animal, too dignified to struggle when you look death in the eye."

Gulo stepped behind Diamond and placed the cold steel at the top of Diamond's spine.

"I am a hunter," Gulo said. "Killing you now would

140

give me as little satisfaction as buying a pound of chopped meat in the supermarket. Do you understand?"

"Yeah."

The knife was gone from the P.I.'s neck. Red barely felt the ropes part at his hands. He moved them in front of him and began wiggling them to restore circulation.

"I will leave your feet bound. You can release yourself. When we meet again I will have the pleasure of killing you."

"I plan to disappoint you."

"You won't," Gulo said, and he was gone.

It took Diamond nearly five minutes to unravel the intricate knots with his benumbed hands.

He was a bit wobbly when he got up. He quickly collected his belongings from the table, reloaded the .38, and moved to the stairs.

Devil lay at the bottom. One of the pitchforks from the gardening rack was standing in his chest. He was deader than an unwatered house plant.

Frank was sprawled at the top. Red couldn't tell if the rope around his neck was tied in a fourfold blood knot or a sailor's breastplate. The rope looked very nice. Frank didn't. His tongue stood as straight up as the pitchfork and he had a ghastly blue color.

Diamond stepped over him and walked to a rear service door. OPEN ONLY IN AN EMERGENCY it read. I guess this qualifies, Red thought as he shoved it open and the alarm went off.

The fresh air felt good. He really hadn't liked Devil's cigar.

Angie was waiting at the Ace of Diamonds.

"A girl saw Gayle over in Paradise Valley," she said.

"Gayle? Oh, you mean Fifi?"

"The girl in the picture," Angie said. "She saw her

141

at Eastern near Tropicana. She was jogging."

"What time of day?"

"Early morning. About seven A.M."

"How did she look?"

"The same as usual. Stuck-up."

"I mean did she look okay? No guys with guns around? Didn't look beat-up or anything?"

"Listen Red, my friend was driving by. She didn't give her a physical. Do I get my money or not?"

Diamond gave her the $50 and his thanks.

She sloughed off his thanks but took the money.

"When you wise up, give me a call," she said, tossing her hair and bouncing away.

Diamond drove over to Eastern and headed south to where it met Tropicana. He didn't have the patience to wait for the next morning.

A thorough canvass of an area could make or break a case, he knew. The cops did it with teams of detectives. He was only one guy, but he had a lot more incentive. Fifi!

He parked near the intersection and began ringing doorbells and flashing her picture. He was chased by property protective dogs and propositioned by lonely housewives. A dozen doors were slammed in his face. Just one more house, Red kept telling himself, imagining Fifi's smile.

His temper was near the breaking point when he rapped on the door of the modest bungalow. No one answered though he could hear a TV on inside. He took out his frustration on the door, pounding it until the house shook.

He heard movement inside and the door finally was opened. A tiny Mexican woman in a baggy housedress gazed at him with curious brown eyes. She looked old enough to remember the Alamo.

"*Si?*"

Diamond flashed the picture and told of a long lost wife. He tried to remember the Spanish he'd picked up on "The Spanish Fly Caper," but all he could recall were *bandito, pistolero, me gusta, no me gusta,* and a half a dozen different food names. He spoke very slowly and gestured frequently.

The woman waited until he was done. "*Que?*" she asked.

He repeated the story, louder this time. Besides not speaking English, she was hard of hearing.

"*Perdido. Mi esposa,*" he said as the words came back to him.

"*Que?*"

He shouted the story a third time and she appeared to understand.

"Wait," she said, and wandered back into the house. She returned in less than an hour wearing glasses.

She studied the picture. "I see her. *Muy bonita.*"

"Where? When?"

They spent ten more minutes exchanging broken English and mangled Spanish.

He finally learned Fifi ran by the house most mornings at about 7:30 A.M.

"*Gracias,*" Diamond said. He was sweating profusely.

"*Por nada,*" she answered, and went back to the TV.

He punched doorbells until his fingers were numb, hoping that Fifi would answer the door. The sun had been in bed for an hour when he finally gave up.

His stomach demanded attention and he drove to the diner where he'd first met the cabbies. Kincaid and a few others were hanging out. They hovered around his booth.

"Are you really a private eye?" Kincaid asked.

"Is it true you're Red Diamond?" "What's it like

being a private dick?" "You ever been shot?" "What about broads?" others fired at him.

Diamond mumbled through his roast beef. Wiping the gravy from his mouth, he leaned back and pulled out a cigarette.

"It's a tough life," he began. "It means sitting in parked cars watching houses, hotels, offices. For hours. Sometimes days. With nothing to keep you company but a bottle to piss in."

He took a deep drag.

"It means rooting through people's garbage for clues. Knocking on more doors than a traveling salesman. Spending hours going over court records."

"What about the broads?" Kincaid asked impatiently.

Diamond gave a world weary smile.

"The dames are nice. They go for a guy that packs a rod and ain't afraid to use it. I been in a couple hundred shootouts and twice as many bedrooms."

"Ah *ooh*-gah," Kincaid said, mimicking a truck horn.

"There was this caper where I met up with a couple of twins. From Siam. Belly dancers they were. They could shimmy in places other gals don't even have. They were held captive in this warehouse in Pittsburgh. This group of Amazons wanted a king's ransom from their father, who was king. I busted them loose. I was the first guy they'd been with. The king kept them kind of sheltered."

"How were they?" one of the cabbies asked, thrusting his index finger into a ring made of his thumb and other index finger.

"I don't kiss and tell," Diamond said. "But if I would've wanted it, I coulda been Prince Diamond."

"Who's your latest conquest?" Kincaid asked. "You dip your wick with Velma?"

"Nah. I got one girl in mind now. A knockout blonde. Name of Fifi. Got legs that go from here to heaven and back again. She makes Betty Grable look like a chicken. Lana Turner look like a guy. Veronica Lake look like a puddle."

"Who're they?" a younger driver asked. The others shushed him.

"But it ain't just looks. I been with enough dolls to know that when the makeup comes off there'd better be more upstairs than a head of hair. She's smart as a whip, got a great personality. When you're with her you feel you're the only man since Adam. And she's nuts about me."

"Lucky bastard," Kincaid said.

"But it ain't been a bed of roses. There's this guy Rocoo Rico wants her."

"Jealous boyfriend?" a driver asked.

"She won't give him the time of day. But Rocco's the kind that'll steal the clock. One time he sicced seven gunsels on me. And my heater only packs pacifiers for six."

"What'd you do?"

"It was a dark night in Detroit. The streets were deserted when the limo pulled up and the hoods jumped out. I knew they were trouble. You didn't have to be Einstein to figure that out. They was carrying enough firepower to wipe out a division."

The drivers hung on his every word. Diamond puffed on his cigarette.

"They were quick. I was quicker. Three of 'em got new navels before they could say 'Stick 'em up.' You coulda sunk a battleship with all the lead in the air. I had to pick my shots. I ran down this alley. I threw a garbage can cover good enough to get me in the Olympics. Too bad for the mug I caught in the throat."

"That leaves three," Kincaid said.

145

"Yeah. So I jumped up on the fire escape. Ran up to the roof. Red Diamond don't run from trouble. I knew this trouble would follow me. And I had to pick the place to shoot it out."

The men nodded, bobbing their heads like toy puppies in the back of a moving car.

"I got to the roof a second ahead of one of them. He came up real fast. He went down faster. With my footprint on his face."

"Boy you're cool," a driver said admiringly.

Diamond grunted. "So there was two left. I had enough in my rod to take them out but these punks weren't worth good ammo. They came at me from opposite sides of the roof. Smarties. It was too dark to see. They were about twenty feet from me, one to each side. Guns drawn. Breathing hard. Ready to kill."

Diamond took a long last puff and ground out his smoke. The cabbies held their breath.

"So what happened?" one finally asked.

"I popped up and yelled 'Peekaboo.' They both opened fire. Automatics. Ten shots. Boom, boom, boom."

Diamond got up, leaving money on the table for his food.

"And?" Kincaid demanded.

"The dummies shot each other. Rotten break for Rocco."

13

When Diamond got back to his suite at the Ace of Diamonds, the message light on the phone was blinking. Mr. Evans had called, and Mr. Augie Dupin had phoned three times, the operator said. Dupin refused to leave a number and said he would call back.

Norris sounded worried when Diamond rang Evans's office.

"Things are in a terrible state," Norris said. "We've had six cases of food poisoning. Someone left the shrimp out. A truckload of linens was stolen. Two small fires were set. An elevator got stuck on the ninth floor for over an hour. With passengers in it. A half-dozen fistfights broke out."

"How's Tex taking it?"

"He's locked in the screening room."

"Who's in charge of security?"

"No one. The staff is running wild. More people phoning in sick than ever before. We can't take another day like this."

"Listen Norris, I'm too close to Fifi to back off and tackle your staff problems. But if I find her tomorrow, I'll see what I can do."

"I hope we're still around," Norris said.

They hung up, and Diamond got undressed. It had

been another full day. His whole body ached from the beating he'd taken and the miles he searched but he forced himself to do fifteen minutes of exercises.

He was soaking in the hot tub when the phone rang.

"This is Augie Dupin. Who's this?" the Professor said.

"This is Red. How are you?"

"How do I know it's you?"

"Don't you recognize my voice?"

"You could be an impersonator."

It took a few minutes for Diamond to convince the Professor he was who he said he was.

"I'm being careful," the Professor said.

"I appreciate that. Now what about your research?"

"There definitely is something going on with the lands," the genius said.

"Is that with a capital *L*?"

"No. Lands as in terra firma, real estate, the ground."

"What's happening?"

"The first tip was an increased percentage of quit claim deeds indicating rapid transfer of property among artificial persons, to whit, corporations. The conveyances produced a number of instruments and piercing the corporate veil involved ascertaining—"

"It's been a long hard day, Professor, and the last thing I need is you beating me over the head with mumbo jumbo. Can you say it so that a poor, dumb, tired dick can understand it?"

"Surely. Someone is buying up Las Vegas."

"What?"

"Someone is buying up Las Vegas. Most notably the land along the so-called Strip. There are numerous straw men and dummy corporations, but indications are that at least thirty-five percent of the land from Tropicana Avenue to East Fremont is within their control. I might note their acquisition has included property north and south of those parameters. In the outer reaches they have acquired seventy-five percent of the property. Often solely mineral rights and not improvements. Repetition of certain company names or mailing addresses seems to indicate one person or a small group is involved."

"Who is it?"

"I ran into a problem there. Liberian trusts. Panamanian holding companies. Delaware corporations funded through accounts in the Grand Cayman Islands."

"Was there anything that struck you as unusual?"

"Well, there was something," the Professor said. "On several of the papers I noted a Capetown attorney was involved. I took the liberty of calling South Africa. But he asserted the attorney-client privilege and I could go no further. He was very curious who I was."

"Did you tell him?"

"I've learned my lesson. I identified myself as Stewart P. Hoover, prominent Los Angeles attorney."

"Is that where you are?"

"Yes. Safely stowed away in the Sunny Motel. But I plan to change residences every other day."

"Where are you calling from?"

"My room."

"Next time use a pay phone," Diamond said gently. "And if you call anyone else, don't tell them what city you're in."

"You're right, of course. There's so much to learn, isn't there? I'll never get it right."

"You're doing fine. Keep up the good work. And be careful."

"Red, you have my eternal gratitude for sharing the excitement of your lifestyle with me," the Professor said, before hanging up.

Diamond turned on the heater in the room and dragged his weary body to the bed. He crawled under the covers naked. Sleep came easily.

Fifi was with him. He felt her at his feet, rubbing herself against his calves, then his thighs. She moved slowly, sensuously, sinuously, sliding up his skin.

Her touch was dry but her movements fluid. Like she hadn't a joint in her body. He grew hard at her touch. Her tongue caressed his flesh, a fast-moving feather of pleasure. She moved higher. Along his ribs. Nestling in his armpit.

". . .hhh baby, you know that tickles," he said opening one eye a crack as he threw his arm over her.

But there was no Fifi under his arm. He was nose to nose with a snake. A snake that shook its tail at his embrace. A rattlesnake.

He froze, instantly awake as only a man inches away from death can be. His dream was gone, replaced by seven feet of terror.

He locked eyes with the snake. The reptile stuck its tongue out at him. The soft flesh of Red's underarm was exposed to the fangs. The arm that had cracked so many skulls felt like whipped jello.

He'd seen what snakes could do. There was that time with Jo Gar and Mallory, when Rocco had trapped them in the room with the hungry king cobras. The snakes had chosen Mallory as their first meal. They latched on with their fangs, giant leeches pumping poison instead of sucking blood.

Gar and Red had strangled the beasts as they clung to Mallory. But it had been too late for him. Mallory had died a horrible death. His screams haunted Red for months.

Red hadn't blinked or breathed. His mind raced through his options. There were none. Red Diamond had

150

met his maker. He wouldn't cry out or empty his bladder. When a snake had your name on it—

Diamond fainted.

When he awoke the newborn sun was streaming into the room. A little past dawn. He shook his head and lifted the sheet gingerly. No snake!

Freudian symbolism. That's what the court-appointed shrink would say. Phallic symbolism. Anything longer than it's wide represented a dingus. And a snake. Wow.

He was caked with dried sweat. He took a hot shower and got dressed. It was warm in the room and he went to shut the heater.

He didn't get to it. Curled near the grill and enjoying the warmth was a mottled gray-and-brown rattlesnake.

Diamond backpedaled to the phone and called the bell captain.

"I got a wildlife problem in my room," he said.

"You got roaches? I'll send housekeeping up."

"Not roaches. A rattlesnake."

"C'mon buddy. It's too early to be pulling my leg."

"This is Red Diamond in the Diamond Suite and I'm telling you there's a rattlesnake in my room."

"A lot of people, they have a few drinks, they see—"

"I'll bet you a hundred bucks I've got a rattlesnake up here."

"Be right up."

Diamond waited outside his room. The bell captain sauntered over with visions of easy money in his brain.

"I'll wait here," Diamond said. "It's over in the far corner. Near the heater. Watch your step."

"Sure. You got that C-spot handy?"

Diamond nodded. The man casually walked in. Ten seconds later he came running out.

"Holy shit! There's a snake in there."

"Make sure the maid wears boots," Diamond said, draping a DO NOT DISTURB sign over the doorknob.

The bell captain wiped his face with his hand. "I don't believe it. All my life I live in this state and I never seen a damn rattler inside. Let alone in a penthouse suite. How'd that damn diamondback get up here?"

"What did you say?"

"How'd a damn diamondback get in your room?"

Diamondback! Gulo had struck.

"Just lucky I guess," Diamond said, leaving the slack-jawed clerk as he hurried to meet his Fifi.

The hardboiled P.I. felt like a schoolboy on his first date as he parked the car near the Mexican lady's house and waited. He chain-smoked on an empty stomach, adding to his giddiness.

It was 7:20 when he saw her in the distance, lifting her legs high as she ran toward him. He leaned against his car and tried to play it cool as she came closer.

She was wearing white shorts that bared sleek, tanned thighs. Her breasts bobbed under a loose T-shirt. Her blond hair was kept from her heart-shaped face by a red headband that was damp with sweat.

He stepped into her path and her baby blues appraised him. She moved to go around him and he put his arms out.

"Fifi!" he shouted joyously.

"Get out of my way or I'll scream," the woman said, jogging in place and breathing hard. "My name's not Fifi. Leave me alone or I'll call a cop."

"Fifi, it's Red. Don't pretend you don't know me."

"You some kind of pervert? I'm warning you—"

"I get it. Rocco's boys might be watching," Diamond said, glancing around cautiously. "You're right to be careful. You're some doll, Fifi."

"My name's not Fifi." She continued to bob.

"I know you're using the moniker Gayle Collins. I know Moe put the arm on you. But don't worry."

She stopped bouncing. "Who are you? How do you know my name?"

"No need for games. We're safe. It's Red, angel."

She gave him a look that could have chilled the ardor of the most practiced pick-up artist. He was oblivious.

"What do you want?" she demanded.

"You. I love you."

"You're nuts."

"Why don't we go back to my room. I've got the Diamond Suite at the Ace of Diamonds."

"You have that kind of bucks?"

"So that's it. I know you don't like me knocking around the P.I. racket. But things are different now. Look," Diamond said, taking his wad of cash out.

She gazed at the fistful of hundred-dollar bills and the man with the fedora on his head and an ear-to-ear grin on his face.

"Just because you wave some money around you expect me to go back to your room with you?" she asked. "You don't waste time, do you?"

"It's dangerous out on the street. Why don't we go for a cup of java?"

"Java?"

"Joe."

"Joe?"

"Coffee."

"Oh. I don't artificially stimulate my body with caffeine," she said.

"Huh?"

"But I know a place not too far from here that serves a nice herbal tea."

"Great. We'll take my car," he said, reaching for her arm.

She pulled back. "Don't get fresh. I've taken kung

fu. My yin and yang are in harmony."

"They always were," he said with a wink.

She allowed him to open the door for her. She got in. He went around and settled into the driver's seat.

"It's five blocks up. The name is The Body Beautiful," she said.

"Your body is beautiful."

"Watch it, buster. I've heard all the lines. And your's are about as old as zoot suits."

"Zoot suits. That reminds me of the time when that riot broke out by the Palladium. It turned out to be a cover for Rocco's heist of the bank. You were caught in the middle until—"

"You're weird," she said. "Just drive."

The Body Beautiful was all wood with plants in the window, on the floor, and hanging from the ceiling. Diamond felt like he was in the Amazon.

The customers and staff were worshippers of the human temple. They recognized Diamond as an atheist among true believers and dismissed him haughtily.

"I changed my mind," his dream gal said. "Instead of tea, let's get the deluxe special."

"Whatever you want."

When the waiter came he ignored Diamond and took the order from the woman. He returned with the special malted, setting it carefully before her and sloshing it down before Diamond.

"What's in this?" Diamond asked her as he took a sip and made a face.

"Brewer's yeast, two raw eggs, carob, Vitamin E oil, a bunch of things."

"It tastes like medicine."

"It's better for you than medicine. It balances your yin and yang."

"I didn't know it was out of balance."

"You probably haven't had a healthy meal in years," she said.

154

"Hell no. I'm not one of those bachelors who neglects himself. I start most days with a couple of scrambled eggs, bacon, and sausages. I have steak and potatoes a bunch of times a week. A thick, well-done steak. And a big potato with a lump of fresh butter."

She looked at him like he'd confessed to child molesting.

"That's disgusting. I don't eat the flesh of dead animals. Especially those that have been pumped up with nitrates and burned. You probably take in enough cholesterol to kill a horse."

"I don't understand you," he said, reaching into his pocket for a cigarette.

"Don't smoke," she ordered. "The body is a sacred shrine that mustn't be defiled like an old chimney."

"And you think I'm weird," Diamond said, stifling his urge for a smoke.

The woman slurped happily at her malted while Diamond made half-hearted stabs at his.

She was even more beautiful close up, her cheeks puffing in and out as she took in the fluid. Hers was a face that didn't need makeup. A healthy red blush called attention to elegant cheekbones. Teeth that sparkled like a Pepsodent ad. Lips meant for kissing. Sparkling glims that cooly watched him.

"Things are looking up, dollface. I'm working a big case. And I got a good client."

"Who?"

"C'mon babe, you know that's confidential."

She stopped slurping and flicked her tongue out for a quick clean up job on her lips. She pouted. "If you don't trust me, then maybe . . ."

"It's not that."

"Then what is it?"

He hesitated. "Just between us," he whispered. "It's Edward Evans."

"Tex?"

"That's right."

"He's got more money than he knows what to do with," she said.

"That's the one. He's hired me. It's a tough job but I know I can do it."

"I used to be in the show at his flagship casino."

"I know. The Ace of Diamonds. That's how I got your picture," he said, showing her the by now dog-eared photo.

"I was in the chorus line. Never got a chance."

"They didn't recognize your talent."

"It's true. I can sing. I can dance. Ann-Margaret gets her own show. I have to shack up with Moe Greenberg."

"Don't talk that way, angel."

"I didn't do anything so bad," she said defensively. "He takes care of me. So I suck the little creep off a couple of times a week."

Diamond looked around ashamed. "Jeez. Fifi. Don't talk like that. What'll people think?"

"I'm not the only one to do it. A girl's got to survive."

"I know. But you don't got to go talking like a long-shoreman. I bet you didn't really want to. You had to, didn't you? He made you," Diamond said plaintively.

"It's true. He made me. He didn't hold a gun to my head but it was sort of like I had to."

Diamond was tight-lipped with rage. "That rat bastard. He'll pay for that."

The P.I. was thinking murderous thoughts when a man came over to their table. He was five feet six and nearly as wide in the shoulders. He had arms the size of Diamond's waist and veins that bulged like radiator hoses.

"Hey Gayle, remember me?" the man asked.

The woman looked up. "Sure. From the gym last week. On the Nautilus. Eddie."

156

"Buzz off," Diamond told the man. "We're talking."

The weight lifter ignored him. "Gayle, you want to ditch this wimp and go work out? They got a new machine, does wonders for your lats."

"It's okay, Eddie. Maybe later."

"You're sure this guy isn't bothering you?" Eddie asked.

"If you're not out of here by the time I count to three, you're gonna regret it," Diamond said.

"Oh yeah?" Eddie said. He laid a heavy hand on Diamond's shoulder and squeezed. It wasn't as bad as getting caught in a hydraulic press.

"Is that your best answer? 'Oh yeah.' You got anything between your ears besides muscle?" Diamond said, trying not to show the pain.

"Get up and say that."

As Diamond got up, he grabbed the malted from the table and threw it in Eddie's face. The P.I. followed up with two quick punches to the man's washboard flat abdomen. They had no effect. Eddie was still wiping gunk off his face when Diamond caught him in the throat.

The weight lifter began to gag. He threw up something that looked a lot like the malted.

"C'mon doll. Let's go. I can tell when we're not wanted," Diamond said, grabbing the woman's arm.

Out on the street, Red smiled.

"What's so funny?" she asked, still disoriented by the violence.

"I was thinking. That drink did turn out to be good for my health. You got to move fast. You never know when one of these deals turn out to be a setup by Rocco." He kept his arm around her as they walked down the street.

"I don't know," she said hesitantly. "I used to go there every day. I can't go back now."

"Don't worry. I'll make sure you eat right. Filet mignon. Juicy pork chops smothered in sauce. Lamb

chops tender enough to cut with a fork. Shrimp New-
burg. Lobsters Rockefeller."

"I think I'm going to be sick."

"You're just excited at seeing me after so long."

"Was it necessary to hit Eddie?"

"He had the look of one of Rocco's boys. And he put
his hands on me. Nobody puts their hands on me. Except you," he said, giving her a tender squeeze.

"I think I better be going. This isn't what—"

"Trust me, cupcake. We'll go back to the Ace of Diamonds and unwind. I've got to talk to Tex."

She was quiet for a moment. "You're really on that
good terms with him?"

"The best."

"Could you get me back in the show?"

"No sweat."

"A solo number?"

"Piece of cake."

They got into his car. "The Diamond Suite?" she
asked.

"We're on our way."

She slid close to him. "Lover boy, call me Fifi."

14

Fifi insisted on stopping off and buying new clothes before she met Evans. Diamond sat in the department store, keeping an alert watch for Rocco's thugs, while she tried on item after item.

After a couple of hours, the P.I. craved a shoot-out in the lingerie department to relieve the boredom. Instead he got a bill for twenty-five hundred dollars.

He paid for her wardrobe, and they went back to the suite, where Fifi modeled her new clothes for him.

"How do I look?" she asked, pirouhetting in front of him in a slinky black dress that barely clung to her lush curves.

"Like a million bucks," he said, grabbing her in a warm embrace.

"Careful. You'll wrinkle it," she said, pulling away.

She took the dress off. She wasn't wearing anything underneath.

Diamond seized her again. His mouth pressed against hers, then traveled down her neck to erect nipples.

"Ohhh, Red," she said. "Can you really get me in the show?"

"If that's what you want, sure," he said in between nibbles.

"Ohhh. Then take me. Fuck me hard."

He stepped back. "C'mon Fifi. That's no way for a lady to talk."

"Don't stop, you great big hunk. Slam it to me."

"Fifi!"

"What's wrong with you?" she asked. "This is the 1980s. Let yourself go. I'm a woman and I have needs."

"There's no reason for you to talk like that," he chided her.

"Aw, Red snookums. Don't be mad at your little Fifi."

"It's been a while, angel. We been apart too long. We won't waste any time arguing."

He returned to kissing her. There was a knock at the door.

"Rocco!" he said, spinning away and drawing his gun. "Quick, hide in the bedroom."

The naked woman grabbed her clothes and scurried off.

Diamond moved briskly to the door and threw it open.

The body hit him with inhuman speed. Diamond was down on the floor, something warm and wet on his face, before he could get off a shot.

But it wasn't chloroform that assailed his nostrils. It was doggie breath.

Bart. And coming into the suite behind the Samoyed was Rosie, with hands on hips and a smile on her face.

The dog let Diamond up after the P.I. tousled his fur. Rosie came over and gave Diamond a hug.

"I found some money in my pocket that wasn't mine," she said. "I wanted to return it."

It was Diamond's turn to smile. "What brings you back?" he asked. "Not that I ain't glad to see you."

"You were right," she said. "You can't run away. I

160

kept thinking about those turkeys making me hightail it out of town. And Tex's offer of heading security. I been working fifteen years and that's the best chance I ever got. No one is going to stop me from taking it."

"I'm glad you changed your mind," Diamond said.

"I'm glad too," she answered.

"Isn't this a cozy little scene," Fifi said from the bedroom doorway.

"Gayle, what you doing here?" Rosie snapped.

"I was about to ask you the same question," she answered. "And my name is Fifi La Roche. Right Red?"

Diamond nodded. "Rosie, this is the gal I was searching for."

Rosie frowned.

"What's this about you giving her money too?" Fifi asked Diamond.

"It was a loan," he said. "She's a friend."

Rosie took the money out and dropped it on the table. "I'm not like you, honey," she said to Fifi.

"What's that supposed to mean?" Fifi asked.

"You know damn well what it means," Rosie said.

The women glared at each other.

"Ladies, ladies, please. This should be a happy reunion," Diamond said.

"Red, can we go see Tex now?" Fifi asked curtly.

"I want to talk to him too," Rosie said.

"Let's go," the P.I. said. "But I'm not walking into his office with a couple of hissing cats. Shake hands and bury the hatchet."

After a few awkward seconds, the women extended their hands for a halfhearted shake.

But Tex was in his locked screening room and refused to come out, Norris told them.

"We've had more trouble," Norris explained. "The plumbing's been sabotaged. Electricity, too. Half the guests have checked out. And he was very upset that someone put a snake in your room."

"So was I," Diamond said. "But I'm not rich enough to spend my life moping about it. Is there any way to get him out of there?"

"The only contact with him is through an emergency intercom," Norris said. "But he left strict orders not to be disturbed."

"Would you show me where the intercom is?"

Norris deliberated briefly. "It may cost me my job."

"I can't give you any guarantees," Diamond said.

"But he seems to respond to you. I'm concerned about Mr. Evans. I'll do it."

The manservant led him to a long-horned cow skull. Norris removed the jaw and a telephone headset came into view.

Diamond picked it up. "Tex?"

"Mmmmn."

"Tex, this is Red. I got to talk to you."

"Go away."

Diamond rubbed his nose. "Listen you yellow-bellied polecat. Get that skinny bottom of yours out here pronto."

The women and Norris were shocked. They heard the mechanism on the time lock spinning. Evans came storming out.

"No one talks to me like that," a red-faced Evans bellowed. "Who do you think you are?"

"I'm Red Diamond. And if you curl up and die because some weasels are giving you a hard time, then I say you're yellow. You don't deserve me working for you. You don't deserve any of this," Diamond said, waving his arm to take in the surroundings.

Evans came over and grabbed Diamond's lapels. "I don't take that kind of cowflop from nobody."

The men locked eyes. The others held their breaths.

"That's the spirit, you Texas yahoo," Diamond said. "If you can get that riled up over a little name-calling, you can handle a few problems with the casino."

Fifi, Rosie and Norris jumped when Tex let out a whoop. Only Diamond and Bart seemed unfazed. "Red, you ol' son of a gun. You was joshing me. Made me stop feeling sorry for myself. You're right. Let's get together a posse and run those outlaws out of town."

Tex spun his six-guns and let loose a dozen shots into the ceiling. Red took out his .38 and fired off a few rounds himself. The men reloaded and Tex threw his arms around Diamond.

"Well, pardner, what happens now?"

"You remember Rosie," Diamond said, pointing to her. "She's decided to accept your offer and take over security."

"Welcome aboard," Tex said. "I'm sure you'll do a slam-bang job."

"And this," Diamond said, pausing dramatically as he indicated the other woman, "Is Fifi La Roche."

"Pleased to meet you, Mr. Evans," Fifi said.

"It's Tex, young lady, to any friend of Red's."

In a stage whisper, Evans said to Diamond, "Gosh darn but she is a purty young thing."

Fifi smiled. Rosie frowned.

"Fifi sings and dances," Diamond said. "I was hoping you could find her a spot in the show."

"A solo," Fifi piped up. "Of course the others could back me up."

"Well little darlin' why don't you show us your stuff," Evans said.

"I don't know if I'm ready right this second," Fifi said demurely.

It took a minute or so to convince her. She launched into a medley of western songs, including "Bury Me Not On the Lone Prairie," "Old Chrisolm Trail," and "Buttons and Bows." Her voice wasn't very strong or very good, but Evans was dazzled by the subject and Diamond was dazzled by the singer. Norris remained expressionless. Rosie and Bart looked pained.

"Well kick my leg and call me gimpy," Evans said. "I'll tell our show director to arrange a number for you. I love that kind of music."

Fifi jumped up and down and gave Evans a peck on the cheek.

"Watch that now. Don't want to make my friend jealous," Evans said, giving Diamond a wink. "We'll get a contract. You have today and tomorrow to rehearse and we'll try it out on the Friday night show. How's that sound?"

"I can't wait," Fifi said.

"Neither can I," Rosie said cynically.

Diamond and Fifi headed back to his suite while Rosie and Bart went down to the security office.

Fifi was just as Red remembered her, bubbling like a happy schoolgirl, but leaning against him in a way that showed she'd graduated. With honors.

He picked her up and carried her across the threshold. She giggled and kicked but didn't fight very hard. He set her down and closed the door. By the time he turned back to her, her dress was gone. She stood before him radiantly naked.

"Do you like what you see?" she asked.

"Come here and I'll show you."

"Make me," she said mischievously.

With a bullish bellow he ran to her. He chased her around the suite until she let him catch her. In the bedroom. He dragged her to the bed and gently tossed her down. She lay spread-eagled, her blond hair splayed on the pillow.

"It's been too long," he said, undressing as quickly as he could.

164

"I'll make up for that," she promised.

Her body was soft fire under his hands. He kept from squeezing her too hard as she nibbled at his ears and neck. Not much foreplay was needed. He was in her and pumping like an oil man sinking his first well. She bucked and writhed responsively. They gushed together.

They had time to rest and make love again before there was a knock at the door. Diamond got dressed and answered with gun drawn.

A serious looking man and woman stood outside.

"Hello sir. Ms. Washington sent us up to provide bodyguard service for Ms. La Roche," the woman said, without any reaction to his weapon.

"Who?"

"Ms. Washington, the new chief of security," the man said.

"Lemme see some ID," Diamond said.

The duo took identification out of their pockets. Diamond compared the photos with the couple.

"Wait here," he said, shutting the door with them still outside.

He checked the in-house directory and called security.

"Rosie please."

"Who's calling?" the crisp female voice asked.

"Red."

Rosie got on the line quickly. "What's up?" she asked.

"Did you send two people up here? A Chick Hill who plays in the band, according to his ID. And a Bucky Murrill from security."

"Bet. I drafted Chick for security. He's a good man. Ex-Marine. And I know Buck, too. She's one of the few I trust. Either Braun was a complete screw-up, or he deliberately did a number. You wouldn't believe these files. It's a good thing I know so many people here."

165

"I can take care of Fifi."

"If you can tear yourself away from taking care of her, I could use you down here," she said. "I'm cleaning house."

"And you're finding a lot of dirt under the carpets," he said.

"You got it. I've already fired fourteen people and transferred twice that. I need help with the interviewing and checking backgrounds. Your lady love's got to go down to rehearsal anyway. So how 'bout it?"

Rosie finally persuaded him. He gave Fifi a long good-bye kiss and headed down.

Pink slips fell like confetti on a Broadway parade. Supposedly reliable employees turned out to be fugitives from justice. Saint arranged for a paddy wagon and they were hauled away. Others with questionable backgrounds were transferred to less sensitive positions. Keys were confiscated and locks were changed.

During their few breaks, Rosie tried warning Diamond about Fifi. Before she could say anything more than, "That girl of yours is—" Diamond would cut her off. Rosie was doing a great job but her opinion of Fifi was tainted by female jealousy, Red believed.

Hours passed as they separated the gold from the pyrite on the Ace of Diamonds staff.

Using her years in Las Vegas, Rosie hired a couple of dozen people she had met and respected. An elite group of ten security officers was set up and promptly nicknamed "Rosie's Raiders."

Hill and Murrill sat on either side of the show room. As Diamond entered they greeted him with barely perceptible nods. They looked like alert bookends.

Fifi stood at center stage, an expression somewhere between a pout and a snarl on her face. She was wear-

166

ing cowboy boots, a G-string, a skimpy vest held together with a leather thong, and a white Stetson.
Sequins on her outfit glittered from the bright lights.
The generous portions of her bare flesh glistened. She
launched into her dance number and the source of her
sour expression made himself heard.

"Stop. Stop. Stop. You look more like a cow than a
cowgirl," screamed a lean young man in skintight
clothes. He had a neatly trimmed beard and plucked
eyebrows.

"Hey you, it's gonna be hard for you to keep that
jabbering up with a fat lip," Diamond said.

"Who are you?" the man demanded, petulantly
shoving his hands on his narrow hips.

"The name's Red Diamond. And that's my girl
you're calling a cow."

Spurs on Fifi's boots jingled as she walked over. "It's
okay Red. He's Roger Tweed, the best choreographer
around, even if he is a pain in the butt."

"Flattery will get you nowhere," Tweed said. "And
neither will boyfriend's threatening me."

"I don't want anyone—" Diamond began.

She cut him off by leaning over and kissing him.

"Don't worry about me," she said, patting his cheek.
"I'm a big girl."

"This is such a cozy domestic scene," Tweed said.
"But if we're going to have a show I won't be ashamed
of, you better get back to practicing. You need it."

Diamond and the choreographer exchanged the
kind of looks cobras and mongooses do. Diamond walked
to a chair in the front row and sat.

"Now do it this way," Tweed said, demonstrating a
half-dozen steps. Fifi tried following him but was unable
to duplicate the moves.

Red wasn't happy about Fifi appearing in front of
hundreds of people in so skimpy an outfit. He knew

she'd knocked around as a cocktail waitress, wearing not much more than fishnet stockings and a bow tie. And a barmaid. And a showgirl down in the Havana casino before Rocco and Batista got thrown out by the Reds . . . .

Tommy guns exploded in the dank night air. Women screamed, men cursed. Inside the casino a pack of over-dressed partygoers clawed at each other, scrambling to grab their stakes and escape.

I stood on the wooden veranda, my .38 in one mitt, Fifi's hand in the other. She was wearing the matchbook-size outfit that had brought the house down. Mosquitos suckled on the delicious pink flesh.

A couple of house goons came through the door. Before they could uncork their chatter guns, I gave them a few ounces of lead. No charge. Bill it to the undertaker.

I scooped up a Thompson. The Commie rebels were getting closer. It made the gamblers yowl like penned sheep hearing a wolf howl.

Me and Fifi had nearly a mile to get to the small plane I'd chartered out of Miami. A mile of swamp and jungle and rebels and mobsters. A mile-long gauntlet of death.

"You ready dollface?" I asked.

"Anywhere you lead I'll follow," she said, slapping a bug that was mountain climbing on her gorgeous globes.

"Let's do it babe."

"I love you Red," she said, and we headed out.

That was the way Red remembered her. It was diffi-cult to imagine the Fifi he saw practicing on the stage following him blindly.

Broads were different, more independent, Red

thought. It probably came from doing men's work while the guys went off to fight the Krauts.

Once he settled down with Fifi, he was sure she'd lose that hard edge. She'd gotten tough, but hell, she'd had to. He'd soften her up. And get her to stop wearing those outfits that made priests want to renounce their vows. It was okay to wear it for him but he didn't want every Tom, Dick, and Harry enjoying what should be his private view.

She was high kicking now, her long legs flying. He liked what he saw. So would the thousand customers who'd pack into the room Friday night.

But Tweed wasn't pleased. "What do you think you're doing? Kicking a field goal?" he asked. He shooed her aside and began doing high kicks. They were graceful and feminine and looked even more obscene when Tweed did them.

Diamond checked that the bodyguards were still alert and then returned to the Diamond Suite. He didn't stay there very long.

The message light was blinking. The operator said a man had phoned an hour earlier and said, "Tell Diamond 'G' called. I want to talk. Meet me at home." The address was in North Las Vegas.

"G." Greenberg. At last. Of course it could be a trap. But Red Diamond never walked away from a skirmish. And he'd get to meet Rocco's main man in Las Vegas face to face, fist to fist, gun to gun.

He checked that his gun was loaded and in place, pulled his hat down rakishly over one eye, and headed to the site.

The only structure at the address he had been given was a run-down field house. It was located on a deserted Little League field that had broken bleachers and walls covered with graffiti that read *NV—5*, *Banger*, *Disco*, and *Mr. Cool*. High-intensity lights towered above the area, but they were powerless and the diamond was bathed in darkness.

He walked slowly down the first base line, his hand ready to grab for the heater at his hip. The bag at first base was torn.

He followed the line to second, then third. As he walked to the plate, he spotted a couple of kids sipping beer and cagily watching him. He veered from the base line and walked over to them.

They were both black, no more than fourteen, with street savvy expressions that belied their years. Both were lean bordering on scrawny.

"You seen anyone around her?" Diamond asked.

They didn't answer.

"I said you seen anyone around?"

"We heard you, man. We was wondering what you doing," the taller youth said.

"Walking the bases. Waiting for someone."

"Who?" the smaller one asked after taking a long swig.

"I'm not sure."

"Say what?"

"I got a message to come here."

"You right, J.C.," the smaller one said to his companion. "This dude is crazy."

J.C. snickered.

"So you haven't seen anyone around?" Diamond asked.

Neither of the boys answered. The shorter one took another sip of beer. Diamond noticed the name *Rocky* crudely tattooed on the back of the youth's hand.

"You Rocky?" the P.I. asked.

"How you know that?" the teenager asked suspiciously.

"I get around," Diamond said.

"Fool. Your name's on your hand," J.C. said.

"We don't know nothin'," Rocky said. "You a cop?"

Diamond shook his head.

"Cops is the only honkies come around here at night," Rocky said. "You got to meet someone, why don't you do it at one of them fancy casinos?"

"I didn't pick the spot. He did," Diamond said.

"Who he?" Rocky asked.

"I told you I don't know. Now tell me whether you've seen anyone."

"What's in it for us?" J.C. asked.

Diamond took out a buck.

"Sheeit," Rocky said.

The P.I. produced a five from his wallet. J.C. snatched it.

"So, you seen anyone?" Diamond asked.

"No," the two boys answered in unison.

Diamond reached for his money and they took off. They stopped after running about ten yards when they saw Diamond wasn't pursuing them.

Diamond shook his head and resumed walking toward home plate. A beer bottle whizzed past his ear. It arced down and rolled until it landed on top of the plate.

The explosion knocked Diamond off his feet. He fell backward on the sparse grass and lay looking up at the sky. His face felt like he'd been out in the sun too long; his ears were ringing like the bells of St. Anthony's.

"What happened, man?" J.C. asked, hovering over Diamond. The teenager's stunned expression made him look like the youth he was.

"I didn't know the bottle was loaded," Rocky said. "You okay?"

"Yeah. Sure," Diamond said, dizzily getting up.

"I didn't put nothin' in that bottle," Rocky said.

"I know you didn't. You probably saved my life. That bomb was meant for me."

171

As he staggered to his feet, the realization hit Red like the force of the blast. *"G"* had been Gulo. If Diamond had stood at "home" he would've been made into more pieces than a jigsaw puzzle.

"You hear me, man?" J.C. asked. "I said, 'Who are you?'"

"The name's Red Diamond."

"I hear 'bout you," Rocky said. "You that private eye investigatin' the lands."

"Word travels quick."

"Everybody knows who you are," J.C. said. He glanced at his companion, who nodded in answer to an unasked question. "I hear that when things go down it's gonna be real hard on us niggers."

"Worse than Alabama," Rocky said.

"I guess bad times hit your people first," Diamond said.

"My people. Sheeit. I hear they gonna skin us," Rocky said.

"What?"

"A couple of the older brothers say they gonna part our hides," Rocky said.

Diamond looked at the teenager skeptically.

J.C. punched Rocky in the shoulder and with a burst of juvenile energy, they ran off.

Diamond's ears were still ringing when he turned and looked at the crater where home plate had been. Sliding into home now would be a real adventure.

Gulo had had two strikes. He'd have to take another swing before Red could strike him out.

15

A guard was posted by the suite door and Fifi was asleep inside by the time he returned. Exhausted, she failed to respond to his fondling. He thought he was too hepped up to sleep but with his arms around the woman he loved, sweet dreams came easily.

He awoke and she was gone. A note on the pillow read, *Off to rehearsal. Love, FLR.* He was lying in bed trying to decide how to spend the day when the phone jangled.

"Huh?" he mumbled into it, his vocal cords not yet fully awake.

"Red, this is Augie . . .pin. How have . . .been?"

It was a terrible connection.

"I can hardly hear you," Diamond said.

"What? Charlie near you? Everything copacetic?"

"Go Pacific? We got a bad line."

"Time? It's about noon. Don't you have a clop?"

After much confusion, the Professor explained he was calling from a phone booth and the number was missing from the dial. He had no change left and Diamond couldn't call him back. The two men found that by yelling, however, they could almost understand each other.

"I've ascertained who is behind the real estate purchases," the Professor said.

"Asked a train?"

173

"Ascertain. Found out. It's a holding company that goes by the name of Dain Enterprises."

"Dain? Is that Deltz-Adam-Ida-Nancy?"

"Exactly. But even more intriguing are the principals. Moe Greenberg and Vincent Van Houton."

"Is that mountain, *M* like in Mary, *O* like in—"

"No. *H* like in Harry, *O* like in Oscar, *U* like in—"

"Umbrella," Diamond interrupted. "That's the cat's pajamas."

"Catch Bahamas? Do you know who Van Houton is?"

"Do I ever. That's great, Prof. I'll give you a hug when I get back to Los Angeles."

"No need for that. I appreciate the generous fee for my services," the Professor said, obviously pleased with Diamond's enthusiasm. "How's it going? Any excitement?"

"A couple of kids threw a bottle at me and I nearly got blown up."

"Lobotomy? Thrown up?"

"I'm getting hoarse. We gotta cut this off."

"Thrown up?"

"Blown up. A bomb. Boom."

"A bomb. I see. These children tried to kill you."

"Not the kids," Diamond said. "The same guy that tried to ice you. The kids were okay. The weird thing is they said this takeover would mean someone would part their hide."

"Far and wide?"

Diamond was getting frustrated. "Part their hide! Part their hide!"

"Apartheid?"

Diamond was gathering air in his lungs to yell. He paused in mid-gasp. "What did you say?"

"Apartheid. The South African cistern wherein blacks and whites are kept. . . "

Diamond didn't hear the rest of the Professor's garbled words. Van Houton. Greenberg. Apartheid. Krugerrands.

". . . .you jeer what I wed?" the Professor asked.

"As clear as a bell. Thanks again. See you soon."

Diamond had been given the package and the ribbon. All he had to do was tie it up with a neat little bow.

Saint was not as impressed.

"So? Moe and this South African guy are involved in buying up real estate. That's not enough for an indictment," the cop said when Diamond called.

"Don't you see? They're causing this trouble to drive down prices, then they pick it up for a song."

"You may know it and I may know it but that don't mean we can prove it in a court of law. The only one who could connect them to an overt act was Fingers. And he's not gonna be able to testify. Except to St. Peter."

"You gettin' at something?" Diamond asked. "You don't sound like the gung-ho guy I spoke to before."

"You gettin' at something?" Saint snapped.

"There's all kinds of pressure that can be put on people."

"Listen Diamond. You don't know what it's like being a cop. Especially here. There's a lot of temptation. A guy's got a wife, kids, mortgage. There's dozens of assholes who'll pay well for you to close your eyes for a few seconds."

"But you never did. The good ones don't. I thought maybe it came from above, that—"

"I don't need you patting me on the back. Let a cop take a few bucks and the shit's all over him. Or let him shoot some citizen and you never hear the end of it. I'd like to see some of those pols in an alley at three in the morning, a guy coming at them with something in his hand. See if they waste him or just blast him with hot air."

"Don't get sore. It's part—"

"Of the job. I know. And then they farm you out with a pension that you can't buy bubble gum with. And you miss the job. You yell at the wife, she takes the kids and runs off with some guy making real money, and you wind up sucking your revolver in a dirty apartment."

"What's bugging you?"

Saint let out a long sigh. "Everything. I just worked through the night. They pulled me off homicide. Some shitheel broke into a display at the Riviera and stole this jeweled gewgaw on loan from a French museum."

"What's it worth?"

"A lot more than I'll ever make. It's a knife with diamonds and rubies and emeralds. Some king had it done up. And the Feds are involved. State Department and FBI geeks breathing down my neck."

"And cooperation is a one way street with them."

"You got it," Saint said. "The Feds got the bucks, the high priced snitches, the computers, the new cars. I got sore feet."

"How long 'til you pull the pin?"

"One year. But what I do then is anybody's guess."

"You want to go into the P.I. business, give me a buzz. Lots of the best dicks are ex-cops. Mugs Magoo, Richard Diamond, Matt Scudder, Quinny Hite. My old buddy Marlowe used to work for the D.A."

There was silence on the line. "Oh, yeah, sure," Saint said. "Is there anything you want?"

"I was curious about Greenberg's place."

"He lives way out on the west side, near Red Rock Canyon. On Buffalo Drive."

"What's it like out there?"

"He's got about fifteen acres. Mini-golf course, Olympic size swimming pool, helipad. Three buildings

176

with eight bedrooms, four-car garage, wine cellar. A cozy little place."

"What's it like inside?"

"Never been there. None of my stoolies either. And he's got more security gadgets than a bank. We used to be able to keep a better watch on him when he lived in Spanish Oaks. That's probably why he moved out. What's your interest anyway?"

"Just curious."

"Curiousity killed the cat," Saint warned.

"But satisfaction brought it back."

"That may work for cats, but not private eyes. Don't do anything stupid. Understand?"

"Sure. Go home and catch up on your beauty sleep."

"You remember what I told you."

"Perfectly," Diamond said, and Saint hung up.

"That no good, lily-livered, sidewinding skunk," was Evans reaction when he heard about Greenberg's purchases. "I'll tar and feather him. I'll string him up like the cattle rustlin' hoss thief that he is."

"I've got Fifi. Greenberg is in touch with Rocco. They'll have to act."

"And then we'll get 'em."

Diamond got up to leave. "You're looking a lot better today."

"Yup," Evans said. "Rosie is a real gem. She set a trap and caught two of the fellas that was sabotaging things around here. They're in the hoosegow, along with a coyote her Raiders snagged using a magnet on the slots. And word spread. It's a new Ace of Diamonds."

Diamond sent his suit, soiled from the explosion, out for cleaning. Clad in his casual outfit, he spent the day traveling from the Sheik, to the Ramses, to the Lion's Den, hoping to lay his orbs on Greenberg.

177

He'd find a spot at each casino that afforded him a view of the entrance to the executive offices, and then keep it under surveillance. To avoid looking too suspicious, he'd play whatever game was convenient. After six hours, he was down eighty-five dollars.

At his final stop, the Lion's Den, he found a bank of twenty-five cent slot machines that allowed him to watch the entrance to Greenberg's private elevator corridor.

It wasn't until he was about to leave that he saw someone he recognized. James Thursby, the flim-flam man. Was Thursby a friend of Greenberg's? Were the two men involved in some scam together? Or was Thursby, as Red hoped, going to bilk Greenberg out of some of his ill-gotten gains?

It gave Diamond something to think about as he drove back to the Ace of Diamonds for Fifi's debut.

16

Fifi was standing backstage, her nervous shuffling making the spurs on her boots jingle. Murrill and another female security guard were a dozen feet away and as alert as ever.

"Where've you been?" Fifi demanded when she saw Diamond. "The show's about to start."

She was wearing the titillating cowboy outfit. Annoyed, Red snapped, "I've been working. You've been at rehearsal. And I know you've got good protection."

"This is my premiere. Don't you care?"

"I'm here, ain't I?"

"Just in time."

"Fifi baby, there's no point in fighting. You got butterflies in your belly. Pre-show jitters."

"I do not," she said petulantly. She stormed away, the security guards trailing her like respectful ladies in waiting. Red decided to let her calm down and prepare for the show.

He peered out at the audience through a crack in the diamond-studded curtain. Busboys were clearing the remains of the dinners from the booths and long tables. The frenzied activity backstage was building.

He felt he should be planning how to trap Greenberg, but all he could think about was Fifi. It hadn't worked out the way he'd expected with her. But hell, it was a difficult time. Things would improve once Rocco and this showbiz stuff were out of the way.

The house lights dimmed and three Super Trooper spotlights hit revolving mirrored balls that hung from the high ceiling. A man walked out on stage and bathed the crowd with a white-toothed smile that was warmer than the spotlights.

"Hello you lucky people. My name is Steve Plesa and on behalf of everyone here at the Ace of Diamonds I want to welcome you to the Sparkling Showroom. For the next hour and a half some of the most talented young men and women will do nothing but entertain you. So sit back, relax, and give a big hand to," he paused and lifted an arm, "The Diamondaires."

The band began to play, Plesa doffed his skimmer hat, and the curtain swung open.

Center stage was taken up by a giant mirrored staircase. Bare-breasted women with feathers coming out of their heads and rumps began appearing. Men in sequined tuxedos joined them. Everybody hurried about showing off their finery in dances that seemed like choreographed running.

Between numbers the performers would run off-stage and grab costumes from special racks. They'd be back in front of the audience in less than a minute while wardrobe assistants scooped up their discarded garments. Besides the quick change artists, stagehands, sound men, and electricians ran back and forth in organized chaos. Diamond had to move three times to avoid getting trampled.

The dozen dress dancers who had been through four costume changes in the first half hour got a chance to breathe when the comedian came on. Dapper in a black tuxedo, Tony Morain warmed up the crowd with jokes from across the USA.

"You know what the difference is between Vegas and yogurt?" Pause. "Yogurt has culture."

Laughter.

"Anyone here from Los Angeles?"

Loud cheers.

"I thought I saw gold chains shining out there. But seriously, you know why El Lay is like a granola bar?" Pause. "If you take away the fruits and the nuts all that's left are the flakes."

More laughter.

"New York?"

A couple of loud yells.

"Don't mug me, please. You know, in New York, trust is just a name on a bank."

Laughter, cheers, and applause.

A well-endowed woman wearing only a G-string brought out a unicycle and four bowling pins.

Morain made a couple of jokes about her outstanding attributes, then climbed on the cycle and began juggling.

"I used to be an accountant. I started juggling books. The IRS said my work was funny. So here I am."

Rapid fire, perfectly timed, Morain kept the crowd chuckling for fifteen minutes.

Breathing hard at the end of his routine, he said, "But you're not here to see some good-looking guy make jokes. I know what you want. Bring on the boobs."

He left the stage while the applause was still echoing in the showroom. The curtain opened wide and the stage was filled with a re-creation of Columbus discovering America, complete with glittering teepees, a mock galleon, and real horses. The men played the Spaniards. The loincloth-clad women played the Indians.

After the final chorus of "America," the curtain closed and Plesa sauntered out.

"Aren't we having a great time?" he asked, with his thousand-kilowatt smile.

The crowd cheered and clapped their hands.

"We love you," he said. "We love you all. And as a special added attraction, because you've been such a wonderful audience, we now present, in her first Las Vegas engagement, the talented, the charming, the sexy Miss Fifi La Roche."

The curtain parted and there she was, bathed in an amber spotlight and clad in her skimpy cowgirl outfit. Behind her was a backdrop of a western town. Two palomino horses pulled a buckboard out and she began singing "Red River Valley."

The man on the buckboard looked at her wistfully.

As Fifi continued with the song, her voice caught twice. She nearly slipped in a pile of fresh dung after one of the horses relieved himself. But she kept her balance and went on with the show. By her final number—"She Wore a Yellow Ribbon"—the stage was filled with a dozen male and female acrobats, eight topless dancers, fifteen showgirls, and as many dress dancers. A monster yellow ribbon was lowered and the women tied smaller versions around their necks as Fifi completed the song.

When the curtain closed the applause was polite but not as enthusiastic as it had been for the comedian. Diamond was pounding his hands together long after everyone else had stopped.

Fifi came off stage and Diamond tried to embrace her.

"The costume," she said, pushing him away. "You'll ruin it."

"Don't worry about it," he said, but she kept him at arm's distance.

She was panting lightly. "How was I?"

"The greatest."

"Really? Do you think so?"

"Really. You knocked 'em dead."

"It didn't sound that way."

Tweed appeared. "You missed your cue twice and your kicks looked like you'd pulled a hamstring. But considering the time constraints and your own limitations it wasn't as bad as it might have been."

Diamond glared at the choreographer.

"Now go back to the dressing room and get out of that outfit before your boyfriend here spills beer on it," Tweed said.

Fifi nodded obediently and started back to the dressing room with Diamond at her heels. He admired the view.

She hesitated at the dressing room door. "They gave me such a hard time before the show," she said. She drew herself up and put on a haughty face before stepping into the room packed with her former peers.

"Look who's here," Angie said as Fifi and Diamond entered. "It's Annie Oakley and her friend."

Fifi strode to a vacant table and began undressing. Diamond tried looking elsewhere but he was surrounded by bare female flesh.

182

Angie noticed his discomfort and came over.

"Could you help me zip up big fella?" she asked, her nearly bare buttock brushing against him.

Several of the women giggled as Diamond fumbled with the fastener.

"Up to your old tricks, Angie?" Fifi said. "You still hooking on the side?"

Angie spun on her. "Aren't we the fancy lady. You still lifting money out of purses or you just stealing wallets now?"

"She don't need to steal. She's a superstar," one of the other women said sarcastically.

"Talent will show," Fifi said.

"I got more talent in my toenails than you got in your whole body," the woman responded. "I don't have a sugar daddy like you."

Sharp words flew like darts in a British pub, maligning appearances, boyfriends, and sexual preferences. When Fifi called Angie a "flat-chested, flat-backed, two-bit bitch," the woman threw an empty soda glass that missed Fifi and shattered one of the mirrors.

"That's seven more years of bad luck," Fifi said. "And you deserve every day of it."

"Ladies, ladies," Diamond yelled. "Calm down, you—"

"Stay out of this," Angie said.

"Don't tell him what to do," Fifi said, dressed and getting up to leave.

"Oh yeah?"

"Yeah."

Fifi and Angie began swinging. The crowd egged Angie on. Diamond got between the two women and tried to find a place to grab them without getting intimate.

He finally succeeded in separating them. He took Fifi's arm and hauled her out sputtering.

183

"My outfit's still in there," she said.

Diamond went back in. Fifi's clothes were lying on the floor, torn in several places. He glanced around. The women avoided his fiery eyes.

"Just because you're friends with the boss you don't got the right to truck in here any time you want," a woman mumbled.

"I wanted to protect her," Diamond said, throwing his head toward where Fifi waited. "She obviously needs it. From her former friends."

"She never was our friend," the woman said.

He picked up the costume and walked out.

After returning the garments to an annoyed wardrobe mistress, the couple went to the Diamond Suite.

"I hate them. I hate them. I hate them," Fifi fumed.

"It's jealousy, doll. Don't let it get to you."

"I don't want to ever see them again."

"You don't have to."

"I want a private dressing room."

"I'll talk to Tex."

"Promise me you'll get me a private dressing room?"

"I can't promise. I'll talk to him."

Unsatisfied, she stormed around the suite. "I don't belong here anyway. I should be in Hollywood. I took a bunch of pictures once. The photographer said the camera was good to my face."

"I'll be good to the whole package."

"I have talent," she said, not hearing him. "I don't want to have to sing and dance the rest of my life. Especially here. They'll always undercut me. Like that horse taking a crap in the middle of my number. They got trainers who make sure that doesn't happen. I want to go where I'm appreciated. I want to go to Hollywood. I want to be in the movies."

"Soon as I finish up here we'll go back to Los Angeles and see about that."

"I want to go tonight."

"Dollface, you know Red Diamond always finishes his job."

She stepped up to him and gave him a long kiss, probing his mouth with a tongue that was slow and sure.

"C'mon, Red honey. Don't you want your little Fifi to be happy?" she asked as they came up for air.

"More than anything. But until Rocco's out of the picture we're gonna have problems. And I don't know about this film stuff. I don't want you out shooting spectaculars full-time. Who's gonna take care of the house? And the kids?"

"What house? What kids?"

"The house we're gonna get. Maybe in Bay City, right by the beach."

"What kids?"

"The kids we're gonna have," he said, giving her derriere a tender squeeze. "Three or four little ones. A house ain't a home without the pitter-patter of little feet."

"Little feet? What about stretchmarks? I've got a career to think of. Let's take the money you've made and go to Hollywood."

"The money stays under the mattress until I finish this case," he said firmly.

"I need to get to the studios. I know I can make it."

After a few minutes of talking, but not communicating, Fifi threw herself down on the couch. "I'm beat."

"We've got to celebrate your performance," he said.

"How?"

He joined her on the couch and pressed his lips to hers. She twisted away.

"Not now," she said. "I've got a lot on my mind."

"It's the best way to take your mind off your troubles."

His hands wandered over her lush terrain, enjoying

185

the hills, the plains, and the valleys. His mouth bore down again and she didn't resist. Her clothes disappeared faster than a honeymooning couple. He put on his matching birthday suit and they got down to business.

Fifi moaned. Diamond grunted. The doorbell rang.

He got up quickly, grabbing his .38 from the table. He pulled his pants on and went to the door. Through the peephole he saw a forest of flowers. He cracked the door open. The delivery boy's smile wilted when he saw Diamond's .38.

"Flowers for Miss Fifi," he said, handing the foliage to Diamond and taking off without waiting for a tip.

The P.I. shut the door and brought the bouquet to where Fifi lay.

She read the card that was attached. *I enjoyed your performance. You'd enjoy mine. Joe. Room 439*, it read.

Fifi giggled and Diamond tore the card up.

"The nerve of that bum," he said, waving the .38. "I ought to go down there and show him my performance. He'll need new teeth."

"Awww. You're jealous," Fifi said, stroking Diamond's brow. "That's sweet. Don't worry, I'm yours. And you're going to take your little Fifi away from here. Right?"

Her hand moved from his face down to his fly and she undid him. Within seconds they were back in position. It was sweeter than honeysuckle wine, more intoxicating than a fifth of bourbon.

"Ohhh, Red, you're the—"

The doorbell rang, Diamond grabbed his gun and his pants, and stormed to the door. He saw a bunch of roses through the peephole.

He yanked the portal open, seized the bouquet from the startled delivery boy, and slammed the door.

I admired you from afar. I'd like to admire you up

close, the note read. It was signed *Fred. Room 732.*

Fifi sniffed the roses while Diamond tore up the card. The pieces fluttered to the floor like busted dreams.

"Isn't it wonderful? All these fans," she said.

"Fans? They're a bunch of dirty old men."

"How do you know they're old?" she said teasingly. "That's why you have to take me to Hollywood. It'll be different."

"I'm gonna have them put a guard by the elevator and stop this right now."

"Please don't. I get a kick out of it."

"You get a kick out of it? Getting dirty notes from creeps?"

"Not the notes. The flowers. It means they felt something."

"I know what they felt," Diamond said, slamming his fist into his palm. "I'm gonna let them feel something else, sending that kind of stuff to Red Diamond's girl."

"They don't know I'm yours," she said. "But I do."

He returned to her embrace. His pants were around his ankles when the bell rang again.

Muttering under his breath, he pulled his pants up and marched back to the door.

He opened it and reached for the flowers. A fist caught his jaw and sent him flying back.

Babe came in with a bunch of flowers in one hand and a .45 in the other. He dropped the bouquet. Red would've preferred him dropping the roscoe. It wouldn't have mattered much. Flip was right behind Babe with a sawed-off shotgun in his hands. The gun had little charm but a lot of persuasive power.

"Hubba, hubba, what have we got here?" Flip chirped, leering at the naked Fifi. "The boss sure knows how to pick his meat."

187

Diamond took a step toward Flip and Babe laid a paw on the P.I.'s chest. "Don't get no ideas."

Fifi sat up, trying to cover her body with her hands. It only made her look more vulnerable.

"We got orders to take you back to Moe's place," Flip said in his distinctive falsetto. "But I don't think the boss would mind if we was a few minutes late." He flicked his tongue across his lips.

Diamond charged and Babe knocked him down with a swing of the .45.

"We got orders to bring you back alive, shamus," Flip said. "But don't push your luck."

Diamond's .38 was lying near Fifi but she was oblivious to the weapon. She was impaled by Flip's stare.

The P.I. got up and rushed Babe. It was like banging heads with a statue.

Diamond let one of Babe's punches carry him backward until he was a few feet from his gal and his gat.

The gunmen moved toward them.

"I always wanted to try you out," Flip said to Fifi. "But you wouldn't give me a tumble. You were gonna tell Moe. Now he don't care what happens to you."

Babe chortled sadistically. The thugs' eyes were on Fifi, who was trying to cower into the couch. Their guns were pointed at Diamond in a lackluster way.

"Get ready for a rough ride, bitch," Flip said, lowering his shotgun and reaching for his zipper.

Diamond braced himself to jump for his gun. Babe saw the movement and lined his .45 up with the P.I.'s chest. Red knew he couldn't make it but he'd have to try.

The door crashed open.

"Police! Freeze!" Saint shouted, framed in the doorway in a classic combat firing stance.

Babe swung his .45 and Saint's gun cracked. Diamond dove for his weapon as Flip lifted the shotgun.

188

Babe's fingers jerked spasmodially on the trigger and sent a few rounds flying. Flip had the shotgun pointed in Saint's general direction. It would've been enough to retire the cop on the spot but Diamond's .38 turned the killer into a killee.

The score stood at Good Guys–2, Hoods–0. Fifi began to scream, a loud piercing wail that didn't stop even when Red took her in his arms.

Saint called the station. While they were waiting, the cop explained he had been coming by to warn Diamond about a tip he had gotten from an informant. Greenberg had acted quicker than Saint expected and when the cop heard Flip's voice, he came in with gun blazing.

"I appreciate that," Diamond said.

"You're not going to appreciate what I say next. I'm putting you and the girl under house arrest."

"What?"

"I'll hold you as material witnesses or whatever I have to do if you don't cooperate. Maybe acting as an investigator without a Nevada license. We got too many homicides in this town. We don't need more trouble. And if you go after Greenberg, you're going to wind up dead."

"You're all heart."

There was a knock at the door and Saint admitted the troop that spends their time looking at dead bodies.

It didn't take the deputy medical examiner long to decide that Babe and Flip had pulled their final shakedown. The police photographer, fingerprint man, and a couple of other technicians preserved the scene.

Since Saint had been a witness to the shootout, the fuss was just routine. Although Saint was not popular with his brothers in blue, the idea of anyone taking a shot at a cop outweighed other considerations.

The bodies were carted out, with chalklines left

where they had been. The guns were sealed in plastic, marked for identification, and laid out on a counter.

Tex came up with the house doctor, who gave Fifi a sedative and put her to bed.

"Can you get a few of Rosie's Raiders to babysit Fifi?" Diamond asked Evans when he got him off to one side.

"That shouldn't be a problem," Evans said. "Where you going?"

"To get some fresh air. But keep it under your hat."

Tex agreed and Diamond drifted casually through the crowd to where the guns lay. When no one was watching, he picked up his gun and hid it under his jacket. He covertly got a box of bullets out of a drawer, grabbed his hat, and walked briskly out of the room.

He nodded confidently at the cop posted in the hall and took the elevator to the garage.

Five bucks slipped to the attendant and Diamond knew which car the killers had come in. The key was in the ignition. When the valet went to move another auto, the P.I. got behind the wheel of the hoods' car and took off.

He felt good. His exit had been smooth. There were two less punks in the world. The tires rubbed the road and moved him onward. He was on his way to a showdown with Rocco.

There could be no doubt that Rocco was behind the summons. Greenberg was a flunkie front man. It was time to go one-on-one with the master killer himself, a man for whom murder was as difficult as flossing his teeth. . . .

I could see only the back of the big chair behind the desk. It was blood red leather, deeper in color than the stream that dribbled from the corner of my mouth.

Two hoods held my arms. I felt like I'd been Joe Louis's punching bag. There were parts of me that weren't sore but I didn't know where they were.

Rocco's goons had taken their time. With blackjacks, fists, feet, and rubber hoses. I hadn't cracked. They didn't know where I'd stashed Fifi.

So the Lord High Executioner himself wanted to see me. I was honored. I was too much for the hired help.

The chair spun slowly and there he was. The man who Al Capone called "Sir." Who Dillinger gave half his take to. A guy with the warmth of Genghis Khan, without the charm.

"You don't look so hot, peeper," Rocco said. He puffed on a cigar that wasn't as thick as a baseball bat.

I spat blood onto his desk. "I think I'm comin' down with a cold."

Rocco's thin lips parted in a grimace that was supposed to be a smile.

"A real tough guy. You know what I do to tough guys? I stuff 'em," Rocco said. He gestured with his cigar to the head of an unlucky deer that was mounted on the far wall, along with a couple of moose, a lion, and a bear.

"Thanks, but I ate already."

The hoods jerked my arms and gave me a new definition of pain.

"I think you need a lesson," Rocco said.

Savoring every moment, he waddled toward me, an evil ugly animal about to play with its prey.

I slumped. As the hoods struggled to lift me, I spat blood in their faces. They let go and I began flailing with the energy I'd kept on hold.

My punches were sloppy but they did their job. I got my hand on the heavy glass ashtray from Rocco's desk and sent the goons to forty winks-land.

Rocco grabbed for the gun in his desk drawer.

Marks had done a nice job preserving that moment, Red thought. But the reverie had to end. He was getting near Greenberg's place and he didn't have a plan. All he knew was that Rocco was there, and he had to get him.

17

Between the mountains and New Forest Drive, where the tract homes ended with no forest in sight, was a flat wasteland of junkyards and cement company silos. By the time he turned onto Buffalo Drive, the only man-made fixtures were the power lines paralleling the road.

He killed his lights. Gravel and small rocks crunched under his wheels. The car complained as he bounced in and out of chuckholes.

He drove down a dirt road past the sign warning PRIVATE-NO TRESPASSERS. He came to a wrought iron gate that locked thick enough to withstand anything short of a Sherman tank. It was attached to heavy brick pillars with a brass plate bearing the letters *M.G.* The property was ringed by a cyclone fence with barbed wire and razor-ribbon topping. An intercom was mounted on the left-hand brick post.

"It's Flip," Diamond said into the box, doing his best imitation of the dead killer's squeaky falsetto.

"It took you guys long enough," a man answered. There was an electronic hum and the gate swung open.

The P.I. drove down an asphalt roadway about as

long as the Hollywood Freeway. Date palms and Joshua trees limited his view.

He drove further. There were no guards. Greenberg was cocky. He hadn't expected Babe and Flip to fail. And no one would dare to breach his security. No one but Red Diamond.

The main house was an impressive sight. High-intensity sodium lights kept the dark desert night off the hacienda-style house. It looked big enough to house the Mexican Army and have room left over for a few hundred federales.

Diamond parked the car and crept up to the window. A half-dozen men were sitting around the living room. Red recognized Greenberg, Van Houton and his bodyguard Mike Gregory, and Braun, the former Ace of Diamonds security chief. The other two looked like the hired muscle found in mobbed-up bars.

They had brandy snifters in their hands and amazed expressions on their faces when Red sauntered in. The logs in the walk-in fireplace crackled.

"Hey guys, can I join the party?" Diamond asked. He waggled his .38. "Here's my invitation."

A Thompson lay arm's distance from Gregory.

"Grab the chatter gun by the butt and kick it over here," Diamond ordered. "Real careful. We don't want it to go off."

Gregory scowled but did as he was told. Red picked up the Thompson and holstered his own gun.

"I hear you guys wanted to talk to me so I dropped in," he said.

"What do you want?" Greenberg asked.

"To talk. First off, where's Rocco?"

"Who?"

"Don't play dumb. I know he's around here."

"I don't know anybody named Rocco," Greenberg said.

"We'll see. What's that?" Diamond asked, pointing

to a sheaf of papers lying on a wooden coffee table in front of Van Houton.

"Nothing," the South African sneered, moving quickly to retrieve the documents.

Diamond stepped in and rapped the barrel of the Thompson on Van Houton's hand. Gregory started to get up and Diamond swung the weapon to cover him.

"You punks better watch it or I'm gonna start playing this Chicago typewriter," the P.I. said.

When Diamond tucked the papers in his jacket, Gregory lunged. The P.I. staggered backward, his finger squeezing the Thompson's trigger. The gun began talking and the house got instant ventilation.

The other men joined the fray. Diamond swung the gun like a club. His enemies kept getting in each other's way and no one was able to land a solid blow.

"What's going on?" a new voice shouted from the stairway. An Aryan-looking man with a pump-action shotgun came running.

"It's Diamond. Get him," Greenberg yelled.

Red heard footsteps pounding down the stairs. He wriggled free of the pile and began crawling to the door. Gregory jumped up and prepared to come down on him with steel-toed paratrooper boots. A spray from the Thompson sent the bodyguard to oblivion.

The Aryan with the shotgun fired a blast over Diamond's head. His fedora was blown away in a buckshot breeze. He tickled the Thompson's trigger.

It took a fraction of a second for Red to realize the gun wasn't kicking in his hands. Before he could get to his .38, he was kissing close to two shotguns and a 30-30 rifle.

Damn automatic weapons, Red thought as two men lifted him roughly and slammed him down onto a hard wooden chair. Someone else got some rope and he was lashed into place.

Less than five minutes had passed since he entered.

194

Greenberg was literally foaming at the mouth. Spittle dripped down on his pale yellow Lacoste shirt. The casino owner was not very big, but what he lacked in size he made up for in fury. He smacked Red until the P.I. felt like he'd stuck his head in a beehive.

"This is going to be a pleasure," Greenberg said, his face nearly as red as Diamond's. "You're going to die. It may take days. And I'll be watching every second."

"Howzabout we let bygones be bygones," Diamond said.

Greenberg's spittle bubbled and he smacked him again. "You nearly ruined everything."

"That's right," Van Houton said, stepping in and planting a fist in the P.I.'s stomach. "A billion-dollar deal. More money than you could ever imagine."

"What's that?" Diamond gasped.

"Don't tell him," Greenberg said.

"Why not?" Van Houton asked. "He's not going to tell anybody."

Greenberg shrugged and looked uneasy.

"Gold. Silver," Van Houton said. "Do you know what the Comstock Lode is?"

"Yeah. It's the big claim found up near Virginia City," Diamond said. "More than a half billion's been taken out of there."

"You're not as stupid as you look," Van Houton said.

"Thanks tons."

"Tons is right," Van Houton said. "A vein twice as rich as the Comstock Lode runs through Las Vegas. Deeper than ever mined before."

"No one has ever had the foresight and resources to get it out," Greenberg piped in. "But we're going to drive everybody out and make millions."

"You're nuts," Diamond said. "The casinos make more than that. It don't pay."

"The casinos belong to other people," Van Houton

195

said. "The gold will be mine. Everyone in my family has made money in mining. Diamonds, gold, silver, uranium. I was the black sheep. Worth only a million or so. Now I'll show them."

"You got a screw loose," Diamond said. "Maybe a few. How come no one else has ever gone after it? There's no gold there."

"Shut up," Greenberg said, hitting Diamond again.

"Not true," Van Houton said smugly. "We had a leading expert, Dr. Felix Goode, do a rather detailed study. The minerals are well within reach."

Goode? The name was vaguely familiar to Red. Greenberg interrupted his attempted recall by grabbing Diamond's hair.

"Shut up! You're trying to confuse him," Greenberg screamed in Diamond's face, showering him with spittle.

"But you're not confused, are you Moe?" Diamond asked. "Did you bring this guy Goode in?"

"Yes he did," Van Houton answered. "But I checked his credentials thoroughly. He's most reputable."

"Don't let him con you," Greenberg said, jerking Diamond's hair.

Con. Con man. Dr. Felix Goode, also known as Sheik Abu Ben Diba and James Thursby.

"Was Goode a fat guy? Snappy dresser?" Diamond asked.

Greenberg put his hand over Diamond's mouth. The P.I. bit down hard. Greenberg screamed.

"He doesn't want me to tell you you've been had, sonny boy," Diamond said. "Goode is a con man with more names than the phone book. Moe's been playing you for a chump."

Greenberg moved to the fireplace and grabbed a hot poker.

"Let him finish," Van Houton said.

"It's a lie. I tell you, it's a lie," Greenberg said.

"Look at him," Diamond said to Van Houton. "All set to finish me off before I can tell you the truth. I thought we was going to talk for days."

Greenberg lifted the poker above his head.

"Drop it," Van Houton ordered, the .32 in his grip a forceful persuader.

"It's a trick," Greenberg said. "We're close, so close. You'll make millions. Think of the people who laughed at you, how they'll eat their words. Remember that sample Goode got us? And what the assayer said?"

"Bring in your own experts," Diamond urged the South African. "Moe's using you in a power play with the wiseguys. Once he gets his way—"

Van Houton fired as Greenberg swung. The bullet hit the casino owner in the shoulder. The poker seared Diamond's hair as it made like Newton's apple.

Braun shot Van Houton. The Aryan shot Braun. Someone else shot the Aryan. The smell of cordite filled the room as the killers settled their differences.

When the smoke cleared, Greenberg and two of his men were the winners.

"You ruined it," Greenberg screamed at Diamond while one of his men patched up his arm. "You'll pay. You'll watch the girl you stole from me die. Then it will be your turn. You'll beg for death. Now where is she?"

"Moe, I decided. You're not a nice person," Diamond said. "Rocco tried finding that out before. You know what it got him."

"Rocco?"

"Sure, Rocco, the guy whose boots you kiss. Don't play dumb with me. I'm not some South African rich boy that was born yesterday."

"Where's the girl?"

"Didn't Rocco tell you how he tried? How we shot it out and he wound up escaping from the hospital?"

Greenberg picked up the poker and put it in the

197

fireplace. When he brought it back, the tip glowed like a demon sun.

"No more talk about Rocco," he growled. "You tell me where the girl is or I fry your eyes. Then your balls. Understand?"

"Who's writing your scripts? We need to get you some new material."

Greenberg touched the poker to Diamond's cheek. The P.I. tried not to cry out. He failed.

"No more kidding around, smart mouth," Greenberg said, smiling for the first time since Red arrived.

A calvary bugle blew.

"What was that?" Greenberg asked.

"The TV?" one of his henchmen suggested.

Glass shattered and there was a thumping noise.

Greenberg spun as more glass shattered, and they all cried and coughed.

"Tear gas!" the third man choked.

A bugle blew "Charge" and the front door was smashed open. Guns began going off. Diamond kicked over the chair he was tied to.

Gas mask-clad figures stormed in. In the midst was an unmistakable figure, his Stetson nearly getting knocked off as he came through the doorway with six-guns blazing. And despite the gas mask, Red recognized Rosie's form as she let loose a blast from a short-barreled shotgun.

Greenberg's two thugs were gasping for air but they kept firing. Greenberg was down on the ground. Only Diamond could see him as he fumbled to attach a fresh drum to the Thompson.

Red rolled until his bound hands were near the hot poker. He touched them to the metal, burning flesh and hemp. His hands were freed as Greenberg lifted the now loaded machine gun.

As Greenberg trained the weapon on Rosie's Raiders, Diamond brought the poker down on his head, splitting his skull like an overripe melon.

One of Greenberg's surviving aides caught a bullet in the head and the other decided it was time for the white flag.

"Look for Rocco," Diamond croaked, his eyes streaming from the tear gas. Someone handed him a gas mask.

Several of Rosie's Raiders swept through the house while others got the air conditioners pumping out the cordite-and-tear-gas-scented clouds. None of the Raiders were injured.

Diamond tried to get up but Rosie shoved him gently back down. She motioned for one of the Raiders. "This is Rusty Steele," she said. "He's got paramedic training. You take it easy."

Steele cleaned Red's cuts and burns. After studying Diamond's pupils, he said, "I think you've got a mild concussion. We better get you out of here."

"Rocco?"

"There's nobody else in the house," Rosie said.

Tex came over. "How's it going, hombre?" he asked.

"I been better, I been worse," Diamond said.

"I reckoned you'd come out here and try and have all the fun yourself," Tex said. "This beats the gunfight at the O.K. Corral."

"I'm glad you came," Diamond said.

"We've got to get him out of here," Steele told Evans. "He needs rest and observation."

"A hospital?" Tex asked.

"No," Diamond said. "I ain't that bad."

"I agree," Steele said. "Most likely he'll be fine."

"Well, you take him back to the hotel," Evans said. "I'll take care of the law."

Steele helped Diamond up and Rosie tucked his .38 into his holster. She gave him a concerned smile, and a tender kiss.

The scene was blurry for Red. He saw the vans his

rescuers had come in and the tow truck they used to tear down the front gate. He felt himself being lifted into one of the vans, and the vehicle moving as Steele put it into gear.

Diamond lay on blankets in the back of the van and gathered his strength. Steele periodically called back to make sure he was awake.

Red heard the sirens as they neared the Ace of Diamonds. The garage was filled with police and fire vehicles. Their flashing lights were brighter than the signs on the Strip.

Red's first thought was that an arsonist had struck again. Although a crowd had gathered, it didn't look like an evacuation. The mumbling mob parted like a Brylcream man's hair when the P.I. began barreling forward. Steele tried to put the brakes on him, but the scarred and determined P.I. kept on moving. The uniformed cop guarding the police barricade put up his arms to stop Diamond. Their collision was averted when Saint spotted him and ordered the officer to let him through.

"I'm sorry," Saint said.

"I ain't in as bad shape as I look."

"Not for that. I had no idea."

"About what?"

Saint didn't answer. He looked over to the center of the show—the charred remains of an unrecognizable sedan.

"I had no idea she'd do it," the cop said. "She slipped out the way you did."

The moment froze in time. The lights, the noise, the smells, everything, like a stuck frame in a movie projector. And then the image began to burn.

"Fifi?"

Saint stood mute. Diamond grabbed the cop's shoulder and shook him.

200

The veteren cop's voice was choked with rage and sorrow. "She got into your rented car. Tried to drive off. Plastic explosive wired to the ignition. Thousands of diamond-shaped darts. She died quickly."

"Noooooooo!" Diamond screamed. He began swinging wildly. Saint parried the blows easily. A couple of uniformed officers grabbed the P.I. roughly and were about to give him the usual treatment awarded cop-bashers.

"Leave him alone," Saint barked. The officers held Diamond but didn't hit him.

"Are you okay?" the lieutenant asked.

Diamond's head hung limply on his chest. He gave a weak nod. Saint waved his hand and the cops released him.

"I want to see the body," Diamond said.

"There's nothing to see. They're still collecting it, I mean her."

Steele had elbowed his way to their side. "Lieutenant, Mr. Diamond has had a bad time. I'd like to take him upstairs and put him to bed."

"Who are you?" Saint demanded.

"Rusty Steele. I'm with casino security," he said, producing identification.

Saint glanced at it and asked, "How did Red get beat up like that?"

"He was in an accident. Mr. Evans will explain."

"Listen Steele, I'm putting Diamond in your custody. I'm trusting you both, even though he walked out on me once tonight. If he isn't available for questioning tomorrow morning, you're both up a creek. Know what I mean?"

"Yes sir, and thank you."

Steele led the lifeless Diamond from the scene, up to the suite, and sat him down on the couch.

"How are you feeling?" he asked.

201

"Fifi."

"I'm going to get you some ice to keep that swelling down. Stay here."

Steele walked away.

Diamond shut his eyes and the events of the night exploded inside his eyelids.

Guns. Shots. Pain. Blood. Screams. Bodies. Explosion. Fifi. Fifi.

I want to get in my cab and go home, Red thought. What? Cab? To Milly. Milly who? Divorce. Sean and Melonie. The kids. Whose kids? Marriage. Long Island. House. Assets. Dependents. Dependence. Descendents. Defendants.

Lost between Simon Jaffe and Red Diamond, he heard Steele say, "We're out of ice. I'm going down the hall to get a bucket."

Why had Fifi gone out? A call, maybe, from someone telling her that Red needed her. That would bring her on the double. The sedative.

He got up and wobbled to the closet. Her belongings were gone. It didn't make sense.

He moved around the suite, not sure what to do with himself. Her scent was still in the air along with the smells of blood and cordite from the gun battle with Babe and Flip. Their chalk outlines remained.

She would've been dopey. They could've fooled her, thinking she was going to meet Red. Instead she'd met the Grim Reaper.

Gulo. The diamond shaped anti-personnel darts. It had to be his trademark. And he'd gotten her. Fifi was gone. Red Diamond was just another lonely private eye, destined for a cluttered bachelor apartment with empty booze bottles on the floor. The hub his life spun around was gone.

The doorbell rang and he moved with leaden feet to answer it. There was no reason to hurry anymore, no reason for anything. He felt a lone tear begin to trickle down his cheek.

There was one emotion stronger than his sorrow. Hate. He would get his revenge on Rocco and Gulo. They would pay. He would happily die if he could collect that debt.

He was wiping the tear from his eye as he opened the door. His upraised arm saved his life. It wasn't Steele with the ice. It was Gulo with cold steel.

The jewel-encrusted dagger plunged downward. Because of his arm, instead of catching Red in the throat, it pierced his left forearm. The blade was buried so deep it was pulled from the killer's hand, stuck in the P.I.'s flesh. The two men fell backward into the apartment. They rolled and scuffled, landing punches wherever and whenever they could.

Diamond had a few inches and twenty pounds on Gulo. The hit man had a lifetime of experience. Both men were fighting for their lives. They thrashed and flailed, knocking over tables, breaking lamps, and smashing into furniture. Diamond's blood left a dark trail.

Gulo got up and kicked. Red caught his leg and the assassin fell. The P.I. pounced, but Gulo rolled aside. Red's injured arm throbbed with every move. Gulo struggled to get his hands on the purloined French knife, to twist it in deeper or jerk it free.

They rolled into the hot tub and the land war became a sea battle—gasping and punching and fighting to hold each other under the surface. The killer grabbed him in a tenacious pit-bull headlock and shoved Diamond's face underwater.

Red weakened and his life flashed before him. Driving a cab. Breakdown. Times Square. Dead bodies. Mr. Brown's gang war. More dead bodies. Manfred's daughters. Vargas. Even more dead bodies.

Red was tired, an overweight marathon dancer in too-tight shoes. He needed a few minutes rest. Just a few minutes. Gulo was winning. The search for Fifi could wait. Fifi. Fifi. Fifi!

The hit man wasn't prepared for Diamond's manic burst of energy. Red got his head above water and gulped in great gasps of air. He was willing to die, but Gulo would have to go first. He pulled his right arm free. Two of his fingers found Gulo's eyes and the hit man screamed. Water sloshed over the rim as the tide turned. His left arm was nearly useless, but Diamond hit Gulo with a flurry of hard jabs.

Gulo refused to give up. He swung blindly, only one in three punches connecting. The P.I. grabbed Gulo's head and slammed it into the side of the tub. Once, twice, again and again. At some point Red realized he was wasting his energy. Gulo would kill no more.

The knife still embedded in his arm, dripping blood and water, Diamond staggered to the phone. He lifted the five hundred-pound headset.

"Help," he said into the mouthpiece, and then the sandman sapped him into oblivion.

18

He was lying in a snowbank without any chill. Rocco stood over him, wearing a white tux. Fifi stood next to the villain. She was wearing a wedding gown and had a diamond ring.

"You thought you were such a smart guy," Rocco said. "You're a stupid little man in a dirty little world. You're nothing."

"Go back to your cab," Fifi said, putting her arm through Rocco's. "Give it up."

"Never," Diamond shouted. "Never. Never. Never!"

Experienced hands were holding him down. The white grew brighter. The faces blurred, then came back into focus. The nurse released him and wiped his brow with a damp wet rag. A name tag reading LINDA was pinned to her generous chest.

"He's coming around," she said.

Evans stood next to her. "I knew he was too ornery to die."

"How long I been out?" Diamond asked. His voice sounded as weak as an old man's.

"Three days. The docs said you were ready for Boot Hill. I told them if you became buzzard bait I'd take away their golf clubs."

Linda stood up. She was a brunette of staggering

proportions. Her large brown eyes, the darkest spots in the room, showed genuine concern.

"Linda used to work at the casino before she became an RN," Evans said. "She's the best there is. In a whole bunch of ways."

"Is there anything I can do?" she asked Diamond, dabbing him gently with the rag. As she bent, her superstructure jiggled like a skyscraper in an earthquake.

Diamond tried shaking his head. He got dizzy.

"You jes' take it slow. Linda and another gal almost as purty will tend to your needs," Evans said with a lecherous wink.

Diamond did a bad job of feigning a smile.

The wounded P.I. was housed in the Tex Evans Wing of the hospital. He got the royal treatment. The solicitous hovering was interrupted only by visits from Evans, Rosie, and the police. Evans and Rosie wanted him to get well. The cops wanted a statement.

Tex put a team of lawyers in between Diamond and the cops. The frustrated lawmen wound up giving more than they were getting.

From their questions, and with information filled in by Evans and Rosie, Diamond learned that his theory was correct.

Greenberg had used the con man Thursby to trick Van Houton. The South African had supplied money and mercenaries to drive out Strip owners, believing there was a massive gold vein running under the city. It had been hokum, set up by Greenberg to force out his mob-connected brethren, and the few innocents that remained in Las Vegas.

"I always suspected Moe was behind it," Evans said. "But I wanted you to come in and prove me right without my prodding."

When Evans visited, he talked continuously, praising Diamond and joyfully recounting the shootout at Greenberg's.

"Reservations are climbing back up," Evans said. "And the crime rate is dropping so fast we might soon be the safest place in the country. The news people are doing all sorts of stories on it."

Rosie's visits were much quieter. She sat by Diamond's bedside and held his hand.

"I s'pose you'll be leaving soon," she said.

"Probably."

"No chance of you staying?"

"I doubt it."

"I think I could get attached to a guy like you," she said.

"Don't think about it," he said. "I'm poison. Look what happened to the girl I loved."

"You're feeling sorry for yourself," she said. "Think of the good that you did. The thousands of people whose lives are better because of you."

"I guess."

And they sat in silence.

When he was alone, he tried not to wallow in his misery. He thought of the many private eyes who had tougher rows to hoe.

There was Dan Fortune, with just one arm; Nat Perry, a hemophiliac who wasn't scared of killers with sharp objects; Nicholas Street, the amnesiac; Peter Quest, who's glaucoma made him virtually blind at times; Ben Bryn, whose powerful upper torso rested on a body ravaged by polio.

It didn't work. None of them had been Fifi's lover, and none of them had lost her the way he had. Only his urge to find Rocco kept him going.

On Red's eighth day in the hospital, Saint brought him the news that no charges would be pressed in any of the homicides.

"You got off lucky, Diamond," the cop said. "You took the law in your own hands and you're walking away smelling like a rose. Between you being a local hero, and Tex squeezing a lot of nuts, you can leave here without a care in the world."

"Yeah."

"And I hear your arm will be good as new in a month or so."

"Life is wonderful," Diamond said sarcastically.

Saint lifted a small, heavy satchel and handed it to Diamond. "This stuff belongs to you," the cop said. "You can thank Tex for getting it out of the property clerk so quick."

Inside was his gun and the money he had kept tucked under the mattress.

"We found the cash in the car with the woman," Saint said.

"The woman?"

"The one you were calling Fifi. Her name was Gayle Collins. We were able to make a positive ID from her teeth."

Diamond sat up abruptly. "What?"

"Gayle Collins. You knew that, didn't you? This Fifi stuff was a nickname?"

The P.I. was woozy from his sudden move. He lay back.

"You want the doctor?" Saint asked. "You look kind of pale."

"No. I just need time to think."

"I'll be going then," the lieutenant said. "There's a big push going on to crack down on the troublemakers. I'll be working a surveillance and I don't know if I'll be able to see you again. It's gonna be a lot quieter with you gone."

Diamond nodded.

"Don't take any wooden nickels," Saint said, walking briskly from the room.

Could it be possible? Red wondered. Was Fifi still alive? Had Rocco pulled a fast one, slipping this Gayle Collins into the car? Kidnapping Fifi. That was like Rocco. Luring an innocent dupe to her death to throw the P.I. off his scent. The foul stench of murder.

The lethargy that had kept Red wallowing in the hospital bed was gone. He had let them pump him full of drugs. Red Diamond, the man who ate saps for breakfast, shivs for lunch, and slugs for dinner. Lying around like Joe Blow in for a gall bladder operation.

Linda came in as he was awkwardly pulling on his pants.

"What're you doing?" she asked.

"Putting on my drawers, angel. What's it look like?"

"You're supposed to stay here another couple of days," she said, stepping up to him and taking his waistband in her hand. "Get undressed."

"Doll, under most circumstances that would be an offer I couldn't refuse. But I got things to do." He gently pushed her hands away.

"Tex said I should give you some special therapy when you were feeling better." She put her arms around him and let him feel the warmth of her body.

They locked lips. She was soft and as inviting as a mattress after a hard day hauling rocks. She gave herself without hesitation. It was Diamond who broke the clinch.

"That was nice," he said. "Real nice. A fella could get used to that pretty quick."

"You get back into bed and I'll tuck you in with something special."

Diamond reached for his shirt. "Is this therapy covered by Blue Cross?"

"Did I do anything wrong?" she asked.

"You've got the moves down pat. I wish I had time for treatment. But I got to go. Now be a sweetheart and help me get this shirt on."

She did. "I really shouldn't be doing this. The doctor won't approve. And Tex will be mad."

He gave her a peck on the lips. "Tell them I made you do it. And I'll make sure Tex knows how quickly I responded to your attention."

"If you need any T.L.C., I make house calls."

"Just what the doctor ordered."

She exited with an appealing bounce, not exaggerated, a woman who knew how to move like a woman, Red thought.

He slipped his gun into the holster and clipped it to his belt. It had more therapeutic value than a gallon of antibiotics.

Evans was waiting when Red returned to the hotel.

"I heard you checked out," Tex said. "The sawbones wasn't treating you right?"

"They were fine. And Linda is a real peach. I ain't been babied like that since I was in knee pants. But I got to get back to L.A."

"What's the rush? Why don't you stick around a while? Things are getting cleaned up. We could use a man like you to keep the bad guys on their toes."

"It's something Fifi said to me. She kept talking about Hollywood. I think she was giving me a clue."

"So it wasn't Fifi in that car?"

"No. Rocco pulled the old switcheroo. I got to hurry before he realizes I'm wise to him."

Evans gave him a hearty handshake and a slap on the back that nearly opened Diamond's stitches. "What do I owe you?"

"Our account is balanced," Diamond said, holding up the bag with the money.

"I'm sorry to see you moseying on," Evans said.

"A guy's gotta do what a guy's gotta do. Hasta la vista."

"Hasty banana, cowpoke. You're one of a kind. A real ace."

"An ace of diamonds?"

"The best suit."

Norris was waiting outside, a round box under his arm.

"We're truly sorry to see you leave, Mr. Diamond," he said. "I'm to expedite your travel arrangements. Do you want to fly out today?"

"I'd rather drive," Diamond said. "I like being behind the wheel. And I could use the time to think. Can I get a car?"

Norris nodded and they walked to the elevator. A car was ready for them down in the garage.

"Are you sure you'll be able to drive with that?" Norris said, indicating Diamond's injured arm.

"Piece of cake."

Norris opened the door and Diamond slid into the yellow Mustang.

"Is there anything else I might do for you?" the manservant asked.

"I'm fine. Take it easy."

"One final matter. This is for you," Norris said, handing the box to Diamond. "With Mr. Evans's best wishes."

"Thanks," the P.I. said, putting it next to the moneybag and starting the engine. He gave a brief wave and was off.

Diamond took his time in the city, checking for tails and getting a last glimpse of the town that Bugsy built. The sun made it look clean, but old, like a fading blonde who had gotten religion, but still turned a few tricks on the side.

The car's engine hummed smoothly. There were only a few hundred miles on the odometer. But the air-conditioned air had an unpleasant smell. Gasoline and smoke. Perfume and blood.

It wasn't the car. The money that Collins had died with was on the seat next to him, the source of a stench as foul as a Chicago stockyard.

He knew what he had to do. The wheels screeched as he made a U-turn and headed back to the Ace of Diamonds. He parked and took the elevator to the office marked ROSIE WASHINGTON—CHIEF OF SECURITY.

The secretary was a beefy guy who looked like he'd be better with a machine gun than a dictaphone. Red recognized him from the night at Greenberg's ranch. The man nodded and buzzed the P.I. into the inner office.

A surprised Rosie jumped up from behind the glass top desk where she was reviewing papers. Clad in a form fitting dress suit, she ran to Diamond and gave him a hug.

"I thought you were leaving without saying goodbye," she said tearfully.

"I'm like a bad penny. I keep turning up."

"I'm glad you did. Do you have to go?"

He nodded. "I know how you feel. It's why I was gonna check out without stopping at your desk. Like pulling off a bandage, the quicker, the less pain."

It was her turn to nod.

"I got a favor to ask," he said.

"Name it."

He handed her the satchel of cash. "There's two kids up on the north side. J.C. and Rocky. Both about fourteen, kind of skinny. Rocky's got his name tattooed on his hand." He gave her the address of the baseball field.

"The kids saved my life," Diamond continued. "And they gave me some good information. I want this money to go into a trust fund. They get it for their schooling."

"You don't want any of it?"

212

"To me it's dirty money. To them it might do some good. Besides, I'm a couple a hundred ahead," Diamond said, patting his wallet. "And they can use it more than me."

She took the money and put it in a wall safe. "Consider it done. I'll put Rusty right on it. He felt bad about getting knocked out by Gulo."

"How's Rusty doing?"

"Fine. Only his pride was hurt."

"Give him my best," Diamond said. "Anyway, as Tex would say, I got to mosey on down the road a piece."

"I wish you didn't have to."

"I do too. You take care."

"You too," she said stiffly. He heard a sniffle as he shut the door behind him.

He was on the road again. He opened the car windows wide and let the fresh air blow across his face. It was getting hot. By the time he hit the interstate, the stench of the money was gone.

The box Norris had handed him was still there. He pulled to the side of the road and opened it. Inside was a gray, ten-gallon Stetson, with a hatband studded with diamonds. *To replace the cap you lost at the gunfight*, the note from Tex read.

He put the hat on his head. A perfect fit.

Tex was a class guy. And Rosie was something special too. He had a feeling he'd be seeing them again.

He was richer than he had been when he arrived in Vegas. How many people could leave the city and say that? He'd put a few more of Rocco's legions on ice, though he had no doubt the killers would be easy enough to replace.

It was time to go back to where he lived, the city of fallen angels. Fifi would be there. And Rocco. And a chance to settle that long overdue bill.

"Giddyap," he said, tapping the accelerator. The horsepower under the Mustang's hood responded.

He began singing "Don't Fence Me In" as he galloped off. He'd reach Los Angeles in time for the sunset.